The English Adventure

The English Adventurer

Book 2 in the Conquistador series

By Griff Hosker

The English Adventurer

Published by Sword Books Ltd 2022

Copyright ©Griff Hosker First Edition 2022

The author has asserted their moral right under the Copyright, Designs and Patents Act, 1988, to be identified as the author of this work.
All Rights reserved. No part of this publication may be reproduced, copied, stored in a retrieval system, or transmitted, in any form or by any means, without the prior written consent of the copyright holder, nor be otherwise circulated in any form of binding or cover other than that in which it is published and without a similar condition being imposed on the subsequent purchaser.
A CIP catalogue record for this title is available from the British Library.

Contents

The English Adventurer i
Prologue 2
Chapter 1 4
Chapter 2 15
Chapter 3 28
Chapter 4 38
Chapter 5 46
Chapter 6 53
Chapter 7 63
Chapter 8 74
Chapter 9 84
Chapter 10 95
Chapter 11 111
Chapter 12 122
Chapter 13 133
Chapter 14 143
Chapter 15 156
Chapter 16 166
Chapter 17 174
Chapter 18 184
Chapter 19 190
Chapter 20 198
Chapter 21 206
Epilogue 222
Glossary 225
Historical Note 226
Other books by Griff Hosker 228

The English Adventurer
Thomas

Prologue

I am Thomas Penkridge and I am a master gunner. The simple title, however, disguises many things. Firstly that I am a master gunner on a Spanish ship and I became one after I deserted the army of Hernán Cortés. I had been a slave and I had killed men. If those things were not remarkable enough I had latterly been conscripted as a spy for King Henry of England by Lord Collingwood and delivered messages to him at his home in Cádiz. My life thus far had been more than interesting and I was now convinced that I had made the right decision when I had joined Captain Pedro aboard the *'Golden Hawk'*. I doubted that I would be of much use to King Henry and Lord Collingwood but my father had been a loyal Englishman who had served the old King Henry and I was comfortable with my motives. I doubted that I would ever return to England for I had tasted the New World and knew that I could make my fortune there.

I was, however, alone. Those with whom I had sailed from England were now all dead. Most of those alongside whom I had fought in what was once the Aztec Empire were either dead or, like Jose's father, Fernando, had settled in a village north of Santiago on Isla Juana. Jose, whom I had trained as a gunner was now a gun captain on another of Captain Pedro's ships, Captain Phillip's ship, *'The Silver Swan'* and whenever our ships docked Jose and I would spend time together but for the most part, I just spent time in my cabin or I trained my gunners.

It was when I was alone that I began to make maps. It was a secretive affair for all captains, Captain Pedro included, guarded their maps jealously. The pen, ink and parchment I used were secreted in my chest in the cabin. There they were safe as there was an unwritten rule about violating the property of another sailor. I found the making of maps to be calming. You needed patience and care. I found that I was good at it and that surprised me for I had never been a studious boy. Whenever I found myself at the steering board. I took every opportunity to look at the captain's maps. I also made a note each time we spied a point of land. I could steer by the stars; most sailors could. As we plied the seas between Spain and the New World, I grew familiar with them. It was all part of my work as a spy. Maps were as valuable as the gold that was found in the New World for they told others where it was hidden. The land called Mexico, conquered by Hernán Cortés and the

The English Adventurer

Castilla del Oro, close to Panama were the main sources of gold but there was a rumour of a land to the south whose treasure dwarfed both of those sources.

When it was too dark to make my maps. I would sit and look out of one of the two tiny wind holes in my cabin. When we headed west, I would think of those I had known, some, like Captain General Hernán Cortés, were men I would be happy never to see again but there was one leader who had impressed me, Francisco Pizarro. I wondered where he was now. He had not been part of the expedition led by Hernán Cortés but had remained at the Isthmus of Panama, that deadly snake and disease-ridden piece of land that seemed to be the gateway to the land of gold and silver. We often met other sailors who had returned from there and they spoke of a city, far to the south and high in the mountains, a land they called El Dorado, the land of gold. I wondered if Francisco had found it yet and then, as quickly as the thought came it evaporated like morning mist for if such a city had been discovered then the sea would have been filled with ships heading there. It was a dream.

The English Adventurer

Chapter 1

    My cabin was my home and I knew I was lucky to enjoy the privacy. One reason I was accorded such favour, I was the only one except for the captain who had his own cabin, was because of my prowess with the guns. We had just four on the ship but I knew guns and I had skills, given to me by my father, that made me hit more times than I missed. That made me valuable for pirates wanted the treasure we carried when east bound. Consequently, I cherished and cared for the guns we used. Without them, we would be easy targets for the many pirates who sailed the waters. Sailing west was normally an uneventful voyage although the seas were as deadly an enemy as the pirates but coming back, laden as we were with riches from the New World, then there were many who thought to take us. To make life safer Captain Pedro sailed with two consorts so that we could mutually protect each other. However, the gunners on the other two ships took their lead from me. It was Captain Pedro who controlled the small fleet and my decisions that determined where we would strike. We had cargo, of course. The settlers in the west needed things from Spain, wine, clothes, weapons, tools like machetes and metal cooking pots. Pirates were unconcerned with those. They wanted the gold, silver and exotica that came from New Spain. Captain Pedro had won the contract with King Charles, the Spanish called him King Carlos, to bring back the gold from the new world and it was making the captain a rich man.
    We had two falcons and two robinets aboard the ship. We could not afford to waste powder and ball actually firing them and so we just practised firing without using either ball or powder. However, on rare calm days, when the wind allowed and with the captain's permission, we would fire one falcon and one falconet at targets we placed in the water. It was not enough, I knew that, but it would have to be enough. I planned when I had made enough money, to buy a couple of harquebuses. The main reason was that the weapon was accurate and fired a lighter ball than even the robinet which fired a one-pound ball. I wanted them as I could train sailors to use them and that would augment our firepower. I had all four guns cleaned every day. My gunners had other duties abord the ship and on those days when they could not be spared then I cleaned them myself. They were my livelihood. Two of the ship's boys, Juan and Alessandro were also attached to my gunners and it was they who had the task of fetching the powder from the powder store. Although a dangerous activity I thought it less hazardous

than racing up the rigging. They preferred the work on the guns to the rest of their tasks for it made them feel special.

The first voyage after I had been recruited by Lord Collingwood was uneventful. The winds had been benign and we had enjoyed a swift crossing. As we carried minimal water and supplies that was a feat in itself for many ships took much longer. I had managed to make a copy of at least one map and when we returned to Cádiz, I could deliver it to Lord Collingwood. We docked at Isla Juana. Our fleet of three ships was ocean-going and had large holds. Smaller ships were built on Isla Juana and it was they who brought smaller cargoes to the most important port on the island, San Cristóbal de la Habana. Jose and I always hoped that the captain would land at Santiago on the south of the island for his father and his mother had a farm there. As we carried letters we normally landed at San Cristóbal de la Habana. Even in the short time I had been away it had grown. There were now other colonies served by the island. Florida lay to the north and the New Spain of Captain General Hernán Cortés lay to the west. I was keen to hear of Pizarro and the lands to the south.

Jose and I headed for the inn on the quay. It was a popular place with those who arrived from Spain. This was a new land and ocean. Sailors met to exchange information. Jose and I spoke of the voyage and the gunnery we had practised. He was young but so had I been when I had been a gun captain. Jose was keen to learn all that he could from me. We were engrossed in our conversation and did not notice a warrior approaching until he spoke.

"Tomas, is that you?"

I looked up and saw a man I vaguely recognised but could not place, "It is me, Pascual de Andagoya. We served together under Captain General Pedro Arias Dávila in Panama."

Dávila had been rewarded for his work by the governorship of Panama. It was a lucrative position. I remembered the young man. He looked to have aged since then, "Of course, I remember. You are still in Panama?"

Nodding, he leaned in, "This is most fortuitous, Tomas." He glanced at Jose.

I smiled, "Jose is my friend and whatever you say to me you can say to him. He knows how to keep secrets."

Pascual nodded, "I need a gunner. I have equipped an expedition to return to Panama for I intend to sail down the west coast of the new land there. Shipwrights have built me a ship. I have heard of a land called Pirú, and it is said it is a city of gold. I have men with swords and

The English Adventurer

a couple of harquebuses but I remembered what you did with a single falconet. Come with me and I will make your fortune for you."

I confess that I was tempted but then I remembered the jungle and the danger it represented. I shook my head, "I have agreed to serve with Captain Pedro for at least a year and I am honour bound to keep my word."

He nodded, "Then I will have to find another. Guns are easy to find but men who can use them well are rare. If you ever get to Panama when your contract is over then seek me out."

"I will."

We chatted for a while and I discovered that Francisco Pizarro was now the Alcalde of Panama and an important man. I was pleased for he was unlike the Captain General I had followed when we had defeated the Aztecs. He was an honourable man whom you could trust.

He also told me of Florida which lay to the north. "I have sailed there and there are opportunities for a man to become rich." He grinned, "Not as rich as I shall be when I return from Pirú and El Dorado but rich enough."

I saw my chance and I took it, "Pascual, do you have maps of the waters around Florida?"

He nodded, "Of course. They are in my chambers upstairs, why?"

"I would pay you to let me copy them. If, as you say, there are riches there then I would need maps."

I saw him debating. Maps were valuable things and men guarded them jealously but Pascual must have decided that the coins I would give him, especially as he had no immediate intention of sailing to Florida, would help him equip his expedition. We agreed on a price and then he took me and Jose to his room where I made a copy of the map and then paid him. I knew that I would be recompensed by Lord Collingwood and I was pleased with myself for obtaining them honestly.

As we walked back to our ship, I could tell that Jose was disappointed in me, "Why did you not take him up on his offer, Tomas? Captain Pedro would have let you go."

"He might but I am not yet ready to leave his service. Besides, do you not remember Tenochtitlán?"

I saw him shudder, "Aye, but the Aztecs were a fierce people. You have been to Panama, were the people there fierce?"

"Aye the tribes I met in Panama were fierce and the jungle too. I am not saying that I will never go but I want to grow richer first serving Captain Pedro."

The English Adventurer

Unlike Jose, I had been offered a share of the profits from our voyage. That was, of course, dependent on our safe arrival in Cádiz and that meant I would have earned my money. It reflected my position as the master gunner.

"And why do you need the maps of Florida? Captain Pedro does not need them."

I hated lying to my friend but I had no choice. I shrugged, "Let us say that I plan for the future. Who knows what may be discovered in this land called Florida? From what I have heard it is just a land of swamps, snakes and crocodiles but one day they may find another El Dorado."

The next day the captain began to load our cargo. Lord Collingwood had paid for certain plants to be acquired for him. He wanted the plants that had been sent to Spain the year before, the Aztecs called them xictomatl and tomali. They were not cheap and I was not sure if they would survive the voyage. Captain Pedro put me in charge of the two dozen plants. They had flowers on them but no fruit. I took the decision to share my cabin with them. I knew that they would need sunlight but I also knew that salt air might damage them. By keeping them in my cabin at night and leaving them in the lee of the forecastle during the day I hoped that some would survive. It was not the plants themselves which had to survive but the fruit that I hoped they would produce.

We loaded the hold with some of the exotic fruits produced in this land. Captain Pedro had every box examined. He did not wish to transport one of the deadly spiders or snakes from this New World. We also had boxes of silver and gold to take back with us. They were loaded late at night for they were the property of the Governor himself and intended for the King of Spain. Secrecy was all. I knew that despite all the efforts we made someone would know and if just one person knew then word would be gotten to the pirates. I had been a pirate and knew that they could wait just beyond the outer ring of islands. The pirates had taken over some of the smaller islands and made them into their own fortresses. I knew that one day the Spanish would tire of the attacks and destroy the lairs but they could not do so yet. They were too busy finding new sources of treasure and filling the king's coffers.

We left the morning after the treasure was aboard. With full water barrels and food for the voyage, we headed east. The journey back was different from the voyage out. We were more watchful and the lookouts who squatted precariously on the mast tops scoured for the sight of any sail. When they spied one then we ran out the guns. We did not load them but my gun crews and I were ready to do so in an instant. We were

The English Adventurer

called to arms three times in the first three days of the voyage. Two of them were innocent encounters for the ships were heading west and were merchants such as we. The third one was more sinister. The sail appeared to the south and west of us and appeared to be shadowing us. It was only when darkness fell that we were able to relax. The captain changed course to lose our follower.

The next day we saw no sail but ahead lay the thick black clouds of an Atlantic storm. I left out the xictomatl and tomali plants as the rain saved me from using valuable water but as the seas became stormier, I took them inside my cabin to save the foliage from damage. I was soaked by the time I had finished. I had used some of the money given to me by Lord Collingwood to buy more clothes and I changed into dry ones. After securing the plants as best I could I went to sleep. The storm was a violent one but I was a gunner and not a sailor. It was the rest of the crew who had to endure the trimming of sails and the replacing of damaged ropes. The storm raged all night and even when I awoke it was still making the motion of the ship dangerous. The plants were still secure and I left the cabin with my oiled cloak around my shoulders. I made my way to the stern where a salt-rimed Captain Pedro was fastened to the steering board.

He gave me a wry smile, "God could not give us a storm on the way west and peace on the way east, could he?" He nodded aft, "We have lost the other two ships. For all I know we may have already lost two-thirds of the profit we might have made. Who would be a sea captain?"

I laughed, "And such storms raise the value of the cargo we have. The other two captains have good ships and crews. We shall find them when the storm abates. I will fetch food."

He smiled his gratitude, "For one so young you are wise, Tomas. Food and wine will be welcome."

I went to the cabin next to the captain's. It acted as a larder and kitchen. I took a ham from the hook upon which it hung and sliced some thick chunks. The bread was three days old but the butter I smeared on it would make it more palatable. I put the ham on the bread and held it in one hand while I took the mug of wine I had poured in the other. When I emerged Captain Pedro allowed his first mate, Fernando, to take over and he grabbed the ham and bread and the wine.

"Fetch some for Fernando, will you? This storm still has some surprises left for us."

He was right, the motion of the ship was only marginally easier than it had been. After I had fed Fernando, I fed myself. I did so in the relative comfort of my forecastle cabin. I was able to examine the xictomatl and tomali plants. I spied a couple of insects and I squished them. It was a daily activity as was the removal of brown leaves. I saw that some of the flowers had fruited. That was good. I was not sure if Lord Collingwood actually wanted the plants or if it had been an excuse to get me aboard the ship. I knew that if he could grow the plants into fruits then it would be worth a fortune. The seeds could be sold on and make Lord Collingwood ten times what he had paid for them.

The storm died out at noon and I went on the deck to survey the damage we had incurred. It was not as bad as it might have been. Already one sail, the foresail, was being replaced and the ropes and sheets that had been damaged were also receiving attention. After ensuring that the four guns were still secured, I went to the stern, "Where are the other ships, Captain?"

He shrugged as he drank from the wineskin Alessandro had brought him. He handed it back to the ship's boy, "Who knows? They could be ahead or they could be behind."

Alessandro proffered the skin to me and I shook my head, "They could be sunk."

He laughed, "No, my friend. That was a hard storm but one torn sail and a few ropes ripped are nothing. They will be doing as we are and repairing the ships. We sail on the same course and we keep watch. The guns are safe?"

"We tethered them well. The wind cannot harm them."

He looked up at the sky. "We are just a day or two from landfall. The storm helped us by pushing us east. The skin is half full."

I risked placing the fruits on deck. The darkness of the cabin could not be doing them any good. I tended the plants for the rest of the day. I collected the rainwater that we gathered on the canvas protecting the guns and used that to water them. As darkness fell, I returned them to my cabin.

I was woken, just before dawn, by what sounded like thunder. I knew it was not as soon as I stepped out and looked east where the first hints of the sun were to be seen. The flashes were not thunder but guns. Even as I peered, I heard the captain shout, "All hands! All hands! Full sail. Tomas." The single word was an order to get the guns ready.

I waved my hand in acknowledgement and returned to my cabin to dress for war. I donned my hose, tunic, sea boots and leather brigandine before strapping on my sword. I would not wear my morion, my helmet. Juan and Alessandro ran to my side, "Juan, fetch powder and Alessandro shot. There is time so do not run and spill not a grain of powder."

"Aye, captain." They chorused. It was still a game to the two boys but I knew that gunfire at dawn was not a good thing. Sailors and ships

The English Adventurer

were being attacked and the odds were that it was one of our ships. I took off the canvas fastenings of the four guns and checked that there was no water fouling them. The boys arrived with the first of the powder and shot. They carefully placed them close to the guns. I went into my cabin and brought out the stone that would contain the fire I needed to use on the linstock. Fire on a ship was dangerous but the stone minimised the risk. I placed kindling in the bottom and then used my flint to get the flames going. In the darkening gloom of pre-dawn, it lit up the ship. The flames soon died and I touched the linstock to the flames. It glowed red. Handing it to Alessandro I began to load each gun in turn with powder. The gunfire ahead meant that we would need our guns and I would not be wasting precious shot and powder.

By the time I had finished loading the guns the sun had risen ahead of us. We would still be in the darkness and hidden from the battle ahead. I looked up at the cross trees of the main mast. The lookout, Antonio, was peering ahead. Suddenly he shouted, "There are three ships and two are attacking one." There was a pause, "It is the *'Silver Swan'* that is being attacked."

The ship was ours and they were friends. I shouted up, "Do they stand off or are they closing?"

"One is standing off and firing. The other looks close enough to grapple."

"Is *'Swan'* still firing?"

"She is."

"Gun crews!" The command brought my four men to join me at my guns. Until they were needed by me the captain had priority over their services but once the linstock was lit they were mine. Alessandro handed the lit linstock to Guido and then lit a second to hand it, when it glowed, to Carlos. I left them to it and headed for the bowsprit. I leaned over it to peer ahead. I saw that one of the pirates was approaching *'Swan'* from the starboard quarter of her stern. There the ship would be safe from Jose's guns all of which were mounted on the sides. The other was some four ship's lengths from her port side. It was the one closing from the stern that was a problem.

"Guido, you and Carlos shift your robinet here." I pointed to the starboard side of the bowsprit. I had asked the carpenter to fit rings there for just such an emergency. The robinet fired just a one-pound ball but it was an accurate weapon and that was what I needed. If one pirate boarded *'Silver Swan'* then we would have no chance of saving the crew. They would be executed and hurled overboard and then we would have to face three ships. The comfort I took was that the pirates would seek to inflict minimal damage to the *'Swan'* and her cargo.

The English Adventurer

"Juan, go and fetch some of the bags of stones we gathered from the beach of San Cristóbal de la Habana." I had my plan. Leaving the two gunners to secure the seven-foot robinet to the rings I hurried back to Captain Pedro.

As I approached, he said, "Will they be able to board?"

I nodded, "They will. Captain, I wish you to sail directly for her stern. When I wave my hand to starboard then you should sail alongside her."

The captain trusted me and nodded, "You have a plan?"

"I do," I explained it to him and he nodded his approval.

Once back with my men I gathered them around me. "I want all of you to man the lee guns. I will have the ship's boys with me on the starboard robinet at the bows. Load with the bags of stones." I had measured the stones into each bag and they were marked with either an *F* or an *R*. "You will have just one chance to fire so wait until we are abreast of her. I do not think they will have their starboard guns manned."

Guido was a thoughtful man and he asked, "And what will you do, Captain Tomas?"

I gave him a cruel smile, "Why, kill as many of them as I can."

The poacher had become the gamekeeper. I went with the two boys and chose the best ball that we had. It was perfect. I lovingly loaded it. "Once this is fired, I need a bag of stones marked, *R*, you understand? Both bring one for we shall keep firing until I say hold."

"Aye, Captain." They hurried off and I began to adjust the gun.

The pirate, she was French by her lines, would feel safe as we approached from her stern. My modifications to our ship were unusual. The Frenchman would not expect guns on our bows. They would assume we were approaching from that direction to prevent her from firing on us. They were in for a shock.

We could now hear not only the cracks of the guns as the second pirate tried to damage, unsuccessfully, the rigging but also the cries of pain as men were hurt. Captain Pedro had as much sail as his ship would take and we were fairly bouncing along the water. It meant the bows were rising and falling alarmingly. This would be the true test of a master gunner.

The boys arrived back and I blew on the linstock to make it glow. Their faces lit up in anticipation for they knew what that meant. We were two hundred paces from the stern when I lit the linstock to the powder. We were on the uproll and even as we were blinded by the smoke Juan was swabbing out the barrel with seawater and Alessandro

The English Adventurer

was handing me the bag of powder. I had just enough time to see the one-pound ball smash into the stern of the French ship. The crack and the shouts told me what a good strike it was. Wood flew high in the air as I rammed the bag of stones into the barrel. We were one hundred paces from her when I fired, again on the uproll and the balls scythed through the already weakened stern cabin. I had one more chance at a shot and we hurriedly loaded. We were just fifty paces when I fired the second bag and then waved for the captain to turn.

"To larboard." The boys ran but I studied the damage. The stern of the Frenchman had been seriously damaged. The rudder was gone and I saw the blood coming from the scuppers. The quarter deck where the captain would have stood was devoid of anything living. As I reached my men the two guns fired. We were just forty paces from her starboard side and the stones slaughtered the gun crews and the pirates on the deck.

Turning my hands I shouted, "Captain, sail to the other ship. We can end this."

He waved his acknowledgement as I watched the Frenchman begin to list as water started to fill her stern.

"We load with ball. The captain will take us down the lee of the other pirate. If *'Swan'* is still firing we will divide the fire." They cheered and I began to choose the two balls. The larger ball of the falcon would do more damage. I would aim it at the water line. The robinet would fire at the mainmast. Such was my confidence that I did not believe for one instant that I would fail. My friend and acolyte, Jose, was aboard the ship that was under attack. Captain Pedro knew his business and as we turned into the wind he compensated and took us further away from the second pirate so that he could use the wind to his advantage. It was as we turned that I realised the pirate was English. For the first time since I had left my home, I would be fighting my fellow countrymen. I had always said that I would never fight a king's ship. Although this was a pirate, I still felt conflicted but the thought of my friend aboard the *'Swan'* steeled me.

The English pirate had three guns on the larboard side of the ship. I saw men running from the starboard guns. I changed my mind about the target and I hurried to the falcon. It would take time for them to load their guns. I saw that the middle gun protruded from the side more than the others. It was the biggest gun.

"Guido, aim the robinet at the first gun." I knew I was asking much of Guido for normally I aimed but the range was less than forty paces.

"Aye, captain."

The English Adventurer

I concentrated on my target. I saw the crews working furiously to load the weapon as I touched the linstock to the powder. Guido's robinet fired a heartbeat later and our side was wreathed in smoke. "Stones." Alessandro handed me a bag of stones as Juan swabbed out the smoking barrel. I looked at the pirate as the smoke cleared. My ball had smashed into the gunwale before ploughing into the gun and upturning it. The shards of wood from the gunwale had swept across the pirate's deck and, added to Guido's ball had effectively removed their gunners.

I heard Captain Pedro shout, "I will bring her around the stern."

I waved my hand and then, as Alessandro handed me the bag of balls, took a risk. "Juan, fetch me a robinet ball."

I saw the question in his eyes but he obeyed and as the captain began his turn, I double-shotted the falcon with a smaller ball and a bag of stones. I would have one chance to disable the ship and I took it. As we passed within thirty paces of the unprotected stern, I fired. The explosion made me think I had damaged my gun but it was well-cast. The explosion came as the stern of the English pirate disintegrated and, as Captain Pedro took us closer to the starboard side of the *'Silver Swan'* the English pirate suddenly exploded. The shock wave made both our ships heel over such was the power. My ball must have struck the powder magazine. The force of the explosion also sent a wave of water to finally flood the Frenchman which was already almost submerged.

"Reef the sails and prepare to help our friends."

I went to our starboard side to see if there were any survivors from the French pirate. I knew that there would be none from the English one. I saw a couple of men clinging to a piece of wreckage. I was about to throw a rope when I saw the dorsal fins of some sharks. Before I could even throw the rope, their screaming bodies sank beneath the waves.

'Silver Swan' was now our priority. We gently bumped into her and I saw bodies lying littered across her deck. Captain Phillip was having his arm tended by the barber who served as a surgeon. As we were secured to the side I leapt over. One of the falconets had been upended and a second would need a new carriage. I had helped Jose train his gunners and I saw that two lay dead. I shouted, "Jose!"

Alessandro had followed me and he shouted, "Here, Captain Tomas."

I found my friend. One of his gunners was binding the stump of his left forearm. Jose looked up at me and with a sad smile said, "We did the best we could." He then, mercifully, passed out.

The English Adventurer

I turned to Alessandro, "Find their firestone and light a brand. Bring it here to me. Juan pour sea water on the deck to disperse the spilt powder." They both obeyed; I was risking much for fire was a real danger. Powder had been spilt upon the deck and as the English pirate had shown an explosion was a real danger. He brought the brand back and I said to his gunner, "Keep his arm still." As he did as I commanded, I placed the burning brand to the flesh. The smell of burning hair and skin was nauseating and had Jose been awake he would not have been able to bear it but I knew that it was the only way to save his life. I handed the burning brand to Alessandro. "Douse it." He plunged it into the bucket of seawater used to swab out the guns.

Just then I heard a cry, "Sails to the west."

Captain Pedro shouted, "*'Golden Eagle'* has returned! Come back aboard, Tomas."

I obeyed despite the fact that I did not want to abandon my friend. If this was another pirate then my guns were all that stood between us and disaster.

We clambered back aboard our ship and as we were untied, I shouted, "Move the starboard robinet back into position." I hurried to the stern to peer at the approaching ship.

Captain Pedro said, "Once more you have been our salvation Englishman. It is a pity we did not get to hang any of the pirates but *'Silver Swan'* is safe."

I said nothing for I had been responsible for the death of a crew of Englishmen. I might have known some of them. I felt sick.

"It is *'Golden Eagle'* captain."

We all breathed a collective sigh of relief. It was our third companion. We could resume our journey to Cádiz.

Chapter 2

We limped into Cádiz harbour. All three ships were damaged to varying degrees. The dead from the *'Silver Swan'* had been buried at sea. I had not seen Jose after I left his ship but as Captain Phillip did not have to stop to bury another, I hoped he was healing. I felt responsible. I tended my burgeoning fruits and plants more as an occupation than anything else. I was still haunted by the killing of fellow Englishmen. They had been pirates but I had begun my life as an English pirate.

As soon as we tied up, I was the first down the gangplank and I ran to *'Silver Swan'*. To my great joy, I was greeted by Jose. His stump was in a sling but he was on his feet. "The wound is healing?"

He nodded, "There is no smell and it itches. The ship's barber assures me that is a good thing."

I was relieved, "And now…" I looked pointedly at the stump.

He gave me a smile and shook his head, "This will not stop me from being a gunner. In fact, it has determined me to be an even better one. I do not need my left hand to be a gunner. Others can move the gun into position and it is my eyes and my skill that will direct the men to shift the aim or the elevation."

I was not convinced by his arguments. I think I wanted him ashore so that he would be safe. I knew that he regarded me as his mentor and guide. I could never forgive myself if he died because of me.

He saw my look and said, "Tomas, I spoke to the others and they told me what you did. Not your ship, or your gun crews but you. You defeated the Frenchman on your own and then directed Captain Pedro so that you could defeat the other. I would be like you. I am healing and I like this crew. They think I saved them from being boarded," he shrugged, "perhaps, but it only delayed what might have been inevitable had you not intervened."

I was aware we were in the way, "I have work to do but tonight we dine ashore, eh? I shall pay."

"Of course. You are the master gunner whose purse will soon bulge."

I returned to the *'Golden Hawk'*. Already the hold had been opened and the goods were being brought out. Captain Pedro said, "I will let you deliver the plants to the Englishman. Take Juan and Alessandro." He leaned in, "He paid for them before we left and I do not think that there is any need to tell him that we paid less than he gave us."

I knew that Lord Collingwood would not argue. "Of course. I may be some time."

"You are a gunner and not a deck hand. Take all the time you wish."

I went to my cabin and secreted my maps about my person. We had a small, wheeled trolley the carpenter had made for us to move the gun barrels around the deck and we used that to transport the exotic plants through the streets of Cádiz. We made quite a spectacle and crowds gathered to see the strange plants. The result was that our arrival was heralded by the noise of the crowd and Captain Hogan and one of his men, Foster, came to the door armed at our approach. I saw the Irishman grin when he recognised me. He shouted at the crowd in heavily accented Spanish, "Be off with you. This is not a show." The crowd obeyed the huge soldier and he grinned at me and spoke in English, "Well, you returned. I hoped you would." He switched to Spanish, "You two boys take the plants through the house to the courtyard. John, feed them at the kitchen and I will take this English adventurer to his lordship." He was mocking me, I knew, but only gently. It was a sign that he respected me; the crew did it and I remembered the conquistadors bantering with one another. It was the warriors' way.

That was how Captain Hogan always referred to me. I was the English Adventurer. It was only much later that I realised why he was giving me a code name and protecting my identity. I was anonymous. Captain Hogan was more than a big, bluff soldier, he had a mind as sharp as any.

He opened the door to the small room Lord Collingwood was using, "Your gunner, my lord, returned from the New World."

I saw his lordship hurriedly cover the parchments he had been reading. Then he turned and grinned at me, "So you decided to be my spy, after all. Good. Hogan, fetch us a jug of wine and some Iberico ham and join us."

"Yes, my lord."

I took the maps from my doublet, "Here are the maps. I have maps of the islands, the harbour of San Cristóbal de la Habana, and Florida."

It was the last that he greedily grabbed, "This one is like gold."

I frowned. Captain Hogan brought in the wine and ham and poured us goblets before standing discreetly .by the door. Lord Collingwood had said nothing but was poring over the last map. I drank some of the wine and nibbled a slice of ham.

His lordship emulated me and then said, "You have not heard of Cabot, have you?" I shook my head and he continued, "He is an Italian and King Henry hired him to take his ship *'Matthew'* to find treasures in the New World. The difference is he went further north and he found

The English Adventurer

new land but, sadly, one without gold. He has been exploring the coast of this new land and was only stopped when he came upon Spanish settlers in Florida. So you see this map completes our picture of this continent that lies north of Panama."

"But no gold."

Lord Collingwood shook his head, "Not yet but we are hopeful."

I took another sip of wine and then related what Pascual had told me, "It may well be, my lord, that there are riches to be had, south beyond Panama. There I saw, with my own eyes, a sea as big as the one we crossed to get there."

"And there is the rub. The only way to that sea is through a world ruled by Spain. King Henry does not want to provoke a war, not yet anyway. The gold the Spanish have taken makes them the most powerful and richest country in the world. King Henry would have England in that position."

I nodded and then said, "My lord we sank an English ship that attacked us on our way east."

He frowned and then said, "A pirate?"

I nodded and he relaxed and smiled, "Such men do not have a country. Do not let it burden your conscience."

I was not convinced but I gave him the answer he wished, "Of course, my lord."

He patted the map, "This is a good start, Thomas. By the by did you get any plants for me and did they survive?"

"Of course. They are in your courtyard."

He beamed, "Let us go and view them. I did not expect you to succeed." When he saw the plants his smile filled his face, "You have brought me my fortune."

I shook my head, "There are but a handful of plants, my lord."

"And each seed from every one of those plants will be sold for silver. When I idly mentioned my gamble, I was offered money immediately by Spanish gentlemen who know how much can be made from such plants."

John Foster appeared with Juan and Alessandro.

His lordship nodded at them and said, "I will be returning to England in a month or so. If I am not here when you return than report to Captain Hogan." He leaned in, "He has gone native and married a Spanish lady. Irishmen are such romantics. He will be your constant here, Thomas. Fare ye well."

I saw the change in Captain Hogan at that moment. His marriage looked to have made him gentler and I watched as he ruffled Alessandro's curly hair, "These are good boys, Thomas, and they have told me how you sank two pirates using just two guns. You might be wasted on a merchant ship. King Henry needs gunners like you for the navy he is creating."

I shook my head, "I think that Lord Collingwood would still have me as his spy and, besides, this is a profitable occupation."

He said, enigmatically, "There is more to life than profit, Thomas."

Once back on the ship I saw that the hold had been emptied and dockside carpenters and shipwrights were swarming over the captain's three ships to repair them. Captain Pedro kept a room in one of the inns that lined the quay and he said, "Let us retire to my room. This banging and hammering stops a man from thinking. At least your booming guns cease now and then but the hammering…" He picked up his chest and swung it easily on his shoulder. The captain had been an ordinary sailor once and had not lost his strength.

As we went to the room I wondered if the innkeeper had evicted someone when he saw **'Golden Hawk'** hove into the harbour. I could not see an innkeeper with an empty room, even though it had been paid for. Captain Pedro must have paid well for without a word given to the innkeeper we were fetched wine and food once we had entered his comfortable quarters. I saw him stare at the room as we entered. He was ensuring all was as it should be.

He did not speak until the door closed and we were alone. He opened his chest and pulled out a heavy purse, "Here is your share of the profits."

I was a gunner and my hands were like scales. There had to be four pounds of coins in the bag, "You have been paid already?"

He nodded, "In the short time you delivered your plants the merchants swarmed over me like ants over sugar. The fruits we brought back were all bought and we were paid ten times what we paid." He laughed, "Even the spoiled ones were taken for their seeds can be used. I suspect that in time those fruits will be grown over here and will no longer be a profitable cargo. It is why we shall sail further west next time we cross the sea and try to find new fruits that we can sell."

I was intrigued, "Captain Pedro, how do you make gold from carrying the king's treasure?" I hesitated, "Does some fall between the cracks?" I wondered if I had gone too far and offended him.

He laughed, "I would not be so foolish. No, the governor sent a sealed document with the precise amounts so, even if I wished, I could not rob the king. Besides, there is no need. Much gold is lost on the voyages east. The pirates, as we know, now gather like shoals of sharks to prey upon us. A tenth of the treasure is paid to us for each cargo we successfully bring. So you see, Tomas, that your payment does not impoverish me. There will be a smaller amount from my other two captains when they join us. All know that it was you that saved three ships. Had you not had the wit to do what you did then the *'Swan'*, the *'Hawk'* and the late arriving *'Eagle'* would have all been taken and it would be the French and English pirates that would have profited."

I was a rich man and I began to imagine buying myself a huge estate in Devon.

The captain's words brought me from my reverie. "Tomas, I asked you for a year. More than four months have passed." He nodded at the bag of gold, "Join my company and you will be able to retire to a country estate, as I plan to, withing five years. What say you?"

It was too good an offer to refuse but I was still guarded, "How about this, Captain Pedro? I will stay on the ship until I tire of the sea," I patted the gold, "and the pay."

He laughed, "Aye, that will do." He held out a gnarled mitt for me to shake and the deal was done. "And now, take this." He pushed over a smaller purse, "This is not a payment but is for you to use to buy more weapons. Use this to buy what you can."

"I can buy anything?"

"You are the gunner and I am the sailor. I bow to you and your skill in all matters relating to gunnery and warfare. You know your business."

"How about the other ships? Do you want more arms for them?"

He frowned, "Mine is the largest ship and we will fit her out first. I do not baulk at the expense but I know that you will train gunners well. I intend for us to sail closer together in future." Leaning forward he said, "There are two places where ships are attacked. One is close to the Portuguese Islands of Santa Maria and then São Miguel and the other is to the east of the island Christopher Columbus had named San Salvador. Between the two is a vast ocean. We ensure that when we near Santa Maria and then São Miguel we wait together. Better to reach Spain late than never at all."

It made sense to me, "So I will be directing the guns of the other ships?"

"Your one-armed friend has already shown his courage and skill. We need a better gun captain on *'Golden Eagle'*."

"If I work with Guido on the next voyage west, he should be able to be the gun captain. He has natural skills and that is never to be ignored."

"I leave it to you, Master Gunner Tomas."

That evening as I dined with Jose, I told him my news. He was not put out by the fact that I would have all the guns. "I am still learning my

The English Adventurer

trade, Tomas, and it will take some time to get used to using just one hand." He smiled, "One of the crew suggested I have a hook made and that is not a bad idea."

I admired his philosophy. I suppose having survived the slaughter in Tenochtitlán had made Jose realise, as I did, that we had been given a second chance at life and we should embrace it.

Buying guns was not as easy as it sounded. The Spanish king was precious about such things and I had to go to a royal foundry to buy what I needed. The alternative was to find a blacksmith and have one cast. That was always a risk. As soon as I entered the richly decorated and furnished office of the perfumed official who sat with an aloof and haughty look made me feel that my visit was a mistake. That I was a foreigner made the official who ran the foundry suspicious and I suspect that I might have been sent on my way empty handed had the master of the workshop not entered the room to collect the work schedules.

He heard the official say, as he waved a dismissive hand, "Go back to your *'Golden Hawk'* and tell your captain that he shall not have any guns from this royal foundry."

I was turning to go when the master asked me, "You are the master gunner from the '*Golden Hawk*'?" I nodded and the man's face broke into a smile. His words told me that he was the superior of the official, "Signior Alcatez, did you not hear of the sea battle where this man and his ship, with just four guns, sank two pirates," he paused for effect, "and saved the King's gold?"

The man's eyes widened, "But this man is an Englishman."

"I know and he serves Spain." He put a mighty arm around my shoulder, "Come with me, and tell me what you wish." He glared at the official, "We are all here to serve Spain and this gunner and his ship do so." He led me out into a courtyard and I could smell the charcoal ahead and hear the noise of the foundry. "I am Miguel and I make the guns. They are the finest anywhere."

"I am Thomas Penkridge and Signior Alcatez was right I am English. You should know that I was a slave for a while but then I was saved and became a master gunner."

"I like you more and more for I too have humble beginnings. I was a young blacksmith in my village when my lord asked me to cast him a cannon." He chuckled, "Either God gave me a natural skill or I was lucky. I made good guns and now I am here with more money than I know what to do with. So, Master Gunner Penkridge," he struggled to get his tongue around my surname, "what is it that you wish?"

We had reached the foundry workshop and he led me to a plain office which was in direct contrast to the official's ornately decorated one. Simply made wooden furniture was all that could be seen and there was a jug of ale and a pair of wooden beakers on the table that was festooned with parchments.

He poured us both a beaker of ale and said, apologetically, "Here I am not a tidy man for I hate the spiders' marks on the parchment but we have to please the officials. You want guns?"

"I have two falcons and two robinets. They are serviceable but I need something bigger. I would have a pair of the new sakers." He took a wax tablet and wrote 2 and the letter S. "I also need four or five harquebuses." I dropped the purse on the table. I would not haggle with him. "This is the gold I have been given for my purchases."

He wrote 5 and H on the wax tablet, "Do you need the carriages for the sakers?"

I had already decided that the ship's carpenter could make what I needed, "No."

"And ball?" he saw my forehead frown and said, "The robinet will take, what? A one-pound ball and the falcon a two?" I nodded, "Then you will need more cannon balls for the sakers will need a three-pound ball. Of course, you could use the smaller balls in the saker."

I shook my head, "The windage would make the gun too inaccurate. With so few guns we have to hit that at which we aim immediately."

He laughed, "You are a true gunner." He emptied the purse and carefully counted out the coins. He nodded, "Two sakers and four harquebuses, twenty cannon balls and one hundred balls for the harquebuses."

It was not enough, of course, but it was fair. I nodded, "Agreed. And when will they be ready?"

He shook his head, "Ah, there you have me. I can let you have the harquebuses tomorrow. We have plenty in stock but," he leaned towards me, "the revolt in Castile has caused a demand for more of my guns and I have been given an order for guns that are intended for war in Italy." He tapped the side of his nose, "Keep that to yourself, my friend. I like you and I admire what you did against the pirates. I will make your two guns but it will take two months. I am sorry."

I shook my head, "That cannot be helped. The four harquebuses will help."

He stood and shook my hand, "I will send the harquebus to your ship. Now the sakers…what names shall I give them?"

I knew he was a true craftsman. Casting names on the guns gave them a soul. It sounded blasphemous I know but the best guns always had names. Naming them was easy. "Mary, it was mother's name and my father named his first gun after her." He nodded and wrote it on the

The English Adventurer

wax tablet. "And Katerina." Katerina had died at Tenochtitlán and I wanted her to be honoured."

"An English and a Spanish name, interesting. This Katerina must have been special to rank alongside your mother."

I nodded, "She was." That was all that I said. I stood, "It may be longer than two months before I return. We sail as soon as our ships are repaired."

"Do not fear, your guns will be here when you return. That I promise. You and I have more in common than I do with that perfumed popinjay. Leave everything to me."

I made my own way out and the glare from the official told me that I had not made a friend. Captain Pedro was a little disappointed that the guns would not be ready but pleased that I had, at least, found harquebuses. "The ships will sail in a week. We have supplies to take to Isla Juana as well as some officials sent by the king. You and I will have to forego our cabins for the voyage."

I shrugged, "It cannot be helped. Officials?"

"Aye, the king, it seems, is less than happy with some of his governors. They are being replaced. We take them as far as Isla Juana."

The harquebuses arrived the next morning. They were brand new and greased. I sat with Juan and Alessandro and Guido to remove the grease and get to know their working. The other men I used as gun crews were too busy helping to repair the ship. "Guido, the captain has given me permission to train you as the master gunner for **'Golden Eagle'**."

His eyes widened, "That is an honour but am I ready?"

"We have this next voyage to make you ready. My cabin is needed for the officials. I will be sleeping with the crew and as we have passengers then every waking hour will be spent with the guns. We will also need to train the crew to use these." I nodded to the guns which looked like matchsticks compared to the cannons. "They have a very short range but used together they can clear the aft castle. Come, I will show you."

After Juan had fetched powder and Alessandro a linstock we went to the side that faced the empty harbour. There were no ships in sight. The tide was on the turn and I had Juan find some broken pieces of wood to use as targets. I showed them how to load the guns. As I did so the last time I had used the weapon came to mind. I shivered, it had been against the Aztecs and that was still a very raw memory. The three of them threw the wood into the harbour and the tide took them away from the ship. Resting the weapon on the gunwale, rather than using the stand provided, I fired at a hundred paces. I was lucky in that the

The English Adventurer

wooden fragments were still close together and I actually managed to hit a piece although not the one I aimed at. The crack of the gun made seabirds take to the air and drew the attention of everyone in the port.

"Now, go and get another of the harquebuses. If we are to train the men then we need you to be able to use them."

Alessandro said, "Even us?"

I smiled, "You would be a ship's boy for the rest of our life?"

"No Master Gunner but…" They ran to get a weapon.

I loaded and then watched them as they did so. The boys had grown in the last year but, even so, they struggled to lift the heavy weapons and rest them on the gunwale.

"Now I shall use one linstock so that the effect will not be as good as it might if we fired together." I shouted to Carlos who was nearby, "Carlos, throw those broken timbers over the side."

"Yes, Master Gunner Tomas." Grabbing an armful he hurled them over the side.

I watched the wood drift away, "Now you must aim slightly ahead of the wood." I waited until the wood was one hundred paces away and then lit, in turn, Juan's, Alessandro's and Guido's guns before my own. Their three balls hit the water at almost the same time. Mine a heartbeat later. One of the timbers was hit although we had no idea which ball had done so.

"Good. Now that is enough for today. Clean out the harquebuses and then store them in my cabin." I knew that I would have to find somewhere else for them when we had the new officials aboard. When we had cleaned and stored them the three of them went about their business for there was still much work to do. I took my satchel of coins and left the ship. I also had a task to perform.

I headed for Lord Collingwood's home. He had told me that he was leaving for a while and I was not surprised when I was greeted by Captain Hogan who took me to Lord Collingwood's inner sanctum. "I take it, Thomas, that there is news for his lordship?"

I nodded, "But as with all the information I gather I know not its value but I am honour bound to deliver it. First, we sail in a week and we have new officials aboard for King Charles is not happy with some of his governors."

Taking a wax table the Irishman made notes. "That is useful information. Is that all?"

"No, the rebels in Castile are still causing the king problems and he is preparing for war with some of the city-states in Italy."

"That is good news. You have done well, Thomas."

"And in return, I would like a favour." He frowned and I said, "You can refuse." I emptied my purses of coins from my satchel on the desk, "This is my treasure and there is enough now that I fear it might be lost if my ship sinks. I would have Lord Collingwood keep it here."

The captain relaxed and smiled, "We can do that but what if you and your ship perish?"

"I have no one save an old comrade, Fernando." I gave the captain the name of the village where he and his family lived, "I would have this given to Fernando if I die."

"You trust us?"

I shrugged, "I will be dead by then but I would hope for honour from his lordship."

He smiled, "I will honour your wishes but let us pray that you do not perish, eh?"

I felt happier knowing that my treasure was safe. We had left a fortune on Turtle Island. At the very worst I knew that if I was robbed it would be by Captain Hogan and I liked him. I did not think either he or his lordship would rob me but my life, thus far, had taught me to expect the worst of people.

The last week in Cádiz passed like a blur. I managed to have an hour with Jose and the sailor who at the moment commanded the two guns on the *'Golden Eagle.'* I brought them aboard our ship so that Guido and my two boys could hear my words.

"Until we have the sakers we are more vulnerable to attack. I intend to have your captains buy harquebuses for you but until then my ship is the best armed. Accordingly, when we go into action we will lead and your task will be to watch our stern. As I realised when we fought the pirates the stern is our most vulnerable place. I intend to permanently mount the robinet at the bows. Now that we have the harquebuses, we can add to the broadside which will only have one falcon."

"What about our captains, Tomas, will they agree to this?"

I smiled at Jose, "These ships are all Captain Pedro's, he will command them but I hope they see the wisdom of this decision. Your task will be to use your guns and ball wisely. Stop any ship from closing with our stern and we will have a chance. We know, already, where we are likely to be attacked. That is when we will be on our guard. Our voyage to the west will be more perilous than normal as we carry important passengers. Your ships will have King Carlos' new officials and if an enemy or even a devious friend were to find out then we might be in danger."

"Devious friend?"

The English Adventurer

"Remember, Jose, that Don Diego Velázquez de Cuéllar and Governor General Cortés hate each other. There may a replacement for either on board our ships and we shall not know who they are. Even Captain Pedro is too lowly for that."

I had just finished speaking with my men when the other two captains arrived on board and Captain Phillip took my arm, "I think you should come with us to Captain Pedro."

I was intrigued but I knew that Captain Phillip would not take me to such an important meeting unless it was necessary. He and Captain Pedro were the oldest of friends and had been one reason why Captain Pedro had been so desperate to save his ship. It was not just the cargo, it was his friend.

As we entered the cabin he gave a wry smile, "I see, old friend that you continue to read my mind. I was about to send for my gunner. We have a problem. As well as the officials and their belongings we have also been commissioned to carry shot, powder and weapons."

Captain Ramon was the captain of the *'Golden Eagle'*. His face became effused like beetroot and I thought he would explode, "We cannot! We do not have the holds specially made for such a contract. We must refuse."

"And if I could, I would but this comes from the king himself. He wants this rebellion put down. Don Diego Columbus is an experienced officer but he knows that his men must be better armed. We all know how rich the New World is but they do not have foundries and they, as yet, produce a poor powder. That will change but not yet. Tomas, you know powder better than any, what do you suggest?"

"Captain Ramon is quite right our ships are not the best but I would distribute the powder between the three ships. Put it as close to the waterline as you can so that the damp will discourage ignition. They can dry the powder when it is unloaded in the New World. Do not have men go near it and those that do should wear slippers and not shoes. It goes without saying that you will not be able to have fires." I knew that damp powder would have to be dried but that would not be our problem.

Captain Phillip shook his head, "That will go down well with men who expect hot food every day."

Captain Pedro said, "Tomas is right and I will impress that on Don Diego when he comes aboard. Yours is a good plan and we will spread the load amongst all the ships: powder, weapons and shot. If any ship is lost then we shall be compensated by his majesty."

Captain Phillip shook his head, "That will be cold comfort to those who die." He had been wounded in the pirate attack and was now well aware of his own mortality.

The English Adventurer

Within an hour the wagons had begun to arrive. Captain Pedro was firm and would not allow a single grain to be loaded until the holds were prepared. Jose and I closely supervised our ships. We used the forrard hold and the sacks were carefully carried one by one and I had them stacked so that there would be little movement. The friction of two sacks could cause an explosion. I used some of the shot, brought aboard in boxes, to hold the sacks in place and then we loaded the rest of the shot by the stern. The weapons were spread out so that the trim of the ship was correct. Captain Pedro worked until dark shifting the odd box of shot or weapons. We left an easily accessible section of the hold for the chests of the officials. Captain Pedro was convinced that they would find some reason to have their servants descend into the hold to fetch out a handkerchief or some trinket without which they could not continue the voyage. My men and I shifted our gear so that we were close to the shot and the powder. It was safer that way. We knew the dangers better than any and we were more used to the stink of saltpetre. There would be many more people aboard the ship than we normally carried. Every official seemed to need at least two servants.

The officials arrived the day before we were due to leave as the most propitious tide would be before dawn. Only one stood out and that was Don Diego Columbus. He was not related to Christopher Columbus as I had expected but I had heard his name and knew he was a warrior, as well as having been the governor of the New World before Diego Velázquez de Cuéllar. He was not going to the New World to replace an official but to put down a rebellion in the Cumaná River area, at the northern end of this new continent we had discovered. It was the easternmost point of the Castilla del Oro which was the most valuable coastline and sending the most experienced soldier showed how serious the king was to protect the gold that made Spain the most powerful nation in the world. The captain told me that the most important settlement was Nueva Toledo but as it had been sacked by the Indians so many times they had renamed it Cumaná. There was something about the name Nueva Toledo that stuck in my mind but it hid in the dark recesses of my memory and I could not bring it to mind.

I had already moved my chest and gear below decks to sleep and eat with my men in the Stygian gloom of the hold. We set sail and headed west with the most valuable human cargo we had ever carried.

The English Adventurer

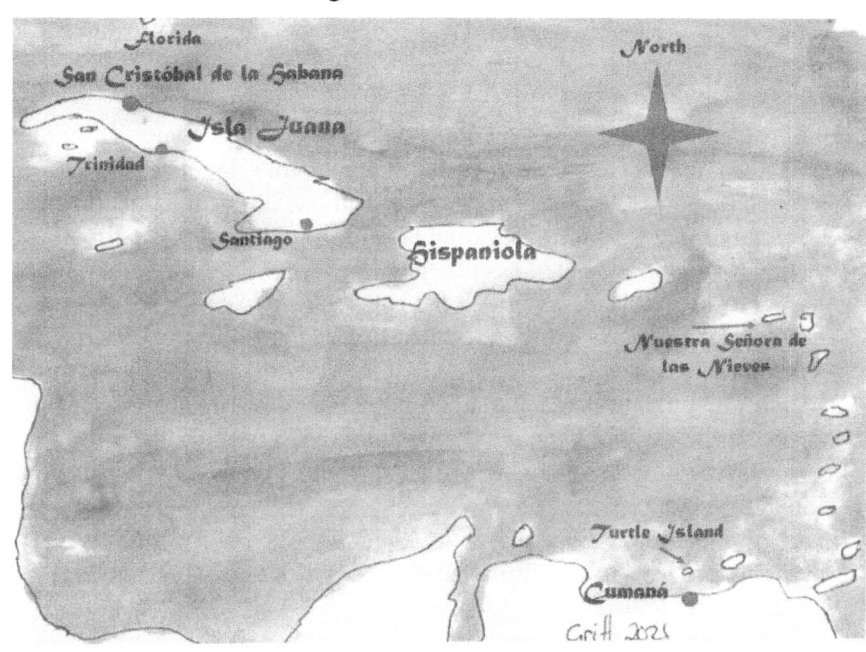

Chapter 3

On the first day at sea, after I had checked the powder, I went on deck. The rest of my men had been busy at their labours before I had even risen. I was the Master Gunner and had more free time than most. Before I ate, I went to check the lashings on the guns. The robinet at the bow looked odd. When I could get one, I would have a second placed on the larboard side as I liked the balance it would provide. As I turned, I met Don Diego Columbus. He was older than I by some margin but unlike the rest of the handful of officials who had boarded our ship, he was dressed as a warrior. He had good boots, workaday hose and a leather brigandine. The oiled cloak had seen service and the hat atop his head was functionally warm rather than decorative and fashionable like the others.

"You are the English gunner I heard about when I was last in Panama." He smiled, "What was it someone called you, 'the English adventurer?'"

I smiled and felt myself blushing. I did not like the attention the nickname attracted. Captain Hogan had said that was how I was described in the busy port that served the New World, "Thomas Penkridge, my lord."

"Francisco Pizarro speaks highly of you and I heard that you recently destroyed two pirates single-handed." He waved a hand at my weapons, "With such a small number of guns that seems remarkable."

"I was lucky but I have a well-trained gun crew and, besides, my friend was aboard the *'Silver Swan'*. I could not allow him to be taken by French pirates."

He smiled, "I can see that you are a warrior. I like you. I will need a Captain of Gunners on my campaign and I know that you served the Captain General." He held up a hand, "I am a professional and I have no opinion about the character of such men but I know that you served him well until…" he smiled, "you suddenly left his service." He leaned in, "Don Diego Velázquez de Cuéllar is a good friend and he speaks well of you. What say you to my offer?"

"I am tempted, my lord, but I gave my word that I would serve Captain Pedro for a little while longer. I have only served him for just over six months. I will consider your offer when my contract is up. You may not want me by then."

"If there is one thing I have learned it is that you can train men to do most things but good gunners are born and not made. We both know

The English Adventurer

that the natives are terrified by two things, horses and cannons." He nodded, "I admire your honour and I will wait."

The crowded ship was a nightmare. Some of the servants seemed to want to descend into the hold at all times of the night and day. I was terrified about an accident and so I took it in turns with Guido to act as a sentry preventing entry to the hold without permission from Captain Pedro. As Don Diego supported all that Captain Pedro said the system worked and we were untroubled.

The hardest part about sleeping so close to the powder was the stink. Urine was used in the manufacture of powder and in the confines of the hold the stench became almost unbearable. Had it been any other than my gun crews I think there might have been a mutiny.

The three captains in our small fleet had sailed these waters enough times to know the winds and to use them to their advantage. Each time I spoke with the captain at the stern and glimpsed both the map and his compass I learned more to add to the map I was making for Lord Collingwood. Even on those days when the wind was not in our favour, we made good progress as we headed west. I often spoke with Don Diego who had a professional interest in the campaigns in Panama and in Mexico. I found him an easy man to talk to for he did not condescend and treated me as an equal. Captain Pedro did the same. They were both in direct contrast to the first Spaniards I had met.

We were nearing the islands known as the Caicos when the attack came. Our route was determined by the winds and the islands, which were largely uninhabited, and they would allow us to replenish our water before the last leg to Isla Juana.

When the lookout reported the four ships appearing from behind one of the islands then, even before I was ordered, I had Juan and Alessandro fetch powder and ball. Don Diego had told me of his fears whilst crossing the ocean. He was not an arrogant man but he knew he had enemies and his death or capture would guarantee that the rebels would succeed. All that they needed was a period of grace and Spain, powerful though it was, would find it hard to recover its lost empire.

He rushed on deck and I saw that he had donned a morion and had strapped on his sword, "Is this usual, Captain Tomas?"

I shook my head, "We are never attacked on our way west."

He nodded, "Treachery." He pointed to Juan and Alessandro as they brought out the harquebuses, "Could I use one of those?"

"You know how?"

He grinned, "I am a soldier. I might not be able to load and fire a falcon but a harquebus is a simple enough device."

The English Adventurer

"Then be my guest." I was happy because I had not had the time to train my gunners as well as I might have liked. Leaving him to load one I hurried to the captain.

Captain Pedro shook his head, "As if having the officials aboard and the powder weren't enough, we now suffer an attack."

"I think that the two are linked, Captain Pedro. The cargo means we might surrender quicker and if they are lucky then the rebellion had more chance of success."

He frowned, "You may be right. I spoke with my captains and they will do as you requested. They will guard our stern."

"Good, then we have a chance." I pointed to the four ships. All were smaller than we were but I saw that they each had guns. Being lower in the water and smaller meant that they could dance around our lumbering ships like terriers around a bull. "Keep us either bow on or beam on to them, Captain Pedro. If they get behind us then we are dead. They will either blow us up or swarm aboard us. Our gun in the bow may come as a surprise to them." We both knew that pirates attracted many ruthless men. The pirate captains did not worry about how many men died. Their loss meant more profits for the survivors.

I hurried back to my gun crews. They awaited my orders. I looked at Don Diego, "If you, my lord, would command the harquebuses I will concentrate on the guns."

"You have a plan?"

"They will try to get to our sterns where they can destroy our rudders and then take us at will. The captain will use our three ships as one and that gives me the chance to destroy them. They are small and nimble but if I bring down a mast then they are helpless."

"You know your business. You men with the harquebus come here and I will give you your orders." He was a general and he knew how to handle warriors.

I went and loaded each gun myself. Guido and the others watched me carefully and it was my way of teaching them. We lit the linstocks and I was acutely aware of the powder keg upon which we sat. The four hunters were skirting around us as they sought a weakness. It was *'Golden Eagle'* that broke first and the cannonball that skipped across the water missed completely. Her gun captain had panicked. The sooner that Guido took over as gun captain the better. Captain Phillip was on our starboard quarter and *'Eagle'* on our larboard. Captain Pedro used the wind well and he made a turn to starboard when the wind turned a little and it brought us beam on to two of the hunters. The other two were on our larboard side and we could not bring those guns to bear. We had a falcon and the second robinet on the starboard side and as the leading pirate was just three hundred paces from us, I took a chance and fired, first the robinet and then the falcon. I fired both on the uproll and that meant a delay in the balls striking. The robinet struck the sail and must have clipped the mast for her captain turned her. It meant the heavier ball from the falcon merely hit the gunwale on the larboard side. The splinters, however, had a devastating effect and hit many men making the pirate turn to starboard, leaving us with just one pirate on the starboard side.

Just as Don Diego shouted, "Masterfully done, Captain Thomas." I heard a moan from my men.

I turned and saw that *'Golden Eagle'* was heading away from us and taking advantage of the wind. Her captain, like his gun captain, had panicked and was fleeing. We had no protection from our larboard quarter but, even worse for the *'Eagle'* and her crew she was now at the mercy of two pirates and they raced after her. Captain Pedro was a brave man and he was also loyal to his ships. He turned to follow. I had just loaded the guns and was ready to repeat the trick with the second pirate on our starboard side but that would not now happen. I ran to the forrard robinet and loaded it with the best one-pound ball I could find. It was now a race and the smaller pirates held the advantage. They closed to within four lengths of the *'Eagle'*, untroubled by any firing. She could not turn for if she did then they would be on both sides. Her captain had made a grave error and her crew could pay the price. I saw my chance and fired the robinet at the nearest pirate that lay just two hundred paces from us. She was turning but I managed to hit her just above the waterline. At the same time, the two ships opened fire on the *'Golden Eagle'*. I deduced that they were using falcons from the sound the guns made and the four flashes told me they had two guns on each ship. I worked out where Captain Ramon had stored his powder when the *'Eagle'* exploded in the biggest explosion I had ever seen. We were half a mile away and the deck was showered with splinters of wood. The only mercy was that none of the crew and her passengers would have known anything about it.

Captain Pedro saw the futility of continuing our present course and he turned. It was fortuitous for as we turned, we caught the pirate to starboard by surprise. I shouted, "Shoot!" as I touched the linstock to the falcon. Guido fired the robinet and Jose and his crew fired their guns at the same time. At least three of the balls hit the pirate that lay just two hundred paces from our starboard side. We could hear the screams as splinters struck the waiting men in the belly of the ship. The sails were peppered too and at least one yard was broken. I saw, as the smoke cleared, that at least one of her guns was upturned.

The English Adventurer

Don Diego shouted, "Captain Pedro, the other two!"

I turned and saw that the two pirates that had done for *'Eagle'* were now racing for us. I saw the smoke from small guns mounted at the bow of each of the pirates. One ball struck towards the stern and I heard a cry from a seaman standing there who was hit by a splinter. I ran to the guns and shouted, "Guido, double shot with a bag of stones." We each rammed a small bag of stones inside the barrel. "You take the starboard ship and I will take the larboard." The starboard pirate had been the one I had struck just above the waterline. I could see what they planned. They were racing at us to make a small target. Bow on the pirates were presenting their strongest parts. They would turn at the last moment and fire four guns at us. They might take hits but as they had twice the firepower, they expected to win the exchange.

"Don Diego, be ready to fire once we have fired."

"Aye, Captain."

"Ready Guido?"

"Aye, Captain."

This was all about timing. As the bows began their turn I shouted, "Shoot!" There is always a delay between touching the linstock and the powder igniting. I had taken that into consideration. The result was that we fired before the pirates and double-shotted balls hit them amidships.

Before the smoke cleared, I heard Don Diego shout, "Shoot!" I smiled. He had listened to my command. I had devised it so that there was no confusion with the other dangerous word on a ship, fire.

We reloaded and waited for the smoke to clear. As it did, I saw two things. The ship I had holed above the waterline had heeled and was now taking on water. Guido's ball had also struck the foremast and men were hacking it clear to prevent it from acting as an anchor. I shouted, "Shoot!" and we fired at the second ship that hove into view. Their starboard gunwale disappeared and I heard the screams as the waiting pirates were hit by splinters and some crushed beneath the overturned falcon. We quickly reloaded but the pirates had had enough. The four of them were all damaged in some way. The one that had been holed would be lucky to make it to one of the nearby islands. We could have pursued them but there would have been no point. I contemplated sending another ball after them but realised the futility of the action. It would merely be vengeful and that would not bring back a ship, a crew and its passengers.

Captain Pedro took us towards the wreckage of *'Eagle'*. We spied bodies and that was all until Juan shouted, "I see an arm waving!"

Sure enough, there was a hatch and someone clung to it. The captain headed for it and Guido hurled a line over. Jesus was one of the

The English Adventurer

ship's boys from the *'Eagle'* and he was the only survivor. That he had managed to survive was a miracle and we all put it down to an act of God. While we hove to, recovering Jesus, the priests who were aboard said prayers for the dead. It was all that we could do and when the sharks arrived to enjoy the unexpected meal, we made full sail and resumed our voyage.

We cleaned out the guns and then secured them. Alessandro, Juan and Guido took the unused powder, stones and ball back to the magazine and I stood with Don Diego. "They were here to kill, Don Diego. They fired their guns to destroy us. They were unconcerned about passengers or cargo. I think that someone does not wish you to get to Cumaná."

He gave me a quizzical look, "Surely they came for your ships."

"This is the first time a westbound convoy was attacked. Someone told them that there were guns and powder aboard and that we carried officials to replace corrupt men. Those two pirates deliberately destroyed *'Eagle'*. True, they could not have known that the magazine would explode but at the range that they sent their balls into her stern they knew that they would kill most of the men aboard."

He nodded, thoughtfully, "You have a good mind and my offer still stands. When we land, I shall see that some of the harquebuses are left aboard the two ships. They made a difference."

"You handled them well."

He laughed, "Had I been allowed to train the men who fired them then we could have reloaded and killed more. I will go and speak with your captain."

Jesus had been comforted by a priest who stood when I approached, "The boy cannot speak. I think the experience was too much for him." He nodded towards Juan and Alessandro who were returning, "I think those two might be able to heal him." He smiled at my raised eyebrows, "I spent some time in an orphanage in Sevilla and I got to know children. Other children are their best healers."

"Thank you."

"No, Englishman, thank you. Don Diego said you were a remarkable man and he is right. I am a man of God and not a man of war but even I can see that it was your skill that defeated four pirates. If not for you we would all have been lost. I shall add you to my prayers."

I took the priest's advice and asked Juan and Alessandro to stay close to Jesus. They were glad to do so for a number of reasons, not least because he seemed to have returned from the dead. That night, as he slept amongst us, he woke up screaming. Alessandro began to sing a lullaby to him and the boy fell asleep. I decided to keep him occupied

The English Adventurer

during the day so that he would not have time to dwell on the loss of all those that he had known. If he was exhausted each night then he might not suffer nightmares. I had the three boys clean out the barrels of the guns and the harquebuses. The latter did not need it as they had only fired one ball each but it was the occupation I needed. That night Jesus did not wake and Juan told me that Jesus had smiled once or twice during the day. He was still silent, but it was a beginning.

I was summoned to the captain during the afternoon watch. He was not happy and he led me to the larboard side. Don Diego and the other passengers were walking in the well of the ship. Don Diego thought that the exercise would be good for them.

"Our journey will not end at Isla Juana, Tomas." I had thought there was something amiss. "Don Diego does not wish to risk damage to his munitions. We will not land and he will report to the governor and then we shall sail to Cumaná."

I knew why he was unhappy and I tried to be philosophical about the matter, "We still only have to unload our cargo once and who knows we may pick up a cargo there."

He shook his head, "Sadly, Tomas, we are commissioned already and with one ship sunk we two will have to carry the cargo intended for three. We will not only be slower but we will also be dangerously overloaded. I like it not. Unless I can hire another ship, and that I doubt, we shall have the most dangerous of voyages home." The captain's depression spread amongst the crew. We had lost a third of our ships and I for one had not thought through the full implications.

The harbour at San Cristóbal de la Habana, on the north side of the island, was full and there appeared to be no berth for us. Don Diego was an impatient man and he cupped his hands and demanded that the **'Golden Hawk'** be allowed to dock. The harbour master must have known the soldier's reputation for a galleon which looked to be recently laden was ordered to sail. That the captain was not happy was clear but he obeyed such was the reputation of Don Diego Columbus.

As soon as we had tied up, he and two of his underlings hurried ashore and Captain Pedro was ordered to maintain a watch on the ship. He turned to me, "You and Guido had better use your harquebuses to discourage any who wish to board," he shook his head, "I had hoped to replenish our supplies but…"

I did not even bother to load the two weapons. Guido and I just stood with them leaning against the gunwale next to the tumblehome and gangplank. It was the first opportunity that Guido and I had to be alone and I spoke to him about his future, "I am sorry that you shall not be the captain of gunners on the **'Eagle'**."

The English Adventurer

"A man cannot be upset about what he never had and besides Captain Pedro has now said that I am your assistant gunner and I have been taken off all other duties."

"And you are happy about that?"

"Captain Tomas, I had friends on the *'Eagle'* and I know that they did not need to die. Had you been the master gunner on her they would be alive. I have only just begun to learn to be a gunner but I see that it is second only to the captain and sailing master of a ship. The best I could have hoped were it not for this opportunity, would be that I might rise to third mate. This is better."

Don Diego seemed to have been away for a long time and when one of his men hurried back to us, I knew we would not be leaving any time soon. "Captain Tomas, Don Diego and the Governor need you. You are to come with me."

Captain Pedro had come to the tumblehome when he had seen the man approach, "You had better go Tomas." He winked at me, "Perhaps some supplies and water might be fetched aboard if Don Diego is delayed." I nodded, knowing what he meant.

The governor's residence reflected Don Diego Velázquez de Cuéllar's ambition. He saw himself ruling, for the king, of course, the empire of New Spain. The fly in the ointment was Hernán Cortés who had disobeyed the governor. I was now accorded, thanks to my service to the king, more respect than hitherto. I was taken by a liveried guard to a room where Don Diego Columbus and Don Diego Velázquez sat at a table, poring over a map. The spy in me knew that such a map would be worth a fortune to Lord Collingwood. There was a table in the far corner where clerks worked on lists and parchments. They were sufficiently far away that they would not be able to hear clearly what was said at the other table.

The Governor looked up and waved me to approach, "Don Diego tells me that you believe the attack on the ships was an attempt to stop Don Diego and his supplies from reaching Cumaná."

"It is just that we have never yet suffered an attack when west bound and the pirates seemed reckless. They came in hard and fast and did not try to dismast us. They normally like to weaken a ship before boarding in large numbers."

The Governor gave me a sharp look, "And you would know such things." I wisely said nothing. "I concur and I believe that snake, the Captain General of Mexico is behind it. He not only denies me my share of the treasure pouring out of that land but he also seeks to undermine me with King Carlos."

The English Adventurer

Don Diego shook his head, "I am not sure that you are correct, my friend, for he is an ocean away from the rebels."

The Governor saw the logic in the argument but he was not convinced. His hatred of Cortés made him blind to all else, "They could be acting in concert."

I saw that Don Diego was tiring of it all but he was a practical man, "Francisco Pizarro is an honourable man?" The question was addressed to us both and the Governor and I nodded. "Then I propose that when I have been safely delivered that the ***'Golden Hawk'*** sails to Nombre de Dios and we ask Captain Pedro and Tomas, here, to ask the Alcalde what he thinks. He is closer to Mexico and may hear what we do not." Nombre de Dios lay some forty miles north of Panama but it was the nearest point at which goods, intended for Panama could be landed.

The Governor turned to look at me and the expression on his face was as though I had stepped in something on my way in, "But this man was a pirate and a slave! We cannot use him as a go-between."

The Governor failed to see the irony of my presence in the meeting.

Don Diego sighed, "Governor, this man has saved the king's treasure as well as the king's men. I think we can trust him and, more importantly, Francisco Pizarro trusts him."

"Very well then."

I had to speak, "Governor, Don Diego, Captain Pedro is anxious to sail back to Spain for he needs another ship. His two ships will be overloaded as it is."

I expected censure but, instead, Governor Velasquez nodded, "You are right and any delay in the delivery of the king's treasure will result in penalties for me." He waved over one of his clerks. The man bent down and the governor spoke in his ear. The clerk nodded and went back to the table. He proffered a parchment to him. Governor Velasquez beamed, "I thought so. When Bilbao was executed, I confiscated two of his ships. I retained the crews but disposed of the cargo. In compensation for the loss of his ship, I will give them and their crews to Captain Pedro. That should satisfy him."

I was not sure it would as he was being given two unknown ships and crews but I knew he would take what he was offered if only to give himself a better chance of reaching Spain.

He took a quill, dipped it in the inkpot and scribbled something on the parchment. He melted some wax and marked it with his seal. "There, give this to Captain Pedro. Don Diego, you will inform Captain Pedro of his new task."

The English Adventurer

Don Diego was a man of action and snatching up the parchment he said, "We have little time to waste. I will send a report back with Captain Pedro once I have assessed the situation."

We strode through the streets in silence. Don Diego's men flanked him. He was the one they would save if we were attacked and I would be the one thrown to any wolves we might meet. I gripped the hilt of my sword.

As we neared the ships he shouted, "We sail at once!"

Captain Phillip had disembarked his passengers and he was ready to sail. Captain Pedro met us at the tumblehome, "Governor Velasquez agreed?" I could tell, from his tone, that he hoped for a different result.

Don Diego put his arm around the captain and said, as he led the captain towards the stern, "Come, for we have a gift for you."

The gangplank was moved aboard and the ship was released from the land as the First Mate ordered the sails to be loosed. We were off to sea once more. This time there would be five ships as there were three carrying the soldiers that Don Diego would lead. They had awaited in the port for our arrival. I had to admire the man for he knew not these men. Some were mercenaries who arrived from Spain and looking for a way to make their fortune whilst some were the sweepings of the island. I did not envy him his task.

Chapter 4

I did not get a chance to speak to Captain Pedro until the next day. I waited until Don Diego and his fellow passengers were marching around the deck before I approached. The captain shook his head, "Have you seen these ships, Tomas, or met their crews?"

"No, Captain."

"And for us to have to sail to Nombre de Dios! Madness."

I offered him a solution, "You trust Captain Phillip, why not have him assess the ships and their crews while we are in Nombre de Dios? He can replace any weaknesses in either ships or crews."

He brightened, "You are a clever man, Tomas. Perhaps this might turn out better than I anticipated."

Jesus smiled more as we headed south but he still remained silent.

It was three days later that I saw Turtle Island. I had known that Nueva Toledo lay south of the island where we had made a home and buried our treasure but I had not expected us to pass so close. It was deserted and storms had taken away all signs of the shelters we had built. I cared not for the treasure we had buried there but the memories that rose in me made me as silent as Jesus. I think I understood, at the moment, Jesus' loss more than any other. I waved him over.

"Jesus, I know that you have lost one family on the *'Golden Eagle'* and we can never replace them but I swear that we will try to be as a family for you. I know that your heart is filled with pain and it stops the words from coming from you. Do not worry about that. When you are ready and wish to speak then we shall hear." His eyes welled up but he smiled and nodded. I ruffled his hair, "Now go and help Juan and Alessandro. Tomorrow, we dock and we will have much to do."

We arrived at a port under siege. Those loyal to the crown had only survived because of the walls around the port and the fact that the rebels had no cannons. Don Diego Columbus had us unload the hold at the same time as his unpredictable army disembarked. The harquebuses were issued to those who knew how to use them. There were six left over. Don Diego sent them back to us. He had kept his word. The powder and the balls were carried ashore and we all breathed a sigh of relief. Lastly, the foodstuffs and the officials left the ship. I heard firing from the distant walls and knew that Don Diego had begun his rule aggressively. Captain Pedro resupplied his ship with water and fresh fruit and vegetables while my ship's boys, Guido and myself swept, carefully, the forward hold. We collected a bucket full of powder. Whilst not of the best quality we could find uses for it and I transferred it to a pot which I sealed and marked. We also found a dozen two-pound balls that had freed themselves from their containers and lodged in the dark recesses of the hold. They were a real treasure.

It was too late to leave the port for the tide was not right and neither Captain Pedro nor Captain Phillip was familiar with the waters. With eight men on watch, we spent a nervous night as guns popped in the distance while we tried to sleep. It was before dawn when Don Diego Columbus arrived back at the ship. He had on his breastplate and helmet. His blackened face told me that he had been close to the cannons that had fired.

"Captain Pedro, I know that you will be sailing west and I would beg a boon."

The captain was suspicious and said, cautiously, "If I can help, Don Diego…"

"It is really your Master Gunner I need. The rebels have fled along the coast. They have begun to build a stronghold ten miles west of here." He took a map from one of the men who had come with him, "Here is a map. The place is called Mochima. I would have your gunner destroy its walls with his guns. It will take me some time to march there and I would like a town which was reduced to be there to greet me." All the time he was looking at me.

I said, "I can do this Captain Pedro."

The captain unrolled the map, "We have to sail down a narrow channel, Don Diego. I will not risk my ship."

Don Diego's face showed that he would brook no argument, "Captain Pedro, because of your service I made this a request but I now command you to reduce the walls of Mochima."

"Then I will obey, albeit reluctantly."

Don Diego softened a little, "I know that you are a good captain and I will forgive you for your comments. More, I trust Captain Tomas to give me an easy victory. Farewell and remember, Tomas, there is always a place for you in my army."

Dawn was still an hour away but as we were awake, we prepared for sea. Captain Phillip was informed of our task. He would leave to sail north again. His task was to ensure that our two new ships were ready for us when we finally returned to Isla Juana. I had powder, balls and bags of stones brought up. The next time we were near a beach I would have the boys gather more stones. They were a cheap but effective weapon.

As the sun came up, we left the port and I joined the captain. He jabbed an angry finger at the map, "See, Tomas, here the channel is less than two hundred paces wide. What if there are rocks?"

The English Adventurer

I smiled, "Captain Pedro, we need not race through the channel. We have all day and looking at the map it is less than four miles from the open sea to Mochima. If God smiles on us, we shall be bombarding by noon and we can be back on the open ocean before dark."

He shook his head, "And this adds a whole day to our journey west, a journey, incidentally, that I do not wish to make."

I sighed, "I know why you are angry, Captain Pedro, you have lost a valuable ship but you are reliant upon men like Don Diego Columbus and Governor Diego de Velasquez. If you wish to make a fortune serving the king then you must obey them."

He nodded, "You are right. I pray that you reduce the walls to matchwood as soon as you can."

The winds were kind to us and the captain pushed us hard along the coast. While he did so I had the second falcon brought to join the robinet and falcon on the starboard side. I wanted all my firepower concentrated in one place. I gathered my small crew around me when the guns were all secured. "We need accuracy and not speed. I want you to prepare each gun. Each time we fire, swab out carefully and ensure that the barrel is cooled and dry. The balls should be perfect. We have more to choose from this time. When the gun is fired then prepare it for another firing. I will use the linstock." I looked at Guido, "If you wish to be a gunner then watch what I do. See how I judge the wind, the range and the roll of the ship."

"We will be at anchor, captain."

"The ship will still move; the firing of the guns, the tide, the wind, all of these will make us move. It will only be a slight movement but it will be movement. Our task is simply to destroy wooden walls so that when Don Diego arrives there will be no defences for the rebels to use."

While we waited, I took a wax tablet and, from memory, made a map of the coast. I would commit it to parchment the next day. Lord Collingwood might need the maps of this coastline. The reason the rebels had done what they had was to become rich men from the gold and silver to be had from it. King Henry had ambitions to become as rich and powerful as the King of Spain.

The captain had been right to be worried. While there were no cliffs and the white beaches and blue waters looked inviting, the passage was narrower than one would have liked and he had two men leaning over the bow looking at the bottom. Luckily there were neither rocks nor sandbanks and we wound our way through a channel that was far from straight. I had told the captain that he needed to moor the ship and allow our starboard guns to fire. I also suggested that this might be a chance for the crew to be taught how to use the harquebuses. They might not hit anything but it would be a good opportunity for them to learn. I merely asked him to use the stern castle so that I was not distracted.

I peered at the wooden walls as we neared the rebel stronghold. The timber had been taken from the hardwood forest and it would not splinter. I saw no guns on the walls and that made sense. Had the rebels been gifted with guns they would have used them in the siege. I shouted, "Captain, moor as close as you can without hazarding your ship."

"I will try."

We edged our way down the channel under reefed sails and with sailors looking for danger. He was a good sailor and we managed to moor less than one hundred and thirty paces from the walls. Even the harquebuses would cause damage. Two anchors were run out, one at the bow and one at the stern to allow us to stay in one place and the sails were reefed. Each gun was loaded and I went to the first falcon and adjusted the aim. I knew that I could hit the wall; Juan could hit the wall but the first ball would tell me the true range. Ideally, I wanted to hit the wall at the base for repeated shots would weaken it and it would be harder to repair. The defenders had some bows, crossbows and a couple of harquebuses but a gunner on a ship tended to kneel down and the missiles that came at us missed as they flew over our heads. However, it was a distraction and I shouted, "Harquebuses, open fire!"

The men were eager to use the new weapons and a huge line of flame, smoke and noise erupted from the sterncastle. I did not even bother to look for damage. They were a distraction for the defenders. Satisfied with my aim I touched the linstock. The boom was much louder than the combined noise of the harquebuses and the smoke hid the fort from sight. I walked to the robinet as Guido and the boys swabbed and loaded the first falcon. I saw that I had hit four feet from the base. I needed to be slightly lower with my next shot from the falcon. There was, however, a satisfying hole and I saw the glow where the ball had ignited the wood. It would die out soon enough but over time the flames might grow. The robinet had a smaller ball and the noise was slightly duller than the falcon. In addition, the harquebus had fired again and the side was wreathed in a fog of smoke. I had to wait longer but the hole, this time smaller, was in the perfect place. It would not need to be adjusted. I went to the second falcon and made a slight change to the aim and lit the linstock. Once again, as the smoke cleared I saw the hole was in the right place and I returned to the first falcon. I adjusted it and fired. Once again it was perfect and now that I had the range, I was able to walk down the loaded guns and use the linstock. It was like rolling thunder in the distance as the guns boomed out. Guido

The English Adventurer

and the boys were now working even faster. After five balls from each gun, I stopped.

"Just swab out and let me see where we hit next." This gave the boys and Guido some rest but it was mainly so that I could assess the damage we had caused. A section of wall twenty paces long was so badly damaged that it was indefensible. I saw men trying to repair it and I said, "Load the guns with bags of balls."

This time when I fired, the balls scythed through men and carried on into the fort. The survivors of the attack took cover.

"Load with ball."

I shifted my aim to the left and we began firing. By noon we had totally destroyed the wall next to the sea and I had managed to send balls and bags of stones to demolish the north wall. We had used half of our supply of balls and I was loath to use them all in case we needed them for a sea battle. Fires burned on the wooden walls and the defenders were forced to waste water dousing them. No matter what they did the walls would be weakened. The fort was indefensible as some of the balls had crossed the fort and damaged the east and south walls. Don Diego Columbus would have no difficulty in taking the rebel base. In addition, our bags of balls and the harquebuses had thinned the defenders numbers by half. Even reinforced by those that Don Diego had defeated already they would not be able to hold out.

Captain Pedro was happy that he had a whole afternoon to navigate the channel and we reached the sea by the middle of the afternoon. My crew and I moved the falcon back and cleaned the guns before securing them for the voyage west. We were all happy. The ones who were the happiest were the sailors who had used the harquebuses. For the first time, they had been able to fight back at a distance. Every sailor had been given the opportunity to fire one and the result was that they had all learned the skill. They would be sad when half of the weapons were given to the **'Silver Swan'** but we could always acquire more.

I retired to my cabin, now vacated by Don Diego and his officials. I transferred the information from the wax tablet to the map I was making. The cabin was secure and no one would dare to search it but I could not help but feel guilty hiding my secrets from my crew and Captain Pedro.

We reached Nombre de Dios just two days later for the winds had helped us. I went ashore to find Francisco Pizarro. Although both the captain and I had both been charged with speaking with the Alcalde Captain Pedro was more concerned with finding a cargo to take to Isla Juana. I changed into what I considered my best clothes and headed through the crowded streets to the residence used by Francisco. I had

The English Adventurer

the usual problem of gaining access to my friend. The guards and officials seemed to think that it was their job to keep people away from the man who ran Panama. I was persistent and insistent. It was when I raised my voice that Francisco himself came out to see what the fuss was all about. His frown turned to a smile when he saw me.

"Tomas! Let him through." The command parted the crowds for me.

I just said, "Governor de Velasquez and Don Diego Columbus sent me, Don Francisco,"

He knew that it was serious and shouted, "Clear my chamber and fetch wine and food for my friend and me."

"Yes, Alcalde."

"You are lucky to find me here. I came to send my reports back to Isla Juana. The journey to the southern sea is easier than it was but it is forty miles through the jungle which, whilst the human enemies are subdued, the natural ones are not.

I hid my smile. The next time I appeared I would be granted an immediate audience. He was all business as we sat down. I told my tale of the voyage and the fight from the time we left Cádiz. We had a brief interruption when the wine and food arrived but other than that I was able to tell my tale without break. I concluded with my thoughts on the motive for the attack.

"You may be right, Tomas, but I cannot agree with the governor's assumption that Cortés is behind this. The rebels are an ocean away. There is more of a threat to us and the Castilla del Oro. I think the threat comes from Don Alphonso del Albuera." He stood and went to a drawer. Taking out a map and using the platters of food to weigh it down I saw that it was a map of the sea that Balboa had discovered. "Pascual de Andagoya spoke to me before he left on his voyage to explore the coast. He spoke of a people who wore gold in their ears and about their necks. Don Alphonso del Albuera tried to join the expedition but Pascual did not trust the man. It was after that incident, some time ago, that I began to ask questions about Don Alphonso. I had not heard the name before then. His family is rich but he is not and he came to this New World to seek his fortune. He has interests in Florida and Nicaragua. It is the latter that is of the most interest. He is an ally of Francisco Hernández de Córdoba. That is a ruthless man who defies all other Spaniards. He has made an empire there and even Cortés is worried about him. There is a rumour that Don Pedro Arias Dávila is already marching south to deal with him."

I shook my head, "I am sorry, Francisco, but I do not understand all of this. How does this explain the attack on our ships?"

The English Adventurer

"Don Diego Columbus is untainted by tales of corruption. Governor General Hernán Cortés is a great warrior but he has ambitions. He has yet to challenge King Carlos and I am not sure that he will do but he has challenged de Velasquez." He went to the map and poked a finger at the coastline I recognised as Florida. "Don Alphonso has interests here. There are few treasures to be had but it is a good base from which to send pirates to raid the gold ships. If Don Alphonso could ensure that Don Diego Columbus would not reach the Castilla del Oro then he would have a free hand to carve out an Empire far to the south while being safe from harm in his stronghold to the north. With de Velasquez and Cortés at each other's throats then who is there to stop him?"

I sipped the wine as I considered his words, "You, Francisco."

He looked shocked, "Me?"

I nodded, "You said that Don Diego Columbus was without a stain, well so are you. Both Don Diego and Governor de Velasquez both sought your advice and it was they sent me here. You could stop this Don Alphonso."

He smiled and spread his arms, "I am Alcalde of this city and, for the moment, that is enough for me."

I nibbled some of the ham. The pigs had been brought over from Spain many years earlier and their New World diet had imparted a different taste. I liked it. "Yet you still yearn to explore do you not?"

"You read me like a book, Tomas, aye, I do. I would explore this southern sea. I believe that the treasures there would make those collected by Cortés seem like the coppers given to beggars outside cathedrals." He began to roll up the map. "I do not wish this to make me rich although I know it would but to make Spain even more powerful than it is. I wish that King Carlos would appoint a stronger hand to rule this land." Putting the map away he said, "So, have I answered your questions now, Tomas?"

"You have indeed all save one, where do we find this Don Alphonso?"

"He is elusive and he left Panama soon after Pascual left with his expedition. He could be anywhere. Knowing his name and stopping his ambitions are two entirely different matters."

"I have my answer then."

"And will you give me my answer, Tomas?"

"You have yet to ask me a question."

"I would have you be my master gunner when I have the funds and the men to seek this southern empire of which I have heard. Will you be that man?"

44

The English Adventurer

I was tempted for Francisco Pizarro seemed to me the most honourable of men. He deserved an honest answer. "I am flattered and tempted but I promised to serve in Captain Pedro's ships and I have gunners to train. Also, I fear the jungles that took so many when I served with Balboa. However, I feel I am obligated to you and if your offer is still there when I have done with Captain Pedro and served him well then, I will be your master gunner."

He beamed, "And that is the answer for which I hoped. It will take me at least a year, maybe two, to find both the funds and the men. You are the first and that gives me hope." He clasped my arm and I had made a promise I had not expected to make.

Chapter 5

Captain Pedro was a happy man for he had managed to find a cargo and it was bound for Isla Juana. The merchant wanted it to be taken all the way to Spain but that would depend on the capacity of the two new ships given by Governor Velasquez. The merchant was happy with the assurance given by Captain Pedro that he would do his best.

Captain Pedro did not ask me about my meeting until we were at sea with a good wind pushing us east. I gave him the information and he nodded, "That makes sense to me. I have heard that Florida is a hotbed of pirates. The islands that ring Isla Juana are now controlled by Governor de Velasquez but Florida is the wild frontier. I will let you tell the governor for you deserve the plaudits."

I said nothing for I wanted to remain anonymous. I did not like this attention. I did not wish to be sacrificed for someone's political ambitions.

Captain Phillip knew his business and as we entered the harbour, we saw that there was a berth next to the *'Silver Swan'*. The two ships tied up further along the quay had to be the ones given to us by Governor de Velasquez. They were much smaller than the one we had lost but from the activity on their decks, Captain Phillip was wasting no time in making them ready for sea. Captain Pedro was a sailor and not a diplomat. After we had tied up, he said, "It is for you to visit the governor. I have much to do to ready my ships."

I nodded, glumly. I was no diplomat either but I knew I had a duty to report to the governor. Once more I dressed in my finest and, after strapping on my sword headed up towards the governor's residence. Over the years, since my father's death, I had developed a sort of sixth sense. It warned me of danger. I wondered if the spirit of my father watched over me. I hoped that he was in heaven but he had died unshriven. What if his spirit still wandered the seas? Whatever the cause, as I walked through the crowded streets of the busiest port in the New World, I felt that I was being watched but whenever I turned, I saw nothing untoward. I was happy when I reached the relative safety of the residence. Here I was known. I was not necessarily liked for I was English and had been a pirate but I was allowed inside the residence and quickly taken to speak to the governor.

Unlike Panama, I was not invited to sit. There were three clerks in the room and they each had a wax tablet. Governor de Velasquez made sure that everything was recorded. I told him what I had learned. He frowned when I spoke Don Alphonso's name but he said nothing at the time. When I had finished, he turned to one of his clerks and said, "Ask Captain Rodrigo to join us." You have done well, Master Gunner and I have heard, from Don Diego, that you were instrumental in defeating the rebels. I was wise to spare your life."

A soldier wearing a breastplate and carrying a morion entered the room and saluted the governor. I took this to be Captain Rodrigo.

"Master Gunner, tell the captain what you just told me." I did and this time there was a reaction from the soldier.

Captain Rodrigo spoke not to me but to the governor, "I have heard of this man. I would not know him if I tripped over him in the street but he has been in Isla Juana. I believe that at the moment he is somewhere in Florida. One of my spies told me that he took ship a week since."

The Governor looked at me, "That would be not long after you arrived with Don Diego." I nodded. "I thought that there was nothing in Florida except for jungle, crocodiles and snakes."

Captain Rodrigo said, "We are in the dark about a land which is closer to us than the Castilla del Oro, Governor, and perhaps the men who are there do so deliberately. They wish us to be in the dark."

The governor nodded, "And with Don Diego and the bulk of our soldiers in Castilla del Oro we can do little about it." He pointed to the door, "Master Gunner, wait without. I will speak with Captain Rodrigo and then write a letter for Captain Pedro to deliver to Cádiz. It is for the king. He should know of this treachery."

I was not offended by being dismissed. The less that I knew the better. I sat and waited. It was Captain Rodrigo who brought me the document. Handing it to me he said, "Guard this with your life. I fear that the pirates will try to attack your little fleet on the way east. You should warn your captain of the danger."

I put the letter inside my doublet, "I think he is well aware of the danger." I smiled, "Would it be possible for us to replenish our stock of balls and powder, Captain? We expended a great deal when we reduced the fort for Don Diego."

He smiled, "I shall come on the morrow and see that you have all you need. Your little fleet will carry the hopes and the gold of the governor to Spain. It would be a shame if they were to be sunk."

As I left, I reflected that the captain had not been concerned about me, or the crew, just the gold and the letter that we would be carrying. It was dark as the gates of the residence were closed behind me and I headed back to the harbour with deserted streets. My sixth sense made my neck prickle and I kept to the centre of the streets. The poor were scurrying about the street, picking through the spoiled food left over from the markets. Their eyes flickered nervously at me as I passed. I

The English Adventurer

had my hands on the hilts of my dagger and my sword so that when the three men burst out of the alleyway and surrounded me, I was ready. I knew that they meant me harm and debate would do little. Drawing my weapons I barely managed to deflect the swords swung at my head. The blade that came at me from behind was hurriedly thrust and merely ripped through my doublet.

Three to one meant that I would die and I cried out, "Treachery! Help!" The cry echoed in the silence of twilight. I repeated the words in English as I twisted my body so that my back was to the wall of the house. None came to help me for this was the poorer quarter and they minded their own business. When my body fell then it would be picked clean before any could find me. I was on my own.

The only advantage that I held was that the three attackers were so keen to get at me that they got in their own way. I swung my sword in an arc and there were sparks in the dark as the blades clashed. Each of the attackers was holding a sword only while I had a dagger. I lunged with the dagger in the dark and was rewarded when it sank into cloth and then flesh. There was a scream and one man stepped back. His movement allowed me an aggressive swing of my sword. I slashed my dagger too and the men stepped back. They had expected an easy kill and now they would use their superior numbers to overcome me. I looked for an escape but there was none. By pressing my back to the wall of the house I had given myself some protection but I had lost any avenue of escape. One of them lunged at my face with his sword and when I riposted it away a second stabbed at my middle, I barely managed to deflect it with my dagger. The wounded man saw his chance and his sword came at my chest. I should have died but for two things. The button took the tip and as the sword sliced through the doublet it found the parchment. Folded parchment is hard to penetrate and only the end of the tip pricked my chest.

It was then that I heard the shout as Guido led half a dozen sailors from *'Golden Hawk'* to fall upon the three attackers. Such was the ferocity of their attack that the three men lay dead before I could halt the slaughter. Captain Rodrigo would want a prisoner and, even as we searched their bodies, he arrived with half a dozen pikemen.

He frowned when he saw the dead men, "They attacked you?" I nodded. "A pity we did not get to question them."

I said, "Had my crew not reached me then I would have been dead."

"The letter?" I took it out. There was a hole and a tiny patch of blood. He gave a thin smile, "Perhaps the cut and the blood will add weight to the contents of the letter. We will escort you back to your ship and I will leave three men to guard it although I think that there will be no repeat of this assault."

As we returned Guido explained that they had heard a shout but it was not until I repeated the cry in English that they knew that it was I who was under threat. There was outrage amongst the whole crew that I had been attacked. Jose came from his ship to ask about my health. I could see that he was shaken to the core.

I held up my hands, "I am unhurt and that is in no small part thanks to this crew."

Captain Pedro nodded, "And we begin loading tomorrow so that we can be, once more, at sea, where we expect to see predators. This is a hell hole."

Captain Rodrigo and his men had not gone directly back to the residence and were descending the gangplank when Captain Pedro's words were uttered. The soldier turned, "And that will change, Captain Pedro. Master Gunner, I apologise, for I should have realised that you were alone and that there are men who wish to see you dead." They left the ship and headed up to the residence, marching in step. They were soldiers.

"I will speak to you on the morrow, Tomas. Have food and get some rest. From what I have learned you were lucky to survive the attack. I need you alert and ready to face the challenges of our voyage back to Spain."

Guido and the three boys ensured that I had both food and drink. There was hot food for we cooked on the quayside. I was not hungry but I knew that they were right and I needed food. As I ate Jesus snuggled next to my chair. He looked like a puppy but he smiled at me reassuringly. It was a sign of a change in the silent survivor.

"Will you want me aboard one of the two ships we have just acquired, Captain Tomas?" Guido waited until his mouth was empty before he spoke.

I shook my head, "I know not if they have guns and besides our plan still stands. We are the heart of this fleet and we will manage the defence. I need you here with me. Did we send the harquebuses to Jose?"

"Yes, captain, and he was grateful."

We might have made better use of them but it was right that Captain Phillip's ship should be as well defended as ours. The fight, long day and general weariness made me fall asleep the moment I clambered into my hammock. The captain did not wake me but I heard the noise as men stamped aboard carrying the cargo we would take to Cádiz. I knew, even before I had left my cabin, that the first boxes would be

King Charles' treasure. It was heavy and would be spread out as low down as possible. It made for greater security and ensured a well-balanced ship. When I emerged Captain Pedro waved me down to his stern cabin. "First mate, take over." He led me into his cabin. Unlike mine, it had shutters at the stern that opened to allow light to flood in. "You slept well."

"I did."

"Your Captain Rodrigo sent a message down that the three attackers had been identified as being members of the crew of a ship that came from Florida. Captain Rodrigo said that you were right. The ship left in the night. Should we be worried?"

I nodded, "The man who is behind this is ambitious. He is building an empire in Florida but he has men working in the south. On our way west he wished to stop Don Diego but on our way east he will be after the gold we carry to finance his empire building and to weaken the position of the governor. We should take a more southerly course back to Spain."

"That will add a day or two."

"Better that than a watery grave."

"Aye. Now the two ships we have been given have good captains and officers but the crews are the scum of the earth. I would not trust them as far as I could throw them. Nor do they have any guns. They can carry cargo and that is all. I spoke with Captain Phillip yesterday and we have devised a plan. His ship will lead our fleet and with, *'Maria'* and *'Isabella'* following him we will bring up the rear. Both the ships we have been given are slow and need the weed cleaning from their hulls. If we are attacked then we will guard the starboard and Captain Phillips the larboard. It is not perfect but what can we do?"

"Then we need to have Jose shift his guns so that they face the larboard side. Now that he has the harquebuses, he can use those if he is attacked on both sides."

The captain nodded, "We sail tomorrow. The balls and powder you requested have been brought aboard. Your man Guido saw to their storage."

I smiled, Guido had been a part of the regular crew but in the last month or so had become part of mine. "I need to send the three boys to seek stones, Captain."

"Aye, I thought you might. When we get back to Spain, I will need to take on more boys."

I waved over Juan and the others, "I need you to find as many stones as you can. You know the kind we seek?"

Juan nodded, "As round as we can manage and the size of a thumbnail."

"Good, now be back here well before dark." I turned to Guido, "Shift the forrard robinet to the starboard side. We need all the guns we can get. A forward-firing gun is a luxury we can ill afford."

I headed for the *'Silver Swan'*. I needed to speak to Jose. He was as busy as the rest of the crew. I was admitted to the deck by the sailor on guard at the gangplank. There were petty thieves who would steal the coins from a corpse. I saw that Jose's stump, while still red, was healing well. "We need you to shift your guns so that they are all on the larboard side," I explained to him the thinking behind the decision. "If you are attacked on the starboard side before you can get into position then have your harquebuses used. If you fire them all at the same time at a ship then some might hit."

"I am in your hands, Tomas, for you are still the master. Even my father acknowledged that. Will we be attacked?"

"We will but there is better news. We do not carry powder and so we should not suffer the same fate as *'Eagle'* and we carry gold. They will try to take us whole and therein lies their weakness. Have you enough bags of balls?"

He nodded, "We went to collect them while Captain Phillip examined the two vessels."

"You have seen more of them than I have, what think you?"

"They have no guns and are much smaller than we are. They are chickens waiting to be plucked."

"Then we will have to guard them. You know that while you do not have the firepower of our ship, I know that you and your gunners will acquit themselves well?"

"I know and Captain Pedro has told Captain Phillip that he will order two sakers for our ship too."

The loss of *'Eagle'* had put any economic considerations to one side. Guns were the only solution for pirates. They had so many crew that the only other way to ensure survival was to carry as many men as they did and that was patently impossible.

I did go ashore but it was with Guido and Carlos. While Guido was now a permanent member of my gun crew Carlos had other tasks to occupy him but Captain Pedro would not risk losing me. We went armed to the market for I wished to buy not gifts but foods that would alleviate the dull diet. I bought a cured ham. I paid more than I would have in Cádiz but that could not be helped. I bought a round of cheese. That too was more expensive than in Spain. The cheap items were the fruits I bought. Papaya fruits and bananas were plentiful. I knew the

The English Adventurer

value of their juice and their sweetness contrasted well with the savoury nature of my luxuries. The papaya would last the longest. I bought a sack of fruit. My gun crew knew that I would share with them my bounty. The fruits would be unlikely to survive more than fourteen nights but it would shorten the time we had to endure the ship's fare.

The boys were already back and were outside my deck sorting out the stones and filling bags. "We did well, Captain Tomas." Alessandro's voice was genuinely excited.

"I collected many white ones." I had never heard Jesus' voice before and I was stunned.

Juan said, "Aye, Captain Tomas, he found his voice while we hunted the stones."

It was a miracle but the priest had been right. The companionship of the two boys had made the difference.

We had fish hooks we had carved from bone and I had bought some cord, "When that is done you can attach the hooks to the cord. While we are in safer waters then you can fish. Fresh fish will augment our diet."

Boys are always happiest when occupied and they enjoyed the competition of seeing who could make the most fishing lines. The next day, as our little fleet set sail we were a happy crew. There would be dangers but for those first three days, as we navigated seas filled with friendly ships, we were happy. I knew that it would change. My map-making had taught me where the danger lay. Once we were to the east of the line of tiny islands that Christopher Columbus had first discovered, then we would be in danger. The open ocean, more unpredictable weather and, worst of all, the pirate predators who preyed on the treasure ships would make our lives hard.

Chapter 6

Perhaps the captain's course further south than was normal confused the pirates for we had two days of peaceful sailing once we had passed the last uninhabited island. The two ships we had acquired were slow but not as slow as I had expected and the captains appeared to be keen to impress Captain Pedro. He had told them that he would decide if he wished to scrap the ships or repair them when we arrived in Cádiz. The two men were eager to be employed by a successful captain like Captain Pedro and they responded quickly to every signal he sent. I knew the problem the pirates had. When I had served with my father, as a pirate, I knew that the sea was empty and that there was a great deal of luck in finding a target. That they would have been waiting for us was clear but we were not where they expected.

We saw the four sails not long after dawn. They were to the south of us and the lookout quickly identified them as the ones that had attacked us on our way west. They had clearly been repaired and they would not underestimate us. The captain's plans were put into action immediately and all four ships took in a reef; we could not outrun them and a stable firing platform might see us survive. We would have to face them first. That pleased me for we were the better armed.

"Boys, fetch powder, balls and bags of stones." The three boys raced away as Carlos joined Guido and me. I lit the fire in the stone ready for the linstock and I turned to Guido. "Issue the harquebuses and have them at the stern. You know who will be the best."

"Aye, come, Carlos."

Everyone aboard the ship was busy and I stared at the four ships as they fanned out to come at us. I knew that they would try to get around our rear and that was why I had the harquebuses there. They would not be able to defeat the pirates but they would discourage them from closing. The biggest danger would be if they tried to disable us and hit our rudder. I did not think they would as it risked an explosion such as the one that had destroyed *'Eagle'*. A more likely threat would be an attempt to dismast us. That took skill and wasted balls. As the balls were fetched, I loaded each gun in turn. The bags of stones would be for when the enemy closed with us.

As we waited, I took the linstock and blew on it. Without turning to look at the gun crews I said, "We fight as we did before. You load, quickly but safely and I will fire. Listen for my commands as to the load." The ships were now half a mile away and had spread out to make it harder for me to hit more than one ship. I would not waste a ball yet

The English Adventurer

but I had decided that I needed to reduce the odds. No matter what they did I would try to hurt one of them and take it from the battle. I gambled that they would not have a forward-firing cannon. As I had discovered it could only be used in the event of finding a stern. That meant I would have the luxury of firing first. One of the pirate ships began to put on more sail and was heading to cross the bows. That made sense for if they fired a broadside, they might hit any of the four of us. A second ship followed her and the other two turned a little to cross our stern.

My father had taught me well and I had an eye for range. The second ship of the two heading for our sterns was four hundred paces from us when I fired the robinet. I deliberately aimed it to bounce across the water like a skimming stone. I was gratified when the small ball slammed into the pirate's side, just three feet or so from the waterline. I repeated the shot with the falcons, hurrying from one to the other. I aimed the robinet slightly higher as the pirate was closer. As my men reloaded, I peered through the smoke to see the results. I saw the holes in her side and it had slowed her. The last ball, from the robinet, had smashed into the gunwale and I knew it would have hurt the pirate.

"Captain, a point or two to starboard."

He waved his hand in acknowledgement. The change in course would allow us to fire for longer and would also bring Jose and his guns into play. The pirates would have to adjust their attack. I knew that my first balls would be slowing down the second pirate and my second rolling volley was aimed at the gunwale. The range was down to three hundred paces and I saw the glowing linstocks from the pirate. My rolling volley was quicker and the balls hit the side as well as the gunwale.

Captain Pedro shouted, "I will turn another couple of points to starboard."

He had seen what I could not, that the move would allow Jose and his guns to do as I had done with the other two pirates. They fired but they were not aiming at one ship but four. Three balls hit. One struck the larboard side of our ship and I guessed, from the shouts, that the other two had hit the new vessels. I concentrated on firing a third time. We were pirouetting around each other and my well-trained crew had every gun ready for me as I went down the line of cannons. The pirate we had hit had been hurt and my third volley ended the threat of the damaged pirate. I saw at least one gun upturned and a two-pound ball from my falcon hit the mainmast. We could hear the crack then the creak and finally the groan as the mast fell into the sea. I had one last chance to fire as the pirate slewed around. My last balls made a mess of her rudder and her stern. She was out of the battle.

The English Adventurer

I heard a ragged cannonade as the other pirate on our side fired at us. His balls slammed into the stern castle. The captain would have to rebuild his cabin. I heard Captain Pedro as he ordered the harquebuses to open fire and then I heard the cannons of *'Silver Swan'* as Jose opened fire. Smoke drifted like fog and therein lay the danger. We no longer had a target and while the odds were now just three to one, one of the pirates was close to our stern.

"Tomas! They are coming between us and *'Isabella'*."

The harquebuses were now our only defence for I could not shift all the guns across the deck.

"Move this falcon!"

It took all six of us to release the cannon from its fastenings, turn it and drag it across the deck to the larboard side. In that time the pirate had fired a broadside into our stern but as there was no cry, I had to assume there was no serious damage. The ripple of gunfire from the harquebuses gave me hope that the pirate was not escaping unscathed. "Load with ball and stones." Desperate times called for desperate measures. The rest of our crew had armed themselves and they lined the larboard side. This would be a test for the captain of the *'Isabella'*. Would his crew fight?

I had no time for such distractions as the pirate was edging up between our two ships. I had angled the gun so that we could fire across the deck. I saw his gun crews as they feverishly loaded their guns. I touched the linstock when they were just forty paces from us and the ball and bag of stones smashed into, first a gun and then, as the ball flew at an angle, across the mainmast and into the sterncastle. The stones ripped through the crews and the waiting pirates.

"Load a bag of stones." I adjusted the aim as soon as Guido lifted his arm, I touched the linstock and this time we were just twenty or so paces from the pirate. His guns had not been reloaded and the bag of stones killed the remaining gun crew.

The grappling hooks from the pirate told me that they had decided to end our threat before taking on the patently unarmed *'Isabella'*. I placed the linstock into the two metal fixings that stopped it from becoming a danger to us. "Arm yourselves, boys reload with stones and then take cover." I drew my sword and dagger. We had thinned their ranks but they still outnumbered us. I was gratified to hear the crack and pop from the harquebuses as they rained death on the pirate's stern. As the boys obeyed me, I stood with Guido and Carlos flanking me. Guido had a pike and Carlos a cutlass. It was Guido who drew first blood as his pike tore through the middle of the leaping pirate. In his falling, he took out a second pirate who fell in a heap at our feet. Carlos ended his life. I blocked the axe swung at my head and then ripped my dagger into the man's guts which spilt across the deck. Guido and Carlos had succeeded in carving a space around the gun and seeing that the boys had run to safety I stuck my sword into the deck and picked the linstock up from its rack, I blew on the end and then, as the ship was on the uproll fired the falcon. It hit the second wave of pirates who were butchered as they prepared to board. Even more of a surprise was that *'Isabella'* had grappled the pirate and her crew were boarding from the larboard side.

There were no living pirates before us and I shouted, "Board them!" I grabbed my sword and leapt over the gunwales of the two ships. It was like a charnel house. We were in no mood for mercy and shocked and stunned pirates were hacked and chopped to death. The harquebuses had cleared the stern of the officers and the pirates who had survived either dropped their weapons or threw themselves overboard. "Back to our ship." I led Guido and Carlos back to our vessel for there were still two ships out there.

Captain Pedro cupped his hands and said, "The other two have been bested and they flee."

I waved my arm and looked to see that the three boys were safe. They were.

The crew of the *'Isabella'* had done well and any thoughts about their loyalty disappeared like the smoke that wreathed us. The well-earned celebrations would have to wait for the pirate ship had been badly damaged in the fighting and was settling into the water. It was Captain Pedro who decided to have the pirate's boat launched and the pirates abandoned. We could not watch them and they were untrustworthy. The guns on the pirate ship were falconets and three of them were salvable. We had to work quickly if we were to save them before the ship sank. As the pirates rowed north in their overloaded boat the crews of both *'Isabella'* and ourselves took all that we could from our prize. The balls and powder were like gold while the supplies of food were an unexpected surprise. The water was lapping over the pirate's deck as the last of our crew clambered aboard. We resumed our voyage. This time more confident in the ability of at least one of our crews.

"What will you do with the falconets, Captain Tomas?"

"We have some sakers coming and I think that the crew of *'Isabella'* deserve at least two of them. Perhaps Jose might have the other one." I found that I was now like Captain Pedro. I thought not of one ship but them all.

The English Adventurer

It took another ten days to reach Cádiz. We knew that the newly acquired ships needed a shipyard as did we for we had also suffered damage and so, as we edged into our berth, Captain Pedro took the decision to give us all three months off. For some, like the ship's boys, that meant staying with the ship and enduring the noise of the work but those, with families, would take the opportunity to visit with them. I did not know what I would be doing but first I had some more coins, the profits from this voyage, as well as my maps, to deliver to Lord Collingwood.

However, before I did anything I visited the foundry. Firstly, it was closer to the harbour than Lord Collingwood's home and, more importantly, I knew that the new guns could be our salvation. Captain Pedro had given me another bag of gold to buy two more sakers for Captain Phillip's ship. Captain Pedro wanted us to be armed to the teeth. The pirates had shown themselves to be persistent. It struck me that the pirates had been bested by us and they would respond. They would get more ships and arm them better. It was as I was leaving the ship that the three boys came to see me, "Captain Tomas."

"Yes, Alessandro."

"What is it that you would have us do while you are away from the ship? We cannot sit idly by. We are your gunners."

I smiled at his enthusiasm, "Stones. We cannot have enough stones. You are right, Alessandro, you are gunners and you can make up the bags of balls for the guns. You now know what is required and I trust your judgement." I saw them swell with pride. "And you will need to keep the guns protected from the weather."

They nodded and Juan said, "You will not be here all the time?"

I shrugged, "I may return, briefly, to England." They looked crestfallen. "But I will return."

Jesus' voice, when he spoke, still surprised me, "I pray to God that you will, Captain Tomas." There was real affection on his face and it touched me.

This time the officious perfumed man did not try to stop me and I went directly to the workshop. Miguel was wearing a leather apron but beneath it, he wore no top. The heat from the burning charcoal almost knocked me over. He waved when he saw me and pointed to his office. I headed there. After the workshop proper, it felt much cooler.

A short time later and wiping his sweaty body with a cloth, Miguel came into the office. He shrugged, "I am a victim of my own success. So many people want my guns that there are not enough hours in the day. You want to know the progress of your guns?"

The English Adventurer

"It is not yet two months and we do not sail for three but I wish to know when they will be ready."

"The end of the week."

I took out the bag of gold, "And we need two more sakers."

His head slumped, "That will be three months, my friend, I am sorry."

"Three months is fine."

He took his wax tablet and made notes. He counted out the coins and pushed a handful back. He smiled, "You are now a regular customer and can enjoy better rates." The business completed, he poured us both some ale. "Tell me of your voyage."

I did so and left nothing out. He heard of the first pirate attack and the loss of our ship. He made the sign of the cross. Then I spoke of our attack on the walls of the wooden fort and that fascinated him. "I can see that you have more skill than most gunners. I should have liked to see the destruction of wooden walls by just four cannons."

I shook my head, "You would not like the heat, my friend. Your foundry workshop is like a cool version of the lands of the Castilla del Oro." I told him of the last attack and the capture of the guns.

"Do they have a maker's mark on them?"

I shook my head, "They are crudely made and if the battle is anything to go by then they are inaccurate. When I train the gunners, it will be for close combat when we can use bags of stones or lead balls to cut down the pirates waiting to board. Your guns will be on the best two ships with the best two gunners."

"Yours?" I nodded. "I like that, no false modesty in you. A man should be proud of his skill. God makes us all good at something and any who does not obey God's wishes is a fool." He stood, "So I will send the guns to your ships. What will you do while you wait?"

"I know not. I may return to my home for I have not visited for some years. I have no family there but it is the land where I was born and it is here." I patted my heart.

"Aye, I know the feeling but you know that you will be disappointed. You have travelled and the world is a wide place. Your island and your home will seem small."

"Perhaps." We clasped arms and I returned to Captain Pedro with the coins I had saved.

"When it is nearer to the time we will sail I shall buy balls. The royal foundry is the only place we can buy cannons but balls are plentiful. What is it that you need?" I told him and he made a note of it. "And what will you do? Take rooms ashore?"

The English Adventurer

I shook my head, "I may travel back to England. I have time. I know not but if not then I will sleep aboard. I will speak with Paulo the carpenter so that he can make the carriages for the two sakers. He can advise the carpenter on *'Silver Swan'*. I will go and speak with Jose now."

Captain Pedro shook his head, "He has left already to visit his uncle. He has news of his father. He said that you would understand his haste."

I did but it made me even more determined to travel home.

It took some time for Paulo to understand exactly what was required. The sakers were bigger and heavier guns with longer barrels. Paulo knew we would need a sturdier carriage. "And one more thing, Paulo, would it be possible to have a hinged flap in the side of the ship so that we do not need to fire over the gunwale? It would mean that the carriage could be lower and less likely to be turned over."

"Cut holes in the side? I would have to ask the captain."

"The gunwale would maintain the integrity of the hull and it would make an enemy think that we were more lightly armed than we are. We would only need to open the flaps when we were in action."

"I like the idea and I will speak with the captain."

It was too late, when I had finished, for me to visit with Lord Collingwood and so I dined ashore and enjoyed a good meal. I rejected the offers of the doxies. I liked women but I would not pay for their services. There were few women other than the doxies around the port. I would be as a monk.

I dressed well and carried my small chest of coins as well as the maps when I headed to Lord Collingwood's home. I dressed like a Spaniard and my Spanish had no English accent. I had to think of the words when I spoke English while Spanish now seemed the language of my life. I knew it was accented but it was the accent of the New World and sailors. I suppose it was the difference between a lord in England and a collier from the north. Both were English but the words and phrases they used were different.

I was admitted immediately by the Englishman, John Foster. He smiled as he recognised me and Captain Hogan also greeted me with a beaming smile when I was admitted to the room, "More coins to deposit I see and maps. Lord Collingwood will be pleased."

"He is home?"

"He is but we leave in a day or two for Madrid." He held his hands out, "Should I put this somewhere safe?"

"If you would." As I handed it to him, I said, by way of explanation for my haste to be rid of my treasure, "One of our ships was blown up

The English Adventurer

on the way out. I know that the captain and the officers kept their gold aboard. Now it lies at the bottom of the ocean. I think that is a waste."

He nodded, "You are a deep one, Thomas. Wait here and I will speak with his lordship."

I did not have long to wait and Captain Hogan took me to the office his lordship used. The Irishman was about to leave when Lord Collingwood arrested him, "Stay, for I would have you hear Thomas' words."

I handed over the maps which the two scrutinised as I told them of the plots and conspiracies I had encountered. I concluded with the sea battle and the news that the damage to the ships necessitated a three-month overhaul. The two men exchanged a glance.

"So, King Charles may be the richest king in Christendom but he is beset by those wishing to undermine him. Interesting. And this land of Pirú, El Dorado?" I nodded, "Do you think it exists?"

I sipped the excellent wine and nodded, "When I was with Balboa, we encountered tribes who had gold and silver upon them but they told us it was the scraps that were discarded by the mighty people from the south." I smiled, "They are not a Christian people, my lord, and they spoke of gods living high in the mountains, in eyries like birds. They are a primitive people."

"And Florida, is that a rich place?"

I shook my head, "If it were then the ships that attacked us would be better armed and, indeed, they would have no need to rob merchantmen."

Lord Collingwood looked disappointed but he nodded, "That is what we have heard. Not all the New World is filled with riches." He leaned forward, "Thomas, what are your plans for the next two months?"

I was surprised at the question but I answered honestly, "I think I will take a ship to England and visit Devon. Why my lord?"

"Hogan here tells me that you use my home as a place to secure your coins."

"I do, my lord, but if that is a problem then…"

He waved an irritated hand as though swatting flies, "It is not a problem but how would you like to add to that treasure?"

I was wary, "Of course, my lord, but how?"

He leaned back and he and the captain drank some wine as his lordship chose his next words carefully, "Thomas, you are unique. You are an Englishman and yet, when you speak. you sound exactly like a Spaniard. You have skills in deception."

The English Adventurer

I shook my head, "I am not sure that is something of which I should be proud, my lord."

"You deceive for your king and your country. You should be proud of that."

I was not sure. My father had served England loyally and then been summarily discarded by one of the ruthless nobles of the land. I wisely said nothing.

"How would you like to spend a month as my servant?" He saw my face and held up his hand, "Hear me out, Thomas. As you know I have enemies in this land. I have to visit Madrid to speak to King Charles. I will be taking Hogan with me but we are both known. In my experience servants are anonymous. You are uniquely gifted. I would have you speak nothing but English so that when you are with other servants, they might speak Spanish openly and you might divine intelligence which would otherwise be hidden." He sipped his wine, "And you have shown that you know how to fight and to use a sword. I would feel safer with you and Captain Hogan watching my back. You would be well paid, Thomas."

It was Captain Hogan who persuaded me, "Thomas, do this for England. Lord Collingwood serves our young king and if England is to be as great as Spain, then he will need our help. It is but a few weeks of work and what else would you do? Go back to sea and travel the stormy seas of Biscay to visit a land where you know nobody? Like it or not, Cádiz and the New World are now your homes. Better to be a rich man here than a poor one in Devon. Regard it as another adventure, a well-paid one."

He was right, of course. If I sailed home I would have to pay for a passage. There would be the expense of hiring a horse and paying for food and a room and for what? To see somewhere that would not look the same after my eight years at sea.

"Very well, my lord, but I am not sure of how much value I can be."

They both laughed, "Do not underestimate yourself, Thomas. Return here tomorrow and we will kit you out as an English servant. You will not carry a fine sword and your dress will be plainer. Can you ride?"

"After a fashion."

Lord Collingwood nodded, "Better and better, for if you look uncomfortable on the back of a horse it will complete the deception."

The deception began when I returned to the ship. I lied to Captain Pedro and the ship's boys. Captain Pedro took the news well but the boys were concerned. To them, England was a wilder place than the New World for to them it was unknown.

The English Adventurer

"Do not fear, I will return and by then you will have sacks of balls for us to use when we sail west again."

That made them smile.

Chapter 7

I slipped away just after dawn and only the sentry on the ship saw me leave. If he wondered why I carried just a small valise he said nothing. Perhaps he was awaiting his breakfast and the end of a boring duty. I headed through streets that were filled with market traders making their way to set up their stalls and people going to buy their food for the day. The phrase the early bird catches the worm was never more appropriate. Wise buyers knew that they would have the pick of the produce and the warmest bread.

Foster was waiting for me and I was admitted quickly and without fuss. I was given a room in Lord Collingwood's house. I had brought my old sea boots rather than the finer boots I had bought in Isla Juana. The rest of the clothes I was to wear were laid out on the bed. Sniffing them they had a musty, almost damp smell and there was something else I could not put my finger on at first and then it came to me. They smelled like my grandfather. That they were not a perfect fit was all part of the deception. The smock I was given was of rough cambric and hung loosely on me. The hose were serviceable if a little rough. The breeches were not new and were very loose. There was a leather jack that came halfway down my thighs and for that I was grateful. If we were placed in harm's way then a leather jack might just deflect a blade. There was an old, oiled cloak with a cowl. The woollen hat I plopped on my head was typical for England but a little warm for Spain. There was a simple belt and a short sword in a scabbard. I still had my dagger and I slipped that into my boot. The last item was a worn leather bag that I attached to the belt. It was empty but I would soon fill it. I took the flint from my valise and dropped that in. I took the handful of coppers that I had brought and put them inside the leather bag. I also put in some dried meat. I had starved when I was a slave and I now always ensured that I had food with me. Chewing dried meat made a stomach think it had enjoyed a meal.

After putting my clothes in it, I placed my valise under the bed. I was ready. I walked down the stairs. Captain Hogan nodded approvingly as I turned around and Lord Collingwood said, in Spanish, "You look good, Tomas." I answered in Spanish and he shook his head, "A mistake like that could be disastrous. Until we return here you speak only English. You look English but your Spanish words do not."

"How do I explain my tanned skin, my lord?"

"You have lived here for some years."

I nodded, "And the clothes, where are they from?"

The English Adventurer

Captain Hogan said, "You are wearing dead men's clothes. Old Henry died of eating bad fish and Walter was just an old man. They both served his lordship."

I now knew why the clothes smelled foisty. I smiled to myself for I was already thinking in English. Foisty was a word from my childhood. My grandmother had used it to describe things that smelled damp and needed airing. I wondered if the smell of clothes that reminded me of my grandfather had done that.

I had never been in the courtyard of Lord Collingwood's house and when Captain Hogan took me to see the horse I would be using I was surprised at how big the stables were. The stables had stalls for six horses although only four were occupied.

He took me to a hackney. It was a better horse than I was expecting, "This is Blade. He used to be Lord Collingwood's horse but he is getting old. He is still a good horse but he can no longer gallop as fast as his lordship would wish. Get acquainted and lead him around the courtyard. We have a long ride on the morrow."

I was left with the grey, almost blue horse. I wished I had brought him an apple or a carrot. I rubbed his forehead, "I will apologise now for my lack of skills as a rider. I beg your indulgence." I found it hard to speak English again. Perhaps my soft tone had an effect for the horse snorted and nodded. It was a good beginning.

When I returned to the house, I passed the servant's quarters and the kitchen. The room I had been given was obviously intended for guests of little importance. I went into the kitchen to introduce myself. There was a cook and two liveried servants. Remembering the role I was to play I said, in English, "I am Thomas and I will be travelling with Lord Collingwood to Madrid."

Foster was the one who run the house but he did not do the cooking. He had servants beneath him. The two servants were older and spoke to me in English. From their accents, they came from the north of England. The older of the two said, "Aye, we heard. I am Harry and this is Rafe." He nodded at the clothes, "They aren't a bad fit."

"They will do."

The cook was Spanish and he said, in Spanish, "Another servant? We do not need one."

I affected a confused expression, "He doesn't speak Spanish, Stephen. He is just hired to ride with his lordship."

The Spaniard nodded, seemingly satisfied with the explanation, "Aah."

The English Adventurer

Harry said, "He's not a bad cook for a Spaniard but he makes the food too greasy and spicy. I am not averse to a bit of lard but I can't abide all this oil."

"Well, I had better find out what I am supposed to do. Pleased to have met you."

"And you."

I liked the two of them and they reminded me of my grandfather. He hated change too. I also wondered if they knew my true purpose. Harry had been quick to let the cook know that I spoke no Spanish."

Captain Hogan was in the office and he covered whatever he was reading when I entered. I was not offended. The fewer secrets I knew the better I like it. "His lordship has a meeting with the Alcalde. Happy with the horse?"

"He seems affable. What time will we be leaving?"

"You have lived here long enough to know that it is too hot at noon to travel. We will leave before dawn and rest when the sun is at its hottest."

"Do I eat in the kitchen with Harry and Rafe?"

"When we are on the road you will eat with the other servants and keep your ears open and your mouth shut but his lordship wishes to use the evening meal to enlighten you about our task so you will dine with us. You have until the evening to yourself."

I nodded, "I had better stay within doors. I do not want any of my shipmates to see me nor do I want to risk someone speaking to me in Spanish."

He smiled, "A real spy. You have not asked yet how much you are being paid."

"As I appear to have little choice in the matter, I will take what I am paid.

"You will be paid four crowns for the four weeks we are away,"

My eyes widened, "That is not an inconsequential amount."

"Trust me, Thomas, you will earn it."

It was Harry and Rafe who served us and their lack of surprise at my presence told me that they knew my purpose. They left the food and closed the door. Lord Collingwood spoke as we ate. "It will take eight or more days to reach Madrid. It is four hundred miles." He shook his head ruefully, "Most cities can be reached by sea but not this one. It is why I need extra protection. As you know, Thomas, the French discovered my identity and will try to stop my efforts to form a stronger alliance with Spain. Then there are those in Spain itself who do not like the English. I think that the danger will come on the road. We pass

The English Adventurer

some lonely and deserted stretches and it is there we will need to be wary."

I nodded, "You think I am good enough?"

They both laughed, "Your skills are not in question. The English gunner who is a magician with his falcons is also reputed to be a fierce fighter who has slain mercenary swordsmen. When people speak of the English adventurer, they speak of a warrior. It is your ears when we stay in our accommodation that might be the difference. Do as you do at sea and garner what you can."

He went into detail about our route and how I might discover the intelligence that might save us. That done we chatted. He asked me about growing up and I asked him about his. It turned out his family came from the north of England and until his grandfather's time had been minor landowners. The arrival of Henry Tudor changed that. Supporting the Tudor monarch rather than the Yorkists meant he was given great swathes of land in the north of England. The burgeoning trade in wool meant that his family became incredibly rich. His younger brother ran the estates and Lord Collingwood was able to support his work for King Henry through the profits from wool. I learned that he had a good head for business. The plants we had brought back for him had yielded another fortune and he invested well. I discovered that he was part owner of a factory that produced gunpowder. I admired him and, from that moment on, saw him as someone I could try to emulate. I would never be a lord but I did not want a title anyway. I could use my money more wisely. Instead of sitting in a chest in his home, I should use it as a farmer uses seed and manure. I began to think of ways to profit from my knowledge of the New World. Instead of taking my whole payment when we returned to Spain, I would ask Captain Pedro for half when we reached the New World. That was the place to make a profit.

I was almost too excited to sleep and I woke before dawn. I heard the watch calling out the time and rose and dressed. It was only when I donned the cambric smock and woollen hose that I realised I had become used to finer clothes. Even as a slave I had still been wearing the clothes I had worn when I had gone to sea. The smock and hose were rough and itchy but I knew that they would be serviceable. I was playing the role of servant and so I went to the stable to saddle Blade and then the horses of Captain Hogan and Lord Collingwood. I did it that way around to ensure that I made no mistakes with the other horses. Then I had to fix the harness to the back of the sumpter. A journey of what might be twenty days necessitated changes of clothes for Lord

The English Adventurer

Collingwood and Captain Hogan. I would simply stink. That done I sharpened my new sword and my dagger.

Rafe came to find me, "Come, Thomas, breakfast awaits. You will need a full belly this day."

I suddenly found I was starving. I went within and joined Harry and Rafe as they ate the simple but homely fare. Freshly made bread and butter that was, as yet, not runny was a delight while the fresh eggs and thick slices of fried ham were a treat none could resist. There was, of course, cheese and it was good cheese. His lordship, it turned out, had a taste for English cheese rather than Spanish and the cheese was more to my taste than that which I normally ate. The two English servants also brewed the beer for the house and it was a reminder of Devon. They made beer in Spain and used the same ingredients as Harry and Rafe but there must have been some difference in technique for the beer I drank at breakfast was like nectar and I knew I would not taste its like again on this journey.

I was ready, cloaked and with a hat on my head when my two charges emerged. Both were dressed plainly and while their hats, cloaks, boots and swords were well-made, they did not ring out as belonging to an important lord. Lord Collingwood wished for anonymity.

Once more I was playing a part and I rode some paces behind the two of them with the laden sumpter on a long lead. I knew that by the time we stopped my buttocks would be red raw. Harry had given me a salve to apply. After fifteen miles I was tempted to put some on but I had no opportunity. The other two were good horsemen and they knew how to ride hard whilst husbanding their horses. I also noted that they were constantly scanning the sides of the road and looking for danger ahead. I forced myself to do the same and discovered that it took my mind from my chafing. We stopped in a small town a half hour before the noon bell sounded from the church. I unsaddled the horses in the inn's stable and fed and watered them before I entered the inn for my food. There was an ostler in the stable and we could have paid him to do what I had done but Lord Collingwood had told me that I was his servant and he would have to act differently.

When I entered the inn, I was directed to a wooden bench with other diners. The man spoke to me in Spanish and told me that Lord Collingwood had paid for my food. I feigned ignorance of his language and he shrugged and then pointed to my place at the end next to two carters. They both inquired about the purpose of my journey and I affected the look of a simpleton with a wide smile. They shrugged and carried on with their food. That first stop was vital for it showed me that

The English Adventurer

I could do as I had been asked. I learned nothing but I would have been surprised if I had. Instead, I listened to the carters as they complained about the taxes they paid and the price of food in inns. I hid my smile as they carped about the bill when it was presented. Their seats were taken by an older couple whom I learned were travelling to Sevilla for a wedding. The man was unhappy about the expense and the time it took from his work. His wife, whose sister was getting married, appeared to be the one in command of that marriage and their arguments entertained me.

When I had finished the food and the watered ale the innkeeper made it clear that I had to vacate my place for other diners. I went out to the stable and found myself a bed of straw in the manger. I dozed rather than slept. I was woken by voices.

"What is an English lord and his companion doing travelling through Spain?"

"I know not, my friend, but we can profit from them. While their servant sleeps let us see what is in their bags."

I had been awake before but now I was more alert. I stretched and yawned, "What time is it?" I spoke in English.

My awakening stopped their thievery. They asked me in Spanish what I had said and I shrugged. One said to his companion, "All Englishmen are imbeciles. I have yet to meet one who can speak our language." The two went about their business turning the hay and removing the fresh dung deposited by the horses. Lord Collingwood and Captain Hogan returned just before the bells sounded two o'clock in the afternoon and I saddled their horses as I was assiduously ignored as we headed north. By the time we retired that evening the pattern for the next eight days had been set. I only spoke to his lordship when we were on deserted stretches of the road and most times I had little to tell him.

He had planned our route well and we avoided staying in major cities like Sevilla. He chose, instead, smaller towns which, whilst having poorer accommodation had less danger for him. The food I was served was far plainer than that which the other two enjoyed. It was largely made up of beans cooked with the bones of sheep or pigs. There was offal and the bread was rough bread but I did not mind. It was hot and after the rations of the open sea, it was like a feast. The pain from my buttocks only lasted a few days for the salve I had been given, whilst pungent, seemed to work.

It was at Guadalupe where I discovered something that was worth reporting to Lord Collingwood. We were staying, not in an inn but in the Royal Monastery of Santa Maria of Guadalupe. Monks had found that providing beds and food for travellers was profitable. This time I knew that I would be eating the same food as Lord Collingwood. I even ate in the same refectory, albeit at the lower end of the long table. There were another dozen or so travellers dotted along the table and I studied them as I ate. The monks around me, having discovered that I spoke no Spanish, were happy to chat with each other openly. I discovered secrets that might have shocked the head of the order but nothing that would help Lord Collingwood.

My bed was the manger with the other horses. I had not seen any other servants in the refectory and there was no ostler. I had managed to purloin four apples from the fruit bowl and I fed these to the horses. I was now comfortable with them and I gave them treats whenever I could find them. That done I climbed above the horses to the hay rack and made a bed using the bales of bound hay. So it was that I was invisible when the two men entered the stables. It was their voices that woke me. There was also something else. They had about them the familiar smell of gunpowder. Was this treachery?

"Do you remember which horses we are to mark?"

"Their servant rides the grey. The other three should be theirs."

I heard our horses become nervous and stamp as the two hidden men approached. "Mark the grey first and then the large black one. That should be enough."

I heard Blade snort and stamp as his hind leg was lifted and I heard the scraping of the file across the horseshoes. There was another snort and then I heard a second file. One of the voices asked, "Why do we need to do this when we intend to ambush them?"

"Did you not hear the Frenchman? This English lord is a spy and he may have tricks to play. If the ambush fails, he will run and this way we can pick up his trail again. The Frenchman not only pays well, but he is also clever and plans ahead."

I let them finish and waited until they had left the stable. I lifted Blade's legs until I found the crudely filed mark on the hoof. It would only be seen if we left the road and rode across the wet ground but if we did leave the road then it would mean we were trying to escape and they could follow us. I found it hard but I managed to sleep and, more importantly, I did not break my cover by entering the monastery to reveal to Lord Collingwood what had just happened.

I kept my counsel until we were on the road to Madrid. I feigned a problem with Blade when I saw that we were alone. Lord Collingwood looked around, "You have news?"

The English Adventurer

"Your horse and mine have had their hooves marked. There is an ambush awaiting us. A Frenchman sent two men to mark the horses so that they can follow us if we leave the road."

I patted Blade and remounted. Lord Collingwood just nodded and we headed up the road once more. "Ride a little closer Thomas and keep your hand upon your sword."

That was easier said than done leading a sumpter but I managed.

The two men spoke so that I could hear their words. "There were two Frenchmen in the monastery last night."

"Yes, my lord, but one had a single companion and the other two."

"Gilles de La Flèche. I do not know the man."

"He smiled too much for my liking, my lord, such men are not to be trusted." I saw Lord Collingwood nod. "If there are just three then they will not risk an ambush. He must have more men."

"And they would need to be found. We have time. The problem is we have no idea where the ambush will take place."

I coughed and said, "Not true, my lord, for if they expect to follow us if we evade them then the ambush cannot be close to houses or roads. They will be expecting us to go across open fields and through woods."

Lord Collingwood turned and smiled, "You are right and that helps us."

We passed along a road that was dotted with farms and small holdings. This close to the river the land was fertile and well-farmed. It was after El Campillo de la Jara that the farms thinned out to almost nothing and, to the north of the river and the road the ground rose and was dotted with copses and small woods as well as rock outcrops that would afford cover.

Captain Hogan was the soldier and it was his instincts that warned us. He slowed a little, it would be imperceptible to any watching in the distance but it was enough. "I think that if there is an ambush, my lord, it will be in the next mile or so. If memory serves there is a hamlet a couple of miles up the road and that rough ground to the west would be a perfect place for them to attack. If we fled to the east, they would see us easily and run us down."

"What do we do, Captain? We are in your hands now." It was interesting that his lordship deferred to the Irishman.

"We do what they will not expect, we charge them. They will have either harquebuses or crossbows and…"

"Captain, they have harquebuses."

"How on earth can you know that, Thomas?"

"I smelled gunpowder last night and ahead, about half a mile away I can see a tendril of smoke. I am guessing a fuze."

The English Adventurer

We were still moving albeit slower and Captain Hogan said, "You have good eyes, you are right."

"They are impossibly slow to reload and very inaccurate, Captain Hogan, A charge will unnerve them."

"When I give the word then release the sumpter. We can collect it later if we survive. Thomas, protect his lordship's right side."

"I need no protection!"

"With respect, my lord, that is why we are here."

I was nervous, as we knowingly walked into the spider's trap. I was not afraid of combat but I normally fought with a gun and from a ship surrounded by comrades and then I remembered Mexico. I had survived there as well as the jungles of the Castilla del Oro. Blade was a good horse and he would not let me down. Having spied the smoke from a distance I found myself anticipating the order to charge. I had moved myself closer to his lordship's right side and saw that the smoke was two hundred paces from our left and was behind a large rock. The harquebusier would be crouching down. He would either have to use his stand or, more likely, use the rock. Of course, there might be two or three waiting for us. They would only need one linstock. I saw the leaves on one of the bushes close to the road move and deduced that someone was hiding there. When Blade snorted and nodded his head then I knew that he had smelled the waiting horses. I almost dropped the reins of the sumpter early so certain was I that the captain would give the order but I did not.

He almost waited too late for, as he shouted, "Now!" A bolt flew from the bushes where I had seen movement. The bolt flashed between my horse and Lord Collingwood's. I had my sword out and instinctively lay low across the saddle.

I saw the two harquebuses rise above the rock and braced myself for what would come next. Captain Hogan had given me a task and I did my duty. I rode at the bush with my sword behind me. The crossbowman was still trying to haul back on the string when Blade crashed through the bush and my sword hit the assassin on the shoulder. My hand jarred when it struck bone and Blade's movement tore the sword across his neck ripping over his throat. I heard the double crack of the harquebuses and the air was filled with the familiar stench of saltpetre and smoke. I saw no one ahead and I wheeled Blade around to my left. He was well-trained and he moved easily. I was now behind the rock and I saw the harquebusiers as they tried to load the weapons quickly. I knew just how hard that was and I dug my heels in to make Blade move faster. I heard the clash of swords as his lordship and the captain duelled with other attackers. I concentrated on the two

The English Adventurer

harquebusiers. They loaded and then lifted the weapons up. I was almost grinning for they were aiming at me and, coming from their side, they could not use the rocks for support. One reached for his stand while the other, panicking, grabbed the linstock to light the fuze. One who was not a gunner might have been afeard but I was not and knew that I had time. The linstock had just lit the end of the fuze when my sword slashed down as Blade's head knocked him to one side. The hand weapon exploded not into flesh but into the air and my sword split his skull. The second harquebusier had managed to rest his weapon on the sand he planted in the ground and was reaching for the linstock when I raised my sword. This time I did not use the edge but the tip and I drove it into his eye. He fell to the ground.

I reined in to look for more enemies but, hearing hooves saw that three riders were galloping away north. From the garb of two of them, they were nobles while the other was a warrior with a leather brigandine. I patted Blade's neck with my sword hand. It was covered in the blood of the dead men. I turned him and saw that the captain and his lordship were whole and had killed their enemies.

The captain shook his head and grinned, "We are both swordsmen and each killed one of our attackers. You are neither a swordsman nor a horseman but you accounted for three." He raised his sword in salute.

His lordship nodded, "Thank you, Thomas, fetch the sumpter and we will search them for anything of value."

By the time I returned, having pulled the sumpter which had been greedily grazing, the bodies had been searched. Lord Collingwood had collected their coins and they were all in one purse, "Here, this is yours by right."

"Thank you, my lord."

The captain waved at the weapons laid out on the ground, "Would you have any of these?"

I dismounted and kneeling, took the stiletto. "I will take this and the two harquebuses if you would allow me. My crew can make good use of these."

We managed to capture two of the ambusher's horses and that enabled me to spread the load more evenly amongst them. It did not make the leading of them any easier. We left the bodies where they lay and headed north. Once we passed the next settlement the road was quieter and we were able to speak.

"I saw three escape, my lord and two were well dressed."

"I shall know the Frenchman when I see him but we will feign ignorance. When we reach Madrid find a smith, Thomas, and have the horses reshod."

The English Adventurer

"Do you think they will try again, my lord?"

"It will be hard to get the men. The ones they hired were professionals. Crossbowmen and harquebusiers do not come cheaply. The road home, unless we can do something about the Frenchman, may be fraught with danger."

Life was as hard on the land as it was at sea.

Chapter 8

We reached Madrid without any further incident. This time we stayed not in an inn but in a house. There was a caretaker and I quickly learned that the house belonged to his lordship. That he did not avail himself of it often was clear from the expression on the caretaker's face who was told that he had three days off and could return to his family. He would be sent for when he could return. The man was torn. He had three days to himself but he would not have the luxury of this fine house. He was sent to buy food for us and then leave. His lordship was being kind although the man might not have seen it as such. He did not know the danger Lord Collingwood represented. I had the luxury of his room. Once within the safety of Lord Collingwood's small Madrid home, we held a council of war.

"My business with the king is important and between here and the palace the roads will be filled with danger." They both looked at me and it was clear that they had discussed the matter at length. "Thomas, it is asking much of you but we would have you follow us, some twenty paces behind. You are to look not only for danger but also for any who are following us. You need to have sharp eyes to identify them. When we enter the palace, we will be safe. If you have the opportunity then follow any who showed an interest in us but do not put yourself at risk. When we have done, we shall wait outside the palace gates and you can resume your duty." I nodded, "I know we ask much of you but…"

I smiled, "I am well paid and I have two harquebuses and an unexpected purse of coins. I will return to my ship a richer man. Do not worry yourself about me, my lord."

"You need not pretend to be English and you can, if you wish, while you are following us, revert to Spanish."

That made sense. If I followed and spoke only English then they would know that I was one of Lord Collingwood's men.

I allowed them to leave by the front door while I used the small gate at the back of the property and went down the small alleyway. It allowed me to join the street lower down and the two were easy to follow in their fine clothes. Both were taller than most of the Spanish men and with their military stride, I would have no difficulty in keeping them in sight. With the cowl of my cloak up over my hat and keeping to the side of the street, I hoped that I was invisible. Certainly, I looked no different from most of the men who walked along the road. It appeared that most were heading either for the palace or for one of the many markets around there. I scanned the road for anyone who appeared to be

The English Adventurer

following and I found none. I wondered if that was my lack of skill. When we reached the palace, I saw that a line of liveried guards was acting as a sort of human fishing net. Well-dressed men, like Lord Collingwood, were allowed to proceed to the gate where they were allowed to state their business. It was as I watched them approach the gate that I saw the watcher. He had not followed but he was waiting close to the gate. As soon as he spied Lord Collingwood, he took off like a hare started by hounds. I marked his clothes, dress and gate. I would have followed but he was on the other side of the crowd who were attempting to gain entry to the palace. I stayed where I was.

Lord Collingwood and Captain Hogan were admitted and I waited. Some of those around me attempted to speak but it was in Spanish and I ignored them. They might be curious, suspicious even, but I would bear that. Time passed. Others came and were either admitted or sent packing. It was then I saw the watcher return with a better-dressed man. I vaguely recognised his build as being similar to the one who had fled the ambush but I could not be sure It piqued my interest. As with the first one I marked his demeanour. His dress alerted the poor around him that he had coins and he was surrounded by men and women with open palms. He and his companion used their fists to disperse them. The guards laughed. There was little sympathy for the beggars. For their part, the beggars resumed their place and watched for the next well-dressed visitor who might slip them a coin if only to be rid of their stink. Some had been close to me before moving to seek a purse and I confess the stench made me nauseous. I was used to sailors who are, generally, clean by nature.

Lord Collingwood and Captain Hogan returned sooner than I would have thought that a meeting with the king would have taken. As they came out, they are surrounded by beggars and I took my opportunity. The other beggars were scattered and the two neared me. I ran out and said, loudly in Spanish, my face hidden by my cowl, "Coppers my lord to feed my family." As Captain Hogan's hand came to push me away, I hissed in English, "Two men, behind you, one is better dressed."

Lord Collingwood's hand clipped my head and that did two things, it made the others who were waiting for entry, laugh and ensured that no others bothered them. I slid away to seemingly melt into the crowd when, in reality, I was seeking the two men. They passed me without a second glance and they followed his lordship. I wondered if Lord Collingwood would try to lose his followers. If he did not then they would know where we resided. I was not privy to his lordship's plan and he led the men directly to our home. The well-dressed man spoke to the spy who had alerted him and then took off, his cloak's hood over his head. I followed, realising that I did not know Madrid well and could easily become lost. I tried to mark my course as I hurried after him. His dress made it easier to follow him at a distance and when he turned to seek if any followed his gaze was always on those within a few paces of him. I was twenty paces back and he appeared to see me not.

He stopped and scrutinised all those around him as we neared a more affluent part of the city. That the crowds had thinned was a testament to the quality of houses. The poorer people had little reason to be there. Caution made me shelter in an alleyway between two houses and I was rewarded when he went to a large and imposing dwelling. The entrance was marked by two huge lemon trees and a guarded gate. I waited until he had entered and then made my way back to Lord Collingwood's. My natural navigational skills meant I made no mistakes and, even more importantly, had spied the names of some of the streets and avenues that led to the house. Avoiding the spy who watched from across the street, I slipped into the house the back way. I was proud of the fact that I managed to enter the kitchen and then the sitting room occupied by Lord Collingwood and Captain Hogan, silently. They both turned suddenly with hands on weapons.

Captain Hogan smiled, "You are a natural at this, Thomas. The man still waits outside?"

I nodded, "I followed the other and he entered a fine house less than half a mile from here." I described the journey and Lord Collingwood knew where it was. "My lord, was it wise to let them know where you lived?"

Captain Hogan said, "The house is secure although the ease with which you entered and surprised us means I will have to improve the security of the rear."

"Captain Hogan is right and had we tried to evade them they might have become suspicious. This way they think that they are the ones in command. The man you followed, describe him."

I did so and added, "I think, my lord, that, from his build, he was one of those who fled the ambush. Not one of the nobles but the other."

"You have done well. Take wine." As I poured myself a goblet of wine Lord Collingwood continued, "We have been granted an audience tomorrow. This night is when there will be danger. Once my business with the king is concluded then all will be well."

Captain Hogan shook his head, "They lost men and there will be an attempt to seek revenge. Our journey home will be fraught with danger."

"Let us get tonight over with. You are the soldier, what is your plan?"

The English Adventurer

The captain rubbed his beard, "An attempt at the front would result in too much attention. They will come from the rear. We will bar the rear gate but they will merely ascend the walls. The rear door to this dwelling is strong but the lock can be picked."

"You could bar it, Captain Hogan."

He smiled and I shivered for it was a cold smile, Captain Hogan was a real killer, "We want to make it hard for them but not too hard. We want them in the house and then we kill them."

"They may outnumber us."

"Oh, they will, Thomas, make no mistake about that but we have an advantage. This is his lordship's house and they know it not. You will wait, hidden, in the stable. They will make a cursory inspection and then enter the house. You will follow." The captain looked at me, "It is them or us, Thomas, and you must eliminate the man or men who watch the back for them. That done, you enter and ensure that none leaves alive."

"You have a greater confidence in my abilities than do I, Captain Hogan."

Lord Collingwood smiled, "We have seen your abilities. I know not whence you have them but you kill like a true warrior."

Captain Hogan said, "And whatever is in their purses is yours."

"A dead man cannot spend coins, Captain Hogan."

"And you will not die. I am counting on the fact that they think we are oblivious to the danger and will be overconfident both in the numbers that they send and their vigilance. They think to catch us sleeping when they will slit our throats."

I emptied my goblet of wine, "I will do as you say for you seem very confident in your ability to read the minds of killers."

Lord Collingwood said, "You have heard the phrase '*poacher turned gamekeeper*'?" I nodded, "Captain Hogan was a great poacher in Ireland if you catch my meaning."

I did and I felt a shiver down my spine. I had thought that the Irishman knew how to kill and now I knew that it had been his profession.

"Eat and sleep between now and dusk." The captain nodded towards my belt, "You might get the chance to use your new stiletto."

I went directly to the stables for I wished, while it was still daylight, to prepare a hiding place as well as to see to the horses. I made myself a shelter above the horses, fed and watered them and then sharpened my sword, dagger and stiletto. That done I went into the kitchen. I was unsure if I was to prepare food for the other two but as I had not been asked, I simply fed myself and ate. The bread was a day old and so I

The English Adventurer

fried it in some oil and then ate it with slices of ham. It was good ham but it needed English mustard. I had not enjoyed mustard since leaving England and it was one of the things I missed the most. I ate well for I was an old campaigner. When there was food you ate, for you knew not when you would starve. That done I made water and then availed myself of sleep. Like food, it was to be taken whenever the chance arose. I had always had the ability to fall asleep quickly and the comfortable warmth of the stable was the perfect place.

Captain Hogan woke me just after dusk, "You could have slept in your room in the house, Thomas."

I nodded, "I know but this way the horses, even the newly acquired ones, will not make a noise in my presence."

The captain's smile told me that he approved. "Come inside, we will eat and we will tell you what we have planned."

I followed and saw that the path from the kitchen to the hall was now littered with objects. They looked like they should be there, a valise, riding cloaks hanging from the hooks and boots lined up along the wall.

Captain Hogan said, "This will narrow their approach and they will have to step carefully to avoid them. We want them looking down. I will be waiting in the kitchen and Lord Collingwood in the sitting room. They may look in the kitchen before they negotiate the passageway but I think not." I was confident that the poacher was right. "Once they have passed, I will step out behind the last one. He should die silently but if not then Lord Collingwood will bar their progress and we will have them between us. No matter how many of them there are they can only fight us one-to-one. Your task, Thomas is to wait until you hear a cry from within before you strike."

"What if the watchers try to enter?"

"Then follow and strike quickly." He saw the doubt in my eyes. "I know it is hard to kill a man by stabbing him in the back but is that not better than one of us dying? They are the ones who will initiate this attack."

"And if they come not?"

Lord Collingwood said, "Then we lose a night of sleep but if they do not come then my message will be delivered to the King of Spain and the alliance against France will be strengthened. The king of France does not want that to happen. They will come."

"Now, take your place."

"I will bar the gate first."

"It is done."

The English Adventurer

I made water before climbing to my perch. I laid my sword at my side for I did not want to trip on it as I descended. I waited.

I did not hear them climb the wall but the horses did and they began to snort and stamp nervously. I heard a voice from below quieten them. The man must have had a treat of some kind for I heard them crunching something. They would not rouse the house. I waited until the man had left the stable and then, clutching my sword, still in its scabbard, climbed down. I went to the door of the stable and peered out. There were six men at the back door. They had weapons drawn but one knelt by the door and was fiddling with something. When the door sprang open, I knew it had been a lockpick. One of the men stood guard at the back door and the others entered.

I knew that I had a moment or two to move for once the door opened the attention of them all was on the house. Unsheathing my sword I slipped along the stable to the back wall of the house. There were too many shadows there for me to be seen and unless I moved quickly then I would be invisible. I saw the sentry's face as he scanned, first the stable, and then the gate. I saw that it had been unbarred. Only one man had been required to climb the wall. I waited until the white face looked the other way and then moved to within six feet of the man. I was hidden by climbing jasmine. The scent disguised both my smell and that of the sentry.

The cry from inside made the man turn and prepare his weapon. Captain Hogan had been correct, it was hard to stab a man in the back but he had prepared me and I slid my sword under his ribs and through his body. It slid to the ground and I stepped into the passageway. Things had not gone as Captain Hogan had planned. There was a body on the ground but the Irishman was being assaulted on two sides and had to use both his dagger and his sword. I did not hesitate but, shouting, "Turn, you assassin!" stabbed at the man to Captain Hogan's left, He was a good swordsman with quick reactions for his blade almost deflected mine but it penetrated his lower abdomen. I saw blood dripping down Captain Hogan's sleeve and I did not hesitate. Withdrawing my sword I lunged at his opponent, sliding my sword across Captain Hogan's front. His enemy was skilled and he had to bring his own sword down to protect him from this new attack. As he did so Captain Hogan slashed his dagger across the man's throat.

Lord Collingwood had been forced back into the sitting room where his opponents could approach from two sides. However, they were oblivious to the fate of their companions. Captain Hogan stabbed one in the back and as the other turned to see the new threat Lord Collingwood ended his life.

The wounded captain looked at me, "Are there more?"

I shook my head, "There were six and six men now lie dead." I nodded to the body of the man whom Lord Collingwood had slain, "This is the one who was with the ambushers and was the one I followed."

"We know where they live."

Captain Hogan shook his head, "We do not seek revenge, Lord Collingwood. The threat is gone and it would do no good to confront the man who lives there. Thomas can find out the name of the owner while we see the king, but better that he remains in the dark about us and what we know. Let him wonder what happened here this night."

"Here, captain, come into the kitchen and I will tend to your wound."

"I am fine, Thomas."

"I know what happens when wounds are left untended. In this, you shall obey me."

He grinned, "Aye, Captain Thomas. Once more you have proved your worth."

The cut was deep. "I will need to sew it."

"Can you?"

I nodded, "I have tended such wounds before but my stitches will not be pretty and there will be some pain." I turned to Lord Collingwood, "If you would fetch me brandy, my lord, I will find the needle and catgut." I went out to the stable and took honey, vinegar and the needle and gut from my saddle bag. I returned and after threading the needle poured brandy on the wound and then on the needle.

"My lord, if you would hold his arm. I know he is a brave man but if he moves whilst I sew then he will undo all my work." In the event, he did not move and he gritted his teeth. I saw his eyes close when the needle entered but he uttered not a sound. When it was done, I smeared honey on it and then bound it. "There."

"Thank you, Thomas."

His lordship was not afraid of getting his hands dirty, "Come Thomas, you and I will move these bodies outside. You may take from them what you will."

I lit a brand and placed it in the sconce in the yard. The man I had followed had a fine sword that had been made in Toledo. I took that. Their purses, especially the leader's, were full. Such men trusted no one and carrying their treasure with them was second nature. That done I took my treasures and secured them in my valise and saddle.

The English Adventurer

Captain Hogan, his arm now in a sling, came out. "We must strip their bodies." I looked at him. "We need to dispose of their bodies and their clothes would identify them."

"Dispose of them, how?"

"We will take them tomorrow night and throw them in the River Manzanares. We will do it at midnight so that by dawn their bodies are well downstream."

"By tomorrow night they will stink."

He shrugged, "Then we wear cloths over our mouths."

That done we retired to enjoy just a couple of hours of sleep before dawn.

The bodies had still to endure a day of Spanish sun but they were still pungent and were upsetting the horses. The three animals we used to dispose of them would be even unhappier.

We ate and then we dressed. I donned my servant's garb and Lord Collingwood and Captain Hogan their finest apparel for they were to visit the king. Captain Hogan refused to wear a sling arguing that a lack of any wound on the two men would only confuse whoever had sent them. "The lack of information helps us and deceives our foes." The Irishman turned to me, "Take care. Better that you return here without knowledge than you give away your identity or, worse, die."

"I will try to stay alive, Captain Hogan." I gave a short bow.

He flicked the back of my head with his good hand, "You have cheek, Thomas Penkridge."

Once more I left by the rear gate but this time I left before they did. I knew that I was disobeying orders but I had decided to become Spanish again. I needed to gain accurate information and if I spoke in English then they would know his lordship sent me. I followed the same route that the dead Frenchman had taken and saw that there were now two liveried guards at the gate. I did not recognise the livery but I noted it for his lordship might be able to use that information. I chose boldness as my weapon. As I neared the two men, who viewed me with increasing suspicion, I exaggerated a limp.

"May I approach the door for I am without funds? I will work for a few coppers."

One swung at me with the haft of his halberd. I deftly ducked out of the way. "Away with you, street rat, lest we do more than swing our weapons at you."

I took a chance and adopted a hurt expression, "I thought that Frenchmen were generous to beggars. Was I misinformed?"

The English Adventurer

The one who had swung at me laughed, "I know not about every Frenchman but the Comte de Valois would not give a sou to place on a dead man's eyes."

I spied a man coming from the next house and I hobbled towards him, "My lord, I am a poor man and the French lord next door refuses to give me a coin."

The man's eyes narrowed, "He is a cruel man. Here." He took a coin from his purse and gave it to me. "Go with God."

I kissed the back of his hand and said, "This will feed me today." He went in one direction and I turned to pass the two sentries. I gave them the sign of the cuckold and when one started after me, took to my legs. I had found that which I needed and hoped that the two sentries, while they might remember me, would do so for the wrong reasons. I reached the house before his lordship and Captain Hogan. I used the time to brush the horses. It calmed them and distracted them from the increasing stench of death that pervaded the yard and stable. When they returned I told them what I had discovered. The name was known to both of them.

That night we wrapped the six bodies in sheets and slung them over the backs of three sumpters. We led them in the dead of night after the watch had passed, and headed towards the river. Captain Hogan had worked out the best place to dispose of them, it was in the poorer part of town. The ones who lived there would not wish attention to be drawn to them. We watched the bodies, now bloating, begin their journey to the sea.

As we headed back, I asked, "Will they not be seen?"

He nodded, "The river is wide and who would seek to retrieve dead bodies? Besides, soon the fishes will nibble at their bodies and the air will disappear. Once they sink beneath the waves a little, they will be hidden. I doubt that much of them will reach the sea."

I could not help but make the sign of the cross and I looked at the captain, "Will their souls reach heaven?"

He shook his head, "Men like that know they are bound for hell. Their only hope is to be successful enough to retire rich and then ask for absolution. Either that or cease to be a night predator."

We packed up our belongings and Captain Hogan fetched the caretaker. Lord Collingwood paid him a healthy amount and we left. I would not say that it was an easy journey south for we had extra, laden horses and we were watching constantly for an ambush. None came. I still played the English servant and my only chance to speak to the others came when we were alone on the road. I asked after we had passed Sevilla and were on the last leg, why the Comte de Valois had not sent men after us.

He shrugged, "I am not sure. Perhaps he has lost too many men or, more likely he is choosing a better time when he can guarantee success. His lordship and the Comte are old enemies. This is a battle of wits between them. Thus far, Lord Collingwood has not returned like for like. He believes that knowing your enemy was better than killing him for who knows who might replace him."

When we reached his lordship's home, he had Foster run a bath for him. Captain Hogan enjoyed one too and, when they had both finished, they allowed me to luxuriate in a warm bath to clean away the stink of horses and rid my body of the lice that had gathered. I even dined in the main dining room with them.

Captain Hogan had dispensed with the sling but I saw that the wound still troubled him, "So, Thomas, do you wish me to store the payment from his lordship and the coins you took with the rest of your fortune?"

I shook my head. I had spent the nights alone on the way south, planning, "I have seen how you, your lordship, make your money grow. I would do the same and the New World is the place to do so. I know not yet how I will use my coin but I will."

His lordship nodded, "And this place, El Dorado, has no master yet."

Captain Hogan said, "Except for the natives who might object to new masters."

Lord Collingwood nodded, "But, as Thomas will attest, they are no match for our modern weapons. As I said, this new land is of interest to us."

"But, your lordship, from what I have heard English ships have yet to sail into the Spanish seas let alone find a way across the Isthmus of Panama."

"When next I return to London, I will speak of this to King Henry. He is young and ambitious. A western empire cannot do us harm. Any information you can bring will serve England, Thomas, as do you."

I left the next day and saw a different future for myself. I had told Captain Pedro he could have me for a year or so. Now I was planning on moving further west to Panama. I still knew not what exactly I would be doing but it would not simply be a master gunner. I wanted more.

The English Adventurer
Paullu

Chapter 9

I am Paullu of the Quechua tribe, but I am not a peasant, I am a noble, an Inca. We are the ones who rule the tribes we have conquered and lead the armies that continue to make our empire ever bigger. Our Empire is the greatest the world has ever known, Tawantinsuyu. Inca Huayna Capac is our Emperor and now that I had seen fourteen summers and came from one of the noblest of families, I was to begin my training as an officer. I would leave my family and I could not guarantee to see any of them again. I did not mind for my father was a soldier and one of the Emperor's bodyguards. He was a Hatun Apu, a commander of five hundred. All knew his rank for with increasing rank came larger gold pieces embedded in his ears. If I survived my training, then I would have a small coin planted in the lobe of each ear and I would become an officer. At first, I might be called upon to assist a commander of a hundred, a Pachaca Camayoc. Hopefully, that period of training would not last long and I would soon be able to learn how to be a leader of men and a warrior who killed many in battle.

I knew that I was lucky for we lived in the holy city of Cuzco and being close to Inca Huayna Capac brought joy and prosperity to our family. I was the third brother to leave to be trained as an officer and as I was the last male my mother would just have my sisters for company. Perhaps that was why she made such a fuss of me as I was leaving. I did not understand the tears she shed. My sisters too wept so much one would have thought it was news of my death they had heard. I was now almost a man and after my training, I would indeed be one. I could not wait. So, I smiled and put my arm around my mother and told her all would be well. She should have been used to this for my father rarely visited the fine home we occupied. I had only seen him six times in the last four years but each time I had interrogated him for information about my training. He had been close-lipped, but he had smiled, albeit grimly, when he said, "If you survive the training then nothing you do after the training will seem hard. Just remember when times are hard that most trainees survive and the ones who are taken… they were not meant to be soldiers. You do not have to undergo the training. It is your choice. There are other things you can do to serve the Emperor."

The English Adventurer

I had stood defiantly and promised, "I swear, father, that I will successfully pass the test and become not only a warrior but one who will lead armies. I will become a Hatun Apuratin."

He laughed and said, "Just pass the test!"

I left early, thinking to be away before my mother was awake but that was not meant to be and she and my sisters had prepared a large breakfast for me which they forced me to eat. Each of my sisters had woven clothes for me as I might be serving high in the mountains where it would be cold. I ate, I took the presents and I thanked them. Once the door was closed, I strode off for the fortress of Sacsayhuamán which guarded our holiest of cities. That was where I would be housed with the other would-be officers and given my instructions. The six days of training would begin once we were taken from the fortress and left far beyond what passed for civilisation. The warm garments made by my sisters would be left behind and with just a simple shift, hat, bronze knife and a waterskin I would have to fend for myself. I only knew that part because my father had told me. As for the rest, he had told me nothing. I assumed I would have to kill my own food and find shelter. I guessed that there would be no trail and I would have to navigate through the jungle. None of that worried me for I had spent some time with the old soldier who worked in our home. Nano had fought alongside my father until a club had rendered one knee useless. He told me how to use the sun and the stars.

"We are lucky, Master Paullu, we live so close to the heavens that our home can always be seen. If all else fails, then know that Cuzco is at the top of our mountains."

I knew that the sun rose in the east and set in the west. Inti was the sun god and he watched over us each day. I knew that some doubted that he had real power save for bringing warmth to our world and the god Viracocha was seen as more powerful. I was not sure, but Inti would be the god who would guide me and help me to find my way to becoming an officer.

I made my way through the city. Everything was organised and orderly. We liked straight lines and order. The closer I came to the pukara, the stronghold, the fewer people I saw and most of those heading to it were going to the warehouses which lay outside its walls. I saw one youth heading down the road towards me. His head was down, and I wondered whence he had come. Then all other thoughts left me as I saw the terraced walls of Sacsayhuamán rising before me. Sitting atop a hill this was our citadel! When I reached the gates to the fortress, the pukara, I saw that they were just two common soldiers who were there. They did not show me any respect and, as I walked up to them, I saw

The English Adventurer

them exchange comments and then laugh. I knew that they were mocking me. When I became an officer then I would remember them, and they would pay for the insult. I kept my dignity.

"I am Paullu Hautpac and I was asked to report here."

"Ready to become an officer are you…sir?" The word 'sir' was imbued with such derision that I thought to slap the man in the face, but I did not.

"I am. Where do I report?"

"Go through the next gate and continue up until you reach level four. Someone will find you…" he laughed, "or perhaps not. It may just be part of the test, eh, Paullu Hautpac?"

The journey up the terraced stone walls seemed to me like all things related to our people and their ways. The guards at each gate were of a higher rank and the rigour was stricter. That I was expected and one of a number was clear to me. The sarcastic comments quickly diminished but as I passed through each gate, I felt more intimidated. I was glad when I reached level four. When I was admitted an official greeted me. I guessed that he came from a noble family, but he had chosen this route rather than a military one. I knew that he had served some time as an officer for he had a gold coin in the lobe of each ear. Every man in the Empire was expected to serve for some part of their life in the service of the Emperor. This official had done his duty. It also told me that he had endured the trials I was about to undertake. Even if he insulted me, he would have my respect.

"I am Aucaruna and I will be in charge of your training and, should you survive, it is I who will assign you to a pukara." I nodded. "You are leaving your ayllus, your family forever. The role of an officer is a lonely one. You will be leading ordinary taxpayers, mitimacs, who may not even be from the Quecha tribe. If you serve on the borders, then it could be soldiers from the conquered army that you lead. Before you undertake this trial, I would have you consider that. When I awake you on the morrow to begin you may withdraw from the trial with no loss of honour."

"I will be a soldier, sir, and serve the Emperor!"

He gave a thin smile, "I will ask you again in the morning. I will take you to the room you and the other candidates will share and after the sun has reached its zenith you will all be instructed in the task you have to perform. You will have one meal this evening and then you will each retire. There will be no talking in the room you all share. There will be no questions. The next words you speak will be to me in the morning when you are asked if you wish to continue."

The English Adventurer

He led me to a simple room in which there were a dozen or so beds. Half were occupied by youths such as me. There was a soldier seated at a desk at the end of the room. "You will rest here until noon when this soldier will fetch you to me. Your test begins now, Paullu Hautpac, and if you speak then you have failed." Again, he gave me a thin smile, "One has already failed the test." He turned and left.

I sat on the bed and worked out that the youth I had passed on my way here was that candidate. I would not make the same mistake. I looked at the others. They were rivals. This test was more than just a pass or fail; my father had told me that. If I did well, better than the others, then I could expect to be assigned to one of the prestigious pukaras. If not then it would be to a border pukara where I would command not Quechua warriors but allies or the conquered peoples, barbarians! The other candidates all looked strong and four of them were bigger than I was. I did not know any of them and that was strange for we lived close to other noble families and while I was not friends with any of the other boys my age, I knew many of them to speak to. The training began on the first day of the new week after you were fourteen. As each trial lasted six days then those that I knew might begin the next week. My father had said that I would need all my strength and so I lay on the bed and looked at the decorated ceiling. I would rest. The ceiling was painted with scenes depicting our glorious battles where we had subjugated the other tribes. We had not lost a battle for almost one hundred years and we were invincible!

Another three candidates were brought, and I knew none of them. At precisely noon the soldier stood and said, "Follow me." He led us through the other gates until we reached the top of the building; it was open to the sun. The terraces zig zagged, and the gates were offset. I could not see how any attacker would reach this high for they would have to endure darts, arrows, and javelins as they did so. The view from the very top was spectacular. The mountains were all around us, but we appeared to be on a level with them. The sun above us looked close enough to touch.

Aucaruna was waiting for us and he smiled, "Congratulations, you have passed the first part of the test. Only one failed." He spread his arms, "We are here for this is what you will aspire to. You will wish to be a great general who is at the top of the mountain having shown the others that he is the best warrior."

We were all standing in a line and, like the others, I felt myself swell with pride. We all stood taller.

"The test is a simple one." He took from behind his back two feathers. One was a white one and one was a red one. "All that you have to do is to find the birds who have these feathers and fetch back one of each!"

He paused and I saw him cock his head on one side. He was waiting for one of us to ask a question. Glancing down the line I saw some frowns. I was lucky Nano had taken me for walks in the jungle and the mountains and he had identified the birds. The red one lived in the jungle and was called the Tunki bird. The upper part of the male was bright red. The other would be known by everyone for it was the largest bird in the land. Its wings were longer than a man and it soared high above the mountains. It was called by many names, but we called it the Inti bird, the bird of the sun god and the white feathers came from its neck. I now saw the cleverness of the test. One bird lived lower down than the other. One would involve climbing while the other would mean travelling through a jungle with snakes, reptiles, and other creatures, not to mention fierce beasts like the jaguar. I now understood why so many failed. I knew that at least four of the others had no idea where to begin to look for the Tunki. The Inti bird was visible now to the west and I knew that they would seek that one first. I would descend to the lower slopes of the mountains and find the Tunki first.

"You will each be given a water skin with enough water for two days. The whole process of collecting the feathers and the rest of the initiation will take six days."

Once again, he allowed that to sink in. If any returned with just the feathers after six days, they would have failed.

"You will be allowed your footwear, shift, hat and a dagger." He smiled again but there was no warmth in it. "If you have no dagger," he paused, "then you have no weapon."

Two of those who did not know where to find the Tunki looked at their feet as though a dagger would materialise. Once again, I was grateful to Nano. He had suggested what I might bring, and my father had given me when I was ten, a finely made bronze dagger. I was armed.

"You are now free to wander until it is time for food which will be served in your bedchamber. You will be watched, and any speaking will result in failure." I saw that another three soldiers had joined the first and they were studying us. Aucaruna left us. Some looked despairingly around. I walked to the western wall for I could see the Inti bird. The best way to get a feather was to get close to their nest. Only a fool would risk trying to take one from a live bird. Taking one from a nest was also risky as they nested high in places that were hard for predators to climb. Shading my eyes from the sun I stared at the birds as they circled. I waited until one plunged to the earth and when I saw it rise

The English Adventurer

with a small animal in its talons, I studied its flight. Three other candidates were also watching, and I knew that they would try to go for the same nest. If I had to then I would use my dagger on them. We had not been told to spare our fellow candidates. I would be an officer no matter what. I did not rely on one sighting and I spent the afternoon identifying a second nest. I was glad I did so for I was the only one who saw the huge Inti bird land closer to the walls of the city. It was still many miles away, but it was closer than the first bird.

I was the last candidate to return to our room and I would have stayed longer but the last guard who remained on the roof was tapping his foot angrily. I had hoped that I might find another Inti bird's nest which would be even closer. I took off my hat and my sandals when I reached the room. I had with me some salve Nuno had given to me. The quest for the feathers and the test would be harder on my feet than I was used to. I was not allowed to take anything with me and so I covered my feet in the aromatic salve and let my feet dry while we awaited the food. I had no idea what the others were doing but, in my head, I was planning a route to the Tunki bird. The quickest way to their nests would be to head directly from the pukara down through the jungle which was constantly attacked to keep it from encroaching on the city. I did not know if there was a trail, but I guessed that some of the mitimacs would be sent into the jungle to gather wood and food. They would have cleared a trail and I would use that.

The earthenware dish was brought in and we all gravitated to the table. As I had expected we were served pachamanca, which was a sort of stew. There was meat, which was probably a cuy, but the majority of the stew was made up of vegetables. The soldier ladled it out for us. It was filling and I ate one whole bowl before looking in the pot for more. I saw the soldier smiling at me. There was none left in. He had ensured we all had the same quantity. We had one beaker of chicha to drink. My mother's brew was more potent than the one we were given but I still sipped it slowly for I would be drinking water for the next six days or more. After I had eaten and drank, I went to make water and then retired. There was nothing else to do until we were woken and allowed out of the pukara. Not surprisingly it took me some time to fall asleep. My mind was racing but eventually, I did.

Aucaruna himself saw us off. We were taken to the main gate not long after dawn. We had not been fed and given no water except for the measured-out skins we were all given. He nodded and said, "When you return… if you return then ask for me and you will be admitted. May those who are worthy survive!"

The English Adventurer

It was hardly a cheery message. I saw the rest of the candidates turn and run down the road which led to the city gate which would take them to the mountains where we had seen the Inti bird. That suited me for it meant I had no competition for the Tunki feather I sought. I headed down a narrow road between houses and after a short walk reached a gate. The gate would be barred at night but as it was daylight it was open and, with my dagger in my belt and my water skin around my back, I stepped onto the faintest of trails. The jungle always smelled. A mixture of animals and rotting vegetation, it was a unique aroma. I headed down the steep slope to look for the Tunki. They tended to forage close to the water and seek fruit. I had seen one whilst hunting with Nano. I knew that I had several miles to walk and while I followed the trail down, I was looking around for the things I might need. Here there would be fruit that I could collect but I also sought a vine so that I could make a sling and use it to make other useful items. I found the liana first and I used my knife to cut a long length. I coiled it around my body after cutting off a piece that I could use as a sling. I cut a small piece of cloth from the hem of my shift and used that to finish off the sling. Finally, I took off my hat and after cutting another length of liana I fashioned a bag. I dropped some of the pebbles I spied into it and continued. I wondered if any of the others would have had the wit to do as I had done. Many would simply race to get to the nest of the Inti bird without any thought of food or how they were going to reach the nest. I had a liana now.

I heard the sound of the Tunki bird long before I saw it. It was in the early afternoon when I reached the area of the jungle in which they lived. I had collected some fruit as I had descended and put them in my improvised bag. The pepino was a refreshing fruit and the other fruit I collected, the guaba, would give me sustenance. They would be a start, but I was determined not to starve. As soon as I heard the distinctive, *tunk* sound which gave the bird its name, I stopped. I saw a rock nearby and I made my way to it. I sat on the top and took out a pebble which I fitted into my sling. Every boy I knew had a sling and knew how to use it. Nano had encouraged me to practise for he said that the skills would help me when I became a soldier. Every soldier, even the officers, used a sling in battle and was one of our most potent weapons. I heard the birds as they made their call, but I saw none. I knew that there was little point in looking for the nest. There would be no red feathers there; the male Tunki had nothing to do with nest building. It was late in the afternoon when I spied one. I had kept still and, perhaps I had blended into the landscape. It flew up towards me and I took my chance. As it neared me, I hurled the pebble. It was not the most accurate of throws,

The English Adventurer

but the size of the pebble compensated for that. I caught the bird a glancing blow and I saw it fall, stunned, to the ground. Leaving my perch, I raced over and, before it could struggle to its feet and fly away, I used my knife to kill it. I hacked off its head, with the red feathers, and put it in my improvised sack.

    Soon it would be dark and there was no way that I was going to risk travelling through the jungle at night. I headed down to the stream I knew would be nearby. The Tunki always lived close to water. I found the stream and while it looked clean I would not risk drinking it. Instead, I looked for dead wood. I would make a fire. Nano had taught me how to find the rocks that, when banged together would make a spark. I soon found them, and I started to gather the dead and dried grasses that would make the kindling. It was almost dark by the time the grass flared into flame and I carefully fed first the dead twigs and then the branches which would feed the fire. They would keep away, I hoped, not only the flying insects but snakes and other animals that might harm me. Finally, I started to pluck the torso of the bird. I did so with my feet in the water. The cool stream refreshed them. With the fruits I had the bird would give me a meal. As it began to cook, I wondered what the others would find to eat. The Inti bird nests high in the rocks. Even with a sling, they were too big to bring down. I guessed that they would have a cold, cheerless and foodless night. I knew that I could eat all my foraging for when I headed back to the city I could gather more of the fruit. My fire worked and I awoke whole and without insect bites. No snake had sought my body for warmth for the fire had burned almost until dawn. There was still heat from it when I rose.

    I reached the city in the mid-morning and headed past the gates of Sacsayhuamán to take the road towards the mountain. The bird's head had begun to smell, and I knew that it would get worse. By noon I was in the jungle once more and I began to climb. This was a thinner jungle, but it still contained dangers. I also discovered that there was less food. I had five or six fruits in my sack, and they would have to sustain me for the rest of the quest. I headed for the tower of rock, which held the nest closest to the city but, by the time the sun began to set, it was still a mile or so away. I found a stream and after gathering wood and making a fire I sat with my feet in the stream. My feet and my footwear were both holding up well. I had walked further in two days than I would normally walk in a week. The sounds in this part of the jungle were different from the ones the previous night. In our land, Tawantinsuyu, no two pieces of jungle are ever the same and there would be different creatures here to my last resting place. I kept the fire burning and although I was woken three or four times by creatures of the night, none

The English Adventurer

came close. I ate some of the fruit and drank a little of the water, but I did not know how long it might take me to get the last feather.

I reached the foot of the precipice where I had spied the nest. As I approached the undergrowth, I disturbed some carrion who flew off. I drew my knife as I approached. There, broken on rocks lay the body of another candidate. I felt his body and it was cold. He must have seen the same nest that I had. From the position of his body and what he had about him I worked out that he had fallen on the way up for I found no white feather. I took his waterskin and his dagger. I did not need to, but I covered his body with rocks so that he would lie undisturbed. When I returned to the city, I would tell Aucaruna where the youth lay. His parents would need to know. The burial also gave me the chance to see how to climb. When the body was buried, I placed the waterskins and my sack on the ground along with my sling. I took the liana and held it, coiled, in my hand and then realised I would need both hands. I slipped the coiled rope around me. Nano had not taught me to climb as such, but he had given me a method to overcome difficulties. I had to make the climb in manageable stages. I saw that the first part was relatively simple. That part of the climb was a quarter of the whole. There was a sort of ledge where I could rest.

Praying to Inti to help me I began the climb. Even though it was relatively easy I was still out of breath when I reached the ledge. I regretted not bringing the water skin for I was thirsty. I had learned a lesson. I wondered if the dead youth had found the first part so easy that he had pushed on too quickly. I waited until my breathing was regular and then began to traverse the cliff. The wall of stone above me was too smooth but a diagonal path had handholds and plant life. The wall was not totally vertical and the slightest of slopes meant I did not have to lean back. It took longer to make the traverse for I made certain that each hand and foothold were secure before moving on. When I found a rock upon which to sit, I saw that I had covered more than half of the climb. The next part was straight up and as I recovered, I saw that I would be able to zig-zag up this part. My hands were already bleeding when I began the next part. This would take me to the nest. I now understood why they had given us this task as an initiation. My bleeding hands were my first wound, and I would have to endure the pain. That was good preparation for becoming an officer. The liana was still coiled around me and afforded some protection from the sharp, jagged rocks. They helped me to climb but they still caused cuts and wounds. I heard a cracking sound some way above me and I stopped and risked a look. The Inti bird had taken to the air and the crack was the first flap of his wings. I suppose that crack, had it surprised a tired

The English Adventurer

youth, might have made him lose his grip. The nest was more than likely to be empty, but I did not rush. The Inti bird would be hunting, and it had a wide range. I had time.

As I approached the nest from below, I stopped and listened. I had assumed there was just one bird in the nest for this was not breeding season but what if there was another? I listened but I heard nothing, and I risked ascending to the top. The nest was huge but the material around the edge was a little fragile and a piece came away as I grabbed it. Luckily, I was leaning forward otherwise I might have lost my balance. The nest was still warm, but I did not spend long examining it for there, in the bottom, were the precious white feathers Nano had told me that the Inti bird groomed themselves every day. I grabbed a handful. The only place I could keep them was in my breechclout. There they would be safe until I could put them with the stinking head of the Tunki. I needed to rest but I suddenly felt exposed. I slipped back over the side and began my descent.

The journey down was harder because I had to look down for my footholds and that told me how high I had climbed. It took me longer to get to my rocky perch. I rested longer than on the way up. I rested so long that I spied the Inti bird returning to its nest with its kill in its talons. The diagonal traverse was even harder than the vertical descent and it was early afternoon before I reached my last staging point. I forced myself to rest as long as possible for although I had the easiest part of the descent the failing light meant that the shadows were deceptive. By the time I reached the grave it was but a short time before dusk and I made a fire. When that was done, I put the white feathers, wrapped in a leaf to prevent the dried blood from the Tunki bird from staining them, in my sack and then I drank. I allowed myself more water for I now had a spare. I ate the last of my fruit. I would be able to reach the city before dark the next day.

As I lay down to sleep, I realised that the dead youth was also preparation for my life as an officer. I would lose comrades in battle and, perhaps, have to sleep close by their corpses. The fruit I had eaten woke me before dawn and the resultant stink after I had emptied my bowels made sleep impossible. I added fuel to the fire and waited for dawn. As soon as the first light shone on the mountainside above me, I set off.

I had walked perhaps a mile when I heard a noise ahead. Hiding behind a tree, I fitted a stone to my sling and waited. It was another of the candidates. I stepped out and he whipped his dagger out. We had been told not to speak and I did not know him. I just nodded. He said, "Have you the feather of the Inti bird." I nodded, "The nest I tried was

The English Adventurer

too difficult. One of our number fell and died. Is there a nest there?" He pointed to the rocky cliff I had climbed. I nodded, "He smiled, "You are taking this no speaking rule seriously aren't you? There is no one here." I shrugged and stepped beyond him. Rules were rules. I was more determined than ever to make it back to the fortress and I ran. My unruly bowels stopped me three more times, but they had quietened by the time I was close to the city. When I saw Sacsayhuamán rising above the city of Cuzco I gave thanks to Inti.

Chapter 10

My early start meant that I reached the gates of the mighty pukara before dark. "I am here to see Aucaruna." This time there were no sneers nor ribald comments and I was taken to the fourth level. I wondered if anyone had beaten me.

Aucaruna was seated at the table we had used and was eating some dried meats and bread. He looked up and smiled. "So Paullu Hautpac, you are the first, but have you done what was asked?" I nodded and he smiled, "Good. You have remembered. Some failed this part of the test. Show me." I opened my hat sack and unwrapped the leaf with the feathers and took out the bird's head. He laughed, "Very imaginative. Only one other had the wit to do as you did." He seemed to see the other water skin. "Did you steal that?" All the water skins were identical. I shook my head. "Found it?" I shook my head. "Then one of your number is dead." I nodded. "When the test is over, and you can speak you shall tell me all." He stood, "Bring your hat and your water skins and follow me."

I was taken to the top of Sacsayhuamán where we received our briefing. There were a dozen mats there. "For the next two days, you will sit here. You will not move from the mat. You may stand but for no longer than it takes to count to a hundred." He smiled, "You will not soil the mat. Do you understand?" I nodded knowing that my bowels could well cost me the chance to become an officer. He pointed to the guards who patrolled the top of the building. "They will watch you. Good luck."

I chose the mat which I believe would keep me from the sun and I sat. I would need to make water but how? Then it came to me. I had two water skins. I would pour the water from one into the other and use the waterskin as a latrine. I almost laughed. I would need to ensure that I drank from the correct one. Night had fallen by the time I had emptied the water. I drank sparingly, for lots of reasons. Fortunately, my bowels appeared to have calmed down. Probably because I had not eaten all day. I slept, albeit badly, leaning forward. I began to topple once and that woke me up. When dawn came, I stood and used the empty waterskin for the first time.

In the middle of the morning, Aucaruna appeared with another candidate. This time his clothes were torn, and his hands were bleeding. Aucaruna gave him the same speech and then he turned to me. "The sentries have reported to me. You have yet to break the rules; keep it that way."

The English Adventurer

The youth chose the mat next to me and his eyes spoke volumes. Two more made it by the end of the day. One was the one I had met and who had spoken to me. The other three all looked in a worse condition than me. I had been lucky or was it something else?

The water skin was almost full by the middle of the next morning. This would be the last morning of the test. Two more candidates had arrived by noon and both were in a shocking condition. My method of making water had been observed by the three who had spent the night with me, and they copied me. They would do without water for the last day. The last candidate arrived in the late afternoon and he limped; he had hurt his leg.

As darkness fell Aucaruna returned. "You are the seven who have passed this part of the test. Follow the guards to the bathhouse. You can use all the facilities there. There will still be no talking."

I knew that at least two of the candidates had died, had others suffered the same fate or had they simply failed?

After we had bathed, we still had to wear the same clothes we had when we had undergone the ordeal. I saw as we dried ourselves that some of the others had been injured in the quest for the feathers. There were bruises as well as cuts. I had been lucky. I think the reason we were given the luxury of the bath was to take away our stink for we were not fed. We were led to the room in which we had first slept. If I thought that we were going to have the joy of a bed I was wrong.

"You are coming to the end of the test. Once that has been accomplished then you can begin the training properly to be an officer of the Inca." He looked at each of us. "Tonight will be a vigil for you. It will be a full moon and just as we serve Inti, the sun god, we must be mindful of his wife, Mama Killa, the goddess of the moon. When Inti rises then you will be brought to the gate and begin your last ordeal. You will follow the six soldiers who will keep running until Inti is gone from the sky. You will keep their pace."

This would be a hard test for me. I was not the fastest of runners and I had a larger frame than some of the others. As I looked at the competition I eliminated, in my mind, the one who had injured his leg. He had limped badly, and he would not be able to keep up. I stared up at Mama Killa as she rose in the sky and as I saw her face take shape, I realised it was not a competition with others; it was with myself. It did not matter if I finished last, just that I finish. I knew that realisation came from Mama Killa and I thanked her. At least my feet, thanks to the salve I had used and the bathing in the water each night, were in better condition than they might otherwise have been. I fell asleep. It was exhaustion but I was saved by the cry of the night owl which jerked

The English Adventurer

my head up. I saw one of the guards staring at me. Had he seen me sleep? If so, then I would be eliminated before the last ordeal. He averted his gaze from me and stared at another. I would not risk sleep again and I began to go through all of my relatives from my father, backwards until I reached Manco Capac. By then Mama Killa had disappeared and Inti was beginning to light the eastern sky.

A new officer came and said, "Rise." I saw he had golden coins in his ears and in his helmet he had the blue feathers which showed his Ayllu. He had done as we had and would have had to endure the ordeal too. He led us down to the main gate. We were not afforded the opportunity to make water or take water. The ordeal was becoming harder as each moment passed. Aucaruna was at the gate but he said nothing. I saw five of the soldiers who would be running with us and saw that they had helmets, shields and weapons. That gave me hope for they would have a harder time than us. My heart sank when servants came out and, taking off our hats, placed a bronze helmet on each of our heads. We were each given a bronze-headed axe. The officer said, "Failure to return with the helmet and the axe means you will not become an officer!" He turned on his heel and started to run. The five soldiers followed him, and we headed down towards the gate I had used what seemed like a lifetime ago to head into the jungle. We had left the roof in the order of our beds and that meant I was next to the last candidate.

While the pace was not fast, the helmet felt uncomfortable and kept banging on the back of my neck. With the axe held in two hands then adjusting it was impossible. When I tried to carry the axe in one hand it upset my rhythm and I almost tripped. I would have to endure the discomfort. The one with the injured leg began to slow. He was three ahead of me and a gap appeared among the others. He was overtaken and was just two ahead. The youth before me sprinted and overtook him and I was forced to do the same to avoid tripping. I saw the pain on his face as I passed. We had to run harder to catch up to the others and it hurt. I wondered how long we would have to run. We passed the stream where I had camped that first night and, after that, I was in an unknown jungle. A mile later I saw two of the soldiers who had begun the run sitting on a log and drinking from a waterskin. I was confused. Did that mean we could stop too? None of the others stopped and I ran on. When a couple of miles later I saw another two of the soldiers drinking I knew what was happening. The soldiers were being replaced. By noon all five of the soldiers had been replaced but not the officer.

We started to climb, and I found it hard to breathe. The helmet had chafed flesh from the back of my neck and insects, attracted by the

The English Adventurer

blood began to annoy me. As the slope became steeper, I found breathing harder and the gap between me and the youth ahead lengthened. I forced myself to run through the pain in my side and catch up with him. I realised it was the one who had spoken to me on the feather hunt. Just when I thought I could run no further we emerged from the jungle into a clearing and I saw the five soldiers and the officer standing with the other candidates. There was a servant who poured water into a beaker for me. I could barely catch my breath and so I waited until I could before I drank. As I did so I saw the officer looking beyond me. I suddenly realised that I was the last. The two behind me were no longer there. I also saw that we were almost back at the city. It lay less than a mile away. We had been taken on a loop and that explained how they had fetched water and changed the soldiers.

I had barely finished the water when the officer said, "If you need to make water then now is the time. We return as soon as I have done so!"

I lay down my axe and took off my helmet. It was a relief to make water, but I had to do it quickly for I determined to make my helmet more comfortable. I found some large leaves and I padded the inside and back with them. It made the helmet slightly more comfortable and the water which was on the leaves dripped down my back cooling me a little. I had just picked up the axe when the officer and the men ran past me. I had been the last but now I was the first and I intended to stay that way. My stomach complained all the way down the slope and rather than finding it easier to run downhill, my knees joined in with my body's moans. I kept up with the soldier ahead and, being at the front saw the first soldier change. It was only a small thing but as the soldiers slowed, it was a relief, and I began to pray for a change of runner. The sun was setting as we began the climb to Sacsayhuamán. Aucaruna was waiting at the main gate to the citadel and he was smiling. As I passed inside the walls he said, simply, "Well done!" The same servants who had given us the helmet and axe took them from us while another gave us water. I say us but as I looked around, I saw that only three others had completed the ordeal.

The four of us were taken to the bathhouse but this time we were accompanied by servants who bathed and oiled us. Salve was applied to our injuries. Our clothes were taken away and we were wrapped in a white robe before we were taken back to the roof where Aucaruna, the officer and a dozen soldiers awaited us as well as some servants. There was a table and on it were various items. We had been given some food and drink in the bathhouse but I was still ravenous and all that I could think of was eating!

The English Adventurer

"Today you have passed your test and you are officers. You have a long way to travel to have ears like Manco here."

I saw that the officer who had run with us was a Gauranga Camayoc, he commanded a thousand!

"Take off your robes."

We did so and stood naked. Eight servants stepped forward and while one held the small coins the other pierced the lobes of our ears to implant the coins which would grow as we ascended the hierarchy of officers. I saw the reason for the nakedness for there was blood when our lobes were pierced. I ignored the pain. Then the servants fetched the breechclouts and fastened them. Aucaruna himself fitted the llantos, the braided royal fringe around our heads. Finally, the soldiers came to give us a shield, a sling and a silver-headed axe. We were officers.

Manco, the soldiers and the servants all left us. Aucaruna spoke, "Your initiation is complete and now you can talk. You will not see each other again unless it is when we go to war for each of you will be sent to a different pukara with replacement soldiers. I will dine with you tonight and answer any questions you might have, and I am sure you have many."

Surprisingly, none of us did and I think it was just the realisation that so few had come through the ordeal which had killed two of our number. I described where I had buried the body and the other three had all seen the other dead candidate. It appeared, from what they told Aucaruna that he had been the first to find the nest we had all seen and, perhaps, he had been too eager and his haste had killed him. As I ate the roasted cuy I thought about all the lessons I had learned during the initiation and how they would help me as an officer. Of course, the real lessons would come when I reached the pukara. Aucaruna would not reveal our assignment. He was a methodical officer who liked to do things properly and that, too, was a lesson. Order and organisation were all. As we had no questions we chatted while we ate. We had all a basic idea of how our tribe, the Quechua, had managed to subjugate so many of the tribes around us. Our empire was so vast that to travel along it from north to south would take months rather than days. Aucaruna put it down to two things, the roads which we built and the pukaras along with their garrisons.

"None of you will serve here, in the heartland of Tawantinsuyu, instead you will be sent to the borderlands and recently conquered people. They are the ones who have yet to learn that acceptance of our rule is the right way forward."

The youth I had met, I learned his name was Tupa, asked, "Will we be given men to command?"

The English Adventurer

Aucaruna laughed so hard that I feared for his health! When he had recovered, he shook his head, "Command? Not for some time. No, the Pachaca Camayoc to whom you will be assigned will have much to teach you. Eventually, you may be given ten men or so to take on a scouting expedition. It will be in the interests of the Pachaca Camayoc to teach you well for when one of his trainees is ready and can be promoted then he can expect to become a Guaranga Camayoc and command a thousand."

I noticed then that Aucaruna had large pieces of gold in his ears, "You are a Hatan Apu, are you not, sir?"

"I am and when the Emperor needs me, I shall relinquish this task and lead an army."

There was little talking in the room when we lay down to sleep. The others were nothing to me and I was nothing to them. When I reached my new posting then I would get to know the others in my position, and I would learn from them. I was on the bottom rung of the ladder and I intended to climb as high as I could.

I learned that I was to be sent to the pukara of Vitcos. It was many miles to the north. Tupa would be travelling with me for a while for he was assigned to Oilantaytambo which lay to the west of my posting. I was envious for he would be more likely to see action and action meant a greater likelihood of promotion. There were more than eight pukara in the Vilcabamba region and the reason had been explained to us by Aucaruna. There were silver deposits in the area and it also produced great quantities of the food which the rich of Cuzco liked. We left with ten soldiers leading llamas which carried our supplies for the eighty-mile journey. They were commanded by Yahuar Roca who was also heading for Oilantaytambo. He would take command of a hundred. Tupa would have to ensure that he kept on the good side of the man who might, quite likely, become his officer. We headed north and east towards the mountains and with our oiled cloaks about our shoulders and our llanos on our heads we both felt like officers, albeit the most junior.

We had still not recovered from our initiation, but no allowances were made and that first morning was the hardest. Aucaruna had made it clear that the main reason for the silence rule was that talking was discouraged amongst soldiers and we marched along the road towards the Vilcabamba Valley. It gave me the chance to study the sacred mountains ahead of us. They almost touched the clouds. I was lucky to be who I was. We passed mitimacs labouring under loads. They came from the subjugated tribes and their purpose was to serve us. Some accompanied us for they would make our food and tend to the animals.

The English Adventurer

They had to clear the animal waste from the road for it had to be kept scrupulously clean! They deposited it in the jungle which constantly threatened to engulf the road. Yahuar Roca ordered them to cut some of it back when we made our first camp for the night.

When we reached Vitcos I was slightly disappointed. I knew it was an important pukara and I had expected it to be larger. There were just six levels. I tried to hide my disappointment. There was an Apu in charge of the pukara and I was assigned to a Pachaca Camayoc, Mayta Huacac. Tupa and the others were taken to their accommodation while I went along with the two soldiers to meet my officer.

Yupanqui Huaca seemed old to be just in command of a hundred. By his age, he should have an Apu. Indeed, the Apu looked to be younger than he was. As I had discovered during my initiation it did not do to act hastily and make rash decisions and judgements. The two soldiers were also replacements and there was a young officer who looked a little older than me. I later learned that Hanan Haullpa had passed his initiation just two years earlier. It was well that I reserved my judgement.

The Apu addressed us, "You three have been assigned to a dangerous place. We have lost twenty men in the last year. We are the central pukara of a complex of four others. Each contingent of one hundred has to spend time in one of the four smaller ones. Now that you three have arrived we will be heading to Yupanca tomorrow. Tonight, you may rest but tomorrow we start at dawn and we will not stop until Inti has gone." The two of them parted and opened the door to a sleeping chamber. "Tonight, you Paullu will share the sleeping chamber with these two men. At Yupanca you and Hanan will share a room."

With that, we were dismissed. I felt let down. I was an officer and yet I would have to share a room with Mitimacs! The two men seemed pleasant enough, but it was not an auspicious start. Once inside I saw that there were ten other men in the room. There were plenty of beds but… I chose the one furthest from any of the others. I arranged my kit first in the wooden box provided. I knew that organisation was of paramount importance. The two new men spoke with the other soldiers. They would be fighting together and they each knew the importance of getting to know their fellows. They spoke as though I was deaf and, once again, I learned that silence could be useful.

"What are the officers like? The Apu looks a little old to have such a lowly command."

"That is because they are both from the Chanca tribe."

The English Adventurer

My ears pricked up. The Chancas had been defeated thirty years earlier. That meant that the two officers had to be of noble blood, but they were not Quechua.

One of the new soldiers asked, "What does that mean?"

"It means, my friend that the only way they can be promoted is if they perform some great deed in battle. That is how our Apu was promoted. He was at Huayna Picchu and was one of only five men to survive an attack. His superior was killed, and he was promoted. He is a good man and as for the young one? We have not seen him yet in battle. That is the only way to judge a man."

The pukara we had been assigned to was even smaller than I had expected. Built in the usual manner with huge blocks of stone and progressively higher levels it was a deterrent to men wishing to attack the main pukara. There was enough accommodation for eighty men, and we had a hundred. It meant that twenty soldiers did not have their own beds. The three officers had two rooms and I would share one with Hanan. My work began immediately for I was assigned a watch on the walls. Yupanqui could have been unkind and given me troublemakers but the twenty men who would watch the walls with me were a mixture of old and young. There were a couple of soldiers who looked as though they could have been a grandfather, but I knew that was not true. One of them took pity on me and guided me through the systems we would use.

"Your job, sir, is to make sure that all the men are doing their duty." He glanced around. "Some will try to avoid work and gamble. You will soon spot them and sort them out. Our job here is to watch for men trying to sneak into the valley."

"Enemy soldiers?"

He shook his head, "Thieves but organised ones. They might come in a warband. The Empire is rich and lazy men would rather steal than work for it. We need to watch the road and the trails through the jungle. The Apu will take you on a patrol tomorrow." He shrugged, "It is a way for him to get to know you. For now, we watch for four hours and when we are relieved, we eat, get some sleep and wait to be called on watch again. With only three officers you will be on watch more than we. That is why they were waiting for your arrival. Now then sir, let me walk you around the walls."

There were men on all three levels of the fortress. The old soldier, his name was Sayri, let me know who the ones I should watch, were. I realise now that he could have been duping me but as events turned out he was honest. I was exhausted by the time my watch ended for I had been nervous about everything. I ate little and my sleep was fitful. I was woken after what seemed like moments by Hanan and I went on watch,

The English Adventurer

relieving the Apu. This time I had a different group of soldiers and before he retired the Apu did what Sayri had done and identified the weaker soldiers.

"That is what all this training is about, young man, learning what your men are like. Then when we go to war, we have more chance of winning."

"But I have not been trained in using my weapons."

He smiled, "I understand that you made a sling and killed a Tunki. That shows skill and as for the axe, that is an easy weapon to use. When you have settled in, we will give you lessons and tomorrow we head into the jungle. That is where you will learn to be a soldier."

My second shift on watch was slightly easier although as it involved part of the night, I did not enjoy that. Who knew what was happening outside the walls? The jungle was far enough away that we would see shadows moving but it was new, and I was uncomfortable. When I went to bed and we had not been attacked then I was happier.

When I left with the twenty-man patrol, I saw that Sayri was left in command. Hanan was asleep. As we waited for the men to check their weapons I asked, "How long is a duty at this pukara, sir?"

He smiled, "A moon. That is considered long enough. We have more than a thousand men and four hundred are in the outposts. The duty in Vitcos is considered easier. Now concentrate. You will follow me and watch how I lead this patrol. One day, before the year is out, you will have to lead a patrol and the men who obey you will be putting their lives in your hands!"

With that intimidating thought in my head, I followed the officer out of the gates towards the jungle. This was not the jungle around Cuzco. That had been a friendly land and the danger came from animals, reptiles, and insects. Here there could be enemies who were doing as we were and scouting. Every bush and tree hid a potential foe. The only good part was that the trail was wider than I had expected. I saw why when I heard the sound of slashing behind us as the soldiers widened the trail. Each patrol widened the trail.

The jungle became oppressively hotter as we descended towards the valley bottom. Yupanqui stopped often and when he did the soldiers ceased their slashing. I had thought to ask him why but then I worked it out for myself. He was listening. While he listened, he studied the trail ahead of him. I did the same, but I had no idea what I sought. We had enjoyed a brief noon break and were about to set off back when one of the soldiers called to him. He waved at me to follow him. I saw the soldier kneeling down.

"Chanca, sir."

The English Adventurer

I saw that he was studying some faeces and I asked the obvious question, "How do you know?"

The soldier did not answer but Yupanqui did. "It is off the trail and intended to be hidden. You can see, within it, the maize he has eaten. We grind ours up and they do not. Do you notice anything else, Paullu?"

I shook my head. The yellow pellets were clear but nothing else.

"It is fresh. Someone was here this day. The beetles have not yet begun to cart it away. He stood and said to the soldier, "Atoc, take four men and see if you find their footprints or their camp."

"Sir!"

Yupanqui said, "Stand to!"

The men showed their experience for stones were placed in slings and they formed a defensive circle around the two of us. Yupanqui looked at me, "Paullu, you are part of this Pachaca, prepare to fight."

I pulled my shield around and took my axe from my belt. I felt foolish. I should have known to do what he had ordered me to. I would have to change the way I behaved for I was being carried not only by this aged officer who was not even Quechua but also by mitimacs!

Atoc returned, "They camped not far away. I would say thirty or forty of them."

Yupanqui nodded and stroked the gold coin in his ear, "So what were they doing? Too few to cause us harm and too many just to cause mischief." He looked at me, "Your next lesson, Paullu; you need to work out what the enemy plans. We do not have enough information. Back to the pukara. Walk with me and I will speak my thoughts aloud. It will help you learn. Atoc, take the rear and watch our backs."

The pace we adopted on the way back was faster to the point that we were almost running.

"The Chanca are a clever people. They know when we change our men, and they might hope to catch us off our guard. We have taken over their lands and they are poorer. We took their nobles and made them part of the Empire. They all did well but the poorer ones, the farmers and the like just lost their land. They seek to hurt us when they can. If they can destroy a pachaca then it is a victory. We are the smallest unit, and it is possible that they outnumber us. Tomorrow I will take Hanan and sixty men to find this band. You will have to command the pukara."

I was not ready, and I wanted to scream *'no'* but I was an officer and I had to take responsibility. How would I do it? When I had walked along the walls, I had observed the whole site and now I ran through it in my mind. The small village and the few fields lay on the Vitcos side of the pukara. The ground on the other side had been cleared for one

The English Adventurer

hundred and twenty paces until the jungle. The three, now seemingly inadequate terraces had one gate on each level and our barracks, temple, storage house and pachaca office and armoury on each level. The padded tunic I had been given now seemed more important than the sling. The Chanca liked to use bows and their range was longer than our spears. I wondered if there were any kumana in the armoury. The spear-thrower would increase the range of a spear. Still not as far as an arrow they might help keep an enemy from the walls. It would be the slings that would be our primary weapon. I knew now that I should have done more when I had first arrived, but I had thought the posting was an easy one.

As soon as we re-entered our fort it was like an ant's nest being disturbed. Everyone seemed to know what to do but me, and I saw Yupanqui glance at me. I said, "I will go and examine the armoury!"

His nod told me it was the right thing to do. Pausing only to deposit my cloak, axe, and shield in my quarters I hurried to the armoury. There were twenty stone-headed spears, thirty throwing spears with fire-hardened tips and four kumanas. That was a relief. There were no bows and that was because none of this unit came from the region which used them. There were bolas but I had never used one and I was unsure of their efficacy. We had plenty of stone-headed maces, but they were a close combat weapon. If I was in command, then I needed to keep the enemy from the walls. There were also plenty of shields.

The bronze tube which hung close to Yupanqui's office was sounded three times. It meant every officer had to report to the office. Hanan and I arrived together. I saw that Sayri was there. It was then I learned his true position. He was the one who acted as the organiser of the men. He was paid more and that was why he had been assigned to me. It was unofficial but, as I later learned, every Apu who had any sense appointed a good soldier to be their eyes and ears and to pass along instructions.

"We have found evidence of a Chanca warband. I intend to lead a large force out tomorrow and quash this rebellion before it can do any damage. I am leaving Paullu in command. I will need you, Sayri and Atoc with me but I want at least ten veterans left with Paullu."

"Sir, Manco is a good man and reliable."

We spent until dusk organising who would stay and who would go. Yupanqui took it upon himself to bear the brunt of the night watch. The purpose of my initiation became clearer with each passing moment. I had gone without sleep for almost six days.

The fort was roused well before Inti even showed his face and Mama Killa was a sliver in the night sky as we made our way to the

The English Adventurer

walls. I was in command and I had taken advice from the others. I put the least experienced six men at the highest level, close to the armoury and offices. Ten men were on the second level and the rest were with me and Manco on the lower level. Every gate had four men manning them. The kumanas were on the lower level. The men of the patrol were taking more than half of the spears and javelins, the rest distributed amongst the men on the lowest level and I made sure that every man had a shield. The ordinary soldiers had helmets, but they were made of wood. Mine was bronze. My cloak would also give me added protection, but enemy stones could still be fatal.

There was no noise as the attack force left the fort. Even the gates were closed quietly as the sixty-two men left the fort and headed into the jungle. They had disappeared before they were halfway to the jungle for a passing cloud masked Mama Killa. I wanted to speak but I knew that it was nerves that made me wish to do so. I had spoken to Manco and the men I would command the night before. Nothing more needed to be said, nor was movement necessary. If the Chanca were in the jungle, then we had to keep movement to a minimum. When Inti rose then I would be happier. My training made even more sense now that I was a serving officer. The time we had spent on the Intiwatanta, the temple to the sun on the top of Sacsayhuamán, had taught me how reliant we were on Inti.

When the thin light of day bathed the jungle I turned to Manco, "I will go to the third level and see if I can see anything."

Manco was much older than I was, and he nodded, "It will help to keep them on their toes. I will have men fetch food and drink. This could be a long day."

The two men I had brought with me were on the third terrace. "Have you seen anything?"

They shook their heads, "No, sir. What are we looking for?"

"Warriors coming to do us harm."

"But we have three stone walls, sir! Besides the Apu has taken the best warriors to find them."

I nodded, "And if he doesn't or he meets a greater number of men than he has?"

One of the other men whom I did not know said, "Sir, we have not lost a battle for a long time. We will be all right."

I became the officer, "And this will not be a battle! This will be a border skirmish. I will not lose the fort." I turned on my heel and descended. While I had been speaking, I had studied the jungle and saw nothing. It was when I reached Manco that it hit me. "Manco, look at

The English Adventurer

the jungle." He did so. "There are no birds flying over the jungle to the east."

He looked and I saw him take in what I had observed. There were birds climbing into the sky before descending back into the jungle. The line of the trail had none but there should have been birds to the east. There the slopes were perfect for the Tunki who liked to hunt there.

"You are right, sir. You have good instincts. What should we do?"

"We maintain a watch but make sure that we have the east covered. You go there and let me know if you see any danger."

As I was left with the two other sentries, I felt the weight of the world upon my shoulders. If this fort fell, then the road was open to attack Vitcos and whilst it had a larger garrison all the farmers who worked the land between here and there would suffer. I would be letting down the Emperor. I found myself looking to the east where Manco was now staring intently at the jungle. I realised that there were no birds between the east and the trail. Instead of looking to the east, I concentrated on the jungle close to the trail. Suddenly I spied something. I knew it could have been a bird but I was taking no chances.

I grabbed the arm of one of the sentries and hissed in his ear, "What do you see close to the trail?"

"What sir?"

I snapped, "Concentrate. There are no birds in the air, yet I can see bright feathers in the jungle, and they are moving. What do you see?"

He stared and then said, quietly, "You are right, sir. There is a Chanca warrior moving towards the trail. I saw the body of one once and they wear feathers like that."

I was almost relieved that I was right and yet this meant that not only the fort but the Apu and the patrol were in danger. "Pass the word that the Chanca warriors are in the jungle. I will find Manco." I headed down to Manco. "Have you seen anything?"

"I am not sure, sir, but there is something there. It could be a big cat hunting."

I shook my head, "I have just seen a Chanca heading west close to the trail." He cocked a questioning eye and I said, "I had it confirmed from another sentry."

"I believe you, sir. The question is, what do we do, sir?"

"They will be waiting to ambush the Apu when he leads the men back. They will be tired and off guard. We have to warn them."

"Easier said than done, sir."

I noticed that many miles down the trail the birds were once more active and that told me there were no men, either friendly or unfriendly there. When the birds disappeared again then it would indicate that our men were coming back. I took a deep breath, "I have a plan. We have rope do we not?" He nodded, "Then I will go with eight men and climb down the west wall. If we make our way to the path, we can work our way back to the jungle. If you watch the trail, then you should be able to see when our men are returning. Ring the alarm bell five times. That will warn the Apu and if I attack from this west side then they may fear that they have been ambushed."

"A good plan but riddled with risks, sir. You will be leaving the fort defended by less than thirty men."

"And that is why I take just eight. Even if we just lead the Chanca away I will still be leaving enough men to guard the pukara." He nodded for the risk was just with me and the men who came with me. "You know the men, go around them and ask for volunteers."

"What if you don't get eight, sir?"

"Then I go with what I have. I cannot allow the Apu and the others to be slaughtered."

"Right sir, I will volunteer then."

I shook my head, "You are to command here but thank you for the offer."

In the end, twelve men volunteered, and I let Manco choose the eight who would come with me. They each took a spear, a shield, and a club. I wondered if I had left it too late for the afternoon was passing. Once more the initiation helped me for I remembered climbing down the cliff and the stone wall was simplicity itself in comparison. As soon as I was down, I headed west toward the jungle. The corner of the pukara hid us from the trail. I did not look behind me and I just prayed that the volunteers were with me.

Once we made the jungle, I led them forty paces into it and then began to head east. I waved my axe to form them into a line. Although the afternoon was passing, I went carefully and slowly, as though I was searching for a skittish Tunki. I looked at the ground to avoid stepping on something which could hurt or trip me and I kept glancing ahead. When I saw the feathers and the feathered cloaks, I knew I had been right. The enemy warriors were fifty paces from us. The Chanca tribesmen had infiltrated the jungle and were planning an ambush. Our soldiers were better but attacked from two sides at once it would be difficult for them to fight back. The Chanca would have the advantage of surprise and cover. I waved my men down to squat on the ground. The Chanca were quiet and all the ones I could see were watching the trail. I counted more than thirty on our side and I had no idea how many were lower down the trail. Had I doomed eight men and myself to an unnecessary death? Then I realised that it would be necessary for we might save the rest of the Pachaca.

I saw the warriors begin to prepare their weapons and then I heard the five notes of the alarm. I stood and waved my men forward. We moved silently towards the Chanca whose own movements and sounds masked any noise we might make. My men had padded armour reinforced with strips of wood and we had woollen cloaks that would slow down missiles. The Chanca were half-naked. Some were loading slingshots while others prepared their shields and clubs. I pulled my as yet unused axe behind me as I swung it. Further down the trail, I heard shouts and some cries. I was ahead of my men and it was I who struck the first blow. The axe was sharp, although I knew it would soon lose its edge and become little better than a club. As it hacked through flesh and jarred against bone, I knew that I had my first kill. Even before he slipped from the axe head, I had pulled it back to swing down across the neck of the next warrior. This time bright blood spurted. My men had used their clubs and spears well and five men had died silently. The other three enemy warriors made a noise and their faces turned.

I knew we could turn and run for we had done what I intended and not only disrupted their ambush but also given a warning to our men but I did not stop for the Chanca did not turn and attack. They stared in terror. I used the spike at the end of the axe to ram into the face of the third Chanca warrior. My men were now screaming as they wielded their weapons. The joy of battle was upon them and we were driving the Chanca away. A cacique, a native chief, I knew it by the gold around his neck, ran at me with his own shield and club. He had wooden armour on his chest and paint on his face and arms which told me that he had killed warriors in battle. I found myself laughing for I had now killed three men and I feared no one. He swung his club at me and as he was taller than I was I dropped to one knee and the club hit the top of my helmet, making my ears ring. I brought my axe across to chop through his left leg just above the ankle. As he fell to the ground I hacked across his throat with the edge of the axe. It ripped it open.

The death of this cacique, I knew there would be others, ended the attack and the Chanca before us fled. I did not follow them for, as I looked, I saw that one of my men had died and another two had wounds. I shouted, "Protect the wounded!"

As we stood with our shields before us one of the warriors grabbed some leaves and mud to staunch the bleeding of one of the wounded. Even I knew that had to be done. I could hear fighting down the trail as the Apu and the rest of our men fought their way through the demoralised Chanca. If nothing else the fort was safe and no matter how many of our men had died it would still be fewer than had I done nothing.

I had thought our skirmish was over but Apu and our men must have charged and some of the Chanca fled our way. "Lock shields!"

We formed a tight half-circle around the wounded men and the warrior tending to them. Two of the others held spears and these helped but the mob of men who ran at us were just desperate to escape and we seemed a lesser threat than the twenty odd men who charged towards them. The spears helped us, and I used my axe like a spear, jabbing the point at the tribesmen who attacked. I hit the Chanca warrior at the same time that his fire-hardened spear struck my cheek. It hurt and I bled but my axe spike rammed deep into his eye and he fell dead at my feet.

For us, that was the end as Yupanqui and some of our men hurtled past us chasing the Chanca. My men were grinning, even the wounded ones when I said, "I think we can go back into the pukara now."

They chorused, "Yes sir!"

"Bring the dead man along with the wounded."

We were cautious as we moved through the jungle in case any Chanca warriors were waiting to attack us. As we emerged into the open the others in the pukara cheered. The sun was beginning to set against a cloudy and gloomy evening as the gates were opened and we marched into the fort. Manco greeted me and bowed, "I thought it madness, sir, but it worked! You have made a good start to your career as a soldier."

I smiled, for he was right.

The English Adventurer
Thomas

Chapter 11

It had been more than a year since I had returned to my ship and my life had changed in that time. I now knew I wished for a new life in the west. Lord Collingwood had told me that whatever I did there would be serving England for I was the only Englishman in that part of the world or the only Englishman who was at the heart of the Spaniards who ruled the land. The other Englishmen were as I had been, pirates. His words made me feel like a lord. Our ships were now better armed, all four of them, and although we were attacked on a few occasions our well-trained gunners with our superior weapons easily beat them off. I had given Guido my old sword for I had the one taken in the fight and I gave Alessandro the short sword I had carried, Juan and Jesus were given good daggers also taken in the fight. Such simple gifts brought such joy that they showed me what hard lives they had. In the year of crossing and recrossing the seas and increasing our treasure, the boys grew and could now aim and fire the guns unattended. That did not happen but as I was planning, at some stage, to leave the ship, it was good preparation for when I did.

I had made my latest report to his lordship and returned to the ship when Captain Pedro sent for me. He was now a very rich man for we had not lost a cargo in over a year. He waved me to a seat and poured a large goblet of wine, "Tomas, you have served me well and helped me to become a rich man and I thought you should know that this voyage will be my last. I have others who can sail my ship and I would enjoy the riches I have acquired. I will retire from the sea. I have a family I rarely see and I am getting old." He patted his stomach, "And fatter." I laughed. "I know that you promised me a year and you have more than done that. If you wish not to sail I will understand."

I was sad for I liked the captain and he had been more than kind to me, "I will sail with you, Captain Pedro, on this last voyage but you should know that I too have ambitions. I have a desire to find El Dorado."

He shook his head, "Many men speak of it but all that it brings is death."

"Nonetheless, Francisco Pizarro believes he can find it and I will go with him."

The English Adventurer

Captain Pedro gave me a strange smile, "Fate is funny, is she not, Tomas? We sail, not only to Isla Juana but also to Nombre de Dios. We carry a new Alcalde for Panama. Your friend, it seems, has itchy feet." That pleased me for if he did intend to sail to El Dorado then this was my chance to be with him. Lord Collingwood had let me know that it was my duty to find out if there was such a fabled land. King Henry coveted such a place.

We had only visited Nombre de Dios once and that had been to garner intelligence. Genoa, with its vast fleet supplied Panama for King Charles used the Genoese banks. No one challenged the Genoese and their fleets were even better armed than Captain Pedro's much smaller one. There were rumours that the Governor, Pedro Arias Dávila, might soon be replaced and Pizarro's replacement as Alcalde was the first move in a wave of changes coming to the Castilla del Oro. The voyage across was an easy one and I had time to speak to my crew about the imminent changes.

"Captain Pedro will leave the sea and I think that I will not be long behind him."

The boys, although technically they were now youths, took the news harder than Guido. Guido knew he would be promoted. He would have my cabin and be paid a good stipend for his work. I knew that Captain Pedro would insist that the gunners for his ships were well-paid. He knew our value.

"And what will you do, Captain Tomas?"

"I am not sure Guido. That depends upon what we find in Nombre de Dios. I have money and I might buy somewhere there. Perhaps even a ship."

Alessandro said, eagerly, "We would join your ship, captain."

I smiled, "And if I did own a ship then I could wish for no better crew than you. We will have to wait but I wanted to tell all of you this so that you would be prepared. I am not deserting you. I am merely taking another voyage."

For the rest of the voyage, I was worked relentlessly, not by Captain Pedro, but by my gunners who wanted to know everything about the cannons and the harquebuses. I did not mind. I had been told such things by my father. I had also passed the knowledge on to Jose. It was only right. I knew that Jose would be upset that I was leaving the sea. Like me, he had become a rich man and I wondered if my news might make him take a different direction.

We did not dock on the north coast of Isla Juana but on the smaller port of Santiago on the south coast. Over the last year, we had used the southern port more than San Cristóbal de la Habana. That had delighted

The English Adventurer

Jose for his father lived a few miles away and he managed to spend a few days with him each time we docked. On the last occasion, we had been in port for a week while we awaited a gold shipment from Mexico. Jose and his father had enjoyed the time together.

When we docked in Santiago, Captain Pedro went ashore to deliver the letters from Cádiz. I met with Jose and we retired to an inn on the quayside. It was of better quality than most and both the food and the wine were of high quality. I was as open and honest with Jose as I had been with Guido and the boys. He smiled, "I have seen this coming for some time. The last time I spoke with my father he said that you would not be sailing in the *'Hawk'* for your whole life. He said that you were meant for something greater."

I shrugged, "I know not about that but once my father died, I wished to leave the sea and the fact that I have continued to sail for so long is a mystery to me. What will you do? Continue as Captain Phillip's gunner?"

He shook his head, "I now have amassed a great deal of money. My father keeps it for me and I have met a girl, in my father's village." He pointed north, "She likes me and does not mind that I only have one hand."

I was surprised, "A girl? You did not tell me."

He gave a shy smile, "A one armed man is cautious about such entanglements. Each time I see her she is more lovely and the last time we spoke of marriage."

"What will you do there?"

"As you know my father's wound weakened him. When I return here, I help him and the last time I was with him I did more work than he did. I was going to tell you that this would be my last voyage when we reached Cádiz. This is better. We will all be happy. I will ask Captain Phillip if I can leave the ship here."

"I will come with you. Captain Phillip will be loath to lose such a fine gunner."

He smiled, "I have trained up Stephano. It was kind of you to let me have him when I lost my arm and he has responded well to my training." He looked sad, "This is an ending, is it not?"

"Perhaps but I intend to stay in the New World and now I have more reason to visit Isla Juana and Santiago."

Captain Phillip was reluctant to let Jose go but I had Captain Pedro on my side and Captain Pedro still owned all four ships. He gave Captain Phillip the title of Commodore and that did the trick. When we left for Nombre de Dios I had an emotional farewell with Jose.

The English Adventurer

Ominously Fernando, his father, was too ill to make the journey and I did not have the opportunity to speak to him.

As we neared the Castilla del Oro, I slimmed down the gear I would take with me. There were some things like my flints, morion, sword, daggers and boots that were vital but over the years I had acquired more than I needed and I gave what I no longer needed to my four gun crews. I found the parting hard when we reached Nombre de Dios. Captain Pedro paid me off and gave me a bonus. He had been more than kind to me and the hand clasp we gave each other was firmer and more sustained than any in recent years. He was a true friend. Poor Jesus burst into tears and before I was unmanned, I left the ship and joined Don Alfonso de Murcia who was the new Alcalde of Panama as we headed to the new residence of the Alcalde of Nombre de Dios. It was a finely made building that had been erected and the new Alcalde insisted that I be given accommodation. Part of our cargo had been horses. Indeed the *'Hawk'* was still in port the next day as the crew cleansed it of horse manure. The eight soldiers who would be Don Alfonso's escort had come directly from Spain and the nine men with whom I would journey the forty miles to Panama were pleased that they had a veteran of Balboa's expedition with them. We had a native guide but as only I spoke his language, and that somewhat rustily, the journey promised to be interesting.

One item I purchased in Nombre de Dios was a breastplate. I already had a morion. I would have taken one of the harquebuses from the ship but I knew that the ship had a greater need than me. I still did not know what I would do in Panama but my feet had been started on that path and it was hard to do other than to head down the road that had now been constructed to take us to Panama, the gateway to the Southern Sea.

There was a road leading south to Panama, Camino Real, or Royal Road, although it was more commonly known as Camino de Cruces, the Road of Crosses. The jungle was very aggressive and there were gangs of natives hacking at it as it encroached on the soil road. I knew that if they did not do so then within a short time the vegetation would have reclaimed the road. I had been told, in Nombre de Dios, that the tribes had been pacified. Don Diego Columbus had been responsible for that. He had ruthlessly executed all those who opposed the rule of Spain. That said there were others who inhabited the jungle, deserters, bandits and brigands who sought to take rather than to work. We rode armed and watchful. The native led and Don Alfonso and I followed. I led a sumpter and each of the eight soldiers held the halter of a laden animal. There were three forts along the road and each had a small barrack

The English Adventurer

block for travellers. It meant we slept safely and I picked up the news from the small garrisons. I learned that the reason a new Alcalde was needed was that Francisco planned an expedition to find El Dorado. The governor of Panama, Pedro Arias Dávila, had, apparently given permission. Some of the garrisons wanted to join Pizarro such was his reputation. It boded well.

The only time I had been at the great ocean that lay to the south of Panama had been when I had served under Balboa. Then there had been no dwellings. The ports now used were just beaches. When I spied Panama, I was amazed at the transformation. Although the buildings were made of wood, I saw a new residence being built in stone. There was a shipyard and the stone quay had small ships tied up there. I knew that Pascual de Andagoya had sailed south and there he had found evidence of El Dorado but it did not explain the presence of other ships. If they were not exploring, what was their purpose?

Once again, I was given accommodation in the residence. I got on well with Don Alfonso who enjoyed the stories I told of my first visits to this land. I was presented to the governor who seemed disinterested and I was quickly dismissed while Governor Dávila interrogated the new Alcalde about politics. I was summoned to another chamber where I found Francisco Pizarro and a priest poring over maps. I had not seen him since our chance meeting in Nombre de Dios.

He leapt to his feet when I entered, "Tomas, when I heard that you were here and had taken me up on my offer, I could not believe my good fortune."

I shook my head, "I was not sure that the offer was still there. I just decided to come here in the hopes of making my fortune." That was a lie and it almost stuck in my throat. I had a fortune and I could have retired, like Jose, and lived a good life. I was serving my king.

"No matter the reason, you could not have come at a more appropriate time. This is Hernando de Luque and he is one of the leaders of our enterprise. The others are the soldier, Don Diego de Almagro, and Don Nicolás Ribera who is helping to fund the venture."

I found myself becoming excited and said, "And what is the venture?"

He waved me over to the map. It had few details on it. He jabbed a finger at a red spot, "This is Panama." He moved his hand south, "This coast is, as yet unexplored. Pascual went there with too few ships and men but he came back from his expedition with stories of warriors wearing gold in their ears. We hope to take more ships, horses and men than he did."

The English Adventurer

The priest shook his head, "Even with Don Nicolás' coins we are still only able to take two ships. That means just fifty men and ten horses. You know we need more."

Ever the optimist Francisco said, "We will ask the Genoese. They have more money than they know what to do with."

"And they would demand a greater share of the spoils."

"Then we will find others."

The priest did not look convinced. I realised that I had the opportunity to make a real fortune. Those who had been with Cortés had all become richer than any noble still living in Spain. I said, hesitantly, "I have money, Francisco."

He gave me a patronising smile, "We are not talking coppers or even silver, Tomas. This needs gold."

I had the bulk of the treasure in my chest but I always carried the gold crowns given to me by Lord Collingwood. I took out the four crowns. "The greater part of my treasure is safe to hand but here is the surety that I do not come into this venture as a pauper."

Francisco beamed and the priest appraised me with new eyes. "Then, my son, there is a chance that we might be able to fit out the expedition as we would wish. I am the treasurer. I will let you know exactly how much you will need to invest and how much you can expect in return." He stood, "I will leave you now to talk."

When he had gone Francisco shook his head, "How did you acquire such a treasure, Tomas?"

"I served as a gunner on a ship carrying the king's gold and I was well rewarded."

"Then why seek to put your life in danger and risk losing all that you have?"

"You are trying to dissuade me, Francisco?"

He shook his head, "No, of course not. I am delighted but if you have enough money to buy into this venture then why not buy somewhere in England or Spain and enjoy it?"

"I am still young and as for danger…It seems to me that sailing a sea without pirates and fighting natives with primitive weapons is easier than what I have done thus far."

"Remember the Aztecs?"

"I do but you are a better leader than Cortés. So, tell me what you know, Francisco. Thus far I have heard rumours only. You seek El Dorado?"

He laughed, "That is the name that others give. The land I seek is far to the south of us. Perhaps more than four hundred nautical miles. I have pieced together a picture of a people who are rich in gold and

The English Adventurer

silver. They rule a land which is bounded on one side by the sea and on the other, according to the natives we have spoken to by an impenetrable barrier of mountains."

"So what is your plan?"

"To do as we did here in Panama. We find somewhere we can build a fort and control the natives and then move on. We know not yet what we will find but I am hopeful that just as the fruits and vegetables we found here made men's fortunes that even before we reach this golden empire, we will have made discoveries that will make us rich."

"You have ships?"

"We have three. Unlike when Columbus first came west, we know that we can sail along the coast. We can load the ships heavily. I hope to establish forts as we go and therefore the vessels will become lighter."

"Cannons?"

"Esmerils, robinets and falconets. They should be a big enough threat. The twenty-eight horses we have will ensure that the natives are cowed. We do not need larger guns. I will not need many harquebuses. Don Diego Almagro has a large number of crossbowmen. Crossbows are lighter than harquebuses and we need not carry much powder." He smiled, "You will be an investor and not needed as a gunner this time, Tomas, although your skill will be much appreciated."

"And when do you hope to leave?"

"If your treasure is sufficient then we will leave when the autumn begins, November. It is not much cooler than it is now but it will make life easier. It will take until then to gather the supplies, horses and men."

My life changed completely in that one meeting. It cost me all but a handful of copper and silver of my hoarded treasure but I became a partner in the venture. I was not worried about the fact that in Panama I was now, effectively, a pauper. I had a fortune in Spain, protected by men I trusted with my life. Although I had invested one-third like all of the others I would only receive one-quarter of the profits. The reason was simple. Diego Almagro was bringing men, weapons and horses as his share of the venture. My life changed because I was now treated as an equal by the Spanish nobles. I had travelled a long and hard journey since I had been a slave. I was accorded a low bow when I visited the ships being fitted out. My words were listened to and my advice was followed.

It was the feast I attended at the residence that showed me the transformation in my life. I had eaten with my betters before now and Lord Collingwood was a much more important person than those around the table but that had been different. When I dined with the

The English Adventurer

governor, the new alcalde and the rest of the principals from the venture I knew that I was part of something that men would speak of in the future, long after we were dead. Balboa had been executed but he was still spoken of in awe when men spoke of the discovery of the southern sea. I found it strange to think of the many natives who had taken the huge expanse of water as part of their lives. It would be Balboa who would have the honour accorded to him because it had been written down. Father Hernando was the one who acted as a scribe for us.

I kept silent as the expedition was discussed. We had the governor's approval but bearing in mind Don Alfonso of Albuera who was still being hunted in Florida, not to mention Captain General Cortés who had totally disregarded his orders, Francisco and the others had to persuade the governor that we had no intentions of emulating the rebels. I studied the others as they spoke. I was the newcomer and largely ignored. Father Juan's motives for the expeditions were simple enough to understand, he wished to bring Christianity to those he saw as lost souls, the natives. Diego de Almagro was another who was easy to understand. He was a soldier and reminded me of Diego Columbus. His face and hands showed signs of battle and, like me, he said little in the debate. I had yet to speak to him but I knew that we would have much in common and when we finally sailed, he would be the one, apart from Francisco, alongside whom I would fight. Nicolás de Ribera, known as 'el Viejo', was a true conquistador. He had made his coins helping to conquer the Castilla del Oro. He had served with Diego Columbus and he was very close to Francisco. Juan Carvallo was the one of whom I was the most suspicious for he was the governor's man. He was feasting with us and yet he had not yet been mentioned. It was towards the end of the discussion that his role was brought up.

Governor Dávila wiped his mouth and after sipping some of the wine said, "I approve your expedition but I have conditions." Even de Almagro looked worried. "Firstly, you go under my banner. You may take yours Francisco and a religious one but you go on my behalf." Francisco and Nicolás nodded. I saw the relief on their faces. "Secondly, to ensure that all is done well, Juan de Cavallo will be the inspector who travels with you. He is my representative on the expedition."

I saw the frown crease on the face of Francisco, "The journey may be fraught with danger."

Juan de Cavallo smiled, "My hands, Don Francisco, are not soft. I am not just a bookkeeper for I have fought both the jungle and the natives. You need not fear for me." I did not doubt his words but he was still the governor's man.

The English Adventurer

Francisco gave a resigned nod.

The governor wiped his mouth again and then stood, a sure sign that the feast was over. "And all the land that you discover will be claimed for God and King Carlos of Spain."

We all stood and chorused, "Of course."

There was one other who became part of our group and he was a priest called Juan de Salcedo. He was the one who would bear the standard of the Virgin that would accompany us. The governor's standard would be the one hanging from our masts alongside that of Spain but when we went ashore, we would be protected by the standard blessed by the bishop.

I was just excited to be deemed as someone important in this venture. The last ship to be purchased, using my money, was a Genoese ship, *'Infanta Maria'*. The Genoese built good ships but the *'Infanta Maria'* was definitely at the end of her career. She was ten years old and I was not sure how many voyages she had left in her but she seemed to be a good ship and her crewmen were experienced. The captain was Guido and it was only sometime later that I discovered the reason the experienced captain was here and not in the Mediterranean. There was a price on his head as he had once been a pirate. I did not know that at first but I liked him from the start and, when I did discover his secret, it merely made me warm to him even more. The guns on the ship were not really what I had hoped. They had four breech-loading berços. They were mounted on the gunwale and were useful in that they could be swivelled and were able to fire in any direction but they fired just a small ball or a bag of stones. It was better than nothing and I took to cleaning and examining them as soon as I boarded.

Captain Guido came to speak to me. He had a puzzled look on his face. Having lived in this land longer than I had, his Spanish was perfect, "Senor Penkridge, why do you bother with these weapons? You are now a shipmaster."

I smiled, "It is Thomas and while I might own this ship, we both know, my friend, that you are the master. I was, I am a gunner and quite a good one. I take an interest in the weapons. Besides, it makes me feel useful rather than just being a walking purse."

He smiled and nodded. From that moment we formed a friendship that helped me in the dark days ahead. I had someone to speak to who had endured a similar life to me. We could talk of ships and storms. We had the craft of the sea and seaman that we could share. I found myself dining and sleeping aboard rather than in the residence. There was another reason for my gradual movement to the ship. There were disagreements and arguments at every turn in the residence for there

The English Adventurer

was not unity amongst the leaders. The collection of leaders was a disparate one and they did not all agree on the same principles. Francisco was the acknowledged leader but Diego de Almagro also saw himself as the military leader while Nicolás, who had invested the greatest share of the funds, saw himself as the one who would make decisions. This was against the backdrop of a governor who was increasingly fearful of allowing the expedition to take place at all.

Once I began to stay aboard, I was given a cabin by the captain. He offered me his cabin. It was the largest and most opulently furnished. I would not evict him and I had the cabin below his at the stern. There were windows to allow in light and it was, compared with what I was used to, a palace. By the end of my first week aboard another of those who would sail with us, a merchant, García de Jerézor Jaren also came aboard and was given the cabin next to me. He was a merchant from Utrera and I learned more from him about buying and selling than any. He had paid to come on the expedition and he showed great foresight. He knew that the first men to land on this recently discovered New World would make the most money. He brought with him four men who could fight but would also help him to establish a trading station. As with Captain Guido, García and I got on well. I began to look forward to this voyage. It would not be like it was with Balboa, hacking through the jungle and fighting wild natives. We would sail down the coast and have the luxury of three floating fortresses.

By the start of the first week in November we were ready to depart. The horses of the expedition had been spread out in the three ships and we had eight of them. I think the age of our ship determined that we should have the smallest number. We also had just twenty-five men. The majority were soldiers but there were some like García who had paid to go on this expedition. They brought their own arms and, in some cases their own food and horses. They would fight under Diego de Almagro but were not obliged to return with us on the ships. They were the true conquistadors. Pedro de Candia was one such adventurer. If I was the English adventurer then Pedro was the Greek one. He was of an age with me and had shared some similar experiences. Whilst I could not recall him, he had heard of me having been in Castilla del Oro at the same time as me. He had fought alongside Diego Columbus on the Castille del Oro and spoke of how my reduction of the fort had saved many lives, including his own.

"Don Diego spoke well of you, Englishman, and valued your skills. He told me once that he owed his great victory thanks to your demolition of the fortress. I, too, was saved as we had no fighting to do and the survivors of your attack simply surrendered. You have abandoned your guns?"

"Let us say, Pedro, that, like you, I have decided to profit from this New World while I can."

He grinned, "With men like you and Don Francisco, how can we fail?"

Chapter 12

We were looking for rivers and places where we might build ports. All three ships' masters made the maps that would help them find the places again. As the owner of the ship, I was privy to the map-making process and the captain saw no problem in my making my own copy. This was real gold for Lord Collingwood. We found a place that we thought would make a good port and Pizarro decided to name it, Puerto Deseado, desired port. We anchored just off the beach and men were sent ashore to search for food, water and natives. Pizarro led the expedition ashore and Pedro de Candia led the six men from our ship. I was not asked to join them and I was happy for the jungle still brought back bad memories. Instead, I joined the other men in building a wooden jetty to make the loading of any supplies that were found easier. Hernando de Luque claimed the land for God and Spain. Pizarro and the explorers arrived back before dark. They hunted for some food and found a village. The village was deserted and Francisco thought that the villagers must have fled. They brought back items from the village and the presence of gold, silver and jewels found in the dwellings suggested that we were on the right path. The food was cooked on the shore but we ate on our ships.

The second day was a repeat of the first and we managed to complete the rudimentary jetty. Some of the merchants and potential settlers had contemplated staying there to complete the port but when Francisco told them that he would not be leaving any soldiers, they accepted his decision but I knew that some would settle in the area. The difference between the first day and the second was that the natives had been warned and there was an ambush. It was close enough to us for the sound of combat to reach us. Only three men suffered minor wounds and the bodies of the dead natives were brought back to the beach so that we could examine them.

I had fought the Aztecs and I saw, immediately, that these natives, whilst they had similar features and colouring, were dressed and armed totally differently. Their hair was festooned with the feathers of the brightly coloured birds we spied in the jungle. They wore no armour of any kind and most just had a loin cloth. They used clubs and stone-tipped spears. The wounds they could cause would be ugly but they had no weapons that could penetrate the metal breastplates worn by those who had accompanied Pizarro. They did, however, have bows and arrows. Whilst the arrows did not look powerful the tips seemed to have been dipped in something. It smelled pungent and my thoughts were

The English Adventurer

that it was a poison of some kind. The greatest discovery, however, was the fact that all had some gold, silver or jewels about them. Some wore then in their ear lobes while others had them as necklets. When I spoke to Pedro he speculated that the natives might think that the jewels and precious metals would protect them in battle.

While Pizarro gathered most of the treasure and stored it on his ship to be shared at the end of the voyage I knew, from experience, that the soldiers who had been ashore would have taken their own share before it could be gathered. It was in the nature of the men who had joined us.

We left in a hopeful frame of mind and headed down the coast. This was not like sailing a treasure fleet back to Spain. Our progress was much slower. We rarely used full sail as Pizarro wanted us all together and he wished to explore the land. He was seeking somewhere to land and I know, from my conversation with him, that he was seeking a mighty river to take him into the heart of the land. We found in the first few days, none that were worth the risk of travelling them. When I was not making the map, I had some of the crew throw lines over the stern to catch fish. None of the other ships did this and I wondered if they anticipated finding food from the shore. My time crossing the great sea that was the Atlantic had taught me to harvest the water's bounty whenever we could. When we pulled ashore to cook food our ship had food to eat even before the hunters had returned.

I know not if the natives had some sort of signalling system but each time we landed and Pizarro and our men explored they found only deserted villages. Pizarro even took to landing horses to enable us to search farther and faster than on foot. The lack of paths and roads meant that it was an unsuccessful attempt to capture live natives. We were in the dark without locals who could act as guides. Even worse was the fact that the hunters rarely brought enough food back to feed us. The horses began to suffer and we ate the first one three weeks into the expedition. We had taken the horses ashore and one had broken free. In its attempt to reach freedom it fell and broke its leg. It had to be destroyed but we were able to eat the animal. Ironically the place we had landed was a potential port. While the horses were brought to try to graze, we built another jetty and the hunters went ashore. The crew of our ship ate the fish we had caught while the horsemeat cooked.

The hunters returned empty handed. Worse, we had lost our first man. One of the soldiers had been bitten by a poisonous reptile and died on the way back. Francisco was saddened by the death. Had this been the Captain General he would not have even given the dead man a second thought but Francisco was different. He named the port, Punta Caballo. The man who had died was Juan de Caballo and as a horse had

The English Adventurer

also died, it seemed fitting. He sat with me on a log we had hewn and we spoke. "This is a tantalizing land, Tomas. It is like an exotic woman wearing veils. You suspect the beauty beneath but until the veils are all removed then you know not what you will see. The mountains where these mysterious people, who have so much treasure that they adorn their bodies with it, are still in the distance. Today has shown me that we need a river. I remember how many men Balboa lost reaching Panama. We have too few. I should have brought more."

I shook my head, "Francisco, without my coins we could have only brought two ships. You know that we need to find something to take back so that more men might invest."

He looked sad, "I know but I also know that this land will yield a greater treasure than the whole of Mexico. We must find a river!"

Fate, it seemed was determined to prevent our leader from finding that which we wished. A tropical storm blew up just two days later and we were swept out to sea. Two horses were swept overboard and everyone on the ship had to fight to save both our vessel and the rest of the animals. Two men were also lost over the side but the ship held and when dawn broke, we found ourselves alone on a blue ocean.

Captain Guido was not only a good captain but a wise one. He came to me, "We need the men's spirits to be raised. I can find the shore and my crew will be busy working but the others, the ones who seek their fortune will need to be comforted. I know that you are a leader and can do this."

He was right. I had heard mumblings, especially after the first death, that we should return to Puerta Deseado which had the potential to be a good base. I went around the ship and whenever I found a hangdog face, I gave the man a job to do. I did so with a smile and I spoke, to those who seemed in the lowest spirits, of the times in the jungles of Panama with Balboa when we thought all was lost and then we found the blue sea. It took time but gradually the spirits brightened and when we saw the green, grey, line that was the land there were cheers. We headed for the shore and Pedro and I led men ashore to ensure that we were not attacked while the captain repaired his ship.

I confess that I went into the jungle with some trepidation. I found myself looking up into the canopy of trees for the reptiles and spiders that might drop on me. One of our minor casualties had been a soldier bitten by a spider the size of a hand. While the man had recovered, he had not left Pizarro's ship since. Pedro and I led with swords in hand. It was the first time I had worn the breastplate and morion and the stifling heat of the jungle made it unbearably uncomfortable. We found a trail and followed it. Thanks to the storm, illness and other losses, we led

The English Adventurer

just ten men. Four of them had crossbows. All wore breastplates and morions. We walked for what seemed like miles but I suspect was little more than a mile and a half and I was about to order the men to rest before returning to the ship when I saw that the jungle ahead lightened. I decided to push on for I did not want to rest in this deadly jungle. It may have been the lack of numbers or perhaps the storm that had hidden our approach but the village we found was not deserted. Captain Hogan might have approached the village more silently than we did but we were just too concerned with the creatures of the jungle to worry too much about the noise we made. I think we expected any village we found to be empty. It was not.

That they were as surprised as we were, was clear. They had no sentries and were going about their normal business when we emerged from the jungle canopy into the clearing. The crossbowmen were the quickest thinkers and I heard them drawing back their strings. Some of the natives saw us and shouted a warning. We were well outnumbered but our strange appearance must have frightened them. The women, children and the old fled while the warriors grabbed arms and prepared to fight. It was they who initiated the attack and they hurled rocks at us.

I was aware that I was the leader and I remembered fighting natives in the jungles of Panama. We had to stay together, "Form a line." It was not much of a command but it was an order and the others obeyed. I took out my dagger too. A crossbowman stepped between Pedro and me. As the natives ran at us the crossbows cracked and four of the natives, just ten paces from us fell. They had now grabbed their bows and arrows hit helmets and breastplates. I remembered the poisoned arrows and shivered as I slashed my sword in an arc before me. It allowed the crossbowman to load his weapon and my sword ripped into two natives. The bright blood that spurted from one told me that he was dead. The other warrior was wounded but he still swung his war club at my head. Although my dagger gutted his unprotected middle the club still struck my morion. A glancing blow, it warned me that these natives could hurt us.

The crossbows cracked again and men fell. Pedro and the others had used their swords well and natives with no armour had no chance. When twelve lay dead and six were wounded the warriors, hurling insults I do not doubt, fled after their families into the jungle.

"Is anyone hurt?"

Pedro looked around and grinned, "No Captain Tomas. We have won the battle!"

I shook my head for we had been lucky, "Crossbowmen, watch the jungle. The rest of you search the huts. We seek food and treasure."

Sheathing my weapons I went into the nearest hut. It happened to be a large one. I found a large, feathered headdress which suggested that this hut belonged to a chief. There were weapons but they were stone made. They looked vicious but I left them. I also found a necklace and it was not only well-made but festooned with gold, silver, as well as jewels. I popped it into my satchel. I found more necklets hanging in another part of the hut. Whilst not as fine as the first one they were valuable. The village yielded a greater quantity of treasure than Pizarro had found and I realised that the reason was that the natives had taken their most valuable treasures with them. We also found food so that, as I gave the order to return, we were laden.

"I will be the rearguard as I have the least to carry. Pedro, you lead." I hated giving that order for I was terrified. I kept glancing behind me and when I saw the brown face following, I knew that I had to do something. "Keep going!" I could not lead the natives to our beach.

"Aye, Captain." Pedro's voice from the front was reassuring.

The trail had been made by the natives and animals. As such it followed the line of least resistance. There were some huge trees that were as wide as three men and when the trail turned around one such obstacle, I stepped behind the huge tree, drew my sword and dagger and waited. I smelled the native before I saw him. No doubt he could smell us but he obviously did not know where I was. As he stepped around the tree, I swung my sword and almost decapitated him. He was a young warrior but well-muscled. He had, not only a necklet but also armbands with pieces of gold and silver on them. I put them in my satchel and looked down the trail. I found myself shaking. The shaking was the fear not of natives but of some creature dropping from above. Satisfied that we were no longer being followed I headed to the beach and I almost cried with relief when I stepped from the Stygian gloom of the jungle onto the bright beach.

"I was worried, Captain Tomas."

I nodded, "Aye, Pedro, we were followed. I fear we can just cook on the beach and then we will sleep on the ship."

He held up some skinned animals we had found. They looked to be monkeys of some type. "We will eat well. With the fish we caught this will make a good stew." I went back to the ship, using the small boat we had. Captain Guido looked up at me, "Well, Captain Tomas?"

"We found a village and fought a battle. We are unharmed and," I emptied my satchel, "we found treasure. The others found some too and we have food."

The English Adventurer

He grinned, "As we are alone then this is ours." His face became serious, "I am sorry. The treasure is yours."

I shook my head, "We will share what we have found for I fear that I will not reap the rewards of my investment on this voyage. How do the repairs go?"

"We can leave at dawn. The men will work all night."

I nodded, "And then do as Captain General Pizarro commanded and keep heading south until we run out of supplies or meet the others."

"If they have survived."

"We did and we have the oldest ship." I smiled to soften the insult, "The best captain and crew but she is an old lady."

He nodded, sadly, "Aye, these seas and this heat ages men more than the waters around Genoa. I yearn for my home. I had hoped that I would find a treasure that would let me retire to the hills above Genoa but perhaps I am fated to die here in this New World."

We used all the sails that we could to hurry south and were rewarded, as the sun began to set by the flicker of firelight that illuminated the other two ships. The sound of hammering confirmed that Captain General Pizarro and the crews were repairing their ships too. I could see that they were both battered and I wondered if this might be the end of the expedition.

I went ashore to meet with Pizarro and the other leaders. There was a heated debate raging as I approached the fire. Dusk meant that they had not seen the slow approach of our ship and when I stepped into the firelight I was greeted with cheers and smiles. I saw the relief on Francisco's face. All of the leaders were there as well as Lieutenant Montenegro who was Diego Almagro's deputy.

"Some thought you had perished." Francisco embraced me and then whirled on the others, "You see, faint hearts, all is not lost. The men and horses we have lost are just a setback. We can still sail south to find this elusive river that will take us deep into the heart of this land of gold."

Nicolás shook his head, "We have found no sign of the treasure we seek. The handful of treasure does not even begin to recompense us for our expenditure."

"Are we accountants or conquistadors?" He glared around him.

The priest, Hernando, shook his head, "We have yet to find a live native that we can convert."

I saw Francisco fight to control his fiery temper, "We have found at least two places where we can establish trading colonies. That is a success. If we were to return now while we would not reap the rich reward we are due, we could argue that we had done what we set out to

The English Adventurer

achieve but I believe that if we push on we may find the river that will take us deep into the heart of this land. I do not call it El Dorado, as many of you do for that suggests we walk in and simply take what we want. We will have to fight and you are all right, we did not bring enough men but when we return with tales of the potential that this land holds then others will seek to travel with us. We take the first steps on a long journey. Let us take the return of one of our number, one who has more to lose than any for he invested his whole fortune with us, as a sign that God is with us."

I did feel guilty for I had not risked all. I had just risked the rewards of serving Lord Collingwood. I knew that this expedition was already a success for me. I had a map that would be more valuable than a galleon full of treasure.

"What say you, another month and then we return home?"

They nodded a reluctant agreement. Francisco waved me to the log upon which he sat. He put his head close to mine and we spoke, "Thank God that you are returned. Some of the men are mutinous."

"We found a village and it was not abandoned."

"You did?"

"We fought them and they fled. We found treasure." I told him of the treasure so that he would know there were no secrets.

He smiled, "Tomas, you keep that for yourself. I am convinced that we will find more and your return is a sign that I am right."

We found Pizarro's river, just a week later. We had celebrated Christmas on a beach but there had been little food and it was the meanest Christmas I had endured since the time I had been a slave. It was the lowest point, up to that time, of our expedition. We named the beach an ironic Puerto del Hambre, the port of hunger.

We were still the last ship in the small fleet and Captain Guido copied the actions of Francisco's captain. We reefed the sails and edged into the river It was very wide at its mouth but narrowed quickly. Francisco pulled into the shore and began to disembark. We followed him and Pedro organised the horses and men to join him. Leading his horse Francisco approached our ship, "Tomas, I intend to explore this river on foot rather than by ship. We will need every man."

I nodded, "I will arm myself and join you."

Captain Guido said as I headed for the side, having armed myself, "Take care, my friend. You do not deserve to die here in this God-forsaken hole."

"We have the banner of the Virgin, how can you say we are God forsaken?"

The English Adventurer

He nodded, made the sign of the cross and said, "I will pray for you."

The storms, accidents and the lack of decent food had halved our number of horses. One was found for me, adding to my feelings of guilt. It took time for us to gather and with scouts at the fore and banners held aloft, we headed along the river. The trail there indicated that the natives used this regularly. We had not seen many boats and we wondered if that was because of the lack of rivers or some fear of the ocean. The natives we had met certainly seemed more superstitious than the Aztecs. Diego Almagro would bring half of the men while Francisco and Lieutenant Montenegro led the other half. I rode at the fore just behind the three men we used as scouts.

Surprisingly the jungle was not as oppressive as we had found hitherto. It seemed more open and we made good progress as we left the river and followed it towards what we assumed was a native village. When we found the unusually large settlement, we realised that our luck had changed. It was, however, once more deserted.

Francisco was delighted for there were ramparts, "We can defend this place. We have found a base from which we can explore." He ordered the men to begin to search the settlement and to make it more defensible. He called over the lieutenant and me, "I think that with Almagro's men when they come, we can hold this place. I would have you two take some men and return to the ships. Tomas, take your ship and return to Panama. I would have you bring more men, ships and supplies."

"Me? I am not an important man."

"You are more important than you realise. Many of the merchants who are with us are here because of you. You are seen as a lucky charm and a good soldier never dismisses luck. By the time you return we will have built a dock close to the river and begun trading with these natives. This is obviously an important place and as we hold it, they will have to bend the knee."

I was not convinced but I nodded and mounted my horse. We headed back to the ship with ten crossbowmen. I rode next to the lieutenant. He admired Francisco, "He is a great man, is he not?"

"He is but I do not like this splitting of forces. Until Diego arrives with the other half of the men then the Captain General is vulnerable."

He laughed, "Vulnerable? The natives fled."

It was precisely at that moment that the ambush was sprung. The natives far from being cowed had allowed us to enter an empty village and now they sought to end our lives. They swarmed from the jungle with bows, arrows, stone spears and clubs. The lieutenant was a brave

The English Adventurer

man and, drawing his sword, shouted, "Crossbowmen, load and release." He charged down the path at the six warriors who with shields and spears ran at us.

I could not let the brave young man do this alone and I drew my own sword and rode at the left of the lieutenant. He had a head start but he was in danger of being surrounded. I heard the sound of crossbows as they were drawn back. There were natives in the trees to my right and their arrows and darts were a worry. If they hit my horse then my falling would end in my death. Most of the missiles missed and the ones that struck pinged off my helmet and breastplate. Lieutenant Montenegro had slashed one native with his sword as his horse crashed into another. I leaned over my horse to cleave the skull of the nearest warrior in two. The lieutenant wheeled his horse to the right and I wheeled mine to the left. I heard the distinctive crack as the bolts were released. Our charge had taken us out of harm's way. Knowing that the reloading of the crossbows took time, we charged again down the trail. The warriors did not know how long it took to reload and they turned to face what they deemed the greater threat, the two metalled monsters riding beasts that they had never seen.

One, obviously a mighty warrior, stepped out and pulled back his arm to hurl an obsidian-tipped spear at me. The spear missed my horse's head by a handspan and then cracked into my breastplate. It was a well-thrown spear and it hurt but the fact that it failed to stop me had an immediate effect. The warriors turned to run. The mighty warrior had no chance to do so and I rammed my sword into his shocked face. The crossbows cracked again as they hit fleeing warriors in the back.

I reined in, "We have to get back to the Captain General. Until reinforcements arrive, he is helpless."

He nodded, "You crossbowmen follow as fast as you can. The Englishmen and I will gallop to the aid of our beleaguered comrades."

As we galloped down the track, we caught up with some of the survivors of the ambush. We slew them but it confirmed the need for speed. We heard the crack of the harquebuses that we had brought with us and the cries and clash of combat. As we neared the village, I saw that my worst fears had been realised. The warriors had entered the village and Francisco was bravely and recklessly leading its defence. I saw the bodies of men in breastplates. That they were surrounded by heaps of native warriors was immaterial. Even as another soldier was surrounded and beaten to his knees the lieutenant and I began to hack and slash our way through warriors who had no defence against our swords. Our horses also did terrible damage. When men fell their skulls and backs were crushed by their mighty hooves. We both whirled our

The English Adventurer

horses as we swashed with our swords. As the crossbowmen who had followed us arrived and began to release their weapons the attack broke down and the warriors tried to retreat. The harquebuses cracked and when three warriors fell, I knew that the harquebusiers had loaded a handful of stones. It shortened the range but was very effective.

I heard a horn and that signified that Diego Almagro was close. With reinforcements and so many enemies dead the village was ours and while the wounded were tended we searched the village. It yielded a great quantity of food. We also found gold, silver and jewels on the dead. It could not compensate for the loss of five men dead and sixteen wounded, not to mention two dead horses but it was a sign that we had found somewhere we could use as a base.

We headed back to our ships the next day. Diego Almagro was in an angry mood. "Next time we come we bring better quality men, Don Francisco. It took too long for my men and me to reach you."

"But you did and for that, I am grateful to you; your valiant charge broke their hearts."

The lieutenant grinned, "I can see that the English adventurer is a true warrior. He fought like a knight."

The Captain General said, "I could have told you that. A man who survived the Balboa expedition not to mention the massacre at Tenochtitlán has no need to prove his courage."

We reached the beach and the treasure and supplies were loaded aboard my ship. Francisco announced to all his intentions of returning to Panama. "I know that men are unhappy and I do not wish to risk a mutiny. Tomorrow, we hunt the forest for a cargo and for food." He nodded towards the mighty trees. "They may not be gold but the timber will fetch a good price. We will find plants we have not seen before and take them back with us."

It seemed like a good plan. Diego Almagro shook his head, "I will take some men back. We will burn that village and it will warn these natives what they can expect when we return."

I knew why he wished to do so, he was angry. It was not just with the men who had been slow but he himself. He was supposed to be the military leader but it was Francisco who had shown real leadership.

I joined the men hewing trees and finding plants. Having cared for the plants taken back to Lord Collingwood, I was better placed than any to know how to not only find the right plants but how to carefully dig them up and carry them to the ships. We were on the beach loading them when the smell of burning drifted over to us. We saw the pall of smoke and knew that Diego had done as he had promised.

The English Adventurer

Francisco said, "That is a sign, we will call this place, Punta Quemada, the place of burning."

When the arsonist finally arrived we saw it had been at a price. Diego Almagro had been hit in the eye by an arrow. The warriors they had encountered had all died but he had lost an eye.

We sailed for home the next day. I had not made my fortune but I had made enough, as had the others, to warrant a second expedition.

Chapter 13

Our return was not the glorious one envisaged by our leaders. The governor was not impressed by the paltry finds we had made and the losses we had suffered. Francisco and the other leaders spent many months trying to persuade him to allow them to fit out a second expedition. When I was not invited to join them I knew that my position had changed. Pizarro apart, the leaders saw me as someone who had provided money. I had little enough left and so I became unimportant. I could have been offended or hurt by the isolation but I was philosophical. I was now the owner of a ship. Captain Pedro had shown me what a man could do with one ship. He had started with one and built up a fleet. Captain Guido was more than happy for me to stay aboard the ship.

My generosity with the treasure I had shared now proved to be vital. The crew had made coins from the expedition and were more than happy to return to the New World. The ship needed repairs and I used the small number of coins I had left to buy the raw materials. The crew worked to repair the ship.

Two months after we had returned Captain Guido and I were dining in his cabin. We were eating a simple stew made of the shellfish collected along the shore, augmented by fish the ship's boys had caught. We knew where to forage wild garlic and onions and with the xictomatl now grown locally, we dined well. The men brewed their own beer. It did not taste like English beer and took some getting used to but we could not afford wine and it was safer than drinking the water.

"Tomas, I can see that you are serious about being a ship owner."

I smiled. I had stripped to the waist and helped the crew when they had hauled the new mast into position, "And why should I not be when I have given my whole fortune to this venture?"

"Then, while we await permission from the governor for the next expedition I suggest we sail *'Infanta'* along the coast to a deserted bay. We can beach her and cant her to enable us to clean the weed from her hull. I know of such a bay and believe that the plants that grow there will allow us to coat the hull and grant us another few years of sailing."

I had been along this coast with Balboa and knew the dangers. I was sceptical, "What about the natives?"

"The ones who were dangerous are now dead and the rest work for us. There will be no danger." He shrugged, "The port fees, whilst not exorbitant will start to eat into your purse, Tomas, I have little enough gold and we can live off the land."

The English Adventurer

I liked the idea. I went to the residence where I sought an audience with Pizarro. He was brought out to meet me. "How goes it, Francisco? When do we leave on our expedition?"

He shook his head, "We do not at the moment. The governor wishes an expedition to the north and he wants our ships."

"Then Captain Guido and I will leave for a month or two to repair our ship. We are heading along the coast to careen her."

"That is good. Even when we do get permission it will take three months or so to complete the preparations. One piece of good news is that we now have the best pilot that I know, Bartolomé Ruiz." I had heard the name but did not recall why. Pizarro saw my confusion and explained, "He was the pilot of Christopher Columbus. He has recently arrived in Panama with his daughter and he is keen to explore a new land. Others made more from his first voyage than he did and he is happy to invest in our venture."

"Good, then when I return, I shall meet him."

As we headed the twenty miles or so along the coast to Chama Bay, I saw that the coastline was no longer wild and rugged. The jungle no longer came down to the sea in a complete line. There were gaps where farms had been built. It showed that civilisation had come to this land. Captain Guido had chosen it because the tide went out a long way and that allowed us more time to work on the ship. He was a skilful sailor and he nudged us in until we were grounded and then half the crew, me amongst them, raced ashore and with many ropes ran to tether us to the trees. I waved the signal and the yards and masts were removed from the ship. It was sad to see the ship thus. It was as though she had been bared naked but we knew that it was necessary. The crew who brought the masts and yards ashore then joined us. When Captain Guido and the handful of crew who remained aboard stood on the sand and waved we began to heave until the ship turned on her side. The captain's signal told us when to stop and we tied off the ropes. We made our camp by the trees and I went with some men, armed with crossbows, to hunt for food.

By the time we returned, with a variety of dead animals and wild greens, the fires were burning and we soon had food cooking. Captain Guido and the First Mate had gone to collect the items he would need to make the coating for the hull. He had told me what it was made of, I confess that I was still no wiser but I was honoured that he would entrust me with what was a secret recipe.

The next day, stripped to the waist and barefooted, we swarmed over the starboard side of the ship and started to scrape the disgusting growth from the hull. Sometimes we found crabs and shrimps living in the mess we collected. They were not wasted and joined the hunter's stew that would sustain us while we worked. The sun burned our backs and had it not been for the salve that one of the crew applied to mine I might have suffered far more than I did. We wove hats to wear keeping the sun from our heads and that made life easier.

When we had finished one side of the hull, the stinking concoction cooked by the captain was painted on the side of the ship. We used the tails of the dead monkeys we had killed for brushes. As we painted the captain examined the ship for any timbers that needed to be replaced. One advantage of this part of the world was the timber that grew here. It was hardwood. *'Infanta Maria'* had been built from such wood and the worms did not seem to like its taste. Even so, there were a couple of planks that needed to be replaced and we did so before giving a second coating to the hull. We had to wait for a high tide to turn the ship and enable us to do the other side. Half of us lay in the shade of the trees while we waited for the perfect tide. The other half waited aboard the ship.

The captain's voice roused us and the ropes securing the ship to the shore were untied. We watched the ship begin to rise as the water floated her. We had to work in unison with the captain as he turned the ship. We kept the pressure on one side as the ropes we had released were attached to the other side and strong swimmers brought them ashore. It took the whole time to turn the ship and as we tightened the ropes and were joined by Captain Guido, the ship canted on her other side. The next day saw a repetition of the work to clean the hull. We were all better and quicker on the larboard side. It took a shorter time. We did not celebrate until we had another abnormally high tide and we floated the ship before we celebrated.

The day after the celebration I went into the jungle to hew down some timber to take back to sell in Panama. It took seven days for the masts and yards, not to mention the sails, to be fitted to Captain Guido's satisfaction for we renewed some of the older ones. The ship's carpenter gave us instructions and we toiled to make new yards. We had enough timbers to make a raft and we would tow it back to Panama. It was almost a year since the Battle of Punto Quemada when we sailed back into the harbour of Panama. We had noticed, despite the raft we towed, a real difference in the ship. She seemed to want to fly and the captain was confident that we would no longer be the slow old lady of the fleet. The First Mate and some men poled the timber to the shipyard and it was he who negotiated the sale with the shipwrights who had exhausted the local supply of shipbuilding timber.

"I will go to the residence and meet with Don Francisco."

The captain nodded and then said, "You know, Tomas, that even if the governor does not allow an expedition, we could sail our ship down the coast. We could find things to trade back here."

The idea did appeal to me but I was a man of honour, "We will wait, Guido. I gave my word to Pizarro."

When I reached the residence, he was no longer there. There was a new governor, Pedro de los Ríos, of Panama and we were directed to a newly built house not far away. I learned later that Francisco had used his own money to have a house built for himself. I found the leaders there along with the famous pilot, Bartolomé Ruiz. They all appeared pleased to see me. I knew I looked different from when I had left. My skin had turned a mahogany brown so that I looked like many of the natives. I had not cut my hair and, instead, had it tied behind my head. The work on the ship had filled me out and, perhaps the healthy diet had made me stronger. Whatever the reason I was a different man from the one who had first been approached to join these conquistadores.

"Tomas, this is perfect timing. We have permission from the new governor and Bartolomé Ruiz has agreed to be the pilot for the fleet." He looked at Diego Almagro and Luque who flanked him. The soldier now wore a patch over his eye making him look more like a pirate than a soldier. "Tomas has earned the right to be part of this expedition, has he not?"

Juan Carvallo laughed, "As he has a ship then he is vital to our hopes."

Don Almagro nodded, "Aye, for he is a doughty warrior and fearless."

Nicolás de Ribera added a word of caution, "But he cannot expect a quarter of the share."

Pizarro said, "Why not? We have, at the moment, just two ships yours and mine for the governor took the other for his expedition." He saw my questioning expression, "As far as I am concerned the division of the profits remains the same. Agreed?"

The heads nodded; Nicolás de Ribera's last of all.

"Now I propose taking just two or three horses. We took too many last time and more died than we brought back. Two or three are enough to cow the natives and to give us the ability to scout further." There were nods again. Pizarro was charismatic and there was no one with a personality to overshadow him. Even Almagro lived in his shadow. "I would have Bartolomé sail aboard the *'Infanta'*. We can carry more men on our ship and with her newly cleaned hull, she can lead" he looked at me, "You have cleaned it have you not?"

The English Adventurer

I laughed, "She is like a foal now and not an aged mare. She will fly and we know that there is no worm in her." I looked at the pilot, "She is a good ship."

"Then when we are done, I will come and inspect her. I am keen to be at sea again. When do you think, Captain General, that we shall be able to sail?"

"The start of March."

We spent another hour or two going over the details of who would be on which ship. It was clear to me that there would be more merchants this time. They were paying for passage and it was their coins that would pay for the supplies. Pizarro was taking more harquebuses this time. I resolved to have at least four on my ship. I could not take cannons ashore but I knew how to use harquebuses.

I left with Bartolomé and we headed to the ship. "It is an honour to meet the man who sailed with Columbus."

He shook his head, "It was the Italian who profited from that voyage." He shrugged, "I may not have gold to show but the woman I married, God rest her soul, bore me a beautiful daughter and for that, I am blessed."

"You have a daughter?"

He nodded, "Isabella. She is living in Don Francisco's home. She will be safer there. She travels everywhere with me."

"And you say your wife died?"

He stopped and looked at me. "She was an Indian."

I knew why he searched my face for answers. He wanted to know if that prejudiced me. I nodded, "There are some beauties. There was one such woman in my life…she was killed by the Aztecs."

He looked relieved, "Then you understand the ache that is in my heart."

Shaking my head I said, "I am not sure that Katerina was the love of my life. We were together too briefly for that and…" I waved my hand as though to dispel the image. "I can do nothing about her death and I would rather forget it."

"Then you are right, my friend, she is not the love of your life or else you would not be able to forget her, no matter how hard you tried." We had reached the harbour and he stopped to look at the ship. "Genoese built?" I nodded. "She looks to be a fine vessel. I can see that she is unladen for she rides high in the water. I like her. And the captain?"

"Guido is as fine a sailor as I have met and I have sailed the seas for many years."

"Good. I believe we shall get on."

The English Adventurer

I heard laughter as soon as we boarded. The crew were all gathered on the deck and I saw that there were jugs. Captain Guido shouted, "The shipwright was so pleased with the quality of timber that he not only paid us the best price but he gave us these jugs of wine, fresh from Spain. We will feast this night."

"And I have good news too. We are to sail at the beginning of March and we have the Fleet Pilot with us," like a conjurer revealing a trick I waved my hand at the pilot, "this is Bartolomé Ruiz." I saw recognition from the older members of the crew but the younger ones looked confused. "The pilot who brought Columbus to the New World."

The expressions changed and the pilot was fetched a chair and a goblet of wine. I went to speak to Guido. "We are given the same share but there will just be two ships. We lead."

He looked pleased, "That is an honour. You bring us good fortune, Englishman."

I drank less than anyone else. I know not why. The result was that only Captain Guido and I were able to stand as darkness fell. "I will take our pilot back to Francisco's. I fear he did not get to see as much of the ship as he might have liked."

Guido smiled, "He did something more important. He got to know the crew. When you get drunk with shipmates it makes a bond. There will be time enough for him to get to know the ship. When we start to take on cargo, he can sail her to get the feel of her."

Bartolomé was drunk but still able to walk. He was also able to speak coherently. I could not allow him to walk alone for Panama had many undesirables on its streets. "The crew like you, Tomas. They admire that you are willing to work alongside them even though you are the owner of the ship. They tell me that you charged a tribe of Indians with just your sword."

"I was not alone and besides, had I not then men would have died."

"That is true courage." He suddenly stopped. "Forgive me." He turned and vomited. I kept my hand on my sword's hilt as I watched for movements from the shadows. There were none. He wiped his mouth with a cloth and said, "That is better."

When we reached the house Francisco and the others were eating. The door was opened by a beautiful vision. "Father, what is the matter?" Bartolomé looked a little worse for wear and he staggered a little as he stepped over the threshold.

"I am drunk, Isabella. I have not been drunk since your mother died so forgive me. This is Tomas Penkridge, the master of the ship I am to

The English Adventurer

pilot. Tomas this is my daughter, Isabella. Did I not tell you that she was a beauty?"

Isabella shook her head in embarrassment, "Father."

I was smitten, "You did not do her justice, my friend." I bowed and kissed the back of her hand, "My lady, you are beautiful."

She squeezed my fingers with her soft hands and said, "And you are the first Englishman I have met. Are they all as handsome as you?"

Before I could answer Bartolomé said, "Isabella, your father feels unwell. Take me to my room. Tomas, we shall see you tomorrow."

I did not want to leave but I knew that I could not stay. "I will count the hours, my lady." Her smile as she closed the door filled my body with a strange warmth.

I woke before dawn, hoping that the pilot and his daughter would arrive early. It was, of course, a forlorn hope but it meant I had plenty of time to bathe and groom myself. I trimmed and shaved my beard. The stiletto I had taken in Spain made a good razor. I wore good clothes rather than my workday ones and I donned my best boots. When I emerged on deck Captain Guido appraised me, "Are we going somewhere special today, Tomas?"

I felt myself flushing although my tanned skin hid it well, "I just thought that I might have to visit with the Captain General again and when I went yesterday, I felt like a beggar."

He seemed satisfied with my explanation, "Will we need to carry horses again, on this voyage?"

I shook my head, "We are the smaller ship and the Captain General only takes a couple."

"Good, I would rather carry people. And we will sail to the same places?"

"Further south. Bartolomé is quite happy to explore the ocean by himself. He found treasure in a New World for Columbus and he is confident he can do so again."

We ate our breakfast. Panama had a bread oven and we ate warm bread as well as fresh eggs cooked on the shore and slices of fried ham. It set us up well. It was almost noon when the pilot and the lovely Isabella arrived. Her skin showed traces of her native background but she bore it like a lady. Bartolomé had bought the finest of clothes and as they approached the ship the crew all stopped what they were doing to stare at her.

Captain Guido saw my dumbstruck look and gave a chuckle, "Now I see why you smell like a pomander." He then shouted, "Back to work and stop staring at the lady."

The English Adventurer

We went to the gangplank and I held out my hand to help Isabella aboard. Captain Guido gave a sweeping bow, "Welcome to the *'Infanta Maria'*."

"This is Isabella Ruiz and you know her father."

As they stepped onto the deck Guido clasped Bartolomé's hand. Bartolomé said, "Today you can explore the ship. No wine for me today."

Captain Guido laughed, "It has all been consumed." He turned to me, "Tomas, if you would show the lady the ship, I will take her father into the hold and the heart of the ship. I am sure he will find it illuminating."

Left alone I found that I did not know what to say. Luckily, Isabella was a confident young woman and she initiated the conversation, "My father tells me that you were in Mexico and fought the Aztecs."

Relieved that I could answer I nodded eagerly, "I did."

"Were they as terrifying as I have heard?"

"More and I will not give you nightmares by describing their barbaric ceremonies. Come, I will do as I was bid and show you the ship."

As we began to walk, she asked, "This is your ship?"

"It is Captain Guido's to command but I own it."

"Then you are a rich man."

"Ask your father. He knows that until we find treasure, we are all poor but with your father's help I am hopeful that we shall both become rich, my lady."

She shook her head, "I had a native mother and can never be a lady."

"Ladies come in all shapes and sizes. It is what is within a lady that makes her so and not her parentage. Besides, from what your father told me, your mother was an important woman."

"She was but only in her village."

"And why should that not make her a lady? Madrid is just a bigger village. If we went back far enough in time then the Queen of Spain's antecedents might have come from a small village."

She laughed and took my hand as I helped her over a coiled rope, "You are a philosopher too. I like you."

I kept hold of her hand and gave a slight squeeze, "And I, most definitely, like you."

She put her left hand to her mouth, and said, coyly, "Sir, do not dally with the affections of a maid."

I let go of her hand and said, "I do not dally, my lady, for I am not that kind of man."

The English Adventurer

She gave me a thoughtful look, "I barely know you and I can see that. Sir, let us slow down a little. My heart beats faster and that is a sign of danger. I would get to know you. Can we not leave it at that for the while?" She waved a hand, "This is not the place for courtship, is it?"

I was aware that faces were turned to us, "Back to work!"

The crew obeyed but with grins. Isabella was right, this was not the place for courting.

When they left, I felt empty. I knew I would have to endure knowing looks and lewd smiles from the crew but I accepted that. I knew that it was just their way. I tried to visit the residence as often as possible but Isabella was seen by Francisco as his housekeeper. I began to feel jealous of him. When, two weeks later, Bartolomé arrived at the ship I felt inordinately excited and greeted him as though I had not seen him for years.

He smiled, "My friend, Isabella is not with me." He held up a hand to silence my questions, "My daughter is wise and she has spoken to me. She is right. Baby steps are what are needed. You and I have a voyage of exploration ahead of us and we can get to know one another. Know that my daughter knows her own mind and heart. She will give her heart when she is ready. You will need to be patient." Captain Guido approached, "Captain Guido, I wondered if today might be a good day for me to see how the ship handles."

We had loaded many of the supplies and all that remained was for the passengers and their belongings to be boarded.

"It is as good a day as any and to be truthful I am anxious to see how she performs when she is not pulling a raft behind her."

I was surplus to requirements and I left the two of them and went to the forecastle. We headed out to sea and sailed towards the islands I had first seen with Balboa, Isla del Rey. I saw that there was a settlement there now. They were just fishermen but I suppose they enjoyed their semi-isolation. They were free from the governor's taxes and could easily sell their catch in Panama's markets. I looked aft and saw that Bartolomé had taken the helm. He was a natural sailor and the ship responded well to his touch. We sailed around the islands and then headed back to port. I waited until we had tied up before I spoke with him.

"How is the ship, Captain Pilot?"

"She handles well. You and your crew did a good job cleaning the hull. She is sound and I look forward to sailing aboard her."

"And Isabella?"

The English Adventurer

He sighed, "That you are keen bodes well but I have said what I have to say and any advances must wait until we return. My daughter is just sixteen years of age. There is time."

It did not sit well but I nodded. I would come back a rich man and then she could not refuse me. For the first time, I regretted leaving my fortune in Spain.

The English Adventurer
Chapter 14

We left on the 10th of March. We had one hundred and sixty men with us. Not all were soldiers but the ones who did so came aboard armed and prepared. Diego's eyepatch was an indication of the dangers we faced. This time we would be leading and not following. More importantly, we would be sailing beyond Punto Quemada so we could take advantage of the favourable winds and clean hull. We were so speedy that Captain Guido and Bartolomé had to reef sails to allow Francisco's ship, admittedly bigger and more heavily laden to catch up with us. We made good time. No one wanted to risk losing men so early in the expedition landing in places we already knew.

Bartolomé showed why he was the most famous pilot. He made immaculate maps. When we had still been in port, he had copied the maps Captain Guido and I had made. Now he added to them. He had a fine hand and I felt embarrassed about the squiggles I had used on the maps I had given to Lord Collingwood. We sailed along the coast and he nodded with satisfaction as we passed Puerto Deseado, Puerto del Hambre and Punta Caballo and confirmed their position on his copy of the map. It was getting on to dark when we reached the river that Pizarro had named when we had last passed it, the San Juan River. We anchored for Bartolomé was summoned aboard the flagship.

I had already appointed the harquebusiers who would use the weapons. One was, of course, Pedro de Candia for we had become great friends. The others were given to those who had been on the previous voyage and whom I had seen fight. We spent an hour each day practising with the weapons. We only fired once a day but we dry-fired to get them into the rhythm. They were keen to use them. Crossbows were all very well but the shock and the sound of the harquebuses were even more of a powerful weapon. As we waited for Bartolomé to return each of us prepared for the days to come. We would be landing and that meant we needed our weapons honed and ready to use. I now had a better-padded jack to wear beneath the breastplate as well as a woollen head protector for the morion. The dents and damage had been repaired in Panama and I felt confident that the natives we found would be more easily cowed than the Aztecs had been. The other purchase had been a machete. These were useful tools and could be used to cut through thick jungle and lianas. They were also a good weapon but I would use mine as a tool.

When he returned Bartolomé was bemused. "Our Captain General, it seems, is keen to have a base here. As we have yet to find natives

The English Adventurer

here he hopes for a better result than the last time you landed. We are to build a port along its river." He smiled, "He knows his own mind."

We waited until dawn and then *'Infanta'* led as we edged our way along the river looking for somewhere we could land. Bartolomé was at the bow sprit and had a lead weight to gauge the bottom. We chose the larger channel. The brown colour of the water did not help us. When we spied a channel to starboard Bartolomé deduced that there was an island there. "I will land us on the larboard side but I think a port on the island would be safer. Still, it is the Captain General who will decide such things."

In the event, the place we landed was also an island. We stopped at a beach and I went ashore with Pedro, Bartolomé and four well-armed sailors. We went on one of the small boats we had brought. Once we landed Pedro and I loaded our harquebuses. I knew that the natives were experts at hiding. If any were waiting and rushed us then an exploding pair of harquebuses would be effective. In the end, it was an anti-climax. No one attacked us and the jungle that Bartolomé had found was not as thick as we had seen further along the coast. The three of us entered the jungle while the others waited for the Captain General. We found no trails but we saw signs that natives used the jungle to hunt and forage. Footprints in the mud and a hewn clearing told us all that we needed to know.

By the time we returned to the beach other boats had landed. Pizarro seemed satisfied. "Tonight we make a camp here and then tomorrow we build Punta San Juan. I will use the boats we have to take forty men and explore the river." He looked at me, "I would appreciate your company, Tomas, and yours, Bartolomé."

"We would be honoured." We both answered together but in my case, there was trepidation in my voice.

It was the same boat we had used to land and the same crew that took us down the river. This time Pizarro led in his boat. I sat in the prow with a loaded harquebus. Pedro sat at the stern and Bartolomé steered. I knew that the journey back would be much easier for we would have the sluggish current to aid us. We spied the smoke in the distance and Pizarro waved us to the shore. We had passed one narrow tributary, heading for the sea and we landed at the only beach that looked large enough for the seven boats to land.

When we stepped ashore Diego Almagro took charge. Leaving one man from each boat to guard our landing site we headed through the jungle towards the village. I had not discussed our intention with either of the two men who were leading us but I now believe that the wound suffered by Diego affected his judgement. As we neared the clearing wherein sat the village, he waved us into a semi-circle. Pedro and I had the only two harquebuses although there were ten crossbowmen with us. It was clear that he intended to be aggressive. Pedro and I flanked Bartolomé. He was the pilot and more vulnerable than any of us partly because of his age and also his lack of experience at this sort of thing. We moved towards the village, now becoming clearer through the trees.

The villager who saw us and shouted out a warning made the mistake of sending an arrow in our direction. Diego Almagro was ready and shouted, "Charge!" Pedro and I both blew on our fuzes and then fired at the mass of warriors who ran at us. Allied to the wall of bolts that were sent at the natives it ended the first attack. As we had seen before, the tendency of the natives along this coast had been to flee when confronted. Their warriors would then return to fight. This was no different. With that fact in our heads, we tried to hit as many warriors as we could. We now recognised the leaders. They had more feathers in their headdresses and they wore more elaborate and precious jewellery. Pedro and I stacked our harquebuses against a tree and drawing our swords ran into the village where forty or so warriors were making a stand. Darts, arrows and spears were hurled at us but our armour protected us. It took less than ten minutes to defeat them and then secure the village.

Francisco then took charge, "Tomas, take your boat and return to the ships. I believe that we can sail a ship here. Make it the flagship. You and Bartolomé finish the port and send my ship here. We will use this as our base."

I was unsure if he was wise but I nodded and we headed back to our harquebuses. We stopped only to take the treasure from four of the men we had slain. We made it back to the camp quickly. I went to speak to Nicolás de Ribera, "The Captain General has taken a village. He wants your ship to sail to it." His face showed his fear, "The river is wide, more than three hundred paces, and seems deep enough. The landing place is guarded by our men and you will easily find it." He nodded. "We are to finish this port."

There was plenty of wood and with no natives, so far as we knew, on what we had discovered was an island, we set to building a port. Half the men built the wooden quay and jetty while the other half-built dwellings for us to use. The only one not involved in the building was Bartolomé. He sat on the deck working on his precious maps, adding the details we had just discovered. None begrudged him for the lack of hard labour. His work would yield us gold and profit. Merchants had stayed with us. Some had brought their own soldiers. They built separate homes and buildings. The ones we built were for communal

The English Adventurer

use. Two weeks after we had begun, we had a crude dock where ships could tie up and enough houses for us to sleep ashore. Some of the merchants had even begun to harvest the land close by the port, gathering the leaves and plants that could be sold back in Panama as well as taking emeralds from the small rivers. This coast seemed to teem with the green gems.

We saw Francisco's ship as it edged back up the river. The captain and the pilot both stopped work and joined me on the wooden quay as the ship tied up. It did not turn to face upriver nor did the crew disembark, instead it simply tied fore and after and Francisco clambered down a rope ladder. He turned and waved, I saw Diego Almagro and Nicolás de Ribera at the stern.

Francisco smiled, "They are going back for more men. This land has potential. Whilst we have yet to find gold and silver, I am hopeful that this land will yield treasure. Captain Guido, I would have you take your ship and explore further south. Bartolomé, use your instincts. Find this land of Pirú for me."

"But that means you will be left without ships here."

He smiled, "We have wood and can build boats but if you would leave me your longboat, Captain, it will augment the three boats left to me by Diego."

"Of course."

Bartolomé asked, quite reasonably in my opinion, "And how long do we explore before we return?"

The Captain General shrugged, "Until you find evidence that this empire we seek is close. If you are away for six months then so be it. Diego will be back in a couple of months. Have you plenty of supplies?"

We had sent men hunting and foraging and I nodded, "We have and if we just take our crew we can manage." I nodded at the merchants, "Is this our first colony? San Juan?"

"Until we have women it is just an outpost of Spain but one day, aye, it may well be."

There was little point in racing away south. We knew not how long we might need to find this land. We gathered more of the fruits we had found and skinned, cooked and salted the animals we had hunted and trapped. Already some of the men we were leaving behind were making salt pans. We would need more salt and it was easy enough to manufacture.

Francisco left before we did. He left Lieutenant Montenegro in command and I was happy about that. The soldier was brave but intelligent. Francisco looked almost evangelical as he was rowed up the

The English Adventurer

river. He was nothing like Hernán Cortés. Francisco truly wanted to find this mystical land but he wished to do so for Spain. I had never seen him show the same greed for power as Cortés. He led through charisma.

We left the next day and I stood at the stern with the pilot and the captain. I knew that we were sailing where no one from Europe had ever travelled. Bartolomé had a small table and camp chair brought up so that he could record what we spied as we sailed. I was aware of the importance of what we did but also the danger our isolation represented. We were one small ship sailing south into a land that was completely unexplored. We had yet to meet any warriors who were not primitive natives but I knew that Francisco was convinced that there was some mighty power in the land and they were the people that we sought. We used the coastline as our guide. Whenever we spied a river, we reefed the sails and edged closer to it so that Bartolomé could add details to the map. If the river appeared wide enough then we entered the estuary but we never sailed so far that we could not turn around if we had to. We saw no natives but, in the distance, we did see smoke from their fires. We did not land.

How he knew it I do not know but one day Bartolomé banged the table and said, "That is it, we have crossed the equator."

I had been at sea most of my life but I had not heard of this term before. "Equator?"

Bartolomé pointed to the sun, "The sun is directly overhead and it only happens here. Imagine a belt going around our world. That is the equator. The clever men half a century ago so named it, '*circulus aequator diei et noctis*', it means '*circle equalizing day and night*'."

"And that is important?"

"To a navigator, it is for it fixes our position." He pointed to his map. "The sun's position in the sky will change as we head south and I can be more accurate with my map."

I confess that I was distracted. The joy I thought I might have had to discover new lands was replaced by distress that I was parted from Isabella. I saw the jungle and the natives as a threat. I wondered if I should, when we returned, marry her and then sail back to Spain. Even if I made not a nugget of gold from this expedition I had more than enough in Spain to give Isabella a home.

It was four days later when we spied another vessel. The lookout was sceptical of what he saw, "Captain I see a sail but it is not a ship. Perhaps I need to be replaced. My head has gone sun blind."

Guido said, "Tomas, you have brains and a good eye. Ascend the mast and see if you can make sense of this."

The English Adventurer

I clambered up the mast, somewhat less lithely than I might have done some years earlier. I joined the sailor, Antonio, and he pointed south. He was right, there was a vessel or a sail at least but it was not a ship that I recognised and then it came to me. It was a raft such as the one we had towed back to Panama. The difference was that they had a sail but it was of the same dimensions and as well as men aboard I saw what looked like cargo. It floated well and seemed to have a large cargo aboard.

I called down, "He is right, captain. There is a raft with natives aboard."

Bartolomé shouted, "Full sail, captain. This raft has been sent by God."

By the time I had descended the sails were billowing and we were easily catching the raft which had turned and was attempting to flee south. Our ship was sleek in comparison and we cut through the water. The captain took us ahead of the raft and turned us into the wind so that we stopped and barred her progress. She bumped into our side.

"Get men aboard her. Tomas, lead them."

I used a rope to clamber down and found six terrified natives who cowered around the mast. They wore simple loin cloths but I saw that they wore gold necklets. I gave orders to the men who had come with me, "Lower their sail and see what is under these covers." There were ropes and covers over the cargo and I was anxious to see what we had.

Bartolomé shouted down, "We will take four of these men back with us. They are as valuable as anything we may find under those covers."

My time in the New World had given me a smattering of the native languages. They were all different but there were some similarities in words. I pointed to one and said, "You, go to boat." He shook his head fearfully and I drew my dagger and pointed it at him. I had no intention of using it but he was not to know that. He climbed the rope and his agility told me that this was not the first time he had climbed a rope. I chose another three and they did not argue.

"Captain Tomas, treasure!"

The covers revealed finely made ceramic ware, textiles and, best of all, ingots of gold and silver. There were only half a dozen in total but they were the first sign, apart from the river emeralds, that we had found real treasure.

"Get them aboard."

The two men we left aboard the raft had a mixture of terror and relief. Relief that we were leaving and terror that their friends were about to be devoured by this strange creature. I was the last to leave and

The English Adventurer

I said, as I climbed the rope, "Safe voyage." I smiled. I know not if they understood my crude attempt at their language but they smiled back anyway. Perhaps that, too, was relief that I was leaving.

Guido's face was a picture when I stepped aboard, "This is a great treasure, Tomas. Once more you bring us luck."

Bartolomé nodded, "It is evidence of a greater treasure to come." He pointed to the four men who were shaking, not with the cold, for it was unbearably hot, but fear. Bartolomé had lived in this land longer than I had and he had more languages he could use. He began to speak to them. I understood about half of his words and gathered that he was letting them know that they were safe and would be well treated. He smiled as did I. Guido and the rest of the crew were moving the cargo to the empty hold. He sent a boy for a jug of our beer and some beakers. When it came back, he drank some and then gave me a beaker of it which I drank and pointedly smacked my lips. When he poured one each for the natives they sniffed it suspiciously before sipping it. Their smiles and chatter told us that they approved. It was the start and over the next few days as we continued to head south, the two of us spent much time speaking to them. Gradually we learned their language and we taught them some of our words. These were the link that Pizarro had sought. We now had the means to ask questions of any natives we found. We sailed closer to the coast and Bartolomé was able to identify the names of some of the places. Until we had more words it was simply a case of pointing and then one of the natives would say a word. Bartolomé would transcribe it as he heard it on to the map. Tumbes seemed to be the port from which they had sailed. When we won over their trust we sailed close to it. As a port it was primitive but then if they only had rafts, the natives called them a Balsa, they would not need well-made quays and could simply drag the rafts onto beaches. It made sense and it told us that this empire, rich though it might be, was more primitive than ours.

It was as we left and headed north that we learned our first facts about this mysterious race that ruled a large empire. We shared no words for size but the four men agreed that if we were to sail, even in our fast ship that flew across the waves, it would take three moons to sail to the southernmost part of the empire. It had taken five days for Bartolomé and to some extent, me to become familiar enough with their words to extract information. A day north of Tumbes one of them pointed to the shore and said, "Cotocollau, Quitoloma and Quito. We had established how to differentiate between men and places.

Bartolomé said, "Places?" And they nodded.

The English Adventurer

Another said a flurry of words. The others nodded in agreement. It had been too fast for Bartolomé and me to understand and Ruiz made them speak more slowly, questioning every word. From what we gathered the two places had been independent as had Tumbes. The Tumpi people, who lived there, had been conquered by another race, the ones who ruled this enormous empire that stretched for three moons to the south. The four natives called them the Inca. When we asked them about the treasure, they did not really understand our questions. When we brought out a gold piece they merely nodded. It was then we saw that how much gold and silver they wore around their necks. They had so much gold that to them it was not treasure. We now had enough information to take to Pizarro. As we sailed closer to our port of San Juan the natives, now seemingly accepting their role as translators, pointed to the shore. We could see in the distance smoke rising from a settlement. We had seen the smoke on the way south and thought it another primitive village. They assured us that it was a city and there were stone buildings. Once more the word Inca was used. Bartolomé and I calculated that it was less than two days south of our port. We had tangible proof now and we sped back to San Juan.

Francisco was even more excited than we were at the discovery. It alleviated his depressed mood. Since our departure, many men had died or deserted the potential colony. Wild animals, reptiles and biting insects had taken their toll. Once again, the natives had fled before Pizarro could speak to them and, worse, took to ambushing the foraging parties. Men were unhappy and wished to leave.

Almagro had still to return and so we abandoned the upstream port and waited at San Juan for Almagro. Pizarro spent every waking minute with the four natives, Bartolomé and me. We pored over the maps and discovered everything that we could. Pizarro's persistence paid off and we learned that the people were led by warriors called the Inca. That word seemed to apply to the leader of the people and his best warriors. The four seemed fearful of them and it was clear that they were not Inca. One of them told us that they were Tumpi, the recently conquered tribe. We also learned the name of the place that they had pointed to that lay just the other side of the river to the south of us. Atacames was newly conquered and marked the northern end of this native empire.

"When Diego returns, we shall sail south and visit this place."

Diego arrived two days later. The men he had brought, however, were few in number and did not replace the ones we had lost. I had learned to gauge the nature of the men quickly. Men like Pedro de Candia and Alonso de Molina were the best of men and you knew that if you were hard-pressed, they would not run. The new men seemed to me like men who had already run, I did not know what from. We had, however, supplies and we would not starve.

There was disagreement about our next course of action. Many wished to return to Panama arguing that the discoveries we had made would guarantee that the governor would be forced to provide more men and ships. We now had proof of this vast empire. Pizarro was persuasive and he won over the doubters. We would visit these cities. Leaving the buildings we had made for a future visit we loaded the ships. The horses having died it was much easier than it had been. Pizarro travelled with us and not on his former flagship. That became Diego's. It was the start of a rift between the two leaders. When I first met them, they seemed as one with the same hopes and dreams. Since the loss of his eye, Diego had changed. I knew Francisco had not but then I spent more time with him.

We passed the first island we had discovered and had considered a good landing place. Francisco looked at the map and said, "What is this place named, Bartolomé?"

"I have yet to write it on the map but I thought Isla del Gallo."

"A good name. It is somewhere we might land but first let us see this wondrous city."

We reached the coast just as the sun was setting. The smell of smoke from the land drifted over to us and we anchored. While we ate on the open deck Francisco spoke to the leaders who were aboard his ship. Nicolás de Ribera, rather than becoming distant from Pizarro had become closer and he was aboard along with Pedro and Alfonso. We had not seen Atacames close up but our natives had said it was only recently conquered. It seemed to us the best chance we had of a peaceful encounter.

"We will land tomorrow but I want only those we know we can trust. I would rather not fight."

Pedro nodded, "Then the best men are aboard this ship, Diego and Lieutenant Montenegro apart, of course. There are just thirty I would trust. We now have four harquebuses and they seemed to cow the natives."

He shook his head, "I would try something different here. If this place has been recently conquered then we may be able to act as allies. If they joined with us, we would have both a base and an army with which to fight."

He turned to me, "Did you not use local Indians to fight the Aztecs in Mexico?"

I nodded, "Although the Captain General was careless with their lives."

The English Adventurer

"But it worked. We will use these four natives for just such a purpose. We will take two in case things go awry."

I gave Pizarro a sideways glance. Was he expecting the men to be killed and was giving himself insurance?

"Who are the best two?"

Hernando had insisted upon baptising them when we had reached San Juan. The four had seemed bemused by the pouring of the water and the chanting. "Felipillo and Martinillo."

"Bring Felipillo and one other. We will go armed but I want the men to know that I hope for a peaceful outcome."

Nicolás asked, "And Diego? What of him?"

Pizarro shook his head, "He can stay with the others. I will tell him that it is in case of treachery."

"He will not like it."

"Until I fail then I command."

As we waited Bartolomé said, "Tomas, I will be aboard the ship and safe. I would urge you to be cautious and careful. I have grown fond of you and know that when we return to Panama you shall have my blessing in your quest to win my daughter's hand. Better an ignominious retreat rather than death."

His words made my heart soar, "I will be careful and so long as Almagro is not with us, I am confident that all will be peaceful."

Pizarro was rowed to the flagship and spent an hour aboard. We were preparing for the landing but the heated words drifted across to us. Eventually, he returned and we descended to the boats. I had loaded the guns on the ship myself. If we had to flee quickly then the gun crews would be able to fire them and cover our retreat. None of us expected that but it was as well to be prepared.

Pedro and I kept the two translators close to us while the boats were tethered. Two men armed with crossbows guarded them and after Felipillo had pointed to the well-marked trail in the jungle we followed our leader. We had learned that the town was a mile or so inland. There was a port of some description along the river but as we did not know the depth of the river and knowing that the rafts used in this part of the world could float on a large puddle, it was decided to approach this way. The jungle had been cleared and we did not need to hack our way through it. It was not farmed and I knew from Felipillo that the people of this land farmed closer to their city. They terraced it and seemed, from his words, to be far more sophisticated than the people we had met on the Castilla del Oro.

There were not many of us but enough to make the brightly coloured birds take flight and warn the town of our approach. The result

The English Adventurer

was that when the jungle ended and we came to tended fields there was an army to greet us. I frowned for the men who arrayed before us were not the usual mob of natives. They were organised. They stood on terraces that were clearly defensive. It was cleverly done for it allowed all their missile men to use their weapons and their general to see us clearly. There were two bands of slingers before a double line of spearmen and archers. The spearmen had shields. I saw that they had been arranged so that similarly armed men were next to one another. The third line was made up of men armed with clubs, what looked like a primitive halberd, and bone swords tipped with metal. There was also one warrior who wore a helmet, the first I had seen. There were feathers sticking from it but this was not the headdress I had seen before. I saw that in his ears, glistening in the morning sun he wore gold. It was not a tiny piece of gold but appeared to be the size of a crown. Next to him were another six men who also wore helmets but without the feathers and they had no gold in their ears. They were a bodyguard.

Felipillo pointed at him and said, "Inca."

Here was proof of this new potential enemy. I knew from my time in Mexico that as grand as this army was it would be nothing compared to the one closer to the heart of this empire.

Pizarro turned and said, "Bring the translator forward."

I edged him closer to the front. Our men had also formed a double line but we were dwarfed by the four hundred men who were facing us. Our handful of harquebuses and crossbows would not stop us from being overwhelmed.

"Tomas, tell him to tell them that we come in peace and wish to trade."

Pizarro knew some of the native's words but I had spent the longest time with him and there would be no misunderstandings. I told him what to say and added, "Speak loudly. Do not fear, we will protect you and your brother."

He spoke the words and it struck me that the army that watched us was silent and waiting for such words. That too was unusual. The helmeted warrior clearly controlled them and I wondered if he would speak. The man in front of him wore a headdress of feathers and I saw him turn and speak to the helmeted warrior. He turned back and shouted. Felipillo translated his words exactly, "Go back to the sea for you are not wanted here. If you go back now then you can keep your lives but do not try the patience of the Apu."

Francisco asked, "Apu?"

The English Adventurer

I spoke to Felipillo who shrugged and told me he had never heard the word before and had just spoken it the way he had heard it pronounced.

Pedro said, "They look better organised, Captain General, what do we do?"

For the first time, I saw the doubt on Pizarro's face. Nicolás said, "It is not dishonourable to fall back in light of such numbers. Even if we landed those that Diego brought, we could not fight these men."

"Perhaps if we had a falconet with us but the harquebuses we have brought cannot stop them."

Just then the spearmen began banging their shields and it sounded to me like the precursor to an attack. Francisco thought so too and he ordered us to fall back. There was relief throughout our party. We fell back in good order with the crossbowmen at the rear watching with loaded weapons. Once on the beach, we were ferried back to the ships. The army followed us but the sight of our ships must have inspired fear for they did not leave the shelter of the trees. The exception was the helmeted leader who walked to the water's edge with his bodyguard to view us. It was either an act of bravery or bravado to show the people that this Inca was not afraid of us.

We sailed close to Diego Almagro and Francisco called out, "We do not have enough men to win this battle. Let us find somewhere safe to camp and we can debate our future."

The one-eyed soldier reluctantly agreed and we sailed back to Isla del Gallo. There was a good beach and no sign of habitation. We landed and made a camp. I say we but it was the soldiers and sailors who built the camp while we debated. The views were as disparate as it was possible to be.

Juan Carvallo had been one of those who had sailed back to Panama with Almagro and had sailed with us to Atacames. Before we disembarked, he had warned Francisco that the new governor of Panama wanted him arrested. I saw the fear on Pizarro's face. It coloured his judgement in the debate.

I listened more than I spoke. Diego Almagro was, as I expected, keen to sail back and fight the natives. I was not sure we would win. It was Pedro and Alfonso who provided the arguments against such action. Pizarro was keen to stay on the Isla del Gallo and await reinforcements. He wanted Hernando Luque to persuade the governor to send more men.

Pizarro was eloquent, "The treasure we have found is clear evidence that there is more to be had. If we send that back to Panama it will convince him."

The English Adventurer

Some of the merchants were also disillusioned and wished to return. The deaths at San Juan could not compensate for the ingots we had discovered. The food had almost been cooked when Pizarro tired of the debate. He took his sword and made a line in the sand. He shouted, "Those on that side of the line can go back to Panama and be poor; those on this side can come to Peru and be rich. Let the good Castilian choose his path."

I knew which side I would join despite my desire to leave the dangers of this land and seek the hand of Isabella. Like me the pilot Bartolomé joined Pizarro. We were few in number. Less than twenty of us were there.

He nodded sadly and said, "Then leave us the supplies that were brought and return to Panama with the treasure. I am still the leader of this expedition and I would have my share." As men drifted off, he grabbed the arms of both me and Bartolomé and led us away. "I am honoured that you would stay with me and there are no two others that I would rather join me but I need you two to ensure that a ship returns for me." He lowered his voice and looked over to Almagro. "I fear that without allies we will be marooned here. Besides, you, Tomas, have a lady to court and you, Bartolomé, need to make copies of your maps." He nodded toward Pedro, Alfonso and Nicolás de Ribera. Those three are as loyal as you two. Return as soon as you can. Tomas, we will need a falconet. It may not be for this voyage but if we are to defeat those who conquered Atacames then we will need more than a handful of harquebuses."

We argued but it was in vain and we would return to Panama. Our presence also meant that the treasure we had found, the gold, silver, ceramics and textiles would remain on *'Infanta Maria'*. The credit for their capture would be accorded correctly.

Before we left, we helped to build the handful of huts that they would need and brought ashore the precious supplies but, the next day as we left, I felt guilt for I knew not if I would see him again.

The English Adventurer
Paullu

Chapter 15

I had learned from my early encounters that I had to obey orders and be prepared to make difficult decisions. The result was that, after ten years, I was promoted to Guaranga Camayoc, commander of a thousand and I was sent to the north to take the land of the Tumpi from them. A thousand men does not sound like many but I had with me another one thousand allies, Chinchaysuyu warriors. They were numbers only but they would allow me to use my own men judiciously. I could afford to be profligate with our allies. When we conquered the Tumpi we would enlist them into our ranks and so our army would grow. At the heart of the army, we still had the great regiments all recruited from the two major branches of the Inca but I was happy to lead my men. They might not all be Inca but I had trained them to be superior to any other regiment. It had, of course, been at a cost. My parents had died and I had not been able to say goodbye and I had a family no longer. I had enjoyed women, of course, but they had been captives. I lived a solitary life. It was a good life but one surrounded by servants and those who served me. I took solace in the thought that long after I was gone the empire I had helped to build would still stand as a monument to our vision and courage.

Tumbes was our first major target. Our allies had been able to sweep the smaller villages aside. It had cost us two hundred men but as none of them were mine it did not bother me. Tumbes was a different prospect. It had walls and it had ditches. There were also more than two thousand warriors who would be able to defend it. The progress of my men had been steady rather than speedy and it meant many survived their attacks and joined the garrison of Tumbes. The first thing I did was surround the town with the camps of my Chinchaysuyu allies. It would ensure that none would escape when it fell and I was confident that it would fall.

I gathered my senior officers around me. Most had been with me for more than a year and we got on well. By that I mean they obeyed me without question and, thus far, had not let me down. We stopped close to the main gate. I pointed, "That is where their leader will be." I turned to Hautpac, he was my second in command, a Pachaca Camayoc, commander of one hundred. "Take one-third of the men and gather them at the north side." He saluted. I turned to Manco. He was a young

The English Adventurer

Pachaca Camayoc but he was clever and the men liked him. This would give him his chance to show me what he could do. "Manco take another third of the men and wait at the south side." I gave them both a thin smile, "It goes without saying that you do not take all the best men." They managed a smile in return. "I will attack the main gate with half of the Chinchaysuyu. When you hear my horn sound three times, we will feign a retreat and you two will attack at the same time. When they take men from the main gate, we will renew our assault. Do not tell the men our plans just divide them and camp. We attack at dawn."

I was more than confident in my own ability. Some of my archers came from the eastern side of the empire and their bows had a much longer range than those of the coastal Tumpi. As every one of my warriors was skilled with a sling then I knew that a shower of stones would decimate their numbers. One innovation I had introduced was the use of padded tunics for my officers. Allied to our helmets it meant we had more protection than most men. I had seen how it affected enemies when stones hit our heads and bodies yet did not incapacitate us.

I did not have the horn sounded I merely waved my axe and pointed at the walls. The stones that fell from our slings were like an avalanche in the mountains close to my home. That we had wrongfooted them was clear. Seeing the three bodies of men forming up they had expected a simultaneous attack. My men hurled their stones in a regular manner and they fell amongst men who had no protection from the falling stones. Men cannot throw stones for long periods and as the defenders rushed men to the main gate I signalled for the attack with bows. Some archers were able to send their arrows deep into the town while others knocked men from the walls. I wondered if I would need my flank attacks. However, having made my plans I would see them through. To do other would be seen as indecisive. When I waved my axe for the third time my men, protected by helmets and shields marched forward. I, of course, led them. As I had expected, their archers and slingers targeted me. I was well protected although by the time we neared their walls I had so many arrows in my shield that I could have used it offensively. While we held shields above us then men began to hack at the wooden walls.

When we had done what I deemed to be enough damage I had the horn sounded. My well-trained men disengaged and began to walk back. The Tumpi cheered thinking that they had defeated us. We stopped just outside the range of their arrows and stones. I had the wounded taken to the rear and called on our allies to form up before us. The two flank attacks struck at the same time and the wail from within told me that we had been successful in confusing them. The two walls that were attacked had fewer men than at the start of the battle and as we marched forward their chief, standing at the gate saw my brilliance. He was brave as were his bodyguards but when we breached the gates the majority of those within fled towards the other gate. Their chief and his bodyguards died to a man. They were outclassed by my weapons and my bodyguards. We won by early afternoon and I was satisfied.

We might have won the battle but I did not slow down. We set the defeated men to begin building the Pukara. The hard labour and obedience to our orders would make it easier to make them good recruits in our army. We had breached their walls far too easily and if we were to make the town defensible then it needed to reflect the other fortresses we had built. Of course, it was not a perfect site. For a start there was no convenient mountain and quarry but my officers worked with what they had to hand. While I set up the civilian administration that would run the town, they levelled the walls and built up terraces. Lacking stone we used wood for the ramparts. My officer utilised what there was and they made it cunningly constructed so that an attacker could not simply run at the ramparts. They would have to twist and turn, exposing their sides to stones and missiles as they did so. Once I was satisfied that it would be effective, I sent a messenger to the Inca to tell him of my victory. Perhaps it would lead to another promotion, maybe Apuratin, the commander of two and a half thousand. I made sure that I accorded praise where praise was due and I was satisfied with my missive. Three moons later and we had almost finished the new pukara. The mighty general Quiz-Quiz who was close to the Inca, Huayna Capac, came himself to speak to me. I was honoured when he marched in with five hundred of his bodyguard and a thousand Chimu warriors. I liked the Chimu if only because they were even better builders than we were.

I took the general on a tour of the town while the Chimu senior officers offered advice, suggestions and help to my men.

"You have done better than we could have expected, Paullu. From your report, you lost few men. Was that true?"

I had been accurate down to the last wound. I knew that any discrepancy could result in my execution. I nodded, "I have the lists in my office and you are more than welcome to peruse them."

He smiled, "That will not be necessary. One thing men cannot say of you is that you lie. You may be the dullest officer in the army but that, in my view, is no bad thing." We had finished the tour and were in the office I had commandeered. I saw that Quiz-Quiz approved its bare appearance. We sat and a servant brought us beer.

The English Adventurer

"I am giving you the temporary rank of Apuratin. It is just that, temporary so do not get used to it. I want you to take your men, the Chimu I brought and the Chinchaysuyu, along with your regiment. Enough survived for them to be a viable force?" I nodded. Their losses had been lighter than we had expected. "I will be leaving an experienced Pachaca Camayoc here with one hundred men. You can make a regiment of five hundred Tumpi. You have a Pachaca Camayoc who can lead them?"

"I do. Hautpac. He would make a good Guaranga Camayoc."

He nodded, cautiously, "We shall see." He handed me the two pieces of gold. They were larger than the ones I wore in my ears already and I felt my heart race. I was being promoted. When you take your next target then you may wear these for you will be promoted. Give yours to this Hautpac." He smiled, "Incentive for you both, eh?"

"And what is our target?"

"Atacames, by the coast. It is stronger than this place was and I think you may find it harder to take. We shall see. When it is done then you can send the Chimu, Chinchaysuyu and Tumpi to Tingasta."

He had surprised me and my face and words made him smile, "But that is at the other end of the empire."

"And far from the homelands of these three tribes. In time Hautpac will bring them back north but by then they will have forgotten their families and their homeland."

We chatted inconsequentially about this and that and then I brought up the health of the Inca, Huayna Capac. It was a risk but I heard that he had been unwell. Quiz-Quiz darted a quick look at me and seeing no hidden meaning spoke, "Between you and I, Paullu, he is far from well. Fear not, however, for we have good doctors and he will be healed. It is good that your loyalty is not in question for the ranks of many of your superiors have been culled. You and I just do our duty and serve the Inca." He finished his beer and changed the subject, "Now, you have six months to subjugate Atacames. Just do as you did here in Tumbes and all will be well. Send me regular reports. I will be in Machu Picchu. The Inca finds it peaceful and he can contemplate better there."

With that, I was dismissed. I went to give Hautpac the good news. He was a good man and thanked me as though I had made the promotion. I had not but I had chosen the best man that I had. We talked until dark about our plans and we still had yet to finalise them. We had to stop for the meal we enjoyed with Quiz-Quiz and his officers. He left the next morning before dawn with his depleted escort. He was an old-fashioned general and I wanted to be like him. After he had gone and while I ate my breakfast, I examined the two pieces of gold I would

The English Adventurer

wear in my ears. They were not new. That, in itself, was not a surprise but there were the marks of a blade and I wondered if they had been taken from some disgraced officer. I would ensure that was not me.

When we left some months later for the march down the coast to Atacames, I had ensured that all my officers knew my mind. The officer left by Quiz-Quiz had made it quite clear to me that his ambitions were now fulfilled. He would not rise any higher and was quite happy to be the garrison commander of Tumbes. He had chosen the easy life and that made me think less of the man I had only just met. The most aggressive warriors had died in the battle and we had ensured that the ones who were likely to be belligerent were in the Tumpi regiment. The garrison commander would have an easy life, especially when we took Atacames.

The Tumpi scouts knew the town well and they appeared to be quite happy to help us to conquer the last independent part of Tumpi land. They even helped us to persuade some of the smaller villages and towns to accept our rule without fighting. It meant that when we reached the town, we had only lost a handful of men and that had been due to the terrain, insects and reptiles. That was not the way I would wish to go. While the three regiments of allies surrounded the north, east and south of the town, I went to the beach to approach from the west. I had yet to formulate my plan but, as always, the securing of the perimeter was always vital. While my regiment made camp I waved over my new second in command, Manco, "I want our best five scouts to come with me.

"Is that wise, sir?"

I snapped, "When I want your opinion then I will ask you."

"Sorry, sir." He saluted and hurried off.

I could have chosen them but this was a test for him. Did he have the skills to judge the right man for the job? He passed the test and brought me the five I would have chosen myself. "Bring your slings, shields and spears. I would scout out the defences."

They were all grizzled veterans. I had stormed walls with them before now. They knew my skill and I was well aware of theirs. We headed along the trail. I doubted that there would be anyone left in the jungle. My army had not been silent in our approach. However, all it took was one hero, willing to risk his own life and my career would be over. I let three of the men lead. They were expendable and two followed, watching my back. As the jungle thinned, I saw the town. They must have heard what we had done at Tumbes and had begun to make a half-hearted attempt at terracing. They were clearly farmers and had made the terraces too small and not high enough. They had only managed one finished terrace and a second one was just begun. It would not slow us. While my four guards watched the jungle for danger, I studied the defences. The gate was new and that was its strength but it had no towers. They had not made the entrance twist and turn. We could make a straightforward assault. As they had tried to copy what we had done at Tumbes I had to assume that they knew of our attack. That gave me my plan. We headed back through the jungle and I summoned the officers of the three regiments. I also had food brought to the beach. The cloying heat and stench of the coastal jungle were not to my liking. When I built the pukara I would ensure that it was light and airy and built well above the jungle canopy.

I waited until the food had been brought and my officers had all partaken. "Gentlemen, we will assault the town from all four sides simultaneously." I smiled, "It will allow me to see our Tumpi and Chimu warriors in action. I want you to have your men sound the drums, cymbals and horns before we attack. It will unnerve them. When you hear my horn then cease the din. The silence will also have an effect. Although we will all be in place at the same time, the first horn blast will be to signal my attack. It will, I hope, draw more defenders to the main gate. The second horn will signal the rest of you to attack. You will prosecute the attack until you have taken the walls. You may suffer casualties but the important matter is to take Atacames. With this in our hands and the river as a border then we can rest a while before we continue our conquest."

I went through their dispositions. If any thought that they were being talked down to they said nothing. I would not risk a misjudgement from one of my officers. They were all required to know exactly what I intended. When I was satisfied, I had my servants build me a shelter on the beach. The breeze from the sea was most pleasant and took the stench of the jungle back towards Atacames. With an overcrowded town filled with refugees and little food, the smell would add to their discomfort and make an early surrender more likely. I rose early and walked into the sea, naked. Turning I faced the east and watched Inti as he rose from behind Atacames. It was a cloudless sunrise and boded well for the attack. That done I came back to my shelter and my servants dried and then dressed me. They knew how to do so and my layers of padding were intended to help me to survive. It was not as though I expected any warrior to best me but it was always as well to be prepared and assume the worst. By the time I was dressed my food had been prepared. I ate well. I had learned over the years the value of a full belly. My junior officers all came to report that their units were ready and in position.

"Good. Return to your officers and await the horn. Inti smiles on the morning and it bodes well for us." Their faces told me that my confident words had put heart into them. I had a bodyguard of twelve men. They followed me into battle and would happily die to ensure that I survived. They were a reassuring wall of weapons and muscle. We moved up along the trail, to our starting positions. Others picked their way noisily through the jungle. Noise would scare away the reptiles and insects, or so the men hoped. The Tumpi in the town would know we were coming and the squawking birds and monkeys would alert them just as well as a drum or horn. We stopped at the edge of the jungle and I nodded to Manco who shouted, "Drums, cymbals and horns."

The cacophony of noise was almost painful but I let it go on longer than was comfortable. I turned to the man with my personal horn. It had a very distinctive note and when he sounded it, he was a good musician, then, in an instant, all other noise stopped. The horn was for the other regiments and my officers all looked to me and my long axe. I waved it forward and we began to move.

"Sound the horn twice."

This time there was a roar as the three regiments of allies charged. I had not told them to shout and it annoyed me. However, they were not regulars and I would have to excuse their lack of professionalism. We all stopped and my slingers started hurling their stones. We were in position first and I saw that whoever commanded was bringing men from the two adjacent walls. When the stones were thrown from the other three sides then confusion reigned inside the town. We changed to arrows and spears at the same moment. My officers had all been drilled well and as the arrows fell my spear and axmen moved forward. My bodyguards had their shields up to protect both me and them. Even so one of them paid with his life for a simple mistake when he stumbled over a rock. The stone from the walls was well thrown and he fell dead.

Their simple terracing was not yet finished and rather than a sharp and steep edge it was more of a slope. We struggled but we were able to ascend and then I joined the other axmen in hacking through the walls. They had not yet finished the walls and we soon entered the town. This time there would be no escape for we were attacking from all four sides. I called a halt to the slaughter when I realised that the Tumpi warriors would not give in.

I called over my translator and he spoke my words, "Tumpi warriors you have done all that can be expected of you. I want no more needless slaughter. Surrender now and you shall live." They hurled back obscenities and I held up my hand. "If you do not then I shall sell every man, woman and child I do not kill, into slavery. It is your choice.

The English Adventurer

Surrender and you shall join the army of the Empire of the Inca. We will make a town that no one will be able to assault. What say you?"

It did not take long and Atacames became an imperial town.

I did not send the three regiments of allies directly to their new posting but, instead, had them build the new terraces. There were three of them and I sourced some stones to make them even stronger. With ditches and clever twists and turns, it would be almost impossible for the town to be taken. The only way would be if there was some machine that could demolish walls. We did not have such a machine and I was confident that none of our enemies would either.

It took three months for the terraces to be built and then I sent the regiments away. Hautpac was more emotional at our parting than I was. That was in our natures, "Do not worry Hautpac. We will see each other again and then we shall both have bigger earlobes."

He grinned for he wore my old ones and I had the ones given to me by Quiz-Quiz, "I never thought I would achieve these, sir. You will soon be a general."

In the event he was wrong. I was still the commander of the coastal region two years later. I had not been passed over for I was now an Apu, captain of two and a half thousand. That only one thousand of them were my best warriors was immaterial. My last battle had been when we took the town. I felt confident enough to send most of my regiment off with Manco to head up the river and investigate the possibility of enlarging the empire in that direction. Of course, I could not simply take unilateral action, I would have to seek permission but by sending such a large force I guaranteed the most accurate information whilst ensuring that my men would not suffer a defeat. Manco had grown into his role as second in command and this was his opportunity to exercise that power. It would do him no harm.

So it was that when the fisherman raced into the pukara and told me of a great wooden bird that disgorged warriors from the sea onto the beach, I was in a difficult position. I had a regiment of Tumpi but the only warriors I had with me were my bodyguard. I took a decision I hoped was wise. I ordered everyone inside the fortress and sent a runner to bring back my men.

I stood at the gate with the new chief of the tribe. He was as mystified about these new visitors as any. When they came, even I was stunned into silence. They wore silvered helmets and had metal about their chests. Some of them carried sticks that smoked. They had strange devices that looked like bows on a stick. They stood there and watched. The chief pointed and said, "Those two, by their dress are Tumpi."

The English Adventurer

I nodded, "Then when they speak you answer but I will tell you what to say."

Sure enough one of the two Tumpi, prompted by the metal-covered warrior shouted, "We come in peace and only wish to trade with you. We come from a land far to the east of here and we will bring you great prosperity."

I understood most of the words but I asked for them to be repeated. Were these sent by Inti? Were they the messengers of the gods? I determined that I could not answer them. I would need to visit with Quiz-Quiz, or even the Inca, I told the chief what to say and he did so, "Go back to the sea for you are not wanted here. If you go back now then you can keep your lives but do not try the patience of the Apu." Warriors from the east remained there and I shouted, "Begin to bang your shields."

Every one of the Tumpi and my bodyguards began to bang their shields. Some even shouted. Our allies had no discipline. However, it seemed to work for the strangers pulled back. I turned to my bodyguard, "Have a hundred men come with us. We will follow them," He saluted and left. I turned to the chief, "Bar the gates when we leave."

I took my weapons and led my small band down the trail. They were all wary, even my bodyguard. When we reached the edge of the jungle even I was dumbfounded. There, standing less than forty paces from the shore was the largest vessel I had ever seen. It dwarfed even the largest Balsa used by the natives who plied the seas of our coast. My bodyguards stayed in the protection of the jungle but I felt obliged to walk toward the sea. I feared them but I was Apu, and I could show no fear. The small boats rowed out and the warriors climbed aboard. The boats were hoisted to the vessel and then, to my amazement, she unfurled so many sails that I thought it was an Inti Bird. It took all my courage to hold my ground as the vessel turned and sped north. I had only seen birds move as fast and that was high in the air. I waited until it was out of sight and then headed back to my men. This was something so important that it necessitated a message to Cusco. I was tempted to go in person but I knew that could be a fatal mistake.

My bodyguards waited until we were back in my home before they spoke, "Apu, what was that? How could it fly across the water?"

"I know not but I fear it does not bode well for us." I would have to choose my words for the missive carefully. I dared not exaggerate but equally, I could not believe what I had just seen. It seemed to me that the white bird was a harbinger of death!

The English Adventurer

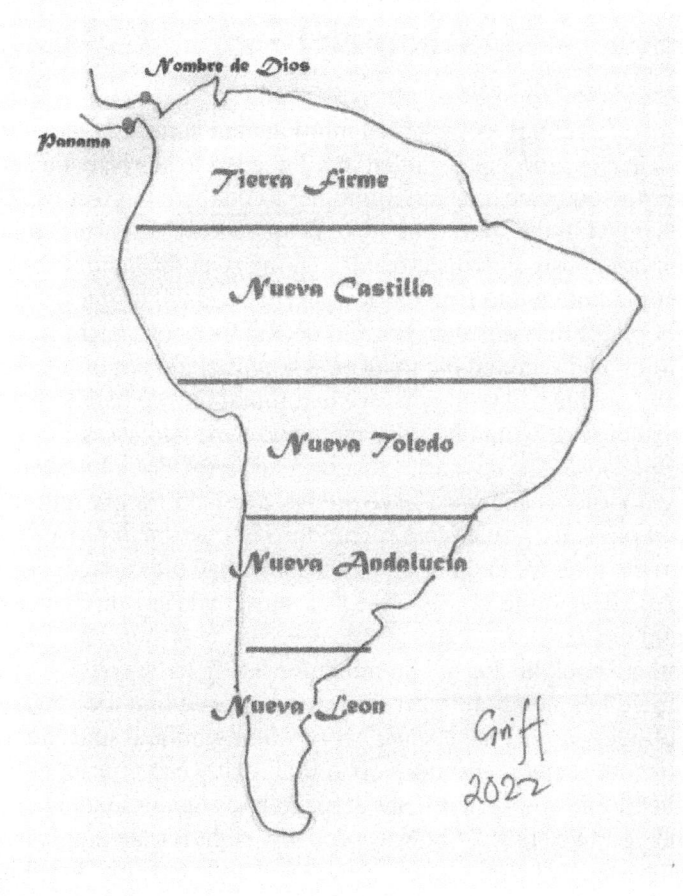

- Nombre de Dios
- Panama
- Tierra Firme
- Nueva Castilla
- Nueva Toledo
- Nueva Andalucia
- Nueva Leon

Griff
2022

The English Adventurer
Thomas

Chapter 16

I had mixed feelings as we sailed into Panama harbour. I had not wanted to leave Pizarro but I wanted, no, I needed to see Isabella and I peered over the gunwale almost willing her to be there to greet us. The port had changed in the short time I had been away. There were more ships and more houses. Civilisation was taking over this land. Diego Almagro could not wait to race to the governor and tell of our finds. He wanted any praise that was due. Bartolomé Ruiz was clever for he and Captain Guido had secreted the treasure where it could not be accessed easily. Many people had seen what we had found but we had it taken to Francisco's house. It would be safer there and we could assess its true value at our leisure. For my part, I just wanted to see Isabella. She opened the door to us and must have prepared herself for our return, The sight of our sails would have spread through the small colony like wildfire. In the time we had been away Isabella had blossomed, or so it seemed to me. Her smile was as wide as a sunset and she threw her arms around me.

Her father shook his head, "So much for trying to be coy."

She turned her attention to her father and hugged him too, "What is the point of being coy? I have spent every waking minute since he left thinking of Tomas and if that does not tell all that we are meant to be together then I know not what." She stepped back and wrinkled her nose, "And you two stink!" She was probably right for the jungle had a stench that permeated clothes and seemed to seep into skin. "I will have a bath run for each of you. Give me your clothes and I will dispose of them."

I shook my head, "Your father and I need such clothes for they are hardy and serviceable. Have them washed."

She put her hands on her hips and laughed, "Not even wed and he gives commands."

I shook my head, "I am sorry. I beg you, my lady, to have my clothes washed so that when I return to sea they will be fit to wear."

She smiled and then a frown filled her face, "You would leave again so soon?"

I shook my head, "Not soon but we left Francisco and some companions marooned on an island."

The English Adventurer

Bartolomé shook his head, "That is harsh. When you are marooned, you have no choice. Pizarro wished to stay there."

"I still know not why, Bartolomé. He could have come home with us and then sailed back."

"You know not the governor. This is all about power, Tomas. I believe that Diego and the governor are working together, they would take what is Francisco's from him. By staying where he is they cannot touch him and when we return he will still be the leader."

Isabella had collected our jacks and smocks. She nodded, "Your father is right. This is still the house where people come to pay their respects to Don Francisco and when they do so they tell me of the machinations of Pedro de los Ríos. He suspects the riches that lie in this southern sea and he wishes them for himself. Tread carefully, father." She left to supervise the filling of the baths.

On the voyages I had sailed with Bartolomé we had spoken of his disappointment in having discovered so much land yet he and his daughter were still poor. He smiled sadly at me, "What I have learned since I first sailed with Columbus is that men like me are given only the crumbs from the high table but since I met you, I am more confident that I may manage to gain the riches my discoveries deserve."

"And however I can help, I will do so."

He gave me a knowing look, "By marrying my daughter you have taken one heavy load from my shoulders and the others are right. You do bring good luck. I am of a good heart. I will go with Captain Guido on the morrow and sell our goods. The merchants who buy them may support us if we do seek a third expedition."

"That goes without saying. What we brought back will hardly compensate for the money we have already spent. If nothing else I will take my ship and return for Francisco."

That was not as quick as either of us would have liked. Pedro de los Ríos proved to be a schemer and it took all the persuasive power of Hernando de Luque to get an agreement to send a ship back for Francisco. However, he would not sanction a third expedition and when Hernando and Diego returned, they were low in spirits. I confess that Isabella and I were busy planning our wedding. I would not sail before we were wed. Captain Guido needed time to make the ship sea ready. Perhaps my mind, being attuned to planning, was sharper than theirs for I came up with a solution, of a sort, "We take more men that we need for the crew. We know that Francisco wants larger numbers of men in case we meet opposition again. We tell the governor that we will bring Francisco back directly but if it takes months then how will the governor know? We are the ones who know this Southern Ocean. You

The English Adventurer

have time for I am to be wed and I need to buy a falconet. Pizarro asked for one and I would not let him down."

I found the gun just a week before I was to be married. I heard of a ship that had been sunk down the coast and Bartolomé and I went with a small boat from my ship and sailed to the beach where she had been sunk in one of the violent storms that destroyed so many vessels. The stumps of her masts still protruded from the water and the two men we had with us did not seem confident. I stripped naked and said, "I will dive beneath these blue waters and see what I can see."

The two sailors were amazed. Most sailors could not swim, "You can swim?"

"Aye, after a fashion but as the masts are proud of the water then I do not think she is deep."

I was not brave enough, or foolish enough to dive in and I lowered myself into the water. Taking a deep breath I dived down to the deck. I was right. The deck lay just eight feet from the surface. I found it hard to stay beneath the water. I used my hands to keep myself moving and I saw the guns, there were two of them and they were falconets. Their carriages had been damaged in the sinking but the barrels looked whole. I knew how to clean them and make them as good as new. I broke surface and found that I was ten feet from the boat. I swam over.

"There are two of them. Row to the place I came up and give me a rope. I will tie it to the first gun and when I give a tug on the rope then pull it up."

Bartolomé growled warningly at the men, "Aye, and do so carefully for I am too old to be spilt into the sea."

I dived down and found that the act of tying the rope to the barrel helped me to stay beneath the water. However, fastening it in two places so that it would not fall back to the seabed meant I almost used all my breath. I broke the surface, gasping for air like a fish. I had no air for my voice and I used my thumb, lifted into the air to give them instructions.

Bartolomé asked, "Are you alright? Do you need the second?"

I had air now and as the two sailors hauled the gun aboard, I nodded, "We know not the condition of this first gun. Besides two falconets are better than one.

It took all four of us to manhandle the cannon aboard. Having done it once the second time was much easier. Our small boat was ominously overloaded and it took all of Bartolomé's skill to sail back to Panama and our ship safely.

Once aboard the *'Infanta Maria,'* I had the carpenter measure the guns so that he could begin work on the two carriages. Then, with the

The English Adventurer

falconets by the forecastle, I began to clean them. The crustaceans we found joined our stew. The weak I threw overboard. The touchhole needed cleaning out but I had a tool for that. It had been given to me by my father and was one of my most precious possessions. We worked every hour of the day to make sure that we had the two guns ready for when we returned to sea. The repairs and arguments with the governor meant it would be more than six months since we had abandoned Pizarro. I stopped work only the day before my wedding. There were still a couple of jobs I needed to do: acquiring the powder and ball but they would have to wait.

The Bishop of Panama himself performed the ceremony in the city's cathedral. I had travelled far since my days as a slave. We used Francisco's residence for the wedding feast and it was Isabella's father who paid for it. He would not hear of me using my money. "I am the bride's father and whilst I have no dowry to give to you I can, at least, pay for the feast."

I know not what I expected of my wedding night but I had never experienced such joy and ecstasy. As Isabella lay sleeping in my arms the next morning, I began to regret my decision to return to Isla del Gallo but I had given my word and Isabella and I had a fortnight only to celebrate our marriage. I determined that I would give no more promises to Francisco. Whatever we found on this voyage would have to do in terms of treasure. We had managed to make back my investment with what we had found on the Balsa and I hoped that this voyage would yield as much. I did not have great demands and living in Francisco's house kept our costs down. Isabella was tearful when we left but the tears were in her eyes and not coursing down her cheeks. She was a strong woman and I was lucky that I had met her. I could not imagine a more perfect wife. She was losing the two men in her life and knew, from our tales, how parlous life was in the sea they were now calling not the Southern Ocean but the Pacific. In my experience, it was far from peaceful.

The ship was well-laden. We only took Felipillo and Martinillo back with us. We left the other two natives we had found to help Isabella whose smile had charmed all three of them. She would teach them Spanish and train them to be servants. The soldiers we had taken on had to hide in the hold until we left the harbour. The governor had spies everywhere and if he thought we had no intention of returning directly to Panama then he might try to stop us. I had no chance to fire the two falconets and I did not wish to waste powder at sea. If we needed them then that would be the time to fire them. They had polished up well and the men I used as gunners were more than happy

The English Adventurer

to have two more guns. I had placed them both on the starboard side. I was still training the gunners and anything that helped them be more efficient was important. Firing the same calibre of ball would help.

Each day we held a council of war by the forecastle. We would eat our cold breakfast and Diego Almagro would give us his views. He was a forceful man. Hernando was still Francisco's ally for, like me, he did not like the belligerent attitude of the soldier. Whilst not unexpected we had with us other soldiers who saw an advantage in peace. Bartolomé and I kept our counsel. We both knew the sea and realised the futility of spitting into the wind. When Pizarro was returned to us then we would voice an opinion.

The belligerent soldier almost spat his words out as commands, "When we return to the city called Atacames we should use Tomas' guns to blast down the walls. It will make them accept our rule."

The priest shook his head, "And how many men do you think we will have to conquer this empire? From what Felipillo has told us its coast is much longer than the coast of France, Spain, Portugal and Italy combined. There are not enough soldiers in Spain to do so. We need to convert the people to God and win their hearts. I agree that Tomas' guns and horses are the weapons that will cow the enemy but once cowed we need to woo them."

It was a good point and we had no horses with us. The forty-odd men aboard our ship were not enough to win a war.

Each morning was the same and the arguments would rage back and forth. Eventually, four days into the voyage Diego took to consorting with some of the men he had brought and Hernando and I would sit and talk at the forecastle. "I see the cross as the way to convert these people, Tomas."

I nodded, "That might work but the Aztecs we fought in Mexico were a fanatical people. They were willing to die for their emperor. Perhaps these people will be the same."

Hernando was also a zealot and he smiled, enigmatically, "God's will, shall be done. I have faith in you and Francisco, Tomas. You are the only Englishman I had met and you are made of stern stuff. Francisco also has a vision. The three of us will prevail and we can make Diego do as we wish and not as his warlike heart desires."

The ragged band of survivors we found on the island were more like skeletons than the hale and hearty men we had left. Some had died and that was mainly through snake bites. Bartolomé and I, at Isabella's prompting, had brought clothes for them and the first thing they did when they boarded was to strip off their old, filthy and lice-ridden clothes and hurl them overboard. After being doused with plenty of

The English Adventurer

seawater they dressed and ate. It was only then that they ate and we waited patiently before speaking. Of course, Diego could not remain silent and it was he who interrupted what I knew to be the most valuable meal the survivors had ever eaten.

"We should sail back to Atacames and use our guns to blast down the walls. Let us start our conquest now and return to Panama with a ship laden with treasures. That will make the governor change his mind."

I saw that the time on the island had bonded the survivors into a closely knit group. Nicolás had always been close to Pizarro and I now saw that the two sat together and when Francisco spoke Nicolás nodded enthusiastically.

"Our time on the island gave us time to reflect." He smiled at Hernando, "We grew closer to God, especially when those snakes killed our comrades. We were able to look a little more dispassionately at what we should do." He pointed to the natives, "Felipillo and the others are the sign that we can win over these people. We know we are not welcome at Atacames. I would sail to Tumbes. It might have as much to offer as Atacames. From what Felipillo told us the people there do not like the rule of this emperor. It is where he came from. Perhaps we can appeal to their nature."

Diego was immovable, "I think it is better to sail to Atacames. There we know what the treasure will be. Tumbes is more of a gamble."

It was at that moment that Pizarro smiled. He had this ability to know the right thing to say at the right time. There were just five of us left from the original group of leaders who had set sail on the first expedition. Francisco said, "I am a reasonable man, Diego. My time on the island has made me calmer. I leave it to you and the other leaders who first joined me in this grand venture. Who wishes to go to Atacames?" Only Diego stepped forward and he glared around, hatefully, at the rest of us. "Tumbes?"

I stepped forward with Hernando. Nicolás stood, as did the other survivors and they roared, "Aye!"

Pizarro had won but that was the start of the crack that appeared between the two men. It would grow to be a chasm.

Felipillo had stayed, along with the other natives, with Bartolomé and me. We had grown close. His Spanish had improved, that was mainly down to Isabella and he had understood most of what they said. He nodded, "Tumbes is good and I shall see my wife and family."

I was surprised. Despite our closeness, he had never mentioned a family, "You have a family there?"

The English Adventurer

He smiled self-effacingly, "I have a wife, a son and two daughters. I hope that they are well. They live in the town. I lived in the town and Don Francisco is right, the people there do not like the rules that we now have to live by." He chewed his lip, "But, there is a garrison of one hundred men. They are led by one of those we saw at Atacames, an Inca. They might oppose you."

It gave me food for thought.

My father in law and I spoke at length to Francisco as we headed past the beach close to Atacames, "Was it hard, Francisco?"

He nodded. He looked too full of emotion to speak and Pedro answered for him, "You cannot believe how hard, Tomas. If we had enjoyed more men we could have built homes where the snakes and biting things would not be able to enter. This is a savage land and we need to tame it."

Francisco nodded, "That is why we came up with the idea of going to Tumbes. It could be as civilised as Atacames and a safer place to use as our base."

I told him what Felipillo had said and added, "We do not have enough men to make war, Francisco. Not that you wish to war."

He rubbed his chin. His normally well-trimmed beard was now wild, "I will give thought to it. When we reach the port then we will anchor and have another debate." He looked over to where Diego was sitting with a group of soldiers, "We need to build bridges with Diego."

Hernando said, "The best way to do that is to show him that the way of peace is the way forward."

We reached the port just before dark and it was the worst time to arrive for we were seen. We had hoped to be there when they woke and hoped that the sight of our ship would make them more inclined to speak of peace. I had been thinking of what we could do and I had a plan but I decided to wait until dawn before I did so.

Felipillo woke me before dawn and brought me to the gunwale. He pointed to the beach and I saw shapes moving, "They are gathering soldiers, Captain, to oppose our landing. I think that they will fight."

He looked to be right. When dawn broke, we saw the beach covered by soldiers. At the heart of it was a warrior who looked like the one I had seen at Atacames on the beach. There were eighty or so similarly armed and dressed warriors with him.

Diego was, of course, triumphant, "See? I was right. We have to fight. I will arm the men and we will board our boats. If our master gunner uses all his cannons then we can clear the beach."

Francisco was not convinced but I could see that he had no better solution. Hernando shook his head and said, "It would make us have to

The English Adventurer

fight tooth and nail. They would take their treasures into the jungle and we would be no better off than before, at San Juan."

I stepped forward, "I have an idea." Every eye swivelled to me. Most were with hope but in Diego's eyes, I saw suspicion. "If I fire every gun, without a ball, it will show the natives just what we can do. It costs us just the powder we would use."

Pedro nodded enthusiastically, "And if we use the harquebuses then the effect will be even greater. I like it."

Francisco added, "As do I."

Diego grudgingly agreed, "But if this fails to shift them then we load with ball and slaughter them."

While we prepared the weapons Felipillo and Francisco conversed together.

"We are ready, Captain General." I thought to give him his full title to remind Diego who was our leader.

"Just wait a moment. Felipillo, say what I told you to say."

Just as Felipillo had learned our language so I had learned his. He cupped his hands and shouted, "Brothers, I bring these men from across the seas. They have mighty weapons and they could wipe you all from the beach. I beg you to allow us to land and to speak of peace."

The helmeted warrior shouted, "No!"

Francisco nodded to me and I walked down the ship touching each gun in turn. They belched flame and smoke. When I reached Pedro and the harquebusiers they fired in turn. When the smoke cleared we saw that the warriors with the better arms had fled and the rest abased themselves on the sand. They were surrendering without a fight. We had terrified them into submission.

Francisco grinned, "Once more, Tomas, you have proved your worth."

Chapter 17

We went ashore armed and with harquebuses. They were unloaded for I wanted no accidents. We were welcomed into the town as though we were gods. I know it is blasphemous to say so but that is the only phrase that does justice to the awe and reverence of our entry to the town. It would have been perfect but for one thing. Felipillo was so excited to see his family that he left the trail to hurry ahead of us. The reptile that bit him was killed by Pedro and Alfonso but he was seriously hurt. We carried him into the centre and while the rest of the leaders greeted the chiefs Bartolomé and I tended to Felipillo.

He gave a wan smile, "I did not get to see my wife. Captain Tomas."

Just then Martinillo rushed up with a woman and three children. When I saw the smile on Felipillo's face I knew who it was. She would know better than any what to do and I stood apart with the pilot.

Bartolomé said, "A clever trick has won us this town but it is a shame about Felipillo."

"He may recover."

Shaking his head my father-in-law said, "He is marked for death. I am sorry. I know that you were close."

He was right and a short while later the man we had taken from the sea died. Martinillo brought Felipillo's wife to us, "She said she wanted to thank you for trying to save her husband." He waved over the boy. "She says her son would do as his father did."

I was touched beyond words and I could barely speak. Bartolomé spoke for me, "The captain is honoured and will watch over the boy as though he was his own son."

She nodded and looked at him as though he was a ghost. I realised then that my translator had been away so long that his wife had thought him dead already. This last visit was unexpected and to be treasured. We left the family to see to the burial and we joined Francisco and the rest of the men in the centre of this fine town. I saw that they had built terraces here too. This was obviously the way that they defended places. As a gunner, it was useful information. The trick with the blank guns would only work once. At some time I might be needed to reduce a fortress' defences and I could see that it would not be easy. There was no sign of the soldiers. The word Inca was repeated when the chief spoke to Pizarro. I was still confused. Did this mean the soldiers or their emperor? I put that from my mind for we were feted. I think that they feared us and respected us at the same moment. We had driven off their

The English Adventurer

invaders and no one had died yet they had seen the potential of our weapons. They brought treasure to us. What they saw as treasure was not necessarily what we did. The gold and silver were equated with the same honour as beans and squashes. The most surprising gift was the small camel. I say camel but it had no hump. It spat in the same way that camels did and so we knew that they were related. The natives called it a lama.

We were given the rooms used by the soldiers. I guess it was a barracks. All the treasure regardless of value was taken to the ship and we enjoyed a night under a roof, waited on by natives desperate to please us.

We held, the survivors of the Thirteen and the leaders, a council of war. "I think we need to explore the area." Francisco was evangelical.

Pedro and Alfonso were as close as any and had a true explorer's spirit. "We will go, Captain General. I will pick the men."

"Take Martinillo with you. I need you back here within fourteen nights. I wish to explore as much of this coast as I can."

Armed with crossbows and two harquebuses they set off and I found myself torn. Part of me wanted to see this new land but, especially after Felipillo's death, my heart had no wish to enter a reptile-riven jungle. Bartolomé found maps in the officers' quarters. They were different from ours but they had pictograms to show the places where they had their forts. He was able to map the castles that defended this land as well as find the roads that seemed to cross the whole of the land. I left him doing what he did best, making maps and I explored the town.

There were similarities between these Tumpi and the people of the Castilla del Oro but it was only in their facial features. The clothes they wore, their language, and their buildings were entirely different. I had been with Balboa and realised that those first natives were primitive in comparison with these Tumpi. Their terraced fields yielded good crops. The people looked to be well fed and happy. They had streets and roads and I was taken to see the great road that led to the rest of the empire that ruled this place. The potential was far greater here than even the Castilla del Oro and the gold we had been given showed how plentiful it was. We even found quantities of it in the barracks. With my share of the gifts they had made I was already well in profit. My investment had paid off. True, it had taken a year or two longer than I had expected but Tumbes promised a golden future.

When our men returned it was with a mixture of good and bad news. We had lost another of our translators. This time it was Martinillo. Pedro and Alfonso had walked into an ambush. The soldiers

The English Adventurer

who had fled must have had second thoughts and some had waited to watch the road. Martinillo died from a hurled stone. The stones that battered Pedro and the others did little harm save make dents and give them a headache while the crossbows and harquebuses slaughtered the attackers. So angry were they with the ambush that any prisoners we might have had were killed by the sword. The good news was that we had more treasure. The gold from the officer's ears was not the only gold that was found and Pedro and his explorers only returned when they were too laden to carry more. It was not just gold and silver that they found but, when they found villages, where the people fled, they discovered well-made ceramics and textiles. All were evidence for the governor.

I had called Felipillo's son, Felipillo. It was partly because it was easier for us to pronounce than his own name but mainly because it seemed to me that it kept the man alive. The youth did not seem to mind and, when we left, I noticed few tears from either him or his family. They seemed to have a different attitude in this land. They were a complicated people.

We headed south for Pizarro was anxious to get as far south as we could before we returned to Panama. We landed many times and each time the places were named and their sites recorded on a map made by Bartolomé. Cabo Blanco, port of Payta, Sechura, Punta de Aguja, Santa Cruz and Trujillo were just names along the coast and although we landed and explored each place, we left no permanent evidence of our visit. It was the map that would help us to find them again in the future. We only turned around when the fresh supplies we had taken in Tumbes were exhausted and we were living from fish caught in the sea and the animals hunted in the jungle. We set off for Panama.

Francisco decided not to call in at Tumbes, "I fear that some of those who fled when we came will have reported to their leaders. As Pedro and Alfonso discovered their roads are so well made that an army could move along them quickly." I saw that Diego was disappointed, he was spoiling for a fight. "Instead we will call at Isla del Gallo and San Juan. Let us see what remains of our first settlements."

We discovered when we revisited the first ports we had built that nature was aggressive. Storms, animals and the seas had rendered the first two useless. Only the crude buildings recently evacuated at Isla del Gallo were recognisable. We headed home against winds that appeared to be against us. Our redoubtable pilot noted the dates and times on a separate document from the maps.

"These are important, Tomas, for it is all very well knowing where you are but if you know when the winds will come then so much the better." He tapped his nose. "While we wait for the news of the next expedition, I will make a copy for you. Keep them safe for with them you can harvest the treasure of this land."

We had with us the other interpreters. One of Felipillo's cousins had also come with us and we named him and christened him Petrillo. Both boys had been christened although I was not sure that it meant much to them. The dousing of their heads with water and the waving of a cross seemed to signify little. They were both younger than Felipillo's father had been and that seemed to make it easier for them to learn. Certainly, by the time that Panama hove into view they were both competent in Spanish.

Francisco had been away, all told, for eighteen months. We had been away for half that time and I wondered if there were any changes in Panama. The first thing we noticed was the increased number of ships. There were now settlements all the way up the west coast of this land. While we had taken great leaps, sailing south, others had simply marched and taken what they wanted. The tribes I had first seen with Balboa had seemed fierce but now I knew that they were not. We now knew how to defeat them and, increasingly, new tribes surrendered without a fight when the metalled warriors were heard to be approaching.

While Francisco and the others reported to the governor's residence Bartolomé and I went with our treasure and the two boys back to Francisco's house. To be honest it felt more like ours than the Captain General's. Isabella had lived in it for longer than he had. In the months we had been away she had blossomed, in more ways than one, for she greeted us with a recently born boy.

She smiled shyly at me, "You were not here, my husband and I knew not what to name him. As he was born in Francisco's house, we christened him Francisco. I hope you approve."

I hugged them both and said, "I care not what you call him. I have a son and he is healthy," I cocked an eye, "is he not?"

"Of course and you, father, are now a grandfather."

Tears welled in the old man's eyes, "And now my days of seeking new lands are done for I have a grandson and I will watch, instead, him grow. You, my son, shall be the pilot of this family."

We went into the large, cool room that we used, especially in the summer and as Isabella fed my son she asked, nervously, "And will you be away again soon?"

I shrugged, "For my part, I know not. Your father has just said that he will stay here. If the Captain General needs me to be his pilot in your father's absence, then I may have to leave again. It depends upon the governor."

She laughed, "Then you will never leave. When you did not return within the month the governor went into a rage. He came here and demanded to know what I knew. I was able to smile and tell him that I was the housekeeper and knew nothing. I do not think that Francisco will be allowed to mount an expedition."

In the event, she was proved prophetic. Francisco and the others returned in low spirits. Despite the baby, Isabella knew her duties and she had a large meal prepared in anticipation of a larger than the usual number of people. The only one of the leaders who did not attend was Diego Almagro. Francisco's face told me the news even before anyone spoke. However, his sadness soon disappeared for he was besotted by the baby. He had no time for such things but that did not mean that he did not yearn for a wife and a family. He waited until we had eaten before the news was fully broken to my father-in-law and me.

"We are forbidden from mounting another expedition. If he had the means then we would all be in gaol now. The empire of the gold will have to wait until we get a new governor."

I had been in Spain more recently than any and I ventured, "King Charles needs gold to finance his wars. Why do you not travel back to Spain? Take some of the treasures we have found and use your eloquence to persuade him."

As soon as the words were uttered then the others joined in. Nicolás, in particular, was keen. "The king will only have heard what the governor wishes him to know. Tell him the truth. I cannot believe that he will not support you in this. It can only make Spain greater."

He did not take much persuading. In fact, we sat up until the early hours working out what and who he would take. We still had two of the natives we had taken from the Balsa and their time with Isabella had made them fluent in Spanish. They would be the best evidence he could take back. They would go as would Pedro, Alfonso and Nicolás. They would take one of the lamas we had brought back as well as samples of the gold, silver, jewels, ceramics and textiles. I slipped away as soon as they began discussing the minor details. I was anxious to share a bed with my wife.

The governor could prevent another expedition for he controlled Panama but he could not stop men from returning to Spain. Francisco was a knight and even the governor, unless he had damning evidence of treason, could not arrest him. Before he left, the Captain General said, "I own the house, Tomas, but I want you and Isabella to regard it as

The English Adventurer

yours. I know not how long I will be away for until I have the support of the king then I shall not return."

"You are kind, Francisco, and is there anything you would have us do while you are away?"

He nodded and leaned in, "García de Jerézor Jaren and Domingo de Soraluce are both disappointed that thus far they have not made their fortunes. We cannot sail to Tumbes and explore this land controlled by the Inca but south and east of Panama are considered Tierra Firme and can be settled without permission. You and Bartolomé know the coast well, find somewhere they can establish a trading post, perhaps two. By the time I return it would be good if there were ports closer to Tumbes that we could use. So long as we have this governor, no matter what the king says, I will not be welcome here."

"We have but one ship, Francisco, and she is old."

He smiled, "And you are resourceful. Men like you and, more importantly, Tomas, they trust you. There are shipyards now aplenty. There are men with money who come here to speculate. We both know where the treasure lies and you can offer them hope that when the time is right, they will be offered places on my expedition."

Francisco, in all the time I knew him, never lost his zeal and his confidence. I smiled and clasped his arm, "And you, friend, take care, for without you there will be no Empire for Spain in this new ocean."

When my friends left, I confess that I did procrastinate. At first, I used the excuse that Captain Guido needed to repair our ancient and battered ship but after a month I knew it was because I was growing comfortable with a baby and wife.

Isabella noticed it too, "Tomas, I love you dearly but I cannot be tripping over you each day as you moon over our son. Did not Don Francisco charge you with watching his business?"

I had made the mistake of telling her all and I now regretted it. She was right, of course, in all the time we were married I could never fault her judgement or her decisions. As it happened both the ship was ready and Bartolomé had finished his map-making. He showed me the maps and the gaps, "It is for you to fill these gaps. See, some are amazingly close to Panama. Making the maps makes your name known for posterity."

I told him what Pizarro had said and he liked the idea. We arranged a dinner with García de Jerézor Jaren and Domingo de Soraluce, whom I knew well, and another six merchants I did not know well but who had expressed an interest in joining a future expedition. Isabella was a wonderful hostess and a good cook. The meal was superb and put them all in a good mood. One of the merchants, Gonzalo, had brought some

The English Adventurer

of the leaves that the natives in Mexico lit and smoked. He had some rolled and he handed them around, "They are called a cigarro and I believe that the smoking has medicinal qualities. Certainly, they keep away the biting insects."

Despite the shutters and the well-made doors, we were always plagued by insects. Isabella had even hired a native to spend the night wafting them away from young Francisco's bed. We all lit them and Gonzalo instructed us on how to smoke them. It burned the throat a little but it induced a pleasant aroma and he was quite right, it kept the insects away. It also managed to make me feel more relaxed. I still do not know how.

As we smoked Gonzalo continued, "And some natives smoke these in a wooden pipe. It prevents the fingers from being burned."

García smiled and said, "There is a point to this, Gonzalo?"

They knew each other well and Gonzalo graciously nodded, "It is no secret that Captain Tomas has invited us all here with a view to trading. I like that idea; I think we all do and that is why we are here."

Everyone nodded their agreement.

"I want to ensure that we have something to trade. These leaves grow well in this climate and yet there are no plantations on the Castilla del Oro. There are places it would grow that are, at present, just jungle. I propose that we find a place beyond the governor's influence and build a port. We know that we can be protected by Captain Tomas. We trade with the natives and seek new treasure but we also have natives clear the jungle and plant the tobacco plants."

García was shrewd, "You have the plants already."

Gonzalo smiled, "Of course. I was looking for somewhere close to the port of Panama but the growth of the city means that there is nowhere suitable."

I liked the idea and I saw Bartolomé smile as I took charge, "Gentlemen, let us form a company. We will each be shareholders on an equal basis." I nodded at my father-in-law, "And I include my father-in-law and Captain Guido in that for without those two we can do nothing."

I saw gratitude in Bartolomé's eyes as they all nodded their agreement. They did not know he would be a silent partner and remain in Panama.

García said, "And the name?"

"The Southern Ocean Company." I know not where the idea came but it did and met with their approval. They babbled on excitedly for a while until I said, "And we will need to commission another vessel. She

The English Adventurer

will not need guns as all that she will be required to do is bring our cargo up the coast to Panama or the Camino de Cruces."

Gonzalo smiled, "The Camino de Cruces, for the less the governor knows the better. He will try to dip his greedy little finger into this honey pot we make."

It was well after midnight when we finished but I was up after dawn for I had much to do. Felipillo was my shadow and, dressed in Spanish garb looked nothing like the village boy who came to us at his mother's behest. We went to Captain Guido who could not believe that I had included him in the company. "It is right, my friend, that you make money. There are conditions." He frowned. I put my hand on his arm, "Nothing of which you will disapprove. You need to train someone to take over this ship and find another to captain our second vessel."

He looked relieved, "I have two such men in mind already." He accompanied me when we went to the shipwright. There were many shipwrights but Alonso was a good one and, more importantly, an honest one. We told him what we needed and I gave him a down payment. The rest would come from the company. Labour was cheap for the natives had grown used to working for their new masters and were undemanding in terms of pay, so long as they had plenty of chicha to drink they were happy. The ship would take three months and that was time enough for what we needed.

We left Panama two weeks later. We had trade goods like tools and machetes in our hold as well as supplies in case we could not find food. Speed was of the essence as Gonzalo needed to get his plants in the ground as quickly as possible. He had hired a man who knew plants and he came with us. Captain Guido and I knew exactly where we would go. Bartolomé had spent hours looking at the coast and discussing various sites. There was a bay three days sailing south and east of Panama that looked suitable. It had a beach and it was sheltered. More importantly, we had seen little signs of natives on our way south. As well as the merchants, some of whom brought their families and belongings, we also had twenty natives who would work for the company. García de Jerézor Jaren and Domingo de Soraluce had selected them and I was confident that they would not let us down. My nervousness at being the pilot soon evaporated when I found it easier than I had thought. It was all down to Bartolomé and his teaching. He had done what my father had done and moulded me in his image. We did the voyage in under three days and that was down to the accuracy of the map. We kept full sail, even at night and we reached a peaceful bay without signs of smoke or inhabitants.

The English Adventurer

One thing we learned after Atacames and Tumbes, was that they were the northern extent of this empire ruled by the Inca. They were many leagues south and I was confident that the firepower of my ship would be more than enough to protect us. In the event the land close to the beach had neither village nor native. It took a month for us to build the port and buildings as well as to clear the jungle. The wood we took helped to make the buildings and the hard part was clearing the roots. The ground appeared fertile. That was not my judgement for I had no idea about such matters but Gonzalo and his plant man looked happy. Leaving them to plant our precious crops the rest of us, armed and with morions and padded jacks headed along the small trail into the jungle. Felipillo was with us and he too was armed. I did not want him to die on his first adventure. We trekked for some miles before we found the village. It was small and mean. The people had settled by a small river and seemed to eke out a living. I had learned from my time with Diego and we approached silently. The result was that when we entered there was shock but not enough time to flee.

Felipillo knew what to do and he quickly told them that while we looked fierce, we came in peace. He did not speak their language but there were enough common words for understanding. I took off my morion and gestured for the chief to sit and speak with me. I could see that the merchants, García and Domingo apart, looked nervous for unlike the two who had sailed with me before they retained their helmets and stood. It mattered not. Through Felipillo I told the chief that we came in peace and wished to trade with them. He looked confused and spread his arm around the village.

Felipillo said, "The chief says that they are poor and have little to spare."

I pointed to the gold and emeralds around his neck, "Ask him about the gold and the gems."

"He says that they have plenty of them but you cannot eat it."

"Where do they find it?"

"It is in the river. They find small pieces although some are too small to be of any use."

I fought back my excitement although Felipillo's words had made even the faint hearted amongst the merchants, smile.

"Tell him that in return for as many of the pieces of gold they bring us we will help his people to clear the jungle and make fields that they can use for crops and we will trade them these." I had kept hidden the machete I had brought. We had chests of them on the ship. The thought of clearing fields did not appeal but the machete brought a smile as wide as a sunrise. We had an ally and we had a source of gold. Within a week of landing, we had made a success of our venture and, as we headed back to the port, we had named Puerta Isabella. I felt proud of myself. I had done this without Francisco and without Bartolomé. I could do this.

The English Adventurer
Paullu

Chapter 18

The disaster at Tumbes almost cost me my life. I was with General Quiz-Quiz when the messenger sent by the Pachaca Camayoc reached us. The fact that he had not returned with his men was ominous. I was saved from execution by virtue of the appointment of the Pachaca Camayoc by the general. He immediately ordered a regiment to prepare to march. "Do you think these are the same people you met, Apu?"

We had questioned the soldier at length before he and the others had been summarily executed for desertion. "From what we were told, yes, General Quiz-Quiz. Their headgear and weapons are distinctive."

"You drove them off with your men?"

I nodded, "But their sailing birds did not spout smoke and fire at us. Perhaps they are…" I did not want to finish the sentence. 'gods'.

The general was shaken too, "None of that. Let us deal with this insurrection and then get to Atacames. Perhaps, in your absence, the same has happened there."

I shook my head and spoke hastily, "Manco is a good man."

General Quiz-Quiz's eyes narrowed, "Meaning my choice was a bad one?" I had said too much and I stood silently. He nodded, "You may be right but never speak that way to me again. You have already used up any favours I might have owed you."

I was angry but I kept my anger to myself. I could have done nothing about Tumbes even if they had sent word when the strangers appeared. I would have to suffer the reprimand. At least I had not been demoted.

We went with more men than we needed. We had two prime regiments and fell upon the unsuspecting town just as the sun rose in the east. It was always the most propitious time to fight. The inhabitants stood no chance for they were not expecting to be slaughtered when they rose. We killed them all and the only loss we suffered was the lack of knowledge about these strangers. There was no evidence of them. Had we not seen the bones of the Pachaca Camayoc and his men on the road we might have believed it all to be a dream. I had studied the bodies and while the men were demolishing the defences to eradicate all traces of the town I spoke with Quiz-Quiz. I was keen to ingratiate myself into his favour once more. "General, the bodies had short bolts

The English Adventurer

in them, some had stones but most were cleanly cut. None had their bones crushed as our weapon might do."

He frowned, "Your point, Paullu?"

"These warriors had long metal weapons by their sides. I thought them too flimsy to be of value but from the wounds they inflicted, we have nothing that can compare."

He was a thoughtful man and I saw that he would consider my words. We left the next morning and marched to Atacames. I hoped that Manco had a good explanation for his lack of interference. We marched into the fortress I had built like an invading army. Our stern expressions and regimented lines did not bode well for the people. They cowered.

Manco had heard nothing from Tumbes, "I am sorry sir, General, but we heard nothing. A fisherman reported seeing a bird-like vessel but he said it was far out to sea."

"And you did not think to send men down to Tumbes?"

He stiffened, "General, my orders were quite clear. I was to ensure that Atacames was protected. Tumbes was the responsibility of another, not me."

He had answered well. The general stayed for another week during which time we saw the stranger's vessel as it flew northwards. Quiz-Quiz was clearly shaken when he saw it. I had allocated a unit to camp at the beach and keep watch. We needed early warning. Thus it was that they came to fetch the general and me to see it as it headed north. The moment he saw it, the attitude of Quiz-Quiz changed. I do not think he disbelieved us but the reality of the vessel was far more terrifying than he had imagined. I pointed to the tubes that I believed had spouted smoke and fire.

The general looked at me and said, quietly, "We have nothing that can defeat such an enemy."

"Nothing save numbers, sir."

Before he left, he gave me new orders. I was to keep patrols to ensure that these strangers did not land again. How I was supposed to stop them I did not know but at least I was back in his favour once more. My men built a lookout post by the beach to make it easier to spot the strangers when they were further out to sea but, as the months passed, we saw nothing. When I was summoned once more to meet with Quiz-Quiz it was nothing to do with strangers in our land but something more pressing. It concerned the Inca. Huayna Capac and his heir and brother Ninan Cuyochi had both died of smallpox a year or so earlier. Huáscar one of his sons had claimed the throne but the arrival of strangers and some unexpected defeats meant that the other son of Huayna Capac, Atahualpa, was now favoured by many generals and a civil war loomed. I was hardly a general but I was summoned along with other chosen Apu so that Quiz-Quiz could discover our allegiances. I had never been consulted before. Both men had the right to be Inca for they were descended from the same man and, ultimately, the sun god.

I knew that I could not change my allegiance from Quiz-Quiz and as he supported Atahualpa, so would I. The war we fought was a disaster for it was fought by the best of the warriors in our empire and being the best meant that it was hard fought. Neither side would give in and that meant the losing side in each battle was massacred. It was down to the best generals. The first battle showed just how bloody it could be. As I led my men I recognised some officers along side whom I had served in my long years of being a soldier. They fought as hard to kill me as I did to kill them. I do not know if it was because I was the better soldier, although I believe I had trained myself well, or simply that Inti wished us to win but as the handful of survivors fled back to Cuzco with Atahualpa's brother, Huáscar, we had won our first victory. I had led my regiment from the front and although it had cost me more than three quarters of my men, it had been seen by both Atahualpa and Quiz-Quiz. As a reward I was promoted and appointed the commander of the bodyguard of Atahualpa who would be, if we succeeded, the new Inca. I had new gold disks fitted to my ears and given a woven breastplate of gold and silver. I had reached as high as I could manage. True I was the inferior of the generals but my task was to guard the emperor and that was the greatest of tasks.

Atahualpa was not afraid of combat and when we went to war against his brother he was at the forefront of every battle. Of course, that meant that the bodyguards I led were there too. They were the best of warriors. Our metal helmets and weapons were the best. I knew how to train men and although we fought in every battle and skirmish we lost fewer men than I had in the first battle. I was learning.

In the end, Quiz-Quiz and his fellow generals prevailed. When Huáscar was defeated, captured and taken for trial, I received my reward from the new Inca; I was made Hatun Apu, the commander of five thousand. I was a general as well as commander of his bodyguard and was given the headdress with the many feathers arched around it. The insignia of the ayllu and my family and clan were honoured. I had reached the top and now I could begin to train more men to fight my way. I knew that I had a sacred duty to protect the emperor. The worry that I had was the strangers who had come to our land. How would we manage to defeat them and their magic? Alarmingly word came that more strangers had been seen. They were not in our lands but beyond

The English Adventurer

the river that marked our northern border. The Inca himself, having heard that I had seen them sent me with one thousand chosen men to leave our land and cross the border. We would visit the land of the Puná. Like the Tumpi they had been recently conquered. We had yet to establish garrisons in their land and that had been the fault of the civil war. Just as the Tumpi had quickly defected to the strangers so the Inca feared that the Puná would too. I had a two-fold mission. Ensure that we did not lose more allies and seek information about the strangers. I had determined to build a pukara as soon as I was able. I would garrison it with half of my men.

Our road system was still very efficient and we reached Atacames quickly. My men still ruled the city and I was thankful that none had been lost in the civil war which had been fought in the heartland and not the borderlands. I took Manco and half the garrison with me and left the weariest members of my new regiment in Atacames. We built rafts and crossed the river. Here there were no roads and we had to hack through the jungle to widen the trail and enable us to reach their settlements. Had we had boats we might have gone directly to their heartland, the Island of Puná, some miles south of Atacames but we had none and while a raft would take us across the river the sea was a different matter. Although the Puná people had their capital many miles away the land through which we passed was where their wealth came from. The rivers yielded emeralds and gold. The fertile land also gave them food. The island was their stronghold but most of them lived on the land just north of Atacames. As soon as I found a village, I set my men to build a pukara while I questioned the headman about the strangers. He was evasive and I did not trust him. I had him executed and then questioned others. I had to execute six of their leaders before I discovered what I wanted to know. There had been no landings but ships had been seen many leagues to the north and the strangers had not only built a port but they had begun to farm. The strangers were coming.

It was then that my mistake came to light. I had cowed the men of Tumbes and Atacames and I thought to do the same here. My executions had, it seemed, made the Puná resentful. Many men left the village and I was forced to use my men to mount a guard on the village to stop more desertions. The Puná I used to help us build the pukara began to sabotage the building and I had to execute more men. Worse, there were attacks on my sentries and morale amongst my men fell to a low ebb. That had never happened before. If the Puná had simply attacked us then I would have defeated them and we could complete our work. As it was, we simply lost more and more men. Added to disease and hunger, three months after we had arrived, I was forced to admit defeat. I burned the village and executed as many villagers as I could and then we made our way back to the river. The Puná warriors were waiting for us all along the trail. We had to fight a running battle through deadly ambushes. We killed more than we lost but that was cold comfort when we reached the rafts. I had lost half of the men I had taken. Many of them had been from my original regiment and they were irreplaceable. Leaving Manco to try to rebuild the morale of my men I left for Kashamarka, the thermal baths where the Inca was now living. It was a long journey of more than five hundred miles but it had to be made. The strangers were getting closer and worse, our grip on the land, thanks to our civil war was slipping.

When I reported to the emperor he was remarkably philosophical about the incident. I deemed it to be a disaster and expected punishment, even death but he saw it as an opportunity to speak to these strangers. He spoke to me, as the commander of his bodyguard, almost as a counsellor, although I knew it was not so, "We have an army, General Paullu, of more than six thousand men. From what you have told me and what we have learned, they have less than five hundred men. Why the bodyguard alone could defeat them. No, we will, when they come, invite them to our heartland, high in the mountains. That will give us time to assess their numbers. We will listen to their words and see if we can make them allies. These tubes that spout fire can be used by us. If I like not the words then we simply slaughter them." He smiled, "You can do that, can you not?"

I bowed, "Inca, give me the word and they shall all die."

"First we shall listen but you know my mind and if we meet them then you know what to do."

The English Adventurer

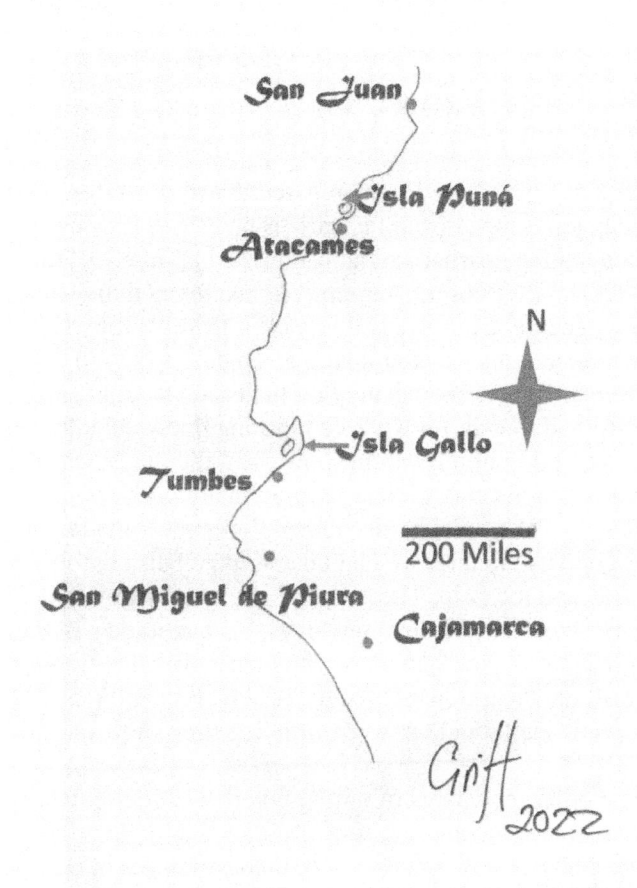

Map showing: San Juan, Isla Puná, Atacames, Isla Gallo, Tumbes, San Miguel de Piura, Cajamarca. Scale: 200 Miles. N compass. Signed Griff 2022.

The English Adventurer
Thomas

Chapter 19

I used the time while the ground was prepared to sail down the coast. I knew the dangers I faced from the natives and I was cautious. Felipillo had proved a quick learner and he had picked up many of the new words used by the natives of this region. We had learned the value of the machete as a trade good and we had plenty of them. While we were protected by hidden guns we would land at suitable sites and wait for the natives to come. By not encroaching on their land we intrigued them. Sometimes we had to wait for a whole morning but eventually, someone would come and Felipillo would show them the machetes and ask what they would trade for them. They brought many goods which, to them, had equal value. We quickly discounted the crudely made pots which were not as good as the ones we had taken on the balsa but we did take the emeralds and the gold. They might have been happy with the trade but we were ecstatic. Within a few days, we had traded all the machetes and I sailed back to our new port with a chest filled with gold and emeralds. Not all the emeralds were of the best quality and many of the pieces of gold were small but they were a tiny fraction of the cost of a machete.

Gonzalo and the other merchants of our company were delighted. We now knew what we needed and I returned to Panama to buy more metal tools and machetes as well as seeds. The land had never been worked and was so fertile that the plant expert thought we might harvest our first crops in a few months. We docked and I had the treasure taken to the house I considered my own. Bartolomé could not believe his eyes when I opened the chest.

"And there is more?"

I nodded, "Instead of marching into their villages armed and ready to fight we simply land and wait for them to come." I patted Felipillo on the shoulder, "Our interpreter here is a marvel. We win them over with the offer of tools. We now know what we need to trade and how much we can expect in return. I fear that soon we will exhaust Panama's supply of tools."

Bartolomé nodded, "Then I will send to Isla Juana for more. It will take time but you can leave the supply of tools to me." He pointed to the chest, "And how is that to be divided?"

The English Adventurer

I had spoken with the others before leaving our new port and we had decided to divide it into twelve. Eleven equal shares for the merchants, Bartolomé, Guido and me and a twelfth for the company. It would provide the funds for Bartolomé to continue to buy trade goods. I told him and he was pleased with the arrangement. We scrupulously divided the treasure into twelve bags and each was named. I gave mine to Isabella while Felipillo took Captain Guido's back to him.

Our new port was a good place to live but it could not compare with my home and after a fine meal, my wife lay in my arms. Francisco had proved to be a good sleeper and we enjoyed a night free from cries. It was as my wife dressed him in the morning that she gave me the news, "And there will be a brother or sister, my husband. Your seed is strong."

I kissed her, "When?"

She laughed, "Not soon, five or six months. I shall need help with the children for I cannot run this house for Don Francisco and two children."

"I gave you the treasure last night. Use it as you will. Pay for servants as you are mistress of my money. There will be more coming. Don Francisco thinks that the land of the Inca is the place we will make our fortune. Your father and I see it closer to home and safer."

When Bartolomé had sent his messenger to order the trade goods we visited the bankers who had come to Panama. They were necessary as they enabled trade with Spain. Instead of sending gold, silver and other treasure to pay for goods we simply paid the bankers and they gave paper which was more easily transported. The paper would be redeemed on Isla Juana. These were the ones who, the king apart, made the greatest profit from this land. The only risk they took was transporting the treasure from Panama to Isla Juana and thence Spain. As there were no more expeditions forthcoming there were many soldiers seeking employment. They were paid well and no gold was lost on land. The sea, as I knew from my time with Captain Pedro, was a different matter. The financial arrangements took a whole day and it was not until a day later that we were able to visit our new ship. **'Infanta Isabella'** was a beautiful little vessel. Intended only to sail down the coast she was fatter and flatter bottomed than **'Infanta Maria'** but she was sturdy and could carry almost as much cargo as her larger consort. We paid Alonso the rest of the money and were told we could sail her the following week.

That gave us a week to buy every tool we could. As soon as we began to buy the prices went up. That was to be expected. I felt sorry for the new colonists who arrived in the city. Unless they had brought

The English Adventurer

tools with them there were none to be had in the city. With the two ships crewed we left Panama a month after I had returned. The new port had grown. I saw that there were balsas tied up. We had begun to attract trade rather than having to seek it. We disgorged our trade goods and, that first evening, I dined with the other leaders and Guido. There was only Bartolomé missing and it was a sort of board meeting. I told them what we had done. I was still new to this and when they all whole heartedly approved every decision I was surprised. García and Domingo agreed with me. Both had been on the Isla del Gallo with Pizarro.

"I cannot believe that we sailed this coast seeking treasure when it was here, right under our noses all the time."

I shook my head, "We know not yet what the world of the Inca holds. Francisco may yet be proved right. I will not abandon him."

Domingo smiled, "You are loyal and I admire that."

García was a clever man, "And we will need that kind of loyalty, Tomas, for when Pizarro returns."

"If he returns."

"Yes, Domingo, if he returns, then the company ships can be used to transport the expedition. Whatever share we get will be divided twelve ways. You can be as loyal as you wish and yet we all profit."

His words made me happy for I still felt that my life and Francisco's were irrevocably bound together. Fate had set me on this course and I would continue to sail it.

Trade was brisk and our profits grew far faster than any of us anticipated. Having spoken to some of the natives further along the coast we negotiated the building of a jetty and the erection of a trading post at two of them. Two of our company left with their families to trade directly with the natives. This was not Diego Almagro's way but it worked. While we saw a financial benefit, we improved the lives of the people who, with metal tools, were able to tame the jungle and increase the land they could farm. What had been subsistence farming now had the potential to provide a surplus that we could trade. As the first year of our enterprise loomed, we all returned to Panama to both celebrate our success and to plan for the future. We had trained natives up to act as foremen and managers of our estates. Some of them even aped our dress and we were flattered.

I returned to a daughter, Maria, named after Bartolomé's wife. It was a double celebration. It was the happiest time of my life. I had everything. A fortnight after our return we had even better news. It came indirectly through a friend who often visited the residence of the governor. Pizarro, it seemed, had met with the king and been rewarded for his boldness. He was given permission to carry on his exploration of

The English Adventurer

the land now known as Peru. Pizarro was officially named the Governor, Captain General, Adelantado and Alguacil Mayor, of New Castile for the distance of two hundred leagues along the newly discovered coast and invested with all authority and prerogatives. We were delighted for him but, even as we celebrated, we heard that Diego Almagro was unhappy not to have been jointly named. I could not see the reason for his attitude. He could have gone with Francisco but he chose not to.

We delayed our return to Puerta Isabella by three days to allow time to debate what we needed to do. We had already ordered another ship from Alonso and now we ordered another. I also suggested that Bartolomé begin to buy every horse he could. Pizarro would need them. I assumed he would bring weapons and men from Spain. My life was filled from dusk until dawn but I had never been happier. It saddened me when I had to leave my family. Isabella suggested that if I thought that the land around Puerta Isabella was safe then I should have a house built and when Francisco returned, she would give up her position as housekeeper. It seemed a good plan to me for the more time I could spend with my family the better.

It was with some relief that we found all well at Puerta Isabella as well as the two trading posts. The natives enjoyed the peace. We heard from the natives that further south, close to the land of the Puná there had been fighting and war. The Inca, they said, were conquering once more. I was still a spy although I could not foresee a time when I would be able to report to Lord Collingwood, I had learned to garner such nuggets of knowledge and store them. It would not affect us directly but when Francisco returned then he would need to know this.

I did not sail south with the ships to trade. Felipillo was more than capable of negotiating the best deal and Captain Guido, with our maps, was able to confidently sail these new waters. My language skills meant I could speak with the natives who lived around Puerta Isabella and I hired enough to clear a large piece of land for my new home. Nothing was wasted. The wood we cut down would be used to build the house and any surplus sold in Panama. The place I picked was on a high piece of ground and had a beautiful view of the sunset. There were also more rocks there. While that made the clearing of the ground harder, it also gave the foundations a more solid base. We had built enough dwellings to have a good idea of what made a fine house. It took a month to clear the land and dig the foundations but it was worth it for I knew that the wooden structure could soon be thrown up. I knew that fine houses in England and Spain had glass in the wind holes but that was a luxury unavailable to us yet. As we began to build, I made larger wind holes

The English Adventurer

that would have the protection of shutters. I also built a veranda and portico. Some of the other merchants expressed surprise for they all had more functional homes.

"I want a home for my family. We will have more children and they will be both comfortable and happy here."

The house was still unfinished when it came time to return to Panama. We had a hold full of treasure and although these waters were safer than the ones on the other side of the isthmus, we would take no chances and our ships sailed together. While Bartolomé organised the sale of the goods, he had learned to become a trader and he did it well, I told my wife all that I had done. She was keen to travel back with me.

Shaking my head I said, "There is much to do. I have another two months of work just to finish it. The roof will be the hardest part. Then we have to furnish it."

It was then that she looked around the room. The furniture she was used to was well made. Francisco had sent to Spain for it. In Panama, the furniture was functional and crude. "We will have to send to Spain for it." I nodded. I could see her mind working as she argued with herself in her head. She shook it as though to clear her thoughts, "We will need to travel to Spain or England for I want the best."

"Spain, then."

She looked surprised. She knew I was English. I had taught her a few words for there were some English phrases which were more appropriate than Spanish ones, "I thought you would have wished to sail to your homeland."

"It has been many years since I lived there and besides, I have to return to Cádiz. When I left there, I had a friend guard my treasure. We will not need to take money back with us for I have a fortune in Spain."

She cuddled me, "I am so lucky to have a husband who can make money so easily. It bodes well for our future."

I only intended to stay in Panama for a month but Francisco returned and with him, his brothers and more conquistadores. He had much to say and this was his house. We vacated all but one room and the four of us endured close company. Bartolomé had bought himself a house so that all of Francisco's guests were accommodated. Whilst I was pleased at his return it brought to the fore thoughts that had been in my head for some time. I no longer wished to be a conquistador. I had been a half-hearted one at best and my family made me now a most reluctant one. I owed it to Francisco to tell him but I knew I would have to pick my moment to do so. He brought with him a clan, his brother Hernando Pizarro as well as two half-brothers from his father, Juan Pizarro and Gonzalo Pizarro and a half-brother from his mother,

The English Adventurer

Francisco Martín de Alcántara as well as his cousin Pedro Pizarro. They were all soldiers and, ominously, Diego Almagro did not join us when Francisco organised the feast. Nicolás de Ribera was there as well as Pedro and Alonso who had accompanied Francisco to Spain. Francisco explained away Diego's absence with a dismissive wave of his hand, "Diego needs to raise more men. I promised King Carlos that I would raise two hundred and fifty men."

I asked, innocently, "And how many do you have?"

He gave me a cheeky grin, "A hundred but there are more here in Panama who will come with us. You will be one will you not, Tomas?"

I was in a most difficult place. I avoided answering directly, "There are many men seeking positions and Bartolomé has been buying horses. I now have more ships. How many do you envisage we shall need?"

He frowned when he realised I had not given him an answer but he went on, "Three ships should suffice. How many horses have you?" He looked over to Bartolomé.

"Twenty-five but I may be able to acquire two more for you."

"Good." I think he thought my reluctance to give an answer was to do with the cost of the expedition for he added, quickly, "And you will be given a large share of the treasure, Tomas."

"Some of those who stayed on Isla del Gallo and I have set up a company. They are our ships but we trust you to be fair in this."

"You know that I shall not be evicting you from this house, Tomas?"

I said, "We need to talk, Francisco. Since you have been away my life has changed."

He nodded, "Tomorrow then."

I did not sleep well and I was up before anyone else. I made my own breakfast and was eating it when Francisco descended. "Food, Francisco?"

He shook his head, "Come let us walk to the harbour while it is still cool and we can speak." I hurried after him, wiping my mouth as I went. He strode purposefully down to the harbour where our three ships were tied up in a line. We went aboard, *'Infanta Maria'* and the night watch gave us the privacy of the forecastle.

He was blunt, "You do not wish to come with us."

"No, Francisco. Isabella and I are building a house along the coast at our new settlement of Puerta Isabella. I need not the treasures of the Incas. I have found my own El Dorado. We have taken it through trade and not by the sword."

The English Adventurer

His eyes pleaded with me, "I need you with me, Tomas. You are my good luck charm and like Pedro and Alonso, your loyalty gives me confidence. Besides, you are now the pilot."

"And I owe you all, Francisco, but we might be away for years and I would miss watching my family grow up."

He pounced on the opportunity and said, "Then give me six months only. I am convinced that will be enough to take this land. We have better warriors and I have a falconet. You could show our men how to use it. I remember that Balboa would not have done what he did in the jungles of the Castillo del Oro without your skill."

I was not sure and doubt filled my face. He had evoked memories of hacking our way through the jungle and hauling the cannon, shot and powder. I had been the only gunner to survive and I did not relish doing so again.

"I need you as a pilot."

I shook my head, "We have good maps and the captains know the waters well."

He said, slyly, "But none as well as you, that is except for Bartolomé. If you will not come then I shall ask him."

I could not allow that. Bartolomé had not been at sea for some time and he might not survive an expedition yet he would feel honour bound to go. "No, Francisco, I will give you six months but I cannot help here with the preparations. I have a house to finish."

He beamed, "Then go and finish your house. You have a month."

It was not enough time but it would have to do.

Isabella was a practical woman and was philosophical about it. "Six months is a long time but not as long as it might have been."

I shook my head, "It is seven months for I need to finish the house."

She beamed, "I will come with you. I have not seen the building and there may be changes I wish to make. Better now than when it is finished, eh?"

I was appalled, "But it is unfinished and the whole settlement is crude. What about the children?"

"If we cannot endure what the head of our family does then it is a poor thing. I am resolved and it will be an adventure."

When she made up her mind there was no arguing with her. She told her women that they would be coming with us and she packed all that we would need. Francisco took it well and told her that there would always be a home for her while I served him.

Guido insisted on giving up his cabin for us and he had the crew on their best behaviour. He regarded my wife as a lady and treated her accordingly. When she saw Puerta Isabella she was impressed. As we

The English Adventurer

tacked our way to the quay she said, "From your words I thought to find mud huts at the edge of the jungle."

She was right, of course. The merchants who had come with us had each built a house for their families and the jungle had been cleared and tamed for more than half a mile inland. There were fields of tobacco and other crops. Even my half-finished mansion looked more impressive than I had thought. We landed and went to the small house I used. It had just three rooms but was comfortable and Isabella was happy.

While they were settling in, I went to the workers toiling away on my house, "Carlos, we have one month to finish it."

His face fell, "Then we will need more men."

It was then that I saw my standing. When they heard the rest of the settlement and the crew of the ship all begged leave to help. The ship's carpenter proved to be invaluable and it was he who supervised the most difficult technical challenge, the roof. Martino was the most unlikely sailor on our ship. He was rotund and far from lithe yet he was one of the most popular amongst the crew. Despite his size he was able to work in the roughest seas and I know that we would not have finished without his help. He even rectified some of the mistakes I had made. Isabella saw, as most women do, flaws in the design and Martino remedied them. When the month was over and we had to return to Panama we had a completed house and Isabella knew exactly what furniture she wanted. It was as we neared Panama that she leaned in and said, "And there will be a third child when you return from this expedition."

The news, welcome though it was, determined that this voyage south, to the land of the Inca, would be my last.

Chapter 20

Diego Almagro did not sail with us when we left Panama aboard our three ships. He stayed to raise more soldiers. There would never be enough soldiers aboard our ships to satisfy Don Diego. We had one hundred and eighty-seven men and twenty seven horses. Sebastián de Belalcázar had thirty men who would not fit on our ship and he would follow when a ship could be hired. We had one falconet and a carriage that would allow us to take it along the Incan roads. Diego and his son would find the rest of the men we needed and we arranged to meet with him at Tumbes. I had ensured that we had plenty of trade goods. We were going armed for war but I knew that trade would yield as much treasure as slaughter. We also had another new member of our expedition, Hernando de Soto, who promised to follow with his one hundred men as soon as the ship he had ordered was finished. I had more confidence that this new conquistador would reach us sooner than Almagro.

I was the pilot and *'Infanta Maria'* was the flagship. Francisco was right, the only man who knew these waters better than me was Bartolomé. My trading experience allowed me to land further south than we had explored and to negotiate with the natives for emeralds and gold. Pizarro was impressed as the natives seemed happy to be given relatively cheap machetes in return for bags of valuable treasure. I think the three ships helped to intimidate them but they would have traded no matter what for word had spread about my ship and, I think, me. We anchored for the night and Pizarro thanked me. "Had Diego been with us then when we landed, he would have been all for conquering these people."

"We do not need to. We could leave men here, Captain General, and make this a port."

He shook his head, "Our destiny lies in the mountains. This treasure is good but as soon as we can I intend to leave the ships and march to meet this Inca. Tumbes is the best place to start as we know there is a road there. We find the road and we will find this mysterious emperor."

We sailed to Tumbes where Francisco hoped to use the Tumpi as allies. It would increase the number of our warriors but when we landed, we saw a town that had been totally destroyed. We went ashore armed to the teeth to try to find out what had happened. I should have had the wit to leave Felipillo aboard the ship but I was not thinking properly. We found the butchered bodies of his mother and sisters, recognisable only by the house and their clothes, amongst a charnel house of a settlement. He was inconsolable and Francisco left him with Pedro and me while he and the others searched for evidence of the perpetrators of this outrage. We gathered the bones of the dead and with Felipillo, buried them. By the time that Francisco sounded the horn for us to return to the ship it was getting on for dark and Pedro and I had to almost drag the interpreter back with us.

Once on the ship I saw the dilemma that faced our leader. He gathered the rest of the principals of the expedition around the main mast. "I think that the Inca did this. From what Tomas has told me they use clubs and axes. The bodies we saw all had evidence of such wounds and they made the place indefensible. We cannot land there but where do we land?"

All eyes were on me and I had an answer. "There is an island to the north of us, Puná. There is no evidence that the Inca have settled there. I believe that there are natives on the island but we can land there and then study the maps to find an alternative landing site. De Soto and Diego will soon follow. Tumbes was not a small place and the army that destroyed it should be approached warily."

He nodded his agreement and we sailed north to the island we had passed many times. I landed on the western side as that was the place that looked to be devoid of people. We disembarked and made a good defensive camp. We cooked hot food and with embedded stakes all around us and armed sentries we slept well. We waited until dawn, when we could scrutinise my maps more closely, before we made any decisions. Francisco, Captain Guido, Felipillo and myself stood at the stern castle and we pondered the map. It was as we did so that we saw a small ship approaching. Too small to be either de Soto or Almagro we deduced that it was Sebastián de Belalcázar whose thirty men could not be accommodated on our three vessels. It was good news and helped us in the formation of our plan.

I pointed at a bay about two hundred miles south of where we were anchored, "As I recall from our first voyage here with Bartolomé we sailed for forty or so miles up a wide river dotted with lakes. It would take us deep into the heartland of this empire." I looked at Felipillo, "Do you know where the Incan capital lies?"

He shook his head but pointed at the huge range of mountains that rose to the west of us. "It is said they live up there as close to the sun god as they can. I know that my father said that visitors from the coast found it hard to breathe up there."

As Sebastián de Belalcázar and his ship moored next to us the lookout on the top of the mast shouted, "Captain! There are armed natives and they are racing to the camp."

The English Adventurer

Francisco was ever decisive and he shouted to de Belalcázar, "Arm and land your men. We have a battle to fight." Cupping his hands he bellowed, "To arms! To arms!"

Pausing only to don my morion and grab my harquebus I followed Francisco down the ladder and into the waiting boat. By the time we reached the camp Pedro and Alfonso had organised the men. I smiled, Pizarro might have brought his brother and half-brothers to help in the fight but it was the old hands who took charge. I stood with Pedro and the other harquebusiers. We were flanked by crossbowmen. The horses still grazed and I know that Pizarro was annoyed that he could not use them. As de Belalcázar's men joined us my regret was that the falconet was still aboard the ship. The natives were of the Puná tribe and we knew them to be fierce and wild. The fact that we had seen no Incan forts in their land was a testament to the fact that the Incas had not truly defeated them. They raced at our lines with clubs, spears and stone edged swords.

I was still the master gunner and the other harquebusiers awaited my order to fire. We would only manage one volley and then we would have to draw swords. I needed to time it so that we punched a hole in their line the width of our ten harquebuses. The crossbowmen had no such restriction. Their weapons had a longer range and could be reloaded more quickly. They began to thin the ranks of the natives and forced more of them into the middle of their attack. When I shouted, "Fire!" the warriors were less than thirty paces from us. The ten harquebuses threw their lead shot at the natives and smashed through flesh, bone and bodies. They tore through the second and third ranks. As we dropped our weapons and drew our swords we saw, as the smoke cleared, that pieces of bone had added to the destructive power of the volley. It was not just ten men that we had felled but more like twenty or so. It made those following slow and that gave time for the crossbows to send another two showers of bolts and then the natives were upon us.

I wore no breastplate but the weapons used by the natives, clubs and swords and axes tipped with stone, would cause more serious wounds if struck at the head. It meant that, as we slashed and stabbed with daggers and swords at bodies lacking armour, we cause terrible and mortal wounds while the odd blow from a club or axe hit our morions and did little harm. Even so it was a frightening battle and brought back memories of Tenochtitlán. It was Captain Guido leading the four crews that swung the battle in our favour. They charged the flank of the warriors using boarding pikes and axes to great effect. The surviving natives fled. It was then that Francisco ordered the cavalry to mount and

The English Adventurer

with their lances pursue and destroy the natives. He was angry and wanted them punished. The look he gave me suggested that he blamed me for landing on this island. Whatever the reason he did not speak to me again until evening when the weary horsemen returned with the news that the only ones who had survived the flight were now in their village.

Pizarro came to me, "If we are to endure battle I would rather it was with an enemy who wears gold. We will tend to the wounded and then sail to the bay you identified when you and Pilot Ruiz returned the last time." The bay had offered the best prospect of sailing deep into the land for we saw it was closer to the mountains. We had not sailed far the first time but we had discovered a series of lakes and that had appealed to Pizarro.

"And de Soto?"

"I will leave de Belalcázar here and he can guide any other ships that follow us. Make a copy of your map for him and he can follow."

I nodded for gone were the days when my maps were a jealously guarded treasure. I had copies for I knew that if I ever returned to Spain then Lord Collingwood would need them.

We had lost five men in the battle. Had this been on the last expedition then it would have been a disaster but although a loss it would not impair our ability. As we prepared to sail Francisco said, "We will need you and the falconet when we next face an enemy. Along with the harquebuses we have a frightening weapon."

It took time to load the horses and for the fleet to leave the island and it was as we did so that we spied a sail. It had to be de Soto and so de Belalcázar was ordered to raise his anchor and join us. We now had a fleet of five ships and more than two hundred and fifty men. We did not know it until we reached land but de Soto also had horses. We would have forty horses and I had seen the effect when our handful had dispersed a whole warband.

Sailing one ship up the river had not been hard but sailing five was more difficult. When Bartolomé and I had visited the last time, we had not landed, now we were looking for a place which we could use as a base. At first it was easy for the lakes made it as easy as sailing the sea, easier for there were no waves. Sometimes the wind did not help and we had to have men disembark and pull us along. It was when the river narrowed to sixty paces that we finally halted. The ship brought by de Belalcázar was the smallest of our ships and the one that Pizarro was happy to risk. We anchored at the end of the last big lake and disembarked. The falconet and one of those I had salvaged were moved to *'Sunrise'*, de Belalcázar's ship. While de Soto's ship would return to

The English Adventurer

Panama to bring Almagro, the other three would wait on the lake and build a defensive camp. Pizarro and the army would march along the river and we would sail up the river. Anticipating adverse winds I had the men cut down branches that we carved into sweeps. We would row if we had to. As we sailed up the river my eyes were drawn to the mountains. They seemed much bigger now that we were closer. I climbed up the mast to afford a better look and saw that while there were trees and forests the tops of the mountains looked to be bare.

That first day we made twenty miles. Felipillo was with Pizarro and he and Pedro were being used as scouts. As we prepared to leave the next morning they returned with the news that they had found a suitable site for a camp. A road passed close to the river and was evidence that the Inca warriors were here. It was a well-made road and not the tracks used by the natives.

Pizarro was delighted with the site and we set about building a camp. The falconets were landed and I had the carpenter of *'Sunrise'* make a carriage for my salvaged falconet. I had to leave him to it as I was needed, along with Felipillo to speak to the natives who had a village close to the road. They were wary but my smile and the offer to trade machetes put them at their ease. After the trade Pizarro told them, through Felipillo, that we were now the masters of this land. They would not be taxed, as such but any surplus that they had would be traded with us. To ensure compliance he had a good captain from our other expedition, Antonio Navarro, and fifty men build a fort and a dock. This would be our first settlement south of Puerta Isabella and Pizarro named it San Miguel de Piura.

We spent a week exploring the area and trading with other natives. We rode horses and that terrified the natives. The Inca people had seemed god-like to them but we, wearing breastplates and morions and riding fantastical beasts they had never seen ensured that they would obey us. We learned that the emperor of this land was called Atahualpa and that he was to be found, the native who told us this, waved a vague arm towards the road heading south and said, "Many days from here."

That decided Pizarro. He divided his forces up, using de Soto as a vanguard. I think Pedro and Alfonso would have relished that role but Francisco wanted his two best warriors with him. Nor was I given a choice. I was the gunner and he needed me and my two falconets. So valuable were they to his plans that he had some natives use their lamas to drag them. It reminded me of the jungles of Panama and Balboa. I resigned myself to the task. I had promised him six months and already one month had passed. I had gathered much treasure but that was of less importance than my survival. We marched along the Incan road and I marvelled at their engineering skills for the road was the equal of any I had seen in England and in Spain, in many ways it was better. I stayed with my two cannons and the men I had been allocated as gunners. Pedro and the harquebusier also marched with us and it meant I saw little of Felipillo. He was at the fore with Pizarro and his brothers.

The horses were what made it an easy journey. There was no opposition and we did not have to fight. The Inca had cleared all the undergrowth close to the road and ambush was impossible. When we stopped, we were fed by terrified natives and it was more like a royal progress than a journey through a dangerous and unknown land.

De Soto was sent, after a week on the road, to deal with a garrison the natives had told us lay ahead. They told us it was a small one and de Soto was confident that he had enough men and horses to deal with it. We waited in the town we had found. Felipillo said it was called Zaran. It was a prosperous place and we took much treasure from it. The horses enjoyed the rest and I wondered if I might get home sooner than the six months.

It was a week later that de Soto returned and this time he was not alone. There was an Incan envoy and with them lamas loaded with gifts from the emperor. He invited us to meet with him, as his guests at a place called Cajamarca. That was the goods news. The bad news was that it was almost two hundred miles away. There was more bad news for the wise Nicolás de Ribera had suffered an injury. He had slipped when dismounting his horse and the priests who were with us bound his leg and told him to rest. He would stay in the village with six men while we headed for the meeting. I feared a trap but Pizarro was in an ebullient mood and we set off the next day, having sent the treasure back to San Miguel. We had just one hundred and eighty men and I did not think that it would be enough. For once I missed Almagro. He might have already joined Navarro at San Miguel.

We no longer enjoyed the advice and company of Juan de Salcedo or Hernando de Luque. Instead we had a Dominican Friar with us, Vincente de Valverde. He was a larger than life character in every way and he always insisted on marching at the fore before even Pizarro's brothers. There had been a time when I would have been at the fore but now I was happy to be with my two guns at the back with the harquebusiers and the marching men. We were among new men now. Pedro, Alfonso and I were the only ones left from the first two expeditions. As we climbed higher and higher into the rarified air of the increasingly high mountains they asked us about the early expeditions and also why we were not rich lords living back in Spain.

The English Adventurer

Pedro snorted his answer, "We found treasure but not enough for us to retire." He nodded to me, "Tomas, here, the English gunner has the right idea. While we gathered men to seek treasure, he simply traded for it." He winked; he was teasing me but I knew that there was no malice behind his words. "Tell them, Tomas, could you retire to Spain if you wished?"

"I could."

One of the younger soldiers asked incredulously, "Then why risk coming?"

I liked Miguel. He lacked a breastplate and his sword and shield were hand me downs but I saw myself in the earnest young man, "Because, Miguel, the Captain General asked me and I am his friend. He likes the way I use my guns."

The road was dotted with their fortresses. Word must have been passed to them for we were allowed to pass but would we be allowed to escape? A few miles from Cajamarca we passed a huge encampment. It was the whole Incan army. It was impossible to count them all but I estimated that there were more than fifty thousand warriors. We were trapped and I wondered if that had been part of the Incan plan all along.

As we neared the town of Cajamarca the scale of the power of this empire could be clearly seen. Like the Aztecs they had well-made homes. Some of them were three stories high. People were well dressed and well fed. This was a prosperous land and people. As with Tenochtitlán there were armed warriors everywhere. I deduced that was not normal but was intended to intimidate us. In my case it worked. We had entered the lair of the emperor and they could shut the door behind us any time they wished. This could all be an elaborate trap and when we slept they would fall upon us and butcher us. I resolved, as we made a camp just outside the town, that if I survived, I would beg permission of Pizarro to return home. My family were more important than a place in posterity. Pizarro placed guards around the camp and held a council of war. I was not invited. The Dominican friar, his brothers along with Pedro and de Soto were summoned but I was not. I was not insulted for in my mind I had already resigned from the expedition. What did concern me was that I was not there and knew not the plans.

Felipillo was not needed at the council and he came to eat his meal with me. We were still close. He shook his head, "I see these warriors, Captain Tomas, and I just wish to kill them. They slaughtered my family, my friends, everyone I knew and for what? They are an evil people."

The English Adventurer

I shook my head, "What they did was inexcusable, Felipillo. but I do understand why they did what they did. They feared us. You saw and heard our guns, what did you think?"

"That they were a magic weapon sent by the gods."

"And to a people who live so close to the skies that they believe they can almost touch the sun god that is a threat to everything that they believe."

"Will there be a battle?"

"I know not but if there is then get behind my guns and the harquebuses. It is there that you will have the best chance to survive."

Pedro, of course, told me Pizarro's plans. He was not being disloyal but he trusted me. He shook his head, "Our captain is a bold one. If you thought that Diego was reckless then you have not met Francisco's brothers. They have a bold plan. Tomorrow Emperor Atahualpa will enter the city with his army and the Captain General intends to have Vincente de Valverde convert him. Once that is done then we will hold the emperor and protect him from his own people."

This seemed to me to be like Tenochtitlán all over again. That time I had barely escaped with my life.

Before I turned in, I was visited by Francisco, "Tomas, a word." He led me away from my men. "I am sorry you were not invited to our council of war but I know that your heart is not in this." I could not lie to an old friend and I nodded. "Nonetheless I need you to be our master gunner tomorrow. Until they belch fire your falconets and the harquebuses appear harmless to these people. They will allow us to take them into their city, of that I am certain, but to make sure that they do you and your weapons will be flanked by the cavalry. If all goes well then you will not be needed but you must be prepared. I want your weapons to be able to clear the plaza where the meeting will be held." His eyes held mine, "When I give the command then you will obey."

"I will but when this is over and not at the end of my terms of enlistment I would go home."

He looked incredulous, "You would give up the chance to conquer an empire that is bigger than any since the time of the Romans?"

"You have no family and I do."

Satisfied with an understandable answer, he nodded, "When we have won then you can go."

I knew what I had to do. I would not enjoy it but if I wanted to get home to my family then I would have to. I would kill as many as I could. If I did not then it would be me who died.

The English Adventurer
Chapter 21

The main road into the city was a wide one and we were easily accommodated between the two lines of horsemen. As we marched in, I saw the buildings rising above the morions of the horsemen and I shuddered for this was the land of the Aztecs all over again. I could hear the murmur of the crowds as we passed into the heart of the city. It was a buzz of wonderment. We were silent for we were few in number but the thousands who watched us babbled as we passed.

There was a large plaza in the centre and that was clearly where the meeting with the emperor would take place. There was a large building at the end and Hernando Pizarro rode up to me and said, "Conceal your weapons in that building. There is cover for you and your weapons will have a field of fire across the whole of the plaza."

I had given my word and I nodded. Concealed by the cavalry we quickly moved the two falconets and harquebuses into the shelter of the porticoed building. It was some sort of ceremonial building, perhaps a temple, for it rose with successively smaller floors for five stories. It was impressive. I wasted no time and had the falconets loaded. As much as I did not wish to do what I knew I would have to, there was no point in being half-hearted. Even with loaded guns I doubted that we could stem the force of an attack if fifty thousand warriors rushed at us. I loaded a ball and bags of stones into each gun. Pedro organised the harquebusiers and we lit enough linstocks to be able to keep up a rapid rate of fire. Sometimes the fuze on the harquebus could go out if not tended well and in the heat of battle that was easy to do. That done Pedro and I went to view the plaza. The cavalry had moved to one side while the pikemen and foot soldiers had gone to the other. Like us, both had taken shelter beneath the porticoed building. The natives knew where we were but our numbers were disguised. Pizarro, his brothers and the priest were before the cavalry holding the banners we had brought.

It took hours for the richly adorned procession to enter and fill the plaza. There were clearly regiments who were the emperor's personal guards. I saw one leader with huge golden discs in his ears and a fantastic, feathered helmet. As he turned to stand, like a rock before his men I saw him scan the horsemen and then his eyes moved across to me. He stared and I realised that this was the warrior I had seen on the beach at Tumbes for he had piercing eyes. I prayed that Felipillo did not recognise him. The youth was just angry enough to try to take vengeance into his own hands. The warrior's eyes continued moving as he took in the foot soldiers. As with our guns more than half were hidden in the building. To the Incas it would appear that our most potent force would be the horsemen and there were just sixty odd of them although the bulk of them were hidden from view. I saw the emperor approach. He was on a litter carried by a dozen bearers and he was glistening with the gold upon his head and body, not to mention the litter itself. This was El Dorado. The litter was a huge one but they carried it easily and in perfect time. He was protected by over five thousand guards. I had worried that he might bring his whole army into the city but that was patently impossible. Even so there had to be at least eight thousand guards for more were tramping behind the personal bodyguard of five thousand men.

Pedro and I moved away from the building to help disguise the hidden guns and, I confess, to watch this mighty emperor approach. I hoped that Francisco knew what he was doing. Felipillo was also with Pizarro and it would be his words that the emperor would hear. The emperor stopped but did not descend from his lofty perch. I was close enough to hear the words spoken by Fray Vincente de Valverde who bellowed them as though giving a sermon in the cathedral at Panama and then translated by Felipillo. The priest announced himself as the emissary of God and the Spanish throne and demanded that the emperor accept Catholicism as his faith and Charles V, the Holy Roman Emperor as his sovereign ruler. After his words were translated, he handed a Bible to the Emperor. The man looked bemused. He opened it, sniffed it and then hurled it to the ground. I had been expecting something to happen but even I was shocked as Pizarro shouted, "Attack! Tomas, open fire!"

I ran back to the guns, shouting, "Roll out the guns!"

I heard horns and hooves as the cavalry charged the litter. Fray Vincente de Valverde and Felipillo ran to take shelter behind the guns. As the two falconets were rolled out, Pedro and his harquebusiers levelled their weapons. He was waiting for my order to fire. We had the guns aimed at the bulk of the warriors, the emperor's guards. I saw the cavalry hacking at the hands and arms of the litter bearers to make them drop the litter. Amazingly they held it up with the bloody stumps of their limbs.

"Now!" I touched the linstock to the two falconets in turn. They and the harquebuses fired. Whilst not as one it was close enough to sweep through the ranks of those trying to save their emperor. We reloaded in a pall of smoke and saw nothing. We had to trust on our skills at reloading. The guns had been aimed appropriately and I fired them again. We kept firing without knowing for certain whom we had struck

The English Adventurer

What we did know was that we were hitting someone for there were screams and cries. More importantly, no fierce warriors wielding clubs and axes came close to us. Although we rammed a damp swab down the barrel between each firing I knew that we had to swab out the guns with soaked swabs or risk a charge exploding prematurely. The harquebuses also needed to be cleaned out. We stopped. The gun crews quickly swabbed out the guns that hissed as they did so and as the smoke began to clear we saw the writhing bodies. The emperor was now held by Pizarro and his brother. The cavalrymen were repeatedly charging the Incas who had no defence against their lances. The pikes to our left were keeping the Incas there at bay but to our fore, the feathered leader I had seen at Tumbes spied me and shouting something led a hundred of his men to race over the bodies of their dying comrades. I am not sure he recognised me but he knew the threat the falconets and harquebuses represented.

"Load!" It was a race and the emperor's guards were desperate to close with us. We had just loaded and I had touched the linstock to the first falconet when they reached to within five paces of us. One falconet fired and then the second but four of the Incas, including the feathered leader, had survived. Swinging his axe he smashed in the head of one of my gunners and I stepped back to draw my sword and dagger. Behind me, I heard the friar intoning prayers. Felipillo was there and I could not allow the last of his family to fall this day.

The feathered leader was a powerful man and he swung his axe down at my head. I was wearing my breastplate as well as my morion but I could not allow the weapon to strike me. I still had a fear of poisoned weapons. I made a cross with my dagger and sword. They held the axe. I was fighting for my life and so, as our bodies closed with one another I brought my knee up between his legs. I hurt him but he did not fall back, indeed he barely registered a blow that had felled men before and so I headbutted him. The tip of the morion drove into his eye and that did make him reel. As he did, I slashed with my sword. He had a gold encrusted piece of material hanging from his neck and that saved his life for while I did cut him, it was not deep. I lunged with my dagger before he could raise his axe once more. Although he managed to block the strike with his axe shaft my blade ripped into his arm. I heard a double boom as the two falconets were fired again and I saw Felipillo with the linstock. For some reason that inspired me and instead of pulling back my dagger I slashed it sideways. This time it tore away the gold-encrusted cloth and I punched with the hilt of my sword at his other eye. It was not honourable but I was fighting for my life. As his head moved backward I drove my sword up and through his body. He slid, lifeless from my blade and I ran to the guns but there was no need. It was all over. The handful of warriors who had survived the slaughter were being charged by cavalry and swordsmen.

I smiled at Felipillo, "Well done, Felipillo."

He nodded seriously and then taking a dagger went and cut the gold from the lobes of the helmeted leader I had just slain. "He may not have been the one to kill my family but he will do." He held the two gold discs to me.

I shook my head, "Take them, Felipillo."

What surprised me was that the army outside the city, more than forty thousand of them, made no attempt to fight us. In fact they remained in their camp. Pizarro worked out that all the generals and the leaders had been in the plaza and we had massacred them. We were able to identify them by the huge golden discs in their ears. The gold was taken as was all the gold they wore. The cost to us was one wounded man. The guns, pikes and horses had won the day and the empire for us.

Emperor Atahualpa, as well as his senior officials were taken prisoner. Pizarro was keen to keep the emperor alive for he wanted no rival to rouse the army and to fight us. He told the emperor that he should fill a room twenty two feet by seventeen feet with gold and silver as surety for his life. It took many days to do so by which time we became increasingly convinced that we would not be attacked. With our guns covering the plaza, so long as we held the centre of the city then the army could not attack. Felipillo discovered that the Incas did not like to attack at night and so it it was only when the sun rose that there was a threat. When Nicolás de Ribera and his escort made it safely to the city then we knew we had won.

A week after Nicolás arrived I went to Pizarro and his brothers. "You no longer need me, Captain General. Let me go home."

Hernando and his brothers shook their heads, "You are a fool, Englishman. We have barely scraped the tip of the treasure this land holds. If you leave then any future treasure will be ours and not yours."

Francisco smiled, "Hernando, you do not know this man. I would not be here but for him and even if he is not here then I will give him his share of the treasure we take. The majority of the ships that brought us here are his." He turned to me, "I am sorry to see you leave but I know that Isabella and your family are your treasure. I envy you that. I beg of you to wait a week for I wish to send some of the treasure back to Panama with you. I need more men. Would you do that for me? I need someone I can trust to take back King Carlos' gold and you have always been the most loyal of men."

The English Adventurer

I could not refuse him and it was only a week. In the end it grew to be three weeks for we had to train men to lead the lamas. Pizarro was loath to lose his horses and until reinforcements arrived, he was sitting on a powder keg. So long as the emperor was alive and the people feared his execution then all would be well. The delay gave me the time to take back treasures that were not gold. They had fine textiles and ceramics. They would serve in my new home. I was also able to say goodbye to the friends I had made. Felipillo, Pedro, Alfonso, and Nicolás de Ribera, were as close to me as had been the crew of the **'Golden Hawk'**.

On the day I left, with the fifteen men and string of one hundred lamas, Pizarro came to me with a parchment, "Here is a gift for you and your family. It is the deeds of my house in Panama. The friar has signed it. I shall not need it for this Peru will be my home from now on. I know not if I will ever see you again, I doubt it, but you should know that I value you as one of my closest and dearest friends. You are the master gunner and the English adventurer without whom none of this would be possible."

"And it had been an honour to serve you, Captain General."

I left and felt sad. I knew that none would ever remember my name for even as I was leaving I saw the influence his brothers had. They did not know me and no matter what Francisco said I would be expunged from any record. This would be the Pizarro family's victory. I did not mind. Anonymity suited me. I would never see the great man again but I was privileged to have known him.

It took a long time to reach San Miguel but we did so safely. My language skills enabled me to negotiate for food and shelter along the way. It was at San Miguel that I met with Diego Almagro. He had with him one hundred and fifty men and fifty horses. Pizarro would have his reinforcements. **'Infanta Maria'** had been one of the ships that brought Almagro and I left Captain Guido to load it while I spent half a day telling my former comrade, Diego, about the victory. Even he was astounded by the level of victory. The treasure being loaded, being a drop in the ocean, told him I spoke the truth.

Like Hernando Pizarro he could not believe that I was leaving. "You have endured more than most and you would leave now? Strange. You English puzzle me."

I smiled, "As did you Spanish when first I met you. If you would take advice from a strange Englishman, I would use some of the men I brought to fortify somewhere on the way back to Cajamarca. We reached here safely but who knows?"

The English Adventurer

He smiled, "And you always had sense. You were, perhaps, too soft but your mind as sharp as any."

I bade farewell to the men I had led from the mountains and boarded my ship. I was leaving Peru and it was without any regret.

It was a month later that we pulled into Puerta Isabella. The house was finished and crudely furnished while Isabella was close to her time. She thought that the babe would come within a week or two and so we decided to head back to Panama. The baby was born a fortnight later and he was a healthy boy with a fine set of lungs on him. We named him John after my father. The birth, however, was not an easy one and Isabella was bedridden for two months. Had I not delayed in Cajamarca then she would have had longer in Panama. I swore I would never leave her side again.

The company's share of the treasure taken and after I had delivered King Charles' share to the governor, the rest was lodged with Pizarro's bankers. That done I felt relieved. I could finally get on with my life. I was so rich now that I could have retired to England but I liked this land. We received regular news from Peru as it was still the company ships that were used to sail to San Miguel and back. When Pedro de Candia stepped off the boat one morning I was surprised. He shook his head, "I bring sad news, Tomas, against Francisco's wishes the Emperor of the Incas was garrotted. It was all those around the Captain General who demanded it and now they will have to fight the Incan army. They will win but it is needless. I will return to Spain and live the life of a gentleman."

He stayed for a month and in that time, I watched him change from the hardened warrior I had always known. Being around my children softened him, somehow. When he left, however, to take the road north he hired good soldiers to guard him and his not inconsiderable treasure and he too was well armed. He smiled as we clasped arms and he mounted the donkey that was the best form of travel for the road. "But when I am in Spain, Tomas, this sword, breastplate and morion will hang in my fine hall."

"And do not forget, Pedro, better to wait for one of the ships I spoke of. They are well armed and you are less likely to have to endure pirates."

I was unwilling to leave Isabella so that when the next meeting of the company took place, it was in my house. I had barely been at Puerta Isabella for more than a year but none begrudged me the time away for, thanks to me, the gold taken in Peru was twenty times the company profits. We were all rich men and it was decided that we needed to hire men to run our business. I left that to others like Gonzalo and García.

The English Adventurer

They were men who would ensure that we were not robbed and those who toiled for us were treated well. Already the tobacco we grew, along with the other produce, was being shipped, not to Isla Juana but to Spain, France and even England. There was a great demand for them. While King Henry and King Charles were allies there would be no difficulties.

The next news we had from Peru, almost eight months after I returned was that the whole Incan Empire was now ruled by Pizarro. He had a capital city high in the mountains but the merchant who brought us the news told me that the Captain General planned on building a new capital by the coast and that made sense for the journey to the mountains was hard. He had also kept his word and the merchant brought my share of the treasure. This was mine and not the company's. We had enough to furnish the new house in Puerta Isabella ten times over.

We waited six months to make the arduous journey back to Spain and purchase what we would need for the house that would be our mansion. Even John was old enough to travel now and Isabella had fully recovered but the doctors had told us that there would be no more children. I anticipated recovering my treasure from Lord Collingwood's but I had to be practical. Who knew what might have happened over the years? Accordingly I took a chest with gold within and I hired men to guard us on the road north. It had been improved since last I had travelled it and there were inns, as well as forts along the way. Even so it was still an adventure for the children.

We had to wait a month for a ship home. The ships I wished to use belonged to my old friend, Captain Pedro. It was with some relief that I saw the **'Silver Swan'** hove into view with four smaller ships behind. Commodore Phillip did not recognise me at first. I now had flecks of grey in my beard and I had filled out, "Is that blank look of suspicion any way to treat an old ship mate?"

He recognised my voice, "It is Tomas, the Englishman who likes adventure so much. Come aboard. We are here to pick up the Peruvian treasure. The governor wanted it all collecting and then sailed back in my fleet. We are the strongest and best armed in these seas."

That explained much. We had seen the huge warehouse surrounded by ten armed guards. They were there night and day. King Charles was taking no chances with his reward from Pizarro.

I told the commodore about my family and what we needed. Commodore Phillip was quite happy to give us passage back to Cádiz and he refused to take payment. Since he had been wounded and I had saved his ship the commodore would do anything for me. "Without you

The English Adventurer

there would be no fleet. Captain Pedro has told all of his captains that he will take no money for the passage of the English Gunner."

"When do you sail?"

"It will take a week, at least and the loading will be more than messy. I would not have your family come aboard while we load the ship. I will send to you when we are ready to sail. It will be a week."

As we left his cabin, I heard a voice I had not heard for some time, "Captain Tomas, you are still alive! God has answered my prayers."

I saw Alessandro who had been a ship's boy but was now a muscled man. Commodore Phillip said, "Alessandro is now master gunner on this ship."

I clasped Alessandro's arm, "Then we are in safe hands. We will have time to speak when I board. For now I need to buy goods that I can trade."

The commodore looked surprised, "A conquistador who trades?"

I nodded, "And I made more treasure by being a trader and hiring out my ships than ever I did firing a gun." I made arrangements for the machetes and tools that were in Nombre de Dios to be sent to Puerta Isabella. I would buy more in Spain but the company needed trade goods now. Word came that we would be able to board the next day and I made sure that we had the finest of meals. I knew that it would be cold fare for the voyage east.

As we boarded the heavily laden and, I was pleased to see, heavily armed flagship, I began to tell my eldest two children what to expect. This was a real adventure for them. When they had sailed from Puerta Isabella we had not left sight of the coast. Once we left the ring of outer islands, we would see nothing until we reached the islands close to Portugal and Spain. I did not recognise any of the smaller ships but I was able to tell them of the features of them. I identified the guns aboard the ships. The flagship now had sakers, ten of them, five on each side. With swivel guns on the forecastle and aft castle we would be a large morsel for a pirate to take. The smaller ships had robinets and falconets. With just four guns on each side they were more vulnerable but when I had spoken to Alessandro, he told me that they used the same methods and ideas that I had outlined and they worked. The ships had been rarely attacked but on the odd occasion that some pirate had risked all they had been easily beaten and in one case, sunk. He had told me of the others who had served with me, all those years ago. Guido and Carlos had made enough in their first year as Master Gunners to retire and both lived on Isla Juana. Juan and Jesus were gunners on two other ships but they were being refitted in Spain. I was pleased that they

The English Adventurer

had all done well and took pride that I had trained them and, more importantly, that they had survived.

The first part of the voyage took us through blue seas and islands now showing the hand of civilisation. There were stone ports and substantial houses where there had once been wooden huts and crude jetties. Heavily laden ships plied the seas carrying cargo. The Castillo de Oro was no longer the only source of treasure and, as I had seen when we had waited for Commodore Phillip, the sea teemed with ships. My family soon tired of what, at first, was a novelty. After a stroll around the deck for fresh air Isabella would take them to the airy cabin we had been given while I stayed on deck for I relished watching the sea and the ships. Once we passed the outer rim of islands, we saw fewer sails and when we met other ships, usually westbound, they, like us were travelling in convoys. What I noticed was how many more ships were to the north of us. As gunner Alessandro had no sea duties I was able to talk to him freely and I asked him where they were bound.

"Florida. King Carlos does not seem interested in the place. It has yielded little in the way of gold. Don Alphonso del Albuera has made it like his own kingdom and he does what he likes. It is said he has the natives growing tobacco for we often see ships heading east laden with leaf but it is rumoured that he is behind the pirates."

I suddenly remembered the name, "Of course. We had dealings with him. I think he was behind the rebellion along the Castilla del Oro all those years ago."

"Yes, captain, he is a pirate although he has a title and is said to be of the nobility. He is a cruel man. None survive the ships he takes. We only know of his work when a ship disappears. At first, we put it down to the storms and the seas but now we know the reality. Any ships sailing north of us are either to be feared for they are pirates or they are friends of the pirates."

"None of our ships…"

He smiled, "No, for Commodore Phillips uses your tactics. Our four consorts will flank our stern if danger threatens and they know his signals. Captain Pedro had them written out. We also sail well south of the Floridian waters. Do not fear, Captain Thomas, we will get you and your family safely home."

"And you? Do you have a family?" He had already told me that Juan and Jesus had families and were happily settled, like Guido and Carlos on Isla Juana.

"It did no harm for you to wait to raise your family. I am a patient man. I am well paid and I waste not my money. My chest in in my cabin in the forecastle and it grows with each voyage. This one sees us

The English Adventurer

carrying the greatest treasure thus far and I will make many gold coins. Another two such voyages and I can buy land and become rich from the crops. The others were happy to buy small farms that need little work. I do not blame them but I would be as you, Captain Tomas."

I now saw why the commodore was so concerned about this voyage. It might be his last voyage too. A sailor had only so much luck as Captain Pedro had realised. The wise ones quit the sea while they could.

It was the sail I spied to the south of us that worried me. I had seen it when I had been speaking with Alessandro. It was heading west as were we and I wondered if it was staying close for protection. The next day it was still there and it did not seem to want to close. If it was a trader then it would be able to sail far faster than five galleons laden with gold. I owed my old shipmates too much to remain silent. I went to the commodore and told him my suspicions.

He was a wise old bird and he nodded, "I have seen her too." Smiling he added, "You have not lost your acute sense of danger. It could be harmless but we will be prepared. Gunner, have ball, shot and powder fetched on deck. If nothing else we can give you a show of our gunnery."

I shook my head, "You need waste no powder on my account."

Alessandro had barely loaded his guns when the lookout shouted, "Ships, on the larboard quarter. They fly before the wind and there are six of them."

I hauled myself up on to the gunwale holding on to a backstay, I used my hand to shade my eyes. They were not merchants. These had to be pirates and were coming in numbers. They were smaller than we were but looked like greyhounds straining at the leash. Their course, with the following wind, would take them across our bows. With no guns to defend us there they could rake us and take down masts and rigging. Incapacitated we would be easy victims for them. I turned and shouted, "Pirates." I saw the commodore nod. I pointed to the sole ship that had dogged us. She was bigger than the other six. "That one stops us fleeing south and must be the leader orchestrating the moves of the others."

I jumped down and went to our cabin. I had my chest and I had brought my morion and breastplate, I intended to sell them in Spain for I thought I would never need them. The men who came to seek their fortune in New Spain would not have the coin to spend. I spoke calmly to my wife, "Isabella, close the shutters and you and the children make a den of the chests." Her eyes widened. I smiled and said, "They are

The English Adventurer

pirates and seek to take us. They will not. This is the strongest part of the ship. Make it a game."

As I strapped on my sword and dagger Francisco said, "Can I come with you and see?"

I shook my head and handed him a spare dirk, "You stay here and protect your mother, brother and sister." He nodded seriously and I saw Isabella's smile of thanks as she began to drag the chests into position. I helped her make the fort in the cabin and then went out on deck. I saw that the six ships had shortened sail and were now in two lines. We had shortened sail. Commodore Phillips knew the futility of trying to outrun pirates in heavily laden gold ships.

I went to the sterncastle. The commodore said, "They want the gold and that means they will try to dismast us." He pointed to the ship on our starboard side, "That one will hope to divide our fire. If Alessandro takes command of the larboard batteries, could you take charge of the starboard?"

I had not commanded such a battery since we had reduced the walls of the fortress when serving with Diego Columbus but a gunner never forgot. "Of course."

I went to the guns and said, "I will command the guns, I am Captain Thomas…"

One of the gunners grinned and said, "Aye we know. You are the English Gunner. Command us, captain, and we shall win."

I pointed to the ship ahead, the pirate leader. She was already positioning herself to start her run and cross our bows. If we tried to turn then the other pirates would be able to turn and to rake our sterns. "That one is our target. She seeks to hit our masts and her shots will fly high. We will aim at her waistline. Some shots will hit the guns while others will hole her. I will aim the guns and all I ask is that you swab out well and load quickly!"

They cheered and I was heartened. They had already loaded the sakers. Until the pirate closed then the swivel guns would be of little use. The saker fired a heavier ball than the falcon. Captain Pedro had bought guns from the royal foundry. I recognised the maker's mark. They would fire true. Alessandro had purchased shot holders, called a monkey, for the ball and I switched the balls around so that the roundest balls were on the top. That done I took the lighted linstock from the ship's boy and watched the pirate. She was waiting. I turned and saw that our taking in of the sails had confused the other six and they had overshot us. They had a choice, they could either take in sail and then turn to take our sterns or continue ahead and try to cross our bows.

The English Adventurer

The commodore must have been reading my mind and he shouted, "Gunners if they try to rake our bows I will turn to larboard." Alessandro and I raised our hands in unison. We knew what to do.

The red and black flag flying from the large, single pirate was enough to tell me that it was the leader. I saw signal flags from her and that confirmed it. The six greyhounds all began to turn to cross our bows. The ship with the red and black flag also turned. She would be bow on to us. Her turn brought her well within range and she was gambling that she would make too difficult a target. I knew that the pirate leader would wait until the last moment to turn and give us a broadside. The balls would clear the gun decks and, if we were dismasted then we would be taken. I decided I would use this as an opportunity to test fire the sakers. In my head I had numbered them one to five. I went to number one gun and adjusted its aim. I lit the linstock and fired. I think it took everyone by surprise. I hurried to the next gun, aimed, and fired. As I went to the number three gun, I saw my first ball skip across the water and catch a glancing blow to the starboard bow of the pirate. As I fired the third gun, I saw the second ball bounce up and smash through the bowsprit. The splintering wood would cause casualties but the greatest damage was caused to her course for the sail on the bowsprit helped to sail the ship. She veered a point or two and the third ball hit her larboard gunwale. The fourth ball managed to hit the yard on her foremast, bringing down part of the sail. The last ball hit below the waterline on the larboard side.

It was not only our ship that cheered the success but all the others. We had only done a little damage but until they could clear away the wreckage then their largest vessel was temporarily out of action. I watched as her captain took her away from our deadly balls. He would make repairs and then come again.

"Reload!"

The gun crews chorused, "Done, sir!"

I could not help smiling. "Have bags of stones ready and when I command then load with ball and stones."

We would now be passing along their line. All six of their ships would be able to fire at us in turn. We would have to endure their fire and I hoped that I had been right and they would try to dismast us. This time I would need to fire the five guns as quickly as I could. I shouted, "Swivel guns, fire as you bear." Their range was much less but firing bags of stones they might get lucky. If one struck a rope and severed it then a sail might fall. You know the calibre of a gun from the sound it makes. The pirates fired first. The first two balls were wasted as our turn made them fire at an empty sea. We were less than two hundred paces from them and were an easy target. I fired five balls in rapid succession. Above us, their balls whistled as I saw our balls smash into gun carriages, the gunwale and scythe across the deck. And then we were on the second one. Alessandro had his sakers firing too and the deck was wreathed in smoke.

Behind us, I heard one of our consorts as she opened fire. The huge explosion that showered us with wreckage told me that a lucky shot had ignited the magazine of a pirate ship. We had shortened the odds but now we had to endure the fire of the next two ships. Although we hit them with every ball and the swivel guns thinned their numbers, a yard crashed down on our deck and I heard cries as men were hit. It was then that the commodore made a masterful move.

"I shall turn to starboard and pass between them. Captain Alessandro now is the time to show your old mentor your skill."

There was laughter in his voice as Alessandro shouted, "Aye, Captain!"

"Load with ball and stones."

The ship heeled as we turned for we now had the wind and we fairly flew. I heard axes and hatchets as men cleared the wreckage. The move had not only taken the pirates by surprise it allowed me the chance to fire at the stern of the second pirate ship in the line. As Alessandro fired at the third pirate my five sakers, aided by the swivels, demolished the stern of the second pirate. The balls and stones tore through wood and emptied the whole deck of men. There were no balls sent in reply as none were mounted there. The commodore continued his turn to larboard and that allowed Alessandro and the other four ships that followed us to pour ball after ball into the remaining pirates. One ship was blown up and one was sinking. A third was low in the water and would not last long and our crew cheered as though we had won. The damage to our ship slowed us and it was then I saw the first pirate, the one with the red and black flag making its purposeful way towards our starboard side. They had repaired their ship and were heading for our stern.

"Commodore!" I pointed.

He nodded and started the turn that would present our broadside. We had prevented him from raking our stern but he would be able to approach and board.

"Stand by to repel boarders."

I held the linstock and shouted, "Turn the guns so that they bear."

It did not matter what was their elevation for I just wanted to rake the ship from bow to stern as it approached. The swivel guns now came into their own and they swept some of the waiting boarders from the

The English Adventurer

shrouds. The pirate's swivel guns, however, also harvested bodies. This day men would die. I ran down the guns as the wrecked bowsprit of the pirate ship nudged ours. I lit each gun as I passed and shouted, "Arm yourselves." So fast was my progress that it was a rolling barrage and balls and stones scythed down the ship. The pirates waiting in the well of the ship were mown down but the pirate I assumed was Don Alphonso del Albuera stood on the undamaged sterncastle with many men. They would board our stern castle and that was where my family was taking shelter. Drawing my sword and dagger I ran to take the steps to the wheel as quickly as I could. I arrived just as the pirates swung over.

I swashed at the bare legs of the pirate whose bare feet came towards my face. My sword was well-made and sharp. It hacked through to the bone and blood spurted, showering the commodore and me. Commodore Phillip shouted, "Swans to me!"

Even with the whole crew, we would still be outnumbered by the pirate. I had to pray that our other four ships were coming to our aid but I was fighting for my life. I simply reacted as the boarding pike came towards my head. I barely parried it away with my sword but even so, it caught the side of my morion. Without my helmet, I would have been a dead man. I rammed my dagger up under the pirate's ribs. I saw the first mate fall, his head split by an axe. Commodore Phillip was fighting for his life against three men. If he fell then the heart would go from the crew. I skewered one pirate through the back as the commodore was struck in the left arm. I stuck my dagger into the naked back of the second and when the third realised that he was alone Commodore Phillip killed him. I placed myself next to the commodore. Blood dripped down his left arm. He could only use his right, "You are wounded."

"We fight on for the alternative is that we feed the sharks."

Don Alphonso del Albuera had just killed three more of the steering crew and he and two men advanced towards us. I saw Alessandro organising the harquebuses. They had not been used but now they would come into their own. I pointed my sword at the pirate leader, "You, Don Alphonso del Albuera, are mine. I have dead comrades to avenge."

He laughed, "The English adventurer! Today your luck runs out, Englishman and the treasure I take will build an empire to rival King Carlos! Florida will become the richest country in the world."

He was confident and I did not doubt that, as a noble, he would have been trained well in the use of a sword. His dagger also had the guard of a swordsman. All I had was the natural skills honed since I was

The English Adventurer

a boy. I knew not the fancy strokes and their names but then all I wanted to do was to kill this pirate king. He nearly did for me with his first strike. His hands were quick and he lunged at my face. The morion afforded some protection but the dagger still sliced into my cheek. I slashed with my dagger and ripped across the back of his finely made gloves. I drew blood and it was on his right hand. At the same time, I hooked my leg behind his and punched at his face with the hilt of my sword. We were so close that I did not have a clean strike but he tumbled backwards, banging into the men who were pressing behind.

I heard Alessandro shout, "Fire!" and the acrid smoke of the eight harquebuses swirled around us. Lead balls struck the pirates but one pinged off my helmet. Alessandro had taken a risk. "Reload!"

The harquebuses had clearly distracted the pirate leader for he stepped back, "Curse you, Englishman. You have no honour."

I laughed, "And you do?" I feinted with my dagger and as he reeled, I deliberately stabbed him in the thigh. He was a good swordsman and his sweep with the sword hit my thigh. It cut the fabric on my breeches but the scratch would not slow me. It was, however, a warning.

I saw the harquebuses raised and even as Alessandro shouted the order I was ducking. I was lucky. The sword swept across the air my head had occupied and the balls from the eight guns smacked into the pirates. One even hit Don Alphonso del Albuera in the backplate he wore. This time he had had enough and he waved the survivors from his crew back to the ship.

Commodore Phillip was not about to allow that to happen and he shouted, "Charge!"

We were few in number but we ran at them. The pirate king had been right, I was lucky for Don Alphonso del Albuera slipped on his own blood that was puddling near his boot. I saved the hangman a job and rammed my sword so hard through his neck that it stuck there in the deck.

"To the guns." I left the pirate bleeding his life out and then helped the crew to double shot the guns. Alessandro and his larboard crew helped and even as the pirate ship tried to pull away the five sakers fired at point blank range. I had aimed one saker to fire below the waterline. As the gunwale and pirate guns, not to mention their crews, disappeared a fire took hold of the sail. The wind began to push the ship away from us and even though we reloaded I knew that we would not need to fire again. Already the pirate was sinking lower and lower into the water. The crew threw themselves overboard and tried to cling to the wreckage from the sunken and sinking ships. They would not last long as sharks were already gathering.

The English Adventurer

The crews of our five ships all cheered until Alessandro saw my bloody cheek and shouted, "Gonzalo, fetch my medical kit."

I went to the gunwale and leaned against it for support. The loss of blood and the excitement had weakened me. I saw that two of the pirate ships were undamaged. They had been at the rear of the column and they were now heading home with a third damaged ship with them. We had accounted for four pirate ships and, more importantly removed the threat of Don Alphonso del Albuera. The cheers brought my wife and family from their fortress of chests. Isabella saw me and raced over.

Alessandro said, "Donna Isabella, I am good with a needle and I will make a scar so small on this hero that it will look, in time, as though he cut himself shaving."

She smiled, "I know well enough that my husband is a hero but now I hope that he can sheathe his sword for good." She looked down, "Where is it?"

Francisco had spied it and he ran to the blade and tugged it free, "It is here. Can I have it father?"

I shook my head, "Let us hope that it is many years until it is yours. Fetch it here."

He first wiped it clean on the finely made clothes of Don Alphonso del Albuera and then brought it to me. He sheathed it for me.

"And now," I said, "when we have repaired the ship we will sail to the safer waters of Spain. I hope that this was my last adventure."

Epilogue

It took longer than I expected to repair the ship and we had dead to bury. We eventually limped into port and Commodore Phillip organised a carriage to take us where we wished to go. Once more he had been wounded but, as with the first time he had survived. I hoped he would take it as a warning and retire.

"I will leave my chests on board until I know where we are to send them." I took only a satchel with coins for expenses and the maps I had made.

"They will be safe here. Once more, Tomas, we are in your debt. Once again, I am personally indebted to you for you saved my life."

When the carriage arrived, I told the driver where to go. We descended outside his lordship's home and I gave him a silver coin. "Wait here and it will be worth your while."

His eyes widened for I had given him a week's wages. "I will wait for as long as you wish."

I had explained on the ship to my wife that this was the house of an old friend. She did not need to know my murky past for nothing would be gained by that knowledge.

Foster, now looking ancient, opened the door and, at first, his rheumy eyes failed to recognise me. When I spoke in English I surprised my wife and children. Indeed, it felt alien to me but Foster recognised my voice and almost cracked his face so wide was his smile, "Master Penkridge, come. I will tell the captain you are here." He saw my face and shook his head, "In the wars once more, I see."

"No Lord Collingwood?"

He shook his head, "The king needed him and this home," he tapped his nose, "and all that goes on beneath its roof are now in the hands of the captain. He will be pleased to see you. He often speaks of you."

"Did he not think me dead?"

"No, for he sought news of the English Adventurer who served Pizarro when ships arrived in port from the New World. He knows you are alive but wondered if he would ever see you again."

When we were ushered into the drawing room I had not seen for some years I saw a much older, grey-haired and bearded Captain Hogan. I recognised his wife but not the three children seated around the room. Foster took great delight in saying, "Thomas Penkridge and family recently returned from the New World."

The English Adventurer

The Irishman jumped up and almost lifted me from the ground. His grey hair belied his strength. "I never thought I would see you again. This is the best of days."

"And there were dark times I thought so too."

"Your family?" I nodded and introduced my wife and children. "And this is my family." He introduced them and then laughed, "We are the only two who speak English in this room! What must your family think? You will stay will you not?"

"I would not impose and I have a carriage waiting."

Shaking his head he said, "John, give the driver a coin and tell him he will not be needed."

I said, "Ask him to fetch our chests from the ship. The captain is holding them for us."

Foster nodded and hurried off. Captain Hogan laughed again, "It is no imposition for you are still King Henry's spy are you not? You will have much to report as well as your treasure to collect." He turned to his wife and spoke in Spanish. I knew she had understood some of our English but not all. "My love, would you take Thomas' family to the guest rooms? I have much to talk about with my old friend."

I had brought maps with me and I handed those over while Captain Hogan poured wine. "There is not enough gold in England to pay for these maps, Thomas, but I am guessing that you do not need it," I told him the political news first. I knew that I would not be a spy after this visit and I gave him everything that I knew. Including the treachery of Don Alphonso del Albuera."

He nodded and scribed everything on a wax tablet. He checked the names with me and then put the tablet away. He would transcribe it later, "You look prosperous."

"I am," I told him of my success as a trader and as a half-hearted conquistador and by the time the table and food were prepared, he had heard everything that he needed to know.

Our wives and children had got on well for both families had such different lives that just speaking of them gave each family an adventure. It allowed the captain and I to speak, "So, Thomas, what are your plans? Do you wish to buy something here in Cádiz?"

I shook my head, "This visit is more of a nostalgic return but a temporary one. The New World is our home. We will buy those things that we cannot get, as yet, in Panama and then return. It is a huge land and there is more profit to be made."

"I am pleased for you deserve something after a hard life."

"And you?"

His face darkened, "I fear that England and Spain might not be allies for much longer. When our king divorced Katherine of Aragon then relations soured. Lord Collingwood was remarkably foresighted. I am not seen as an Irishman now. Only Foster and I use English and that is rare. Instead, we gather intelligence. If there is a war then I can still do my duty." He left it at that and I wondered what that would entail He looked at me and his eyes bored into my soul. "And you, are you Spanish or English now, Thomas Penkridge?"

I confess that I knew not and I answered him honestly. "I will not fight my homeland but nor will I sit by if my family is threatened. Let us hope it does not come to that."

"Amen to that. Let us hope we both enjoy peace for the rest of our lives."

We stayed not just for a month, as I had originally planned, but six months and then I needed a whole ship to return to Panama. It was easily organised and one of the reasons we stayed for six months was to await the return of **'Silver Swan'**. Captain Phillip would have an almost empty ship and he was keen to repay what he saw as his debt to me. I had the hold filled with all sorts of trade goods. We had machetes and tools as well as seeds for plants that did not grow as yet in the New World but that I knew would do well in the fertile soil that allowed, sometimes, for three crops a year. The prices for everything were much lower in Spain. My wife had bought fine clothes and furniture we could not buy in Panama and we set sail in a convoy of well-armed ships. My children had seen Spain and they dressed like young lords and a lady but they would grow up in a New World. My father would not have recognised either that world or me but I hoped he would be proud of me. I had a fortune but I had been a master gunner admired by all and I had a name that would outlive me, I was the English Adventurer who had been at the heart of the conquest of two empires. Thomas Penkridge might be unknown but the English Adventurer was not.

The End

The English Adventurer

Glossary

Ayllu- Incan family or clan
Burgular – burglar
Chicha- beer
Cuy - Guinea Pig
Gong scourers – the workers who collected human faeces at night
Inti bird- Condor
Isla Juana – Cuba
Kashamarka – Cajamarca
Lama- how the word llama would have been spoken by an Indian
Morion- a Spanish helmet
Kumana- a device to throw a spear further
Pukara – An Incan fortress
Sweating sickness – A disease that ravaged England from 1485 - 1551 and then disappeared. The symptoms/disease either lasted a day or resulted in death.
San Juan Bautista – Puerto Rico
Tomali - green tomatoes
Tunki – Andean cock of the rock (Peru's national bird)
Xictomatl – red tomatoes

The English Adventurer

Historical Note

Mexico was known as New Spain until 1521 after which time it became known as Mexico, named after the heartland of the Aztec Empire.

The Famous Thirteen

Nicolás de Ribera "el Viejo", born in Olvera, Andalucía
Cristóbal de Peralta hidalgo of Baeza
Antón de Carrión born in Carrión de los Condes
Pedro de Candia, a Greek born in Candia, Crete
Domingo de Soraluce, or Soria Lucina, a Basque merchant from Vergara
Francisco de Cuéllar from Cuellar
Joan de la Torrey Díaz Chacón, born in Villagarcía de la Torre de Extremadura, near Llerena
Pedro de Alcón from Cazalla de la Sierra north of Seville
Garcia de Jerézor Jaren, Utrera merchant
Alonso de Briceño, born about 1506 in Benavente
Alonso de Molina born in Úbeda
Gonzalo Martín de Trujillo, born in Trujillo
Martín de Paz
Bartolomé Ruiz- pilot

Historians have noted inconsistencies in reports of the identity of the Famous Thirteen and have identified as many as nineteen candidates for the thirteen spots. As Bartolomé Ruiz was the man who rescued Pizarro from his island I think we can discount him but I have included his name as he was one of the most important of the men identified as Pizarro's famous 13.

King Carlos was the king of Spain but I have the English men in the story call him King Charles.

Francisco Pizarro became the first ruler of Peru and built Lima. He married Atahualpa's wife, 10-year-old Cuxirimay Ocllo Yupanqui and she bore him two sons, Juan and Francisco.

Diego Almagro and he fell out and the dispute had to be settled by the Bishop of Panama. One side story to that is that it was the Bishop who discovered the Galapagos islands when he was blown off course. The king, through his bishop, settled the dispute by awarding the Governorate of New Toledo to Almagro and the Governorate of New

The English Adventurer

Castile to Pizarro. It did not end the enmity. When Almagro and the Pizarro brothers fell out and battled Diego Almagro was defeated, captured and executed by Francisco's brothers. Three years later, however, Diego Almagro's son, also called Diego, stormed Francisco's palace and after a hard fight slew him. Diego Almagro II was caught and executed the following year.

When Francisco Pizarro met with King Carlos in Toledo the Captain General told the king of the exploits of Bartolomé Ruiz. The king awarded Bartolomé the title and honours, 'Hidalgo, Knight of the Golden Spur, Pilot of the South Sea,' and a salary of 75,000 maravedis per year, and perpetual Regent of Tumbes. He also won the title of Clerk of Tumbes for his children. He truly deserved the title.

The conquistadores were hard men but my research led me to believe that they were not the monsters that they were made out to be. What I found remarkable was that two very small groups of soldiers conquered empires which had many thousands of well-armed and organised warriors themselves. The rate of fire of their weapons was so slow that they could, as the British Army was at Isandlwana, have been easily overwhelmed. That they were not is truly amazing.

The English Adventurer

Other books by Griff Hosker

If you enjoyed reading this book, then why not read another one by the author?

Ancient History

The Sword of Cartimandua Series
(Germania and Britannia 50 A.D. – 128 A.D.)
Ulpius Felix- Roman Warrior (prequel)
The Sword of Cartimandua
The Horse Warriors
Invasion Caledonia
Roman Retreat
Revolt of the Red Witch
Druid's Gold
Trajan's Hunters
The Last Frontier
Hero of Rome
Roman Hawk
Roman Treachery
Roman Wall
Roman Courage

The Wolf Warrior series
(Britain in the late 6th Century)
Saxon Dawn
Saxon Revenge
Saxon England
Saxon Blood
Saxon Slayer
Saxon Slaughter
Saxon Bane
Saxon Fall: Rise of the Warlord
Saxon Throne
Saxon Sword

Medieval History

The English Adventurer

The Dragon Heart Series
Viking Slave
Viking Warrior
Viking Jarl
Viking Kingdom
Viking Wolf
Viking War
Viking Sword
Viking Wrath
Viking Raid
Viking Legend
Viking Vengeance
Viking Dragon
Viking Treasure
Viking Enemy
Viking Witch
Viking Blood
Viking Weregeld
Viking Storm
Viking Warband
Viking Shadow
Viking Legacy
Viking Clan
Viking Bravery

The Norman Genesis Series
Hrolf the Viking
Horseman
The Battle for a Home
Revenge of the Franks
The Land of the Northmen
Ragnvald Hrolfsson
Brothers in Blood
Lord of Rouen
Drekar in the Seine
Duke of Normandy
The Duke and the King

New World Series
Blood on the Blade
Across the Seas
The Savage Wilderness

The English Adventurer
The Bear and the Wolf
Erik The Navigator
Erik's Clan

The Vengeance Trail

Danelaw
(England and Denmark in the 11th Century)
Dragon Sword
Oathsword
Bloodsword

The Reconquista Chronicles
Castilian Knight
El Campeador
The Lord of Valencia

The Aelfraed Series
(Britain and Byzantium 1050 A.D. - 1085 A.D.)
Housecarl
Outlaw
Varangian

The Anarchy Series England 1120-1180
English Knight
Knight of the Empress
Northern Knight
Baron of the North
Earl
King Henry's Champion
The King is Dead
Warlord of the North
Enemy at the Gate
The Fallen Crown
Warlord's War
Kingmaker
Henry II
Crusader
The Welsh Marches
Irish War
Poisonous Plots

The English Adventurer
The Princes' Revolt
Earl Marshal
The Perfect Knight

Border Knight
1182 - 1300
Sword for Hire
Return of the Knight
Baron's War
Magna Carta
Welsh Wars
Henry III
The Bloody Border
Baron's Crusade
Sentinel of the North
War in the West
Debt of Honour
Blood of the Warlord
The Fettered King

Sir John Hawkwood Series
France and Italy 1339 - 1387
Crécy: The Age of the Archer
Man at Arms
The White Company
Leader of Men

Lord Edward's Archer
Lord Edward's Archer
King in Waiting
An Archer's Crusade
Targets of Treachery
The Great Cause
Wallace's War

Struggle for a Crown
1360- 1485
Blood on the Crown
To Murder a King
The Throne
King Henry IV
The Road to Agincourt

The English Adventurer

St Crispin's Day
The Battle for France
The Last Knight
Queen's Knight

Tales from the Sword

Conquistador
England and America in the 16th Century
Conquistador
The English Adventurer

Modern History

The Napoleonic Horseman Series
Chasseur à Cheval
Napoleon's Guard
British Light Dragoon
Soldier Spy
1808: The Road to Coruña
Talavera
The Lines of Torres Vedras
Bloody Badajoz
The Road to France
Waterloo

The Lucky Jack American Civil War series
Rebel Raiders
Confederate Rangers
The Road to Gettysburg

Soldier of the Queen series
Soldier of the Queen

The British Ace Series
1914
1915 Fokker Scourge
1916 Angels over the Somme
1917 Eagles Fall
1918 We will remember them

The English Adventurer

From Arctic Snow to Desert Sand
Wings over Persia

Combined Operations series
1940-1945
Commando
Raider
Behind Enemy Lines
Dieppe
Toehold in Europe
Sword Beach
Breakout
The Battle for Antwerp
King Tiger
Beyond the Rhine
Korea
Korean Winter

Tales From the Sword II

Other Books
Great Granny's Ghost (Aimed at 9-14-year-old young people)

For more information on all of the books then please visit the author's website at www.griffhosker.com where there is a link to contact him or visit his Facebook page: GriffHosker at Sword Books

Printed in Great Britain
by Amazon